Why Are You Crying, Mama?

by

Thang Za Dal

A Historical Romance Novel

Copyright: © 2021 Thang Za Dal

Publisher: tredition GmbH, Hamburg
Halenreie 40-44
22359 Hamburg

978-3-347-28115-8 (Paperback)
978-3-347-28116-5 (Hardcover)
978-3-347-28117-2 (eBook)

Dedicated to my Parents, Brother, Sisters,
my wife and our daughters

CHAPTER 1
(7th May 1934 – Monday – 8 p.m.)

The place was Florenville, Belgium.

"Why are you crying, Mama?"

The small girl's faint voice was filled with sorrow. She meekly stood at the door of a living room, quite spacious, luxuriously decorated, and dimly lit. The woman quickly dried the tears on her cheeks and turned toward the little girl.

"Oh, my dear, I didn't know you were there. Come hug me."

The girl was about six years old and biracial, African-Caucasian; she seemed to have slightly more prominent African features than Caucasian. She went to her mother, who was sitting on a large sofa. Her mother, who held a book in her hand, put it on a nearby table, stretched out her arms, and took the child tenderly to her side. Outside it was not yet fully dark. The clock on the wall read nine o'clock.

The woman was in her mid-twenties and Caucasian. In a soft voice, she asked her child, "How often do you see me crying, darling?"

"Quite often. Whenever I see you crying, I am so sad, Mama."

"My child, I'll have to repeat what I've often told you whenever you asked me this question: Women are very odd beings.women are very odd beings. They cry for many reasons. They cry when they are happy; they cry when they are sad; they cry when they reminisce about old memories, good or bad; they cry when they see beautiful things; sometimes, they cry without even knowing why."

"Really?"

"Yes, you will know when you grow up and become a woman."

"But why are you crying right now, Mama?"

"I'm crying right now because I'm so happy to have a lovely and intelligent daughter like you."

"I don't believe I'm intelligent and lovely. All the boys and girls I meet on the streets call out, 'Hey, you ugly, stupid nigger.'"

"Don't take them seriously. They're just children like you."

"Even many adults call me the same thing."

5

"Oh really? I'm so sad to hear that. But try to be strong, okay?"

"That's what I've been trying to do for years. I have secretly cried alone many times because I don't want to make you sad with my own sorrow."

Upon hearing these words, the woman could barely contain her emotions. With a trembling voice, she said, "I've always thought so, my child, but I never dared to ask you."

Both of them sobbed for some minutes. Then, the child spoke with a broken voice. "Mama, you said you were crying out of happiness because you've got a lovely and intelligent daughter like me. Would you still cry with happiness if I were an ugly, stupid child?"

The woman was quite surprised and saddened by the child's unexpected question. She answered with an effort, "Even then, I'd still cry out of happiness, my child."

The woman was interrupted by her daughter. "I don't believe that. You just said you're crying out of happiness because I'm a lovely and intelligent child, but that means you'd not cry out of happiness if I were ugly and stupid."

Tears were streaming down the woman's face.

"Even then, I'd still love you because you're mine. Beauty and ugliness are superficial things. For example, when you see a stranger, you might think they are beautiful or handsome at first glance. But if they said or did something awful to you, you wouldn't find them beautiful or handsome anymore. In the same way, you might find a stranger ugly at first glance, but if he is kind to you and does nice things for you, you'd find him ugly no more, and you'd like and love him. To you, he could become the most handsome guy. The most handsome or beautiful guy in the world is the one who likes you, who loves you, who cares for you and who helps you when you're in need."

"Do you really mean it, Mama?"

"Yes, I really mean it. But you'll find out that it's true when you grow up and have more experience in the world. Sadly, countless people leave the world without ever having learned this priceless lesson. Just one example: If I saw your papa on the street somewhere, I wouldn't find him handsome or attractive, although he's not ugly. He

6

was not the type I'd fall in love with quickly. If he had not saved my life, I'd have been hit by a car and most likely killed on the spot, or I could have been handicapped my whole life. He not only saved my life, but he's so kind and warm that he became one of the most handsome guys in the world to me. And I wonder if my love for him is also partly the result of my feelings of pity for his hard life. Some people say that if you love someone out of sympathy, it's much stronger than a love that results from physical beauty or attraction."

The child was attentively listening to what her mother was telling her.

"Mama, is there anything about him that you don't like – at least sometimes?"

"Before I met your papa, I always dreamed of having someone humorous and exciting as my husband. Sometimes, I find him a little bit boring because he rarely says 'No' to whatever I do or say. But then I've slowly become used to his behavior. His whole life, he has had to fight all kinds of hardship, like racial discrimination and poverty, so he always says he needs peace as much as possible. And he feels very insecure."

"Mama, what does that mean – to feel insecure?"

"He's not sure whether I truly love him deep in my heart. He sometimes thinks I pretend to love him simply out of gratitude for saving my life. And he's worried about whether our marriage will last, and so on. But over time, he's become more convinced that my love for him is real."

"Mama, you and Papa used to tell me some years ago how he saved your life, but you said you'd tell me about it more in detail when I was a little bit older. Would you tell me about it now?"

"Yes, we did promise you that every time you asked us. I think we can tell you about it soon. In the past, we've hidden many secrets from you because we didn't want to burden you with problems that we were – and still are – confronted with."

"Mama, when is Papa coming back from Paris?"

"Tomorrow evening, around six o'clock. We'll pick him up at the station. Now, it's getting late. Let's go to bed, okay?"

"Mama, I'm happy you're going to tell me about you and Papa."

"We won't exactly *tell* you about it, but I've written our life story up to now as a novel, and I'm going to keep on writing it as we go on living. So far, I've written seven chapters. It's something like an autobiographical novel. I'll read these chapters aloud to you, okay? But let's go to bed now. Good night, my dear."

"Good night, Mama. I'm already very excited about it."

The next evening, Jane, the mother, and Jennifer, the young girl, went to pick John, the father, up at the train station. After dinner, Jane, Jennifer, and John were comfortably sitting together on two sofas around a table in the same spacious living room where Jane and Jennifer had sat the previous night. John was a stoutly built, medium-sized man, about 170 centimeters, just a few centimeters taller than Jane, in his late twenties. Jennifer was the right height for her age. The clock on the wall read eight o'clock sharp.

"Mama, yesterday evening, you promised to read me the seven chapters of the novel that you've started writing about your meeting Papa and how you got married. I've been thinking about it the whole day, and I'm very excited to hear it. If possible, could you please read it now?"

"Yes, I promised I would do that . . ."

Jennifer was curious. "Mama, what will you call it?"

"I don't know yet. I'm thinking about three titles. Maybe I'll call it *Why Are You Crying, Mama?* Because it's the question that you ask me most. Or simply *Jane* – my first name. Or perhaps another thing you often say to me: *Whenever I See You Crying, I'm So Sad, Mama.* I'll probably let you choose, okay? Which one do you like most at this moment?"

"I like the first one: *Why Are You Crying, Mama?* But I don't know why."

"Let's discuss it when I finish the whole manuscript, okay? What happened yesterday and today between us in this room will become Chapter 1. Now, though, I'm going to read chapters 2 to 7. Listen!"

CHAPTER 2
(24th December 1926 – Friday)

On the evening of 24th December 1926, a Friday, the time was about ten o'clock. The whole town of Bastogne was well lit with Christmas decorations; it was covered with thick snow and extremely cold. The main streets were full of pedestrians, and the mood was very joyous. Church bells were ringing out through the town. Jane was in town with her mother and a couple of her cousins to spend Christmas with their maternal grandparents.

They were on their way to the Church of St. Francis, on the Avenue de la Gare. The rest, all except Jane, had already crossed the road, but when she started to cross the street at the junction of Avenue de la Gare and Rue de Neufchateau, someone suddenly grasped her from behind and swept her forcefully aside. She was unsure of what had happened. Then she saw a young black man, and now she realized that he was the one who had swept her aside. What she did not see was that an old man had been driving relatively fast toward them, and when he'd tried to turn to the left, he'd lost control of the car and careened toward her. Jane did not see this, as she was looking in the opposite direction. If the young black man had not acted at the last moment, she could have been hit from behind and perhaps killed on the spot. When she realized this, she was overcome by shock. Trembling and looking at the young man, she could barely utter a single word.

"Hello!" the young black man greeted her in English. "Hello, my name is John. Good evening."

She also replied in English, still shaking from shock. "Hi. Good evening, John. I'm Jane. Oh John, I don't know how to thank you. If you hadn't saved me, I'd be dead now, or at least severely injured."

"Good evening, Jane. It's God and not me who has saved you. So please, thank God and not me."

"But I only see you. So, for me, you're the one who saved my life."

9

As people started to gather around them, John looked worried. "Jane, I'm sorry. I'm rather in a hurry. So goodbye and good luck."

"John, could you at least give me your address so I can contact you?"

"I'm an American visiting this country. I'm living in Brussels at the moment. I cannot give you my address now."

"Why not, John?"

"I simply can't. There's a reason, Jane."

"I see. Okay, then. At least take my card. Please contact me as soon as possible, okay? Goodbye and take care. Thank you so much once again. I'll think of you, and I hope we'll meet again someday."

"Goodbye and good luck, Jane. May God bless you."

John hastily took Jane's card and disappeared into the crowd. Jane was upset and shedding tears. Many people were helping the elderly driver. Jane's mother and cousins hurriedly came back to comfort her, and then in a few moments, they were all heading toward the church. After the worship service, they all went to Jane and her cousins' grandparents' home. Jane could not sleep the whole night for she way thinking about what had happened all night. Her mind dwelt in particular upon her young black rescuer, and she wondered whether she would ever meet him again. The family stayed there until the New Year and went home in the first week of 1927.

CHAPTER 3
(March–June 1927)

Jane thought about John day in and day out and waited for a phone call that never came. She often waited for the postman, too, and when he came, she frantically checked her mail. Three months had passed, and nothing had happened; she became restless and depressed. Whenever those who knew the story and her obsession with him wanted to know why she felt like that, she told them that she would like to thank him more profusely and that she wanted to know a little more about his life and so on.

On 20th March, she decided to revisit the town where the accident had happened. She stayed with her maternal grandparents again. Every day, she went into the town center around eleven o'clock in the morning and remained in the vicinity until three or four o'clock in the afternoon, hanging around near the spot where the accident took place, hoping that perhaps her rescuer might revisit it. She also went out in the late evenings and observed passersby around the same site. Every time she saw black people, she ran after them and asked them if they knew a black American named John in Brussels. But as her search for him proved fruitless, she returned to her hometown after three weeks on the 21st April - sad, exhausted, and depressed.

She was so obsessed with John that she could not concentrate on her work at home. Her parents, grandparents on both sides, and close friends and relatives tried to console and persuade her in many different ways to forget about him, saying that he must have a good reason for not contacting her. But she counter-argued that it could be that he had lost her card and that she wanted to know the reason. Her obsession was so intense that her relatives began to suspect that her motive might be more than just gratitude. So her parents advised her to go to Brussels and continue her search for him there. She thought she would never find peace in her life if she didn't find him, so she was determined to continue her quest, no matter how long it might take until every effort had been exhausted.

After two weeks of rest at home, she went to Brussels by car on 4th June and stayed with Maria, her mother's youngest sister, who lived in the city center. Jane decided to stay for at least a couple of weeks. On the day of her departure, her parents and cousins gathered to say goodbye to her. Just before she left, her mother said, "Jane, I wish you the best of luck in your search for him. If he is just a normal human being and not an angel, you'll surely find him. By the way, the other day, one of your aunts said she thought you might have fallen in love with him, at least unconsciously. Although you don't believe in God, if I were you, I'd pray to him anyway. I'll pray for you every day, darling. Take care, and good luck and goodbye."

"Mama, I don't think I've fallen in love with him. Although he's not ugly, he's not the type with whom I could fall in love. And our encounter was so brief. Thank you so much, Mama, Papa, and all of you for giving me support and strength during the last few months. I'll inform you immediately if I find him again."

They hugged and parted. Jane drove straight to Brussels. Maria pitied her so much that she promised to help her in her search. As she had done in Bastogne, Jane left her aunt's apartment every day at different times and walked around or hung about, observing all the black people she came across. Maria accompanied her several times, and they asked nearly every black man and woman they met on the street if they knew a black American named John. Days had come and gone, but nothing happened. Jane had already spent four weeks in Brussels. She was sad and exhausted, both physically and mentally. So she finally decided to go home. But she first wanted to go to Barbara's birthday party at the well-known restaurant *Chez Leon*, located at Rue des Bouchers 18, not far from Maria's apartment. Jane and Barbara studied economics together at the Free University of Brussels. There were about thirty invitees.

Jane and Maria arrived at the restaurant at about eight o'clock. Nearly all the other guests had already arrived, and they introduced themselves to each other. After they had finished the luxurious dinner at around ten o'clock, people formed groups here and there and started making small talk. Jane and her aunt chatted with some guests. At around half past eleven, Jane, Maria, and a few other guests prepared to go home and said goodbye to those around them. Then, Jane excused herself from the group and went to the toilet. On her way, she inadvertently peeked into the kitchen through a half-open door, and there, to her great surprise and excitement, she saw John washing the dishes. She shouted out, "Hi John!"

John looked back at her blankly, perplexed, and said nothing.

Jane continued, "It's me, Jane! I'm the one you rescued on Christmas Eve! Don't you remember me?"

John recognized her now and was very excited too. He rushed to her and shook hands with her and said, "Hi Jane, now I recognize you. Oh, how nice it is to see you again so unexpectedly."

"Oh John, how happy I am to see you again." She could only utter these few words and was so excited that she suddenly hugged him and, at the same time, burst into tears. John also hugged her back. Then, with great effort, she said through her tears, "Oh John, I've been looking for you everywhere, in Bastogne and here in this city, for several weeks. You don't know how happy I am!"

John's eyes were also full of tears. After a short while, John freed her from his arms and said, "Yes, I'm also so happy to see you again, Jane."

Those in the kitchen just stared at them without having any idea what was happening between the pair. Jane looked deep into his face, still tightly holding his hands, and said, "John, I have waited for a call or a letter every day since the accident. Why didn't you contact me?"

"Jane, I wanted to, but I've overstayed my visa and am working illegally in restaurant kitchens, trying to earn money for my return journey."

On hearing these words, Jane once again burst into tears. "John, why didn't you contact me and tell me about it? I could have helped you. I thought you might have lost my card, and I didn't know where to look for you."

"I'm so happy to hear your kind words. Thank you so much for your willingness to help me, Jane. But I think I can manage on my own."

"John, I'm going back home tomorrow. I've got many things to do, so I cannot stay here longer. Can you come with me? My parents and other relatives would be very pleased to see you. You can stay with us as long as you like."

"Thank you so much for your kindness and generosity, but I can't do that. I have to work for at least two more weeks in this place. Then I could probably visit you for a few days. But I must avoid traveling as much as possible because I could get caught at any time by the police for overstaying."

"Would it be possible for the restaurant owner to find someone to take your place now?"

"No, I don't think so. And I can't leave my aunt and uncle so suddenly. I'm living with them, and they're not feeling well at the moment."

"Oh, I see. Yes, I understand your precarious situation. Should I come back here and pick you up and drive you to my home?"

"No, I don't think you'll need to. Three good friends of mine are going in your direction soon, and I could ask them to take me with them and drop me at your place. If that doesn't work, I'll take the risk and come by train."

"Are your friends black or white?"

"They're white. Two are Americans, and one is Belgian."

"Do they know that you've overstayed your visa?"

"Yes, they know about it. But traveling with whites is much safer than traveling alone or with other blacks."

"Aren't they racist?"

"They were somewhat racist when we met. But I won their friendship with my patience, humility, forgiveness, and friendliness."

"That's very interesting … All right, then. But if you'd prefer me to come and pick you up for any reason, please just let me know, okay?"

"Yes, I'll do that."

"Here's my card again. Please call me, and we'll arrange your visit. Well, it's rather late, so we'll have to leave now."

Jane then introduced John to Maria. Observing the pair, Maria silently shed tears of happiness. Jane reached into her purse and took out some money and handed it to John.

"John, here are a few hundred francs for your train ticket if you have to come by train, and the rest is for your other needs."

John refused to take the money at first, saying that it was too much. But Jane insisted that he accept it. Tears streaming down her cheeks, she hugged him affectionately once again and said goodbye, and then hurried out of the kitchen with Maria. His eyes were also full of tears.

CHAPTER 4
(1st July 1927 – Friday)

It was six p.m. on a sunny day. In their large and luxuriously furnished two-story house, Jane and her parents waited in the upstairs guest room for John's arrival. He was on his way, and if everything went well, he would be arriving at any time. Jane went to the window now and then and looked for any sign of him. And then, suddenly, there he was, rounding a distant corner and walking toward the house, carrying a small bag in his right hand.

As Jane saw him, she shouted, "Hey, John, is here!" and ran down the staircase to greet him. They met each other at the garden gate. She heartily hugged him. He hugged her back, but with some slight hesitation.

"Oh John, I'm so glad to see you again. I hope everything went all right on your journey."

"Yes, I'm also delighted to see you again. Everything was okay on the way here."

Jane's parents came down and met him at the main entrance of the house. She introduced John to them. "John, this is my mother, Christine, and here's my father, Paul."

"Hello John, we're thrilled to meet you. You're most welcome here; please make yourself at home right away. Where are your friends?"

"I'm equally pleased to meet you, Christine and Paul. I asked them to drop me at the corner before they went on to their destination."

Christine and Paul were as tall as John and in their late forties or early fifties. They entered the house and went straight into the living room. John was seated in a corner close to Jane. He discreetly observed the whole living room and said, "You've got a very nice house and a huge, beautiful garden. When was it built?"

Jane answered, "Thank you. It was built more than a hundred years ago. My father inherited it from his parents."

"Oh, I see. Since I was a child, one of my dreams has been to have a house and garden of my own."

Jane said, "John, someday you may have such a house and garden, or even one much bigger and more beautiful than ours — who knows? You're still young."

"No, I dare not have such an ambitious dream. My simple dream is to have a small house with a small garden where I can plant vegetables and fruit trees. And above all else, to have a small library and earn a modest sum so that I can afford to buy the books I'm interested in and have enough free time to read them. How lucky you are that you've got such a huge library."

The living room was indeed full of books. Paul commented, "Yes, you're right. Other rooms are also full of books."

"From when I first learned to read, I read all the books that I could get my hands on. Although we're poor, I'm fortunate enough to have had time for reading. My parents are also passionate readers, and we've got a small library at home. Even so, I could not afford to buy many of the books that I wanted to read. And the small local libraries in our neighborhood don't have them. You've got many books in English that I've always wanted to read. If my family could have supported me, my strongest desire was to go to college or university and become a teacher, even a professor. I was always the brightest student from the beginning of my schooling until I left school. But I know it'll remain just a daydream in this life…"

John's words moved Jane, Christine, and Paul to tears. They immediately noticed that John was brilliant. After a few minutes, Christine said, "John, we've prepared dinner. When we've finished eating, we'll sit down here again and get to know each other better. Is that all right with you?"

"That's all right with me, Christine."

"Good. Well, it's not polite to ask you this question, but to arrange our time together here – what's your plan? You may stay with us as long as you like."

"That's very kind of you, but my friends are passing through again on Sunday around two o'clock in the afternoon, and I'll have to go back with them. My aunt is not feeling well at the moment, and I need to look after her."

"I see. After dinner, let's discuss how best we could spend our time while you're here."

Jane showed John the guest bedroom. They then went into the dining room, and Jane and Christine prepared dinner. They finished dinner an hour and a half later and entered the living room again, and took their seats as before. It was eight o'clock.

Jane began the conversation. "John, first of all, my parents would like to tell you how indescribably grateful they are to you for saving my life."

Paul said to John, "Yes John, we don't know how to express our thanks to you for saving Jane's life. Our oldest child was a boy, and he and I were caught in a battle ten years ago in the Great War, and he died from his wounds. I was also severely wounded, but I partially recovered after a long course of treatment. I still have difficulty walking long distances, though. Jane is our only child now. If you had not saved her life, we'd be alone, and how sorrowful we would be without her."

Paul's words visibly moved John, and he expressed his sympathy. "Christine and Paul, I'm so sorry to hear about your son. But you don't need to thank me for what I did for Jane. I am so glad that I could, but it was no effort on my part. It happened in a second. And I'd have done the same for anybody else as well. As a deeply religious Christian, I firmly believe that it was not me that saved her life but our God. So please thank Him, not me."

Christine spoke out. "Yes, as a devoted Christian myself, I also believe it to be the work of God. But I believe that he used you in particular, John, to do it on his behalf. So you also deserve our gratitude."

Just as John was about to say something, Jane interrupted him. "John, please excuse me, but I can't wait to reiterate what I told you when we met again in Brussels and also on the phone – that I cannot describe how happy I am to have met you again and to have you here now. John, please let me tell you very briefly what happened between the incident in Bastogne and when I met you again in Brussels. After we parted from each other, I expected a sign from you – a letter or a call. I waited and waited. I wanted to thank you more, and I wanted to know who you were and where you lived, and about your life. Not a single day passed when I didn't think about you. Then, slowly, as I lost hope of ever hearing from you again, I decided to go to Bastogne again to search for you. I stayed at my grandparents' house for two whole weeks and went out every day to hang around the place where you rescued me in the hope that you might be there. After that, I spent five months here at home and then went to Brussels to continue my search for you. I stayed with Maria and looked for you for four full weeks, in vain. Very often, Maria accompanied me. We ran after every black man and woman we met on the street and asked them if they knew a black American named John, and we described your physical features. So I'd already given up all hope of ever seeing you again in this life when we met again by chance. That's my story. Now, if you don't mind, would you please tell us something about yourself? And we'll also tell you about us. You may tell us only what you're comfortable sharing. Would that be all right? Or should we start with our story first?"

"I don't mind starting with my story, Jane. I've got nothing to hide from you. But I'm afraid I may not have much to tell you that could be of interest to you. I was born on February 15, 1905, a Wednesday. I've got a younger sister named Betty. Andrew, my father, was a Methodist pastor in our small community until two years ago. My mother, Anne, is a teacher in a small primary school. We've been liv-ing in a shabby, three-room apartment in New York City since my childhood. I finished high school four years ago. As my father's health deteriorated four or five years ago, I had to start working part-time when I was still in school to support my family, sometimes as a carpenter's apprentice and sometimes as a farmhand. We're descend-ed from slave families more than three hundred years ago."

19

Jane immediately liked him for his honesty and humility, and she deeply sympathized. John continued, "About ten months ago, I came to visit my paternal aunt, who married a black Belgian more than ten years ago. They're childless. I'm staying with them and working illegally in restaurant kitchens to pay for my journey home and perhaps also for some savings for my family back home. I've already overstayed for six months."

Jane, Christine, and Paul listened attentively, and their eyes were filled with tears. Then Jane asked, "John, if you get caught by the police, what will happen to you?"

"I don't know for sure because nearly every case is handled differently. I could be put in jail for some months and then deported, or I could be fined and deported—provided, of course, that I've got enough money to pay for my journey."

"But what if you don't have enough money for your return trip?"

"I could still be deported at the Belgian government's expense because it'd still be cheaper for the government to deport me than to put me in jail since sooner or later, they'd have to send me home anyway."

Jane continued the conversation. "How much have you personally experienced racial discrimination here and in your country?"

"Oh, racial discrimination? I don't even think about it anymore because it happens every day and everywhere."

"How do you do it? How do you survive the bitterness, the hardship?"

"We blacks don't have any alternative except to commit suicide if you're not strong enough to withstand the humiliation. If you dare not kill yourself, then you have to try to survive against the odds. In my case, it's a bit better, thanks to a very wise grandfather. He passed two pearls of wisdom down to his children and grandchildren, including me. One of those is not to blame white people too much for what they're doing to you because if you were white, you yourself would most likely behave similarly. The other pearl of wisdom is to react to every case of discrimination with patience and forgiveness. I've earned the admiration, even love, of many white racists who mistreated me when we first encountered each other with these simple rules. Jane, do you remember what I told you in Brussels about my three white friends? I won their friendship with such positive attitudes on my part. In the beginning, it was very hard, but I can apply them quite easily now. In this way, I make my life a bit less painful to bear."

Jane, Christine, and Paul were fighting back their tears.

After a few moments, Jane spoke with a broken voice. "Yes, John, I immediately noticed your smiling face when we saw each other again in the kitchen in Brussels, regardless of the dire situation you were in."

"I've even been told a couple of times by racists who later became my friends that they've rarely seen blacks so friendly, so it was a great surprise for them. I explained that since we encounter all kinds of hostility every day, we cannot afford to be friendly to everyone all the time—that deep down in our hearts, we're suffering every second, every minute, every hour."

Now Paul began to speak. "John, it's very laudable to have such positive attitudes and such patience. Such qualities can help blacks in your situation and all human beings, regardless of their ethnicity or social background. Those who have such qualities are much happier in their lives and are generally more successful than those who don't. John, yours is a fascinating yet heartbreaking story at the same time. I'm pleased to know someone like you. And I'm sure Jane and Christine share my feelings. Do you want to tell us more?"

"No, Paul. For the time being, that's all I have to say. As I've already told you, I've nothing special to tell you that could be interesting to you."

"What you've just told us is entirely new to us. If I'm honest, I have never tried to find out how blacks feel deep down in their hearts. I can only imagine how they feel. Okay John, now I'm going to tell you our story. First of all, our close relatives already know what happened with you and Jane in that town, and they also want to meet you. But since you said that your visa expired a long time ago, we decided not to inform them about your coming here; otherwise, the house would be full now. Most of the people in this small community are our relatives. Christine and I were born in 1879. Jane was born, precisely like you, in 1905, on July 14. So you are the same age – an extraordinary coincidence, isn't it? When we married in late 1902, we were only twenty-three years old. And, exactly like you, we – that is, on my side – had a very wise forefather four generations ago. He passed his wisdom down to his posterity.

"His wisdom was that human beings have been oppressing, exploiting, even torturing and killing each other from the beginning of our existence in the name of religion, skin color, political ideas, money, and hatred of all kinds. And even without any reason at all on uncountable occasions. As a result, countless innocent people have lost their priceless lives for nothing. Human life is very short. So why should one waste one's precious life for something that would not benefit him or his loved ones? Therefore, since this great-grandfather's time, our relatives have been trying to collectively analyze the political, religious, economic, and social factors where they live and those of the neighboring countries to take some effective measures in time. We try to stay away from all kinds of conflict and ideology as much and as long as possible if they would not benefit us in one way or another. That's why many people quite often accuse us of being egoistic. Therefore, very few of our close relatives, for example, are involved in any political or religious activities. But we try to be as fair as possible in all our social dealings. Just as we don't want to be hurt by other people, we don't want to hurt other innocent people. Look at Christine and me as an example. She's Flemish, and I'm a Walloon.

"As you know, although we're a nation in name, there are almost no intermarriages between the two ethnic groups. The division is mainly along the linguistic line. So when we fell in love, we foresaw the great obstacles that we would have to overcome. Since I loved her so much, I learned her language, and she also learned mine. So we communicate with each other in both languages. When we got married, nearly every relative on both sides, and most of our friends, bet that the marriage would last five years at the most. But we've just celebrated our silver jubilee earlier this year. Like every other marriage, ours is not perfect, but our conflicts have nothing to do with linguistic or religious or racial issues. And here's how we solved the spiritual obstacle: Christine is a devoted Catholic, and I have no religion. So we made a compromise that each of us should pursue our own beliefs freely. But then, when we were about to get married, her bishop insisted that it should be a Catholic marriage. To make the process smooth, I started to go to church again – I was also a churchgoing Catholic until I was some twenty years old, but then I lost all my religious beliefs and left the Church. She is still endlessly thankful for this gesture of mine. And I must also add something here about Christine's side. I'm very fortunate to have found someone with almost the same philosophical, enlightened background. She also had some wise forefathers, who had nearly the same outlook on life as those on my side. So the overall atmosphere on both sides is quite harmonious, and our married life benefits from it enormously. But there's one thing that might surprise and disappoint you: Jane does not believe in the biblical God, and we don't criticize her for that or try to persuade her to be religious. We fully respect each other's opinions and rights, whatever they may be."

John was suddenly curious and asked Jane, "Is that true, Jane? And if so, why?"

"Yes, it's true, John. And the reason is rather simple. I also used to be a devoted Catholic, like my mother, in my childhood. I regularly went to church with her. But when I was about fifteen or sixteen, a young black girl surprised everybody by asking the bishop, who was preaching about God's never-ending love, a question. Her question was: 'If God is so loving and powerful enough to create the whole universe, why did he make human beings with different skin colors?' All the churchgoers were shocked and stared at her. The bishop himself was surprised and was uncomfortable, but he replied in a very tender voice that God must have had a good reason for doing so, but we humans would never be able to find out what that reason was. After I heard the girl's question, I became very critical of God and decided to go my own way without religion. That question remains in my mind until today. Every time I see black people being discriminated against just because of their skin color, I feel so sad and very often cry. If God had created all humans with the same skin color and the same physical features and the same or nearly the same levels of intelligence, there would be much less suffering and hatred in the world. So my conclusion is: God must be not as powerful as he's supposed to be, or he must be a discriminating God."

John was moved to tears by her words. Then, with a choked-up voice, he asked her, "Jane, you're a wonderful person. I admire you so much for your thoughtfulness. But have you ever asked any theologians for an explanation?"

"I've asked a number of them, and I've read many books concerning this matter, but I found all the explanations absolutely nonsense."

"But Jesus Christ is said to be so loving that he gave his life to save us from our sins."

"John, I'm so sorry to disappoint you, but I'm only interested in what God is supposed to have done with us. So whenever I have to write down the word 'God', I write it with a small 'g'."

"Then are you perhaps more interested in the theory of evolution?"

"No. I may be too simple-minded to be interested in such a theory. I'm only capable of thinking about people's day-to-day survival. Maybe some time in my life, I will want to think more deeply about religion or scientific theories. Who knows?"

"So you don't believe in anything, Jane?"

"Religiously speaking, I believe in nothing. But I believe in the positive qualities of human beings, like sympathy, sincerity, honesty, love, kindness, compassion, and so on."

"But I wonder if these qualities could also be the result of religious morality."

"No, I don't think so, because if you look at what has been happening in the world, innumerable ruthless acts have been committed in the very name of religions and gods by those who claim to be highly moral and religious. I've heard that Buddhism is the only major religion in whose name no war has ever been waged. Hinduism also seems to be peaceful, but I find its caste system cruel. I'm sorry to say that. When I get older, I may look more closely into some religions, as my father is beginning to do now."

John shared his opinion. "I've been thinking about what you just said, Jane – why the biblical God created different colored skins and different levels of intelligence and different physical features and so on. Nevertheless, I remain a religious person because, unlike you white people, we blacks don't have anyone or any institutions to turn to protect us or give us hope. But may I ask you, Paul, a very personal question? Why did you lose your religious beliefs? I'm just curious."

"I'm glad that you asked me, John. For me, the world is full of great mysteries, and I don't rule out the idea that a powerful God exists somewhere in the universe. But I want to do my own search for the answers to these mysteries, if there are any satisfactory answers at all. I don't want to believe blindly in what is written or preached. I started my search some twenty years ago."

"I see. Perhaps could you tell me some of the mysteries you have in mind?"

"The Bible itself is full of great mysteries. And then there's the concept of reincarnation in Hinduism and Buddhism, the mysterious meanings of numbers or numerology, Western astrology, Chinese astrology, Indian or Hindu astrology, the *I-Ching* or *Book of Changes*, palmistry, the Nadi or Palm Leaf astrology of the Tamils in southern India, mediumship, and so on, to name just a few."

"Oh, these subjects do sound interesting, but I've never heard of the last two: the *I-Ching* or Nadi astrology. Could you please tell me a bit more about them, Paul?"

"Well, I came across those two methods of divination only very recently, though they were known among a few European scholars in the early 1700s. An influential German translation was done in 1923 by Richard Wilhelm. And I first heard about Nadi astrology only a couple of years ago from some British colonial officials who had come back from India. So I can only tell you about them very roughly. The *I-Ching* is an ancient Chinese divination text and the oldest of the Chinese classics. It's believed to be more than 2,000 years old. The *I-Ching* uses a type of divination called cleromancy, which produces random numbers. Six numbers between six and nine are turned into a hexagram, which can then be looked up in the *I-Ching* and arranged in an order known as the King Wen sequence…And the Nadi astrology of the Tamil people is thousands of years old. It's said that individuals' destinies have already been written since time immemorial on palm leaves. So if someone wants to know what is written about his destiny, he goes to a Nadi astrologer or Nadi reader. The reader lets the person give him his or her thumbprint (right-hand thumbprint for men and left-hand thumbprint for women), and the reader locates the right palm leaves from piles of stored dried leaves in his custody by reading the thumbprints. When the right palm leaf is located, the reader will make his interpretation of what is written on it."

"Thank you so much for all this fascinating information. Paul, could you perhaps also tell me what you think about creationism and evolution?"

"Before we go on to the issue you've just raised, shouldn't we talk a little bit more about astrology – I mean Western astrology?"

"That'd be great, Paul. I have almost no idea about it. I only know that there are twelve Sun Signs for us human beings."

"Good, John. You must have read or heard about determinism and predestination in theology, I suppose."

"Yes. But since I'm not that interested in theology, I've never explored those subjects deeply. So what do the twelve Sun Signs have to do with determinism and predestination?"

"Well, we'll need hours and hours – and since you don't have much knowledge of them, I'll tell you briefly what I think. So far as I know, the concept of predestination in theology arose in the 1st century AD. It is the doctrine that God has willed all events – the biblical God, that is. The concept of determinism had already been introduced in the 7th and 6th centuries BC by the pre-Socratic philosophers Heraclitus and Leucippus. It was later dealt with by several prominent philosophers, theologians, and scientists – among them Niels Bohr and Albert Einstein, to name just two. I'll tell you what I think about them very briefly. How is it possible to predict individuals' future destinies – or those of nations – by divination if our destinies are not predetermined or if events happen randomly? And everybody has his or her own characteristics according to his or her Sun Sign. So the question is: How could that be possible if something, some being or some force, had not caused it to be so? And how is it possible to predict our destinies by divination methods if we are just products of evolution? Then, when we talk about these mysteries, we naturally have to think about one of the most debated subjects among theologians and philosophers: *free will*."

John was deeply absorbed in Paul's words but visibly perplexed, but then his face suddenly lit up when he heard the words *free will*.

"What you're telling me is so fascinating. Now and then, I've met people who told me that some people are compatible while some are not, depending on their Sun Signs. Is that true? If that's true, then we may have to accept the concept of predestination. Don't you think so?"

"Yes, I think that's true to some extent. But we won't discuss it now. Your next question, please?"

"Oh yes. Would you please explain how you interpret the idea of free will?"

"As you may know, different philosophers, scientists, and theologians interpret it quite differently. The main point here is whether humans still have free will or not if our destinies are already determined. I believe in predestination to some extent, but I also believe that we still have some room for free will. It'd depend on several fac-

27

tors, such as who you are, where you are, in which era you live. Furthermore, the religious, cultural, economic, educational, and political backgrounds of the country or society in which you live will also play some crucial roles. Further, your gender, the types of decisions you have to make, the timing, your level of intelligence, and whether you are a brave or a cowardly person, et cetera, will also surely influence your decision-making process. Even then, if I'm honest, sometimes I'm doubtful if individuals' free will could change the final destiny of the whole of humankind. And there's one thing that disturbs me very much: Nearly all the philosophers that I know use the word *we – we, we, we –* as if all people see and think exactly in the same way. But that's not true at all, in my opinion. So whether every one of us has free will or not – and how much of it we have – will depend greatly on the various factors I mentioned. Please let me say only this much for the time being."

Paul continued after a few moments. "As I've told you, I began my search some twenty years ago for answers to the mysteries I've just mentioned – that is, if there are any answers at all. But what I can tell you now from my little knowledge on these subjects is that I think it's easier for me to accept creationism than evolutionism. A very simple reason is that until now, evolutionists cannot yet convincingly explain which of the following things come first – the chicken or the egg, or the female or the male – of any living being. But since the evolutionary theory is still in its infancy, we'll have to wait and see how scientists try to prove the theory in the long run."

"Does that mean it's easier for you now to accept that a creator God exists forever, without a beginning or an end?"

"Yes. That's what I'm thinking, given what I've found out through my research. But I still have to do plenty more research in the future. Someday, I might go to India and the Far East to expand my search over there concerning the concept of reincarnation and other hidden knowledge. What I've learned up to now shows that the more you try to find answers to these mysteries, the more mysterious they become. I'll give you one example. My curiosity about the mysteries in the

Bible started with the numbers that are so frequently used: 7, 12, 40, 49, and 70. I wanted to know why it was so and why they played such crucial roles. So I began to look at the stories in the Bible from an occult point of view –"

John abruptly interrupted. "Why did you start to look at these stories from an occultist perspective? Many Christians said that any form of occultism was Satan or Lucifer's work or some other 'dark forces'. So how do you explain that? Sorry for interrupting you."

"So far as I know, that's the official line of all the Christian Churches. Some verses in the Old Testament strictly forbid the use of necromancy, astrology, witchcraft, sorcery, mediumship, et cetera. But in biblical times, what are now known as prophets were called 'seers' – an occult term. And when the Philistines surrounded King Saul's army and he was helpless, he was forced to consult the Witch of Endor because the prophet Samuel had already died, and God did not communicate with him in dreams or by any other means. The witch, therefore, summoned the spirit of Samuel at the request of the king. The spirit of Samuel told him through the medium that he and his sons would be killed the next day in the battle and that his army would be completely destroyed."

This story dumbfounded John. It took him a little while to respond to Paul. "I've never heard this story before. I find it so fascinating. Could you please tell me where I can find it – the Witch of Endor – and where I can find the seers and prophets as well?"

"Well, I don't want to quote any biblical verses in this discussion; otherwise, it could easily become a theological debate. I'll make one exception, though: 1 Samuel 28:1-25. But I won't cite the verses where you'll find the terms 'seer' and 'prophet'. So far as I know, both terms are mentioned in about thirty verses in different chapters of the Old Testament. Even if these occult means are Satan's work, and interest in or use of them is against God's laws, I wonder why there's no mutual love and harmony among those who don't use such methods. Certainly, such practices are not as sinful as waging wars against each other in His name. Here's another interesting thing: In astrology, you only need to calculate the positions of the planets on the day and at the time and place of your birth, and the time when you ask an astrologer to make predictions for you. Nothing more than that. There's no black magic, no mantras, no rituals of any kind."

"Thank you very much, Paul. Please continue."

"Thank you, John. So I want to find out for myself if such occult means are the work of Satan. One can argue for that being the case, but my simple counter-argument would be this: Why didn't other numbers also play equally important roles? We could perhaps discuss these mysteries in the future, when and if I find some satisfactory answers, but not now. My knowledge of these topics is still too minimal, and even if I tried to tell you what I've learned so far, it'd be too complex for you to understand. John, I think the moment you begin to believe in any form of existence beyond this human life, you can no longer look at things from a worldly perspective. All the stories in the Bible are so strange if you examine them from a non-believer's point of view."

"I've never thought about these things before, Paul. But couldn't you perhaps find answers to these mysteries by studying theology? Or the Bible itself?"

"No, John. If you look at those who founded the thousands of Christian Churches worldwide today, they are people who could recite many parts of the Bible by heart. Even then, they interpret the texts completely differently. That's the main reason I want to try to approach the biblical God from a different perspective. And another very crucial fact that we should not forget about this subject is that since the existence of Christianity, countless religious wars have been fought between Christians, mainly by those who vehemently condemned the belief in or practice of occultism by claiming that it was against God's law. Perhaps the worst thing God could do to those who believe in occult practices would be to punish them while they're still alive or send their souls to hell when they die. Unlike those who initiated religious wars, such people don't pose a threat to humanity at all."

"How about approaching these mysteries through philosophy, Paul?"

"No, I don't think that would work. I have studied philosophy. By the way, John, I think you might also want to know why Christine is a devoted Catholic. She accepts her Church's doctrine unconditionally."

John turned to Christine and said, "So far as I know, nearly all the Protestant Churches say bad things about your Church. So I'm curious to know how you see your Church and why you remain a devoted Catholic. If that's too personal, you don't need to answer the question, Christine."

"No, it's not too personal at all, John. I'm glad that you asked me. There are some simple reasons why I remain a Catholic. Many of my best friends, who belong to different Protestant Churches, have tried to persuade me to leave the Roman Catholic Church by saying all kinds of bad things about it. But I asked them these questions in return: If Protestantism is better than Catholicism, why are there so many different Protestant Churches, and why isn't there more love and harmony among them than among the Catholics? These friends don't have a satisfactory answer. And my second argument is that a great number of Catholic theologians, cardinals, archbishops, bishops, and priests were and are among the world's brightest people, so they all cannot be wrong. And furthermore, I'm also fascinated by the rituals, rites, liturgies, and my Church's clergy's robes, absent in the Protestant Churches. After all, it's my life."

John was delighted with Christine's explanation. "Thank you so much, Christine, for explaining all this. May I ask you and Paul another question that just came to my mind: What do you think about Jane's point of view on the biblical God and religion in general?"

"John, as Paul told you a few minutes ago, we're a family, but we don't try to influence each other with our religious or philosophical or political or social points of view."

"Thank you very much, Paul. I respect you all for your spirit of freedom."

John now turned to Paul again and said, "Excuse me, Paul. An idea suddenly popped into my head concerning the Bible. It's often said that Judaism and Christianity are religions of prophecy. What would you say about that?"

"I agree with that, John. It is also part of my research. But to my mind, prophecies are, like dreams and visions, too mysterious to decipher. Yet the leaders of many Churches claimed in the past, and still claim in our time, to be able to interpret them correctly. We know that these attempts have caused the death and suffering of countless innocent people. I'm especially fascinated by the so-called end-of-time prophecies, and I've looked into other non-biblical prophecies as well. One of the main problems with the prophecies in the Bible is that they are scattered through several chapters with a time-span of thousands of years. So it's an almost impossible task for us mortals to draw concrete conclusions about them all that could be accepted by all Christians, or even a large portion of them. It's extremely dangerous to make one's interpretations of the prophecies public because countless self-proclaimed biblical experts in every era have tried and are still trying to interpret these prophecies according to their whims and to serve their interests. The result was and is all those religious wars. So my interpretations are only for myself. I'll tell nobody else."

"Thank you very much, Paul. I'm interested in what these interpretations of yours could be. Why do you think what you've mentioned is so mysterious to us?"

"I'm quite sure that there must be other dimensions or laws or forces in the universe that are unimaginable to the human mind but are in many different ways influencing us directly or indirectly. Just one example is the question of how it's possible to predict the future by divination, as I said a while ago."

Paul continued, "John, by the way, let's go back to your interest in reading. May I know the subjects that interest you most?"

"I love novels. But my main interest is history, especially slavery. I've also read many books on the histories of some major European countries, including yours."

"Well, that is very interesting. In that case, you're surely well-informed about the countless bloody wars that white people have been fighting against each other since the beginning of time."

"Yes, to some extent."

"You see, we white people are ruthless not only toward colored people, but our brutality toward each other is also beyond description. The Great War ended recently, yet fresh tensions between nations are gathering momentum everywhere, here in Europe and worldwide. So it's likely that we're going to experience major conflicts again very soon. If that happens, it could be several times worse, with our modern weapons, than the ones that we've had in the past. It'd be devastating beyond our imagination."

Paul continued, "John, since you're interested in history, you surely must have read about communism. What do you think about that?"

"I'm sorry, Paul, I'm not yet knowledgeable enough to go into such an abstract subject. Even for studying the topics in which I'm most interested, I don't have enough time. Talking about future conflicts around the world, though, I'd like to ask you one thing. A while ago, you told me that at every critical moment in history, the members of your community – or your relatives – made thorough analyses of the overall conditions and then decided how to react in the best way. In that way, you could prevent yourselves from being sacrificed in time for a cause that wouldn't benefit you. So my question now is, have you done that yourself or are you going to do it soon since the situation everywhere seems critical already?"

"John, I'm glad that you asked that. Yes, we did it earlier this year. We invited some distinguished people from many academic disciplines and institutions and had them do the analysis. The conclusion was that we're rapidly heading for several major armed conflicts around the world in this or coming decades."

"Paul, didn't they think that they could find some solutions to avoid these conflicts?"

"John, if I'm to be honest, every member of the analysis group was very pessimistic about our immediate future. Since there are so many powerful rivals in the world these days, it'd be almost impossible to find rational solutions. Look, the white man is against the white man; the white man is against the yellow, the brown, and the black man; the yellow man is against the yellow man; the brown man is against the brown man; the black man is against the black man; the powerful man is against the powerless; the rich man is against the poor man; the intelligent man is against the ignorant; the man is against the woman, and so on. And if that were not enough, hundreds of millions of people are divided into many religions. Even among the Christians, for instance, there are divisions into several rival Churches, and so on. Oh, it's endless if you start looking. So it's so crucial that you keep calm and don't look at things around you with emotion, but logically and rationally, if you don't want to be sacrificed for a cause that would not be beneficial to you. The world has been full of all kinds of hatred since the beginning of human existence, and this will come to an end only when there's no longer a single human being on earth, as heartbreaking as that is, John."

Paul's words moved John deeply. "Paul, thank you so much. I'll think about all these things very carefully. You have given me a lot of food for thought. Have you considered the measures you could take to prevent yourselves from being sacrificed for nothing?"

"No, not really, John. We cannot do that yet. But we've decided to closely observe world events and make preparations for if and when the conflicts should become a reality. But John, since we're living in societies that are ruled by laws and traditions, it's not always possible to isolate yourself from the society in which you live and act independently. For example, where there is a law of conscription for a young man to serve in the armed forces, you have very little chance to do otherwise. And if you can't look at things from a logical point of view and act emotionally instead, or if you aren't courageous enough to defend your rights, you'll be sacrificed for nothing even though you had a chance to avoid it. Well, what I'm telling you could be too complicated to understand because you're still young and you haven't had a great deal of life experience yet. But someday, you'll understand more clearly what I'm talking about."

"Paul, thank you so much for these wise words – although, as you've just said, they're difficult for me to understand right now."

Paul continued, "John, your own family story has also moved us deeply. You have our deepest sympathies. And now I'll tell you a little bit more about us. Until very recently, we had about one hundred hectares of farmland not far from here, but we sold them, and we're concentrating now on our small construction company. My paternal grandfather started it more than a hundred years ago. Jane is working in the office, managing the daily business as my assistant. We've got another branch in St. Vith – about a hundred kilometers from here in the north. And we've got a permanent staff of twenty at both branches. If you hadn't saved Jane's life, we'd most likely have had to reduce our business or completely give it up. Or we might have to employ some of Jane's first cousins…"

Suddenly, John became curious and interrupted. "Excuse me for interrupting you, Paul. But I'm curious how many cousins Jane has. I've got not even a single cousin, and that's why I'm just curious. But I hope it's not too personal for you."

Before Paul could reply, Jane answered, "No, it's not personal at all. I've got altogether fourteen first cousins. Nearly half of them are from my mother's side and the rest from my papa's side."

"Thank you very much, Jane. Paul, would you please continue now?"

"The problem for us is that most of them have their own professions or those who don't have jobs aren't interested at all in working for a company like ours. Well, we're concentrating in the private sector – the construction or restoration of small and medium-size houses that were ruined in the Great War – and we also build new flats or houses to order. Except in winter with thick snow, about fifty to eighty carpenters and masons regularly work for us. So if you're interested in working with us, too, you can stay with us and help us.

35

We've got a couple of spare rooms; you can choose the one you like most. You'll be treated as a family member, not as an employee. And we'll reward you much better than we would a typical employee. But we'll first have to find out if we can arrange with the Immigration and Labor offices for your stay and work permits."

John was overjoyed on hearing these words. He could not hold back his tears. "Oh, I cannot express how happy I am. God has finally answered my prayers."

Jane asked, "John, what were your prayers, by the way? I'm just curious."

"There are always two: to be healthy and to meet many kind people like you. But Paul, I must admit that I'm a Jack-of-all-trades but master of none. I have never attended any vocational schools."

"John, don't worry about that. You'll learn by working. Many of our employees learned their trades with us over the years." Paul continued, "How do your aunt and uncle live? I mean, how do they earn their livelihood, and what kind of flat are they living in?"

"They live by menial jobs – cleaning offices and homes, or babysitting. And at the moment, neither of them are in good health, so their existence is very precarious. They're living in a cellar flat with two rooms. In winter, it's so cold because they can barely afford to buy coal."

"How old are they?"

"My aunt is about fifty and my uncle fifty-five."

"I see. If we can arrange for your permits and come to work with us, they could also move here. The woman who has been running the household for more than forty years is retiring soon, so your aunt and her husband could take over her job. And even if we cannot secure the permits for you and you have to leave the country, we'll take care of them. We've got a few vacant flats in Brussels, so they can move there until they move here. The flats are sufficiently heated. And we'll make some arrangements so that they won't have to work hard to survive. So don't worry about them anymore. By the way, what are their names?"

"Elizabeth and David." John was so overwhelmed with joy and gratitude that he could not utter a single word for several minutes. Then he said, "May I say a few words about what I'm feeling now?"

Paul signaled for him to go ahead.

"I've never dared to dream that such loving and generous people existed in this world."

"John, keep in mind that we're not the only ones who sympathize with the suffering of the blacks. Even in our immediate surroundings, I know many people among my friends and relatives whose hearts bleed whenever they see blacks being unfairly treated. Their only crime is that they were born with black skin. So we, at least – that is, Christine, Jane, I, and our relatives in this community – believe that we should treat the blacks as fairly as we can. After all, we owe a great deal to the people in our colonies. So if you stayed and worked for us, you'd have peace of mind, at least in this small community. I suppose you may also be curious about what kind of people Christine's relatives are. Since nearly all of them live quite far away from here, we don't know much about their attitudes. Her mother, for example, is a Dutchwoman from Holland, and they live in South Africa. When you rescued Jane, they returned to Belgium for a few months to visit friends and relatives. Some of Christine's relatives were strongly against our marriage, but when they realized how much we loved each other and saw that we could successfully handle the prejudice on both sides of the ethnic and linguistic divide, they're now the biggest supporters of our worldview. We know only that much about them. Meanwhile, you'll have ample time to read all the books on the bookshelves that you want. You can borrow books from the nearby libraries as well. John, on behalf of Christine, Jane, and me, I'd like to tell you that you've impressed us deeply with your hunger for knowledge and your tenacity."

John was so glad to hear Paul's words that he could barely speak. John had to fight back his tears. After a while, he tried to express his feelings. "Christine, Paul, Jane, this is the happiest moment of my life. I've never experienced such happiness before. Believe me."

John's words equally moved Christine, Paul, and Jane. Jane assured him that if the stay and work permits could be procured, she would immediately inform him, and she would arrange his journey, too. But even if the two permits could not be secured, her family would buy the ticket for his return journey to America and give him enough money to buy a spacious house with a garden, plus enough for himself and his family for their whole lives.

John was picked up on Sunday afternoon by his three friends. On reflection, Christine, Jane, and Paul were impressed by John's way of speaking: He spoke very quietly, and his manner was very composed.

CHAPTER 5
(15th August 1927 – Monday)

It was already a month since John had visited them. Jane was sitting in her office in a building next to her home. The time was one o'clock in the afternoon. As Jane was about to leave, the telephone rang. She snatched it up, and as she was about to speak, she realized that it was John.

"Good afternoon, Jane, it's me. I received your letter yesterday evening, and I was so excited about the good news. So you mean I'll be fined a thousand francs for my overstay, but I could stay and work for a year first?"

"Good afternoon, John. I'm glad you received it. You'll have to go to the Immigration Office where you live as soon as possible. We've arranged everything, so you don't need to worry. Just go there and when you've got your permits, come here as soon as you can. We'll arrange everything else when you're here. We'll also make arrangements for your aunt and uncle later. Just give me a call as soon as you're ready. Okay? I wish you a nice day, and please convey my greetings to your aunt and uncle. Oh, by the way, we're very pleased to hear from your letter of last week that your aunt and uncle appreciated our offer."

It was 10th September, a Saturday, and cloudy. Around three p.m., Jane went to the railway station to pick John up. They greeted each other joyously and then headed home. Christine and Paul and a number of their relatives were waiting for them at the main entrance. Jane introduced him to them, and they all entered the house. When they were in the living room, Jane said to John, "Make yourself at home. You're family now. We're preparing something exceptional for dinner to mark our reunion. A few more relatives will come later. They want to get to know you better, so after dinner, we'll sit and talk more. When you were here last time, you looked at the spare rooms; choose the one you like most. Tomorrow, we'll discuss plans for the next few months. And if you want, you can start work on Monday."

"Jane, everybody, thank you so much for what you've done for me. I'm already feeling at home. Yes, I'd be happy to start work on Monday. My aunt and uncle asked me to convey their heartfelt greetings to you. Again and again, they asked me to tell you how thankful they are for your generous offer. They've seen the flat and were simply speechless. They're making preparations now so that they can move in before winter comes."

"I'm glad about that. I'll arrange it so that they can move into the flat in early October. We'll then invite them here. We would all like to see them."

Christine, Jane, and a few of her cousins were busy preparing dinner. At seven o'clock, about fifteen relatives joined them at the table—the last guest left at ten. John chose a spacious and comfortably furnished room on the second floor with a view over the backyard.

The next day, Christine, Paul, Jane, and John were sitting in the living room at two o'clock, after lunch. They arranged that John would work as a carpenter's and mason's apprentice for six to eight hours a day and would have Saturdays and Sundays off. During the first few months, Paul discreetly observed how John worked both as a carpenter and mason. He was much impressed by John's skill.

CHAPTER 6
(13th January 1928 – Friday)

John had been with Christine, Paul, and Jane for five months and felt comfortable in his new family. And he and Jane had become quite intimate. Those in the broader community had also fully accepted him as one of them. Then, on the 13th January, when John came back from work and was about to enter the house, Jane, who stood at the front door, greeted him and said, "Good afternoon, John. I've been waiting for you. How about taking a holiday for a week, since there's not much to do here these days? My parents are going to spend a couple of weeks in southern France. They'll leave on the coming Monday. We can also leave on the same day if you want."

John was surprised and excited by the offer. "Hi Jane, good afternoon. That would be great. Where shall we go?"

"I'll think about where we might best spend our free time. I'll let you know this evening. After dinner, would you please come to the office?"

"All right, I'll be there. But Jane, won't your parents be suspicious if we take a holiday alone?"

"It was their suggestion, so don't worry about that."

John was visibly relieved and even more excited now.

After they had dinner together with other family members, they went into the office together.

"John, I've planned for us to depart from here on the same day that my parents leave. They'll go by train at nine o'clock in the morning. We'll send them off to the station, and we'll leave by car at about ten. I don't know yet for sure where we'll be going – we'll drive around according to our mood and the weather without fixing particular destinations. I have already assembled various hotels' names and addresses in a few towns and villages where people of color are welcome. By the way, may I ask you a question, John?"

"Ask away, Jane."

"It's possible that circumstances will oblige us to stay at the odd hotel which is not friendly to colored people. If so, would you mind if

I treated you as if you were a household servant to avoid awkward reactions from the whites?"

"Don't worry about that, Jane. I'll behave as the situation demands."

"Thank you, John. We'll travel in our oldest car to avoid attracting attention."

"I think that's a perfect idea, Jane. I won't be able to sleep tonight for thinking about the holiday."

"Nor me, John. If we enjoy it, we'll extend it another week, okay?"

John could not hide his excitement. They hugged each other and said good night, and separated. On Monday, Jane and John took Christine and Paul to the railway station, and after the train had left, they left home in Jane's old car.

"John, we'll first go to Bastogne and look at the place where you rescued me. From there, we'll drive north. We'll travel only about a hundred kilometers today."

They drove to Bastogne, and when they arrived at the junction where the accident nearly happened, they got out of the car and walked to the site. It was the first time they had revisited it together. Visibly emotional, Jane took John's hand, and they stood there in silence for ten minutes. Jane tenderly looked at John and shed tears. John's eyes were also full of tears, but they uttered not a single word. Then they continued their journey, enjoying the snow-capped landscapes along the way. Around noon they arrived at a small restaurant.

"John, it's lunchtime already. Let's walk a little bit farther over there where the small hill is, and when we come back, let's eat our lunch in this little restaurant, okay?"

They got out of the car and walked at a leisurely pace in the direction of a small hill some 400 or 500 meters away. They climbed the hill and enjoyed the beautiful snow-covered sights that lay below.

"John, how do you like the views from here?"

"It's a pity snow covers the landscape; if it were spring, summer, or autumn, it would be fantastic."

"We'll come back here in every season to find out how the land-scapes around here change, okay?"

"Yes, that'll be great. But I think the views are also beautiful in their way now. If there were no winter and no snow, we might not be able to fully appreciate the beauties of spring, summer, and autumn. Don't you think, Jane?"

"Yes, you're right."

"I'll always remember this place, this date, and these views – and also, of course, you, Jane, my whole life."

"Me too, John. Let's take a seat here and enjoy the beauty of nature."

After brushing the snow from a bench, they sat down. Jane started the conversation.

"John, we've known each other for quite a long time, and we like each other very much, but I've never dared to ask you about your personal life – I mean your intimate life. So would you mind if I asked you a few very personal questions?"

"Yes, that's true. We've known each other for quite a while now. Jane, please go ahead. Ask me anything you like."

"Thank you. Do you have a girlfriend back home? I'm sure you've noticed that I'm rather direct in my dealings with people."

"I noticed it very early on, and I like it very much. No – but I met two interesting girls with whom I could have fallen in love."

"Are they black or white?"

"They're black. They're around my age."

"That means you haven't told them that you're interested in them?"

"I haven't. I'm rather shy."

"I sensed it immediately when we met again in the restaurant kitchen. Have you ever met a white girl with whom you might fall in love?"

"Sure, one or two. But I dared not show my feelings for them, alt-hough they were very friendly and kind to me; I thought perhaps they were only interested in friendship."

"Are there any black and white couples in your community back home?"

"Yes, there are some, but it's very rare."

"Are they happy? Are their marriages happy?"

"I don't know much about them. But so far as I know, they've got many problems, mainly caused by the colors of their skin."

"Have you ever thought about being married and how many children you'd like to have?"

"Yes, now and then, I think about such things. My parents, and especially my mother, said a couple of times that they'd like to have grandchildren as soon as possible. But I'm not sure whether I'll ever decide to get married and have children of my own."

"Why is that?"

"I don't know whether I'd be psychologically strong enough to see my children being discriminated against every day."

"John, I can understand your feelings."

"Thank you very much, Jane. Any more questions?"

"For the time being, no. You'd like to ask me some questions in return, I suppose."

"Yes, if you don't mind."

"Go ahead."

"Thank you, Jane. Could you perhaps tell me more about your life?"

"Yes, sure. Well, I've fallen in love with three men. All of them were white. But our relations were not very harmonious. One was a racist, one was too religious, and one was too political. For almost a year, I haven't had a boyfriend."

"When would you like to get married, and how many children would you like?"

"Well, if I find someone I could love, I think I could get married right now. As for the number of children, I've no idea – at least two, perhaps."

"What do you mean by 'if you find someone you could love'? What kind of qualities would you expect in your life-mate?"

"He would have to love me. And he must not be too religious, too political, or a racist. He must not be too possessive; he must not be too greedy or stingy. And he must not be too talkative. I don't care about nationality or skin color. How about you?"

"As I'm not yet sure whether I'll ever marry, I haven't thought about such things. But with your charm and beauty and qualifications, I'm sure you'll easily find a life-mate of your choice, Jane."

"John, have you ever noticed that my interest in you might be more than just friendship?"

John was quite surprised by Jane's words. He tried to remain calm, but without much success. Then, after a long while, he tried to express his feelings. "I dare not speculate about that, Jane. I only know that you and all of your relatives have been extraordinarily good to me."

"John, I think *you* could be my life-mate."

John could not believe what he'd just heard. He began to get even more nervous. "No Jane, you must be kidding."

"I'm very serious, John."

He thought for a long moment. "Jane, I'm so pleased to hear this, but we're worlds apart. I know you are very humane and not a bit racist, but I cannot imagine marrying you."

"Why not?"

"In your family and among your relatives, I find happiness and peace. I know how much you all care about me. But if we were to get married, their attitude toward me might change. I won't find another haven like this in my life. So let's be good friends."

"I'm quite sure their attitude wouldn't change much. So you don't need to worry about that. I've been thinking about a life with you and the obstacles we'd have to confront. And I'm quite ready to make any sacrifices, John."

"No Jane, think about it carefully. I don't want to ruin your peaceful life or that of your relatives. They'll surely think that I've seduced you."

"They know you very well, so they wouldn't think that. And I don't care what the world thinks about me or us. You know they like you very much."

"Yes, I know that, and I'm so thankful for it. But they like me as a friend and not as a future son-in-law. And think about the fate of our children. They would suffer."

Jane looked deeply and longingly into John's eyes and, at the same time, shyly took his hand and asked him in a seductive voice, "John, would you take my hands and hold them? I want to touch you."

John did not know how to react. He was very nervous and withdrew his hand. "No, no, Jane. I've got nothing against it, but if I did that, I'd get very excited. I haven't touched a woman for years. I'm already electrified."

Jane was somewhat disappointed, for she had expected a passionate embrace and a tender kiss. But she did not insist.

"John, look, our children will not be on their own. We know that innumerable blacks and biracials suffer discrimination every day in many countries around the world. Our children will find peace and love, at least at our home and among my relatives."

"Jane, I don't know what to say. You know how much I love you. If I were white, I'd have expressed my love for you long ago. Please let me think about it, okay?"

The duo returned to the restaurant. After lunch, they continued their journey to Hotel Paradies, where they were going to stay. It was located just a few kilometers on this side of St. Vith. Both of them were silent throughout the journey. At four o'clock, they arrived at the hotel. It was a small but very nice-looking place. Before they got out of the car, Jane told John that she had booked one bedroom for them because it was the only room available. John asked her if they could perhaps find separate rooms in another hotel in the neighborhood. She said that every room had been booked out as there was a big cultural festival in the vicinity. John realized that this was Jane's secret plan to spend some days and nights together alone. He was quite uncomfortable with the arrangement.

"We don't have an alternative. We won't show any intimacy between us. We'll behave as if we're just good friends. But you don't need to worry too much; I made an effort to get us a room in this hotel because it accepts all nationalities. So let's hope that the white guests will be tolerant."

To their great relief, the hotel guests were a mixture of whites and coloreds. Very few people paid attention to their presence. Even so, they did not exhibit any intimacy. Except during meal times in the morning, noon, and evening, and a few short excursions into the surrounding areas, they stayed in their hotel room most of the time. They extended their holiday for one more week, as they enjoyed it so much.

Jennifer was silently shedding tears as Jane was reading. Jane stopped reading further and said to her daughter, "Jennifer, I'm sorry, but I'll have to skip a few passages because there are some intimate conversations involved. But you may read them when you reach a certain age, say twelve. Is that okay?"

"Mama, that's okay."

Jane skipped the following passage:

When they breakfasted together after the first night at the hotel, they discreetly looked around them to check whether anyone was seated nearby. There were a few people behind them, but none of them paid them any attention. So Jane spoke to John in a whisper.

"How do you feel now, John?"

"Fantastic. And you?"

"The same. I've been dreaming of just such blissful moments since soon after you moved in with us. You're very strong, John."

"You are too, Jane. And we're still young, so it's quite natural. But I'm not sure whether you were pretending to be enjoying it so that I'd not be disappointed. As I've never been with a woman so intimately before, I feel clumsy and inexperienced. I was so excited that I came in a few seconds the first two or three times, as you noticed."

"Why should I pretend, John? I'm not that experienced either. You did well. So don't worry about it at all. We'll experiment to find the best ways to fulfill each other's needs, okay? We have plenty of time ahead."

"Thank you, Jane. I feel relieved by your soothing words."

"John, have you ever slept with white women before?"

"Yes, a couple of times. But they were professionals – prostitutes."

"What were the differences between them and me?"

"The two are worlds apart, Jane. There were no feelings at all between them and me. They just slept with me for money. But now, with you – I cannot describe the difference in words."

Here, Jane continued reading for Jennifer.

At the end of their holiday, they headed home. They had become much closer now than before and were in an exuberant mood all the time. On their way back home, they discussed several topics.

"How shall we behave at home, Jane? I think your parents will notice that something special has happened between us, even if we pretend to be as we were before."

"Yes, I think so, too. My mother even teased me a couple of times about whether my attitude toward you was more than simple friendship. Let's behave as normal. We should not show too much intimacy unless I get pregnant."

"Okay. Let's pretend that nothing happened between us."

"But it'll be difficult to hide our feelings. And they won't believe that nothing happened. Well then…would you like to have a boy or a girl?"

"I don't have a preference. I pray that we have a healthy baby."

"If I conceive," Jane said, "I'll inform my mother first and then my father."

"And if you don't get pregnant?"

"Let's think about it. We could perhaps wait a little longer to tell them about us."

"I agree, Jane. What shall we do tonight and in general before we make our new relationship public?"

"We shouldn't sleep in the same room. Come to me at eight o'clock and leave at nine or ten. Is that okay?"

"Yes. I like the idea."

They were cautious about their behavior in front of their relatives and friends and succeeded in hiding their relationship.

CHAPTER 7
(27th March 1928 – Tuesday)

More than two months had passed since Jane and John's holiday at the Hotel Paradies, and Jane noticed that she had missed her periods. She spoke with her mother about it and wanted to tell John what her mother told her, so she invited him to her office for breakfast. It was at nine a.m. He entered the office, and after having passionately kissed each other for several minutes, she said, "John, I have some good news. I haven't had my period for two months, so I think I'm pregnant. Yesterday evening I informed my mother about it. She said she would speak to my father."

John's reaction was a mixture of joy and worry. "Oh really? I'm happy to hear that. But how did she react?"

"She simply said that she and my father had sensed a long time ago that I was interested in you as more than just a friend and that they had prepared for something like this."

"Was she sad or angry?"

"No. She was happy. And she said, 'Jane, it's your life. We cannot decide what you should do with your life. You're a very mature person, and you see the consequences of your actions. We'll support you in every possible way to make your married life a happy and successful one.' She also said that we would all sit down together, either this evening or in a couple of days, and discuss what to do."

"I see. I feel much better now. Yes, we'll wait for the discussion."

At that moment, someone knocked on the door, and John opened it. It was Christine. She greeted him and Jane joyously, as she always did. John was glad because he did not sense any change in her mood.

"Mama, I've just informed John about our conversation of yesterday evening."

"Good. I've come to tell you both that we'll all meet in the living room after dinner. Your papa was also happy about the news. Till this evening. Bye-bye."

Christine left, and John and Jane petted and cuddled each other passionately again. After a few moments, Jane said, gently holding his hands, "John, please don't go to work today. Stay with me, okay?"

"Okay. Now we can be together more often, and for longer. I'm so glad."

"No, John. My mother wants us to keep behaving like before and not show too much affection in public. She wants to arrange everything before we make it widely known. You know she's very religious, so she wants us to get married before my pregnancy becomes visible. For her, it's shocking to have a relationship before marriage. But she's full of understanding in our case. Nevertheless, she wants to arrange your permits, and the procedures of marriage between a Belgian and an American, because we have no knowledge or experience of that."

"I understand. We'll be discreet. Let's see what your father has to say this evening."

Jane was busy in the office the whole day. John sat nearby and lovingly observed her all the time. Then it was dinnertime. When the clock on the wall pointed to half-past six, Jane and John left the office and headed for the house. They went straight into the dining room. Paul was already there and greeted the couple as heartily as ever. When they all started eating, Paul spoke. "John and Jane, your mother told me that she had informed about our after-dinner meeting."

Both answered at the same time. "Yes, she has informed us about it."

"Good."

Then John spoke. "I was very unsure how she would react, and when I knew that she was not against it and I saw no change today in her attitude toward me, I couldn't have been gladder and more thankful."

"Good, John. As you know, we aren't concerned about the color of a person's skin or social status. We only care about his character and his heart."

At eight p.m., they went into the living room and took their seats as they usually did. Paul started the conversation. "Christine, and I are happy that Jane has found her ideal life-partner. We noticed a long time ago that she was delighted whenever you two were together. We'll do everything we can to make your married life as happy as possible. The only thing we're worried about is the timing. By this, I mean that the political situation worldwide is getting more and more complicated with each passing day. A major war may break out again sooner rather than later. But such things are beyond our control; the only thing we can do is try to steer our lives away from such dangers as much as we can. You've been with us for more than half a year, and your stay and work permits are going to expire in a couple of months. Jane and I will make every effort to get them extended, and at the same time, we'll make inquiries about the necessary procedures for your marriage. Hopefully, we'll get all the required information in a few days. As soon as we do, we'll make arrangements for the wedding, before Jane's pregnancy becomes too visible."

Christine interrupted, "Are you thinking about having only a civil marriage or a religious marriage as well?"

John answered before Jane could. "We've discussed it, and as you know, I'm a church-going Christian, so I'd very much want to have both marriages. Jane naturally wanted to have only a civil marriage, but she said she would not object to having both, as Paul and you did. It depends on her. I won't force my wishes upon her."

"Well, as I've told you before, John, I won't change my mind. If you're happy, I'll be happy as well, and our marriage will benefit as it did with my parents. I could convert to your religion, but it'd not be sincere and genuine. I would probably feel guilty toward your God. I mean, if He or She does exist, He or She probably wouldn't appreciate it. Mama and Papa, do you have any ideas to solve this dilemma?"

Christine expressed her feelings. "Jane, I think John is very fair in giving you the freedom to decide for yourself. I'm sure he loves you even more because of your compromise. I loved your father even more for how he approached our marital arrangements. If you do that, John and his parents and relatives will be so delighted. And if you and your children are happy, God and your father and I will be happy. I don't think you need to feel guilty about it. Even if it's a sin in God's eyes, He'll surely be merciful enough to forgive you, Jane."

"Thank you very much, Mama, for your kind words. "

John's eyes were filled with tears of happiness and gratitude. "I'm so happy to hear these words, Christine and Jane."

Paul continued, "As soon as we get the information we need, let's discuss the wedding in detail. I suggest that we invite only our immediate relatives and closest friends and make things as simple as possible. And John must also decide who he wants to invite."

"Thank you very much, Paul. I think I'll invite the two Americans and the Belgian and their girlfriends." John then got an idea and continued, "Christine and Paul, may I ask you a personal question?"

Paul signaled him to go ahead.

"Thank you very much. You have both overcome all kinds of obstacles in your lives and even celebrated the silver jubilee of your marriage recently. Jane and I'd appreciate it very much if you could tell us the secrets of a happy and lasting marriage."

Jane, Christine, and Paul were much amused. Paul turned to Christine and jokingly said, "It's beyond my expertise. Honey, you're the expert. Tell them about our secrets."

Everybody was heartily laughing. Christine said, "No Paul, it's very unfair that you give me all the credit for our happy marriage. We both deserve equal credit."

They roared with laughter once again. Then Christine continued, "Well, since Paul has authorized me to speak on his behalf ..."

More laughter interrupted her. Then she continued, "I'll tell you the few basic rules that have enabled us to make it work. One: We have never used sex as a weapon. During these long years, we rarely had sex-related problems, even when our relations were sour. Even when one of us was not in the mood for sex, we still tried to fulfill each other's desires. For example, if I was not in the mood, but Paul was, I would say to him, 'I'm not in the mood, but try to arouse me if you want.'

"In the same way, he allowed me to arouse him when he was not in the mood, but I was. And almost every time, we succeeded. Sex has powerful healing and reconciling power, so we used it fully. Two: Everyone must have a certain amount of freedom. Three: One should not be too possessive. Four: You should never impulsively threaten each other with divorce – if you did that, you'd make your partner very insecure, and the wound could be hard to heal. We've never used this word against each other even once in our entire married life, even when our marriage seemed to be beyond repair once or twice. Five: You must try to develop a culture of open discussion and compromise."

Christine's words made Jane and John tremendously happy.

"Thank you so much, Christine. I'm quite sure we'll make a good start with these valuable guidelines. But you might have some more good ideas?"

"Yes, John. When we decided to get married, we agreed upon these five rules. We discussed these things very openly. Of course, there are many other important factors that one has to observe, but everybody's situation is different. I don't think you can lay down universal rules for all married couples. You'll have to try to adjust as problems arise over time. Oh, I nearly forgot to tell you another crucial factor that you should not overlook or underestimate: When you're angry with your partner about something, you should not nurse your grievance and sulk. Let him or her know it right away and try to find a solution as soon as possible. This can mean a great deal for a long-lasting relationship."

John responded, "Thank you so much, Christine, for your invaluable ideas. Could you perhaps tell us a bit more about the things that you've had to adjust to?"

"Okay, here are a few that we – especially I – had to adjust. I used to be very lively and quite flirtatious. I had had more boyfriends than Paul. At the beginning of our relationship, he was always so serious that I found him rather boring. But then, when I found out that he possessed the many qualities that I wanted in my future life-partner, which none of my other boyfriends had, I tried to adjust my lifestyle to suit his. He was very tolerant and did not try to dictate how I should behave. But I discerned that he was silently suffering because of my way of life."

Jane also expressed her views. "Mama, you've never told me about the intimate side of your early life before. It's so fascinating. Hopefully, we will benefit from the basic tenets you've just mentioned." She then turned to John and jokingly said, "John, please write down Mama's advice before we forget it, and let's hang it on the wall, okay?"

"Don't worry, Jane. Although I've got very poor memory, I'll surely remember them."

Everybody laughed heartily again.

John got another idea and turned to Paul. "Paul, I'd like to ask you a brief but important question. You once said that some people are compatible, whereas others are not, depending on their Sun Signs. So would you please tell me whether Jane and I are compatible or not? I'm curious."

"John, it's good that you asked me that. Christine and I are not compatible according to our Sun Signs. But when we got to know each other's strong and weak points according to astrology, we tried to overcome our weaknesses and strengthen our existing strong points. So no, I won't tell you whether you're compatible or not. I've got quite a lot of books on the subject that you can read. But even if you're not compatible according to astrology, don't be discouraged. Several other factors play vital roles in making a married life a success or a failure. I've met many happily married couples who are not compatible according to astrology, and I know many couples whose marriages are miserable, even though they should be compatible according to their Sun Signs. But you have nothing to lose by getting some basic knowledge of astrology; it could be helpful to learn the innate characteristics of your Sun Signs. On the other hand, you mustn't become too dependent on it."

Jane was curious about what Paul was saying. "Papa, if it's not too personal for you and Mama, could you perhaps tell us what your strengths and weaknesses were and what kinds of compromises you had to make for a happy and successful marriage?"

Paul turned to Christine again and half-jokingly said, "Darling, over to you again. Tell them the deep secrets that we've been keeping between us during our married life!"

Another roar of laughter.

"Paul, it's not fair that you ask me to speak on your behalf once again."

"Christine, you know that I'm not very good at betraying such deep secrets. Women are more gifted in discussing such sensitive topics diplomatically. So please go ahead, darling."

Another rapturous burst of laughter.

"Okay. Listen, Jane. As you know, my Sun Sign is Scorpio, and Paul's is Aquarius. The first time we met, I immediately sensed that your papa was obsessed with me. He later confessed that he found me extremely erotic, but when he knew that I was a Scorpio, he distanced himself from me. The reason was that, according to astrology, Scorpios are possessive and jealous. So he was afraid to fall in love with me. But he could not ignore me for long ..."

Jane impulsively interrupted her mother. "And Papa, being a typical Aquarius, I suppose you love freedom at all costs, hence the detachment. It's interesting how you could strike a compromise between these polar opposites."

Christine continued, "I was surrounded by a lot of handsome men nearly all the time. He knew that. But when I began to think seriously about finding a steady life-mate, I realized that nearly all the men who were interested in me were interested in just one thing. Do you know what I mean? But your papa played it cool and mysterious. I was very disappointed, but on the other hand, it was a great challenge for me to get his love. I had expected a love letter from him for a long time, but it never came. And he did not even once try to date me, although he showed me in many different ways how much he cared for me whenever we met. So I couldn't wait any longer for him to take the initiative. Well, to cut our story short, I seduced him. Please don't ask me how! Paul, now it's your turn to tell the rest. I won't say any- more."

They all broke into laughter once again. After several moments, Paul spoke.

"I'll tell you about your mama's strong points. She's visionary and has solid business acumen. We owe her a great deal for our family's business successes. She's an expert at dealing with people, especially our business partners and employees. It's no wonder that she's such a person; she must have inherited those strengths from both parents. She came from two successful business families. And as I'm so re- served, she knew that I wouldn't have a chance with another woman, so she could live in total peace without the fear of losing me. Isn't that true, honey?"

Everybody was greatly amused. Jane became more inquisitive. "Is he reserved in your most intimate moments, too, Mama?"

"Far from it. He can also be the warmest and most tender person in the world."

"Mama and Papa, thank you so much for sharing your intimate se- crets with us so frankly. I appreciate it very much."

Christine got an idea and said, "By the way, just for your knowledge, I'd like to tell you one more thing that I think could be very important for a long-lasting marriage life: mutual respect. By this, I mean both partners must have some qualities for which they can respect each other. For instance, we both are very generous with the needy. I don't know if our marriage would have lasted this long if one of us had been selfish and stingy."

John and Jane thanked her profusely. It was 9:30 p.m., so they all went to bed. Over the next few days, Jane and Paul sent several let- ters of inquiry to different departments. And to their great relief, the authorities concerned informed them that they would extend John's stay and work permits, and they would give his application for per- manent residence special consideration. The civil marriage department gave them the green light within a week, so they immediately planned the wedding ceremony.

The civil marriage took place on 12th April, a Tuesday, and the religious ceremony in the small Methodist church in Florenville at noon on 22nd April, a Sunday. The wedding party was held at Christine and Paul's residence on the same day between four and nine p.m., with about one hundred guests. They invited only their relatives and best friends. Among them were John's American and Belgian friends, who had offered him a ride when he first visited Paul's family, with their girlfriends; Maria, Jane's maternal aunt; and Barbara, Jane's former classmate from Brussels, and her boyfriend. Elizabeth and David and Jane's maternal grandparents were also present. Christine and Paul gave short speeches detailing the couple's history, starting from the near-accident through which they first met each other. Everybody enjoyed the party tremendously. The last guests left at nine o'clock.

Jennifer was born at home with a midwife's help on 24th October 1928, a Wednesday, at ten o'clock in the morning. Her physical features were quite biracial. She was very healthy. Anne, John's mother, chose her first name. The birth was a great joy to everybody in the family and friend circles.

Jane had just finished reading Jennifer chapters 1 to 7 of her novel. While she read, Jennifer silently shed tears several times, but she did not interrupt her mother. John's eyes were also full of tears throughout the reading. After a long moment, Jane said to Jennifer, "Jennifer, we've come to the end of Chapter 7. As I said, I'll keep on writing as our lives continue to unfold."

"Thank you so much, Mama. What a wonderful story it is! You could become a famous writer, Mama. Who taught you storytelling?"

"Actually, I wanted to study literature so that I could become a writer. I've read a lot of novels, and I keep reading. If I'm successful with this novel, I'll write more. I have so many ideas in my head."

"Papa, what do you think about Mama's novel?"

"I found it so fascinating. I've had to fight back my tears nearly the whole time. Your mama has never given me any hint that she was writing such an excellent novel. Honey, I'm sure that you'll be successful with it. My strongest wish right now is to live long enough to be able to read the whole thing when it's finished. I'm very proud of you, and I always will be, honey."

"Thank you very much for your compliments. I'll try my best. Well, it's already ten o'clock. Let's go to bed."

Jennifer wanted to know more about her father, but Jane suggested that they discuss it the next day, as it was already late.

CHAPTER 8
(9th May 1934 – Wednesday)

Jennifer, Jane, and John were seated together in the living room as they had been the previous evening. The time was seven o'clock in the evening. Jennifer started the discussion by asking, "Papa, would you please tell me a bit more about your background?"

"My child, you've heard that I came from an African slave family. I'll make my story very brief; I don't think I should burden you too much now with how the slaves suffered during the past three or four hundred years and how we're still suffering from racial discrimination. When you grow up, you'll learn about it in more detail, whether you want to or not."

"What is a slave, Papa?"

"A slave is someone who is owned by another person and has to work for a master."

"Papa, how can someone own another person?"

"Well, in the case of the African slaves, they were rounded up in their native villages by slave traders, many of them white people. Not only that but various warring African tribes sold their prisoners of war to the whites. And they were taken in chains to America by ships and traded like animals in slave markets. They were not regarded as human beings, but merely as material possessions."

"How long ago was this, Papa?"

"The first African slaves arrived in the United States three or four hundred years ago. They were forced to work on tobacco and cotton plantations."

"How many slaves were there, Papa?"

"When slavery was finally abolished following the American Civil War of 1861 to 1865, several million slaves were freed."

"Papa, what is a civil war?"

"A civil war is a war in which the citizens of a country are fighting against each other because of their different political or economic or religious or racial ideas."

"Was the civil war in America only because of slavery?"

"There were other important issues, but that was the most significant one. It was caused mainly by the attempt to abolish slavery."

"Papa, how many is a million?"

"A million is many, many, many. You'll learn when you're in the third or fourth grade."

"Who freed them?"

"Overwhelmingly, the whites, but the slaves themselves also played significant roles in gaining their freedom. President Abraham Lincoln, who was the sixteenth president of America, is said to have played a key role as well."

"What is a president, Papa?"

"A president is like a king or queen who rules a country. But unlike a king or queen, he has to be elected every four years by the people."

"Papa, why are white people so bad?"

"Jennifer, though there are many bad white men and women, there are also many good white men and women. And there are also many good and bad black people."

"Papa, please go on. Please tell me more about how the slaves suffered."

"No, Jennifer. You're still too young to know how much the slaves suffered. The brutality is beyond description. When you grow up – say sixteen or seventeen – you can read about it. It's also crucial for you to know that we blacks are not the only ones who suffered as slaves: Throughout human history, slavery was – and still is – almost everywhere worldwide. Countless other slaves also suffered just like us. Now, let me tell you some of my own life stories very briefly, okay?"

"Please go ahead, Papa."

"When my forefathers were freed from slavery, they had to struggle very hard to survive. My grandparents and parents had to work as manual laborers or house servants. Fortunately, my father's only sister, your aunt Elizabeth, met her future Belgian husband, David, on a journey, and they later got married. They invited me to visit them here in Belgium in 1926, two years before you were born. Then, as your mama has described in her novel, our story started when that accident happened."

"Yes, your aunt and uncle love me so much, and I also love them very much. Papa, your aunt also used to tell me how much she suffered in America."

"Yes? I begged them not to tell you too much about how the blacks have been suffering for the past four hundred years."

"Mama and Papa, if God is so loving, why did he allow people to do such bad things to each other?"

John tried to answer. "Jennifer, people have asked that question for generations, but nobody has a satisfactory answer. That's one reason why your opa and your mama don't belong to any Church."

"But Papa, why do you and other blacks still worship a God that has caused so much suffering?"

"Well, we don't have any other choice. The white people have most of the wealth, technology, and so on; they can afford not to believe in God. But we blacks – no one in this world can give us hope except God. He is the only person to whom we can turn for hope."

"But does God really exist?"

"Nobody knows for sure."

"But Papa, if he doesn't exist, what's the use of worshipping him? How can someone who doesn't exist give you hope?"

"Jennifer, as you heard in Chapter 4 of your mama's novel, your opa, for example, believes that God probably exists because there are so many mysterious things in this world that we cannot explain."

"I see. Now I think I understand a bit better. Papa and Mama, may I ask you a question?"

Jane told her to go ahead.

"You knew that I'd suffer discrimination my whole life. So why did you let me come into this brutal world?"

Jane and John were shocked and saddened by Jennifer's unexpected question. Jane tried to answer in a soothing tone while holding back her tears. "Jennifer, as I described in the novel, that's exactly what your papa was always worried about. He was not even sure if he wanted a child of his own. It was my decision to have a baby. I hoped that I'd be able to give you, and your papa as well, some peace and love and security. As long as my parents, aunts, uncles, cousins, and I are alive, both of you will have peace, love, and security."

"Mama, I know that you love Papa and me very much. And I know that Papa and I find love and security in the community of your relatives. Papa and Mama, by the way, are you planning to have more children?"

Again Jane and John were quite taken aback by Jennifer's words. Jane answered with a counter-question. "Well, as the political situation around the world and especially in Europe has been getting worse since you were born, we'd like to wait. What do you think about that? Do you want sisters and brothers?"

"Mama and Papa, if you ask my opinion, I don't want you to make more babies who will only suffer like me – but it's your life, so it's up to you."

Jane and John remained silent for a long while, overcome by sorrow. Their eyes were filled with tears. Jane tried very hard to fight back her tears and took Jennifer tenderly to her side. They were silent until Jennifer asked her mother again in a broken voice, "Mama, do you ever look down on me because of my skin color?"

All of a sudden, Jane burst into torrential tears.

"Oh, Mama, I'm so sorry. I didn't mean to hurt you. Please forgive me, Mama, okay?"

It took Jane several minutes to recover from her sorrow. She then spoke in a trembling voice. "Jennifer, please don't ask me this question again if you love me, okay? It hurts me so much, you know. It's not that I blame you – if I were in your position, I'd most likely ask my mother the same question. Honey, believe me, if it were possible, I'd share my skin with you or exchange it with yours completely."

Jennifer, too, was sobbing now. "Mama, I'm so sad that I hurt you with this stupid question. Please forgive me. I promise I'll never ask you this question again. I love you so much, Mama."

Jennifer gazed at her father, who was also silently shedding tears. "Papa, I notice that you're so happy when you're alone or with Mama. I've often asked you how you manage it, and you say that if you're friendly and polite to other people, they will react in the same way. I try to do the same, but most people don't change their attitude toward me."

John answered in a soothing voice. "But darling, the situation would be even worse if you didn't try. In general, friendliness and politeness will make your life easier. As your mama says in Chapter 4, my paternal grandfather passed two pearls of wisdom down to his children and grandchildren. And by observing these pearls, our lives become a bit more bearable in the face of discrimination. Before I get the chance to speak to someone, they may be rude toward me, but I can nearly always turn their hostility around – or at least neutralize it. Remember that this is the only weapon we black people have. If we try to respond to hostility with hostility, the situation will worsen, and life will get harder. And we should not merely blame those who are hostile to us for their racist behavior. You should try to accept that you might do the same thing if you were they. If you take their way of treating you too seriously, you're only ruining your life. These are the pearls of wisdom that my grandfather passed down to us."

"Thank you very much. Papa, what is wisdom?"

"There are many different ways to explain it, but one of the simplest definitions is 'knowledge of the difference between good and evil'."

"But Papa, I think everybody knows what is good and what is evil."

"No, Jennifer. Not everybody knows the difference. Many people do awful things and believe they're doing good things. You'll know what I mean when you grow up and have more life experience."

"Another explanation of wisdom, perhaps, Papa?"

"Let me think it over … Well, here's a very simple one: Live and let live! Does that make sense? Let others live as you wish to live. Jesus Christ preaches: Do as you would have others do to you."

"Thank you, Papa. Now I understand it better. But Papa, I try to be friendly to whoever I come into contact with, but it's not always easy, and I am not always successful. So what should I do?"

"Jennifer, I know how hard it is, especially when you're young, but as you grow up, you'll manage somehow. You'll get used to it. It'll become very natural someday. Don't give up, okay?"

"Thank you very much, Papa. I'll keep trying. I promise you."

CHAPTER 9
(19th September 1934 – Saturday)

It was a bright, sunny day, and the time was around five p.m. Jane, Jennifer, and John were preparing to go to Paul and Christine's house. After Jennifer's birth, the family had moved to a house a few kilometers from Christine and Paul's. Christine and Paul had recently come back from New York City, where they had a six-room flat in Brooklyn. They had been there for the past two years. Jennifer was very excited to see her grandparents again; Christine and Paul heartily welcomed them.

After dinner, they gathered in the living room. Paul started the conversation. "Jennifer, you've grown up fast in our absence. How's life with you now? We missed you a lot while we were away. Are there any questions you want to ask your oma and me?"

"I missed you very much, too, Oma and Opa. Well, my life in general is okay, but my perception of the things around me has developed quite remarkably. I've lately been thinking critically about many things. For example, a few days ago, Mama read me some chapters from the novel she's writing. So I got to know quite a lot about both of you and my parents' lives before I was born. It was fascinating. After what Mama read, I've got a few questions I'd like to ask you, Opa, when you have time."

Before answering Jennifer's question, Paul turned to Jane. "Jane, are you writing a novel? You've never told us about it."

"Yes, Papa. I'm writing a novel based on our lives, an autobiographical fiction."

"I think that's an excellent idea, Jane. Keep up the good work. It might even become a bestseller someday—who knows?"

"That would be great, Papa, but I dare not hope that much."

"Have you chosen a title? What is it called?"

"No, I haven't, Papa. But I'm thinking about three titles: *Why Are You Crying, Mama?* is one. Another is *Whenever I See You Crying, I Am So Sad, Mama.* Another option would be simply *Jane.* You can read it, too, if you want to, Papa."

"What are the reasons for choosing the first two titles?"

"The first title is what Jennifer most often asked me. And the seccond title is also what she often said to me."

"In that case, I think both of themselves quite good."

"Thank you very much, Papa."

"I do want to read it, but not yet. If I read it now, the suspense will be too much. I'll read it when you've written half or two-thirds of it. Would that be all right?"

"I think that's a good idea, Papa."

"Jennifer, I'm so glad your mama is writing a novel. We could be famous if it becomes a bestseller."

"Opa, what is a bestseller?"

"A bestseller means a book that's bought by many people and thus becomes very well-known." Paul continued, "First of all, heartfelt greetings from John's parents and sister to you all. As we've told you on the phone a couple of times, we visited them twice, and they visited us three times. They are extremely nice, polite people. We're delighted to buy them a new four-room house with a garden in a much better area. If John goes back to America someday, he'll be able to start planting fruit trees and vegetables, as he's dreamed of since childhood. They asked us to send their love, especially to their granddaughter Jennifer."

"Oh, thank you so much, Opa and Oma. I'll write them a thank-you letter soon."

Paul then encouraged Jennifer to ask him any question she wanted. "Jennifer, I'm happy that you have some questions for me. I'm curious about what your mama has written."

"Opa, my first question is: Why don't you belong to any Christian Church? Why aren't you a Christian anymore? In Mama's book, she gives many reasons, but I want to hear them from you."

"When I was young, say until about I was twenty years old, I was a church-going Catholic, like your oma. But then I started seriously reading the Bible and the literature of other major religions of the world. It's not that I don't believe in the possibility of the existence of a powerful being called God somewhere in the universe, but I just can't blindly follow the doctrines of the existing Christian Churches –"

He was interrupted by Jennifer while Christine, Jane, and John listened attentively. "May I interrupt you, Opa? How many major religions are there in the world, and what are they?"

"Well, so far as I know, there are about ten: Hinduism, Buddhism, Judaism, Islam, Shintoism, Christianity, Confucianism, Jainism, Taoism, and Zoroastrianism."

"Why are there so many major religions, Opa?"

"I don't know, Jennifer, if I'm honest. Of course, one can discuss it endlessly. For example, Hinduism is practiced mainly in India; Buddhism in most Asian countries; Judaism by the Jews; Islam in several Asian and Middle Eastern countries; Confucianism and Taoism are practiced mainly in China or by the Chinese. Shintoism is practiced only in Japan. Zoroastrianism is practiced mainly in Iran – and so on."

"Thank you, Opa. Now please tell me a little more about why you're no longer a church-going Catholic."

"Well, there are several Christian Churches, and every one of them preaches the love of God and his son Jesus. All were founded by people who claim to be experts on the Bible. But many of them started wars against each other in the names of God and Jesus. In the same way, there are also many different branches of Islam and Judaism. When I realized that, I stopped going to church and started reading books on the other religions that I've just mentioned."

"Have you found the best religion for you?"

"No, not yet. I'm still searching."

"Could you perhaps tell me in brief about these religions?"

"Well, I'd love to do that, but we'd better talk about it later, okay? I promise I'll tell you about them in more detail someday."

"Could you perhaps tell me briefly about the differences between them? I'm curious."

"Okay. I'll tell you very briefly. Judaism doesn't take Jesus to be the son of God. The Jews don't even believe him to be a prophet.

Those who practice Islam accept Jesus as a prophet like Mohamed, who founded their religion, but not as God's son. Hinduism and Buddhism are also very old religions. Buddhism is 2,500 years old, and Hinduism is even older. These two religions believe that human beings are born again and again, either as humans or animals. About other religions, we can talk again in the future. Is that all right?"

"That's okay. Do Hindus and Buddhists believe human beings are born again and again? How could that be possible, Opa?"

"Even the high priests of those religions don't know exactly how it happens. The process is known as 'reincarnation'."

"Opa, do they also believe in heaven and hell?"

"For the Buddhists, for example, human existence is just an illusion and all about suffering. So they try to do good things in their lifetime so that they will not be reborn as animals or will be reborn as better human beings. Or they will not be reborn at all. Their heaven is called 'nirvana', and if you are no longer reborn, it means you have attained nirvana. Or the other way around: if you attain nirvana, you exist physically no more. Birth and rebirth are called 'samsara'. You're born again and again because you crave it. You don't realize that it's just an illusion. So, in other words, their final goal is to attain the state of nirvana."

"What is an illusion, Opa?"

"An illusion is something you believe to be real, but it isn't real."

"That's opposite to what we Christians believe. We believe in eternal life in heaven. Am I right, Opa?"

"Yes, you're right."

"Oh, Opa, it sounds so strange; it's too much for me to understand that people can be born again and again."

"It's probably not that difficult for those who believe in it to understand, Jennifer."

"Aren't the Buddhists and Hindus sad because they'll exist no more someday?"

"Here's a fascinating fact. When Christian missionaries first went to Buddhist and Hindu countries to convert the people to Christianity, they were under the illusion that Buddhists and Hindus would convert to Christianity en masse thanks to the concept of eternal life in God's kingdom of heaven. But so far as I know, only a very few have become Christian in proportion to their populations up to now."

"Oh, what a pity, Opa."

"A very strange thing happened to me recently. I met an old friend of mine who came back from India and a few Buddhist countries. He said he observed how Buddhists and Hindus there reacted when their loved ones died. He was surprised to find that they could more easily and quickly overcome their sorrow than Christians, who believe in eternal life, and also that they were more philosophical about death."

"What does the word 'philosophical' mean, Opa?"

Paul stood up and took down two dictionaries from a bookshelf and read from them.

"Jennifer, listen: 'Someone who is philosophical does not get upset when disappointing or disturbing things happen'; and then we have: 'the ability to accept an unpleasant situation calmly because you know that you cannot change it'."

"Thank you very much for telling me these stories, Opa. So they're not afraid to go to hell?"

"Buddhists and Hindus also believe in the existence of a 'hell' called Naraka or Niraya. But it's different from the Christian version of hell on two points: First, the souls of human beings are not sent to Naraka as the result of divine punishment; and second, the length of a being's stay in Naraka is not eternal, though it is very, very long."

"And you, Opa? Do you believe in the Christian hell?"

"I'll say no, for the following two reasons. One: So far as I know, the versions from the various Christian Churches on this subject are not the same. Two: Throughout human history, no one is said to have seen it and come back to tell us how it is."

"That means you've not been doing good things because you're afraid of hell, right?"

"Yes, exactly. We've been trying to do good things, yes, but not because we expect some reward from God, or we're afraid to be punished in hell. We're just happy if we can make somebody else's life better through our deeds. Simple as that. Well, I've enjoyed our discussion very much, Jennifer. Let's discuss all this again when you're a bit older, okay? I don't want to influence your thinking too much with such complicated ideas yet. But I admire your hunger for knowledge. You're very mature for your age, and I'm very proud of you."

"Opa, Mama mentioned other mysteries in which you're interested."

"Yes, that's true. Let's talk about numbers. When I read the Bible, I found out that certain numbers played crucial roles, especially 1, 7, 12, 40, 49, 70, etc. But shall we discuss such mysteries when you're older?"

"That's okay. But may I ask you one or two more questions, Opa? Now, I know that you've studied the Bible and the holy literature of other big religions, so why do you think God made human beings with different skin colors, different physical features, and different levels of intelligence? These are the reasons Mama cannot believe in the biblical God."

Christine, Jane, John, and Paul himself were quite surprised by Jennifer's question. Paul tried to explain calmly. "So far as I know, there's no satisfactory answer. Like your mama, I myself am still confused deeply by it. As I told you a while ago, those who practice Judaism, Christianity, and Islam all claim to worship the same God, but they have different definitions of the God they worship. In Buddhism, there's no creator-god. It was founded by the Buddha in India 2,500 years ago, but he did not claim to be a god. In Hinduism, there are several gods. And so on."

"Opa, do those these religions also have Satan?"

"So far as I know, only Christians, Muslims, and those who adhere to Judaism have Satan and evil spirits who cause humans to do bad things against other humans."

"Really? Very interesting. Thank you, Opa, for your patient explanation. I'll seriously think about what you've just told me. From what

Mama says in her book, I know that you've got a very wise forefather who passed down his wisdom to his descendants. And Papa also had a wise grandfather who passed down his wisdom. So I think I might be one of the luckiest people in the world, having such wise people on both sides. I cannot imagine how my life would be without you, Oma and Opa. You give me strength and hope. I love you so much."

"Jennifer, we love you so much, too. We are also happy to have such an intelligent granddaughter. Do you have any more questions?"

"Yes, Opa. I've got two more simple questions. How long are you going to stay here this time, and when are you going back to America? And why did you stay there for such a long time when you went?"

"We'll stay here for at least two or three years. Your mama has surely told you about the wound that I got during the Great War. Since then, I can no longer fully concentrate on our family business. I need a lot of rest. So your mama has to run it almost single-handedly most of the time in our absence. Your oma and I make only the most important decisions. We've got a small community over there, so we can lead a more relaxed life there. But while we're here, you can always come to us any time you want, okay?"

"Oh, I'm so glad about that, Opa. I wish I could come with you to America someday."

"Jennifer, we'd love to take you with us. But you'll be very sad to hear that racial discrimination there is even worse than here in Europe. Everywhere – in buses, trains, restaurants, schools, and even in the churches – whites and blacks are strictly segregated."

"Yes, Papa has told me about that, and whenever he told me about it, I cried. So he did not want to tell me about it anymore."

Paul looked up at the clock on the wall said, "Oh, it's already eight o'clock, Jennifer. You go to bed with your oma now. I'll stay here for a while with your mama and papa, okay? Good night."

"Opa, I have one last question: How did you get rich?"

Paul, laughing heartily, said, "You're so brilliant to ask me that. We're not rich. We've got enough to survive. We always try to do our best not to get rich at the cost of innocent people's suffering. We earn our money fairly and honestly. So we don't need to feel guilty. We don't have a guilty conscience."

"What do you mean by to feel guilty or to have a guilty conscience, Opa?"

"Well, the simplest way to explain it is if you cause someone to suffer through your words or actions and you feel bad later for what you've done, that means you've got a guilty conscience. I'll give you an example. For generations, we've always tried to help people in need as much as we can. During the Great War, we set up a relief center and helped the helpless, elderly, and orphans who did not have someone to help them. We gave away almost half of what we had. We did this social work not because we wanted to be popular or loved or admired. It had nothing to do with any religious convictions. We've never accumulated – nor are we accumulating – a fortune unfairly. You cannot take your wealth with you, anyway, when you die."

"Now I think I understand a bit better. Thank you very much. Good night, Opa and Mama and Papa! I love you all so much."

At the last moment, Paul had an idea and said to Jennifer, "Wait a minute, Jennifer. I want to tell you one thing: Although we've got more than we need, we're very humble, and we don't let strangers know the extent of our wealth. Good night and sleep well."

"Thank you very much, Opa. Good night."

Paul turned to Jane and John and said, "We should all be so glad that Jennifer's psychological development is very fast."

"Yes, Papa. Her maturity is really fast. She very often surprises and even shocks us with her questions."

Jennifer and Christine went out of the living room. Paul was full of worries for the future. They were sipping wine as Paul continued the conversation.

"As both of you are aware, the political situation around the world is getting worse with every passing day, especially in the major European countries. The atmosphere is becoming almost like it was before the Great War. I don't like how things are evolving, especially since the National Socialists came to power. The Germans are openly and defiantly building up their military might again. We're seeing and hearing what is going on in Germany every day against the Jews, the coloreds, and those who think differently from those in power. I've got a very strong feeling that the next world war is already looming on the horizon. We'll have to prepare ourselves for the worst. If another great war broke out in Europe, we'd most likely be its victims again …"

"But Paul, Belgium is a neutral country."

"Yes, John, we're a neutral country, but we're a small country. In a conflict that involves great powers around us, none of them will respect our neutrality."

"Paul, may I ask you a personal question? Are you Jewish, or do you have any Jewish relatives or Jewish blood? If it's too personal, you don't need to answer."

"No, it's not too personal at all. As you know, the definition of Jewish identity is still controversial. It was generally assumed to be just religious until very recently, but the National Socialists' racial ideology defines it as an ethnicity. As far as I know, we're not Jews and don't have Jewish relatives or Jewish blood. If we're to use the National Socialists' criteria, that is. But I can only confirm that looking back four or five generations. Who knows? People have intermarried in Europe for thousands of years. But we've got some good friends among the Jews."

"Paul, in your personal opinion, how dangerous is the Nazi ideology?"

"It could be extremely dangerous for all non-Germanic people. The ideology is an extremely complex thing that goes back several centuries, John. So far as I know, many factors play in it, among them, for instance, religious, political, economic, historical, cultural, social, and racial."

Then Jane spoke out about how she saw the situation. "Papa, I'm also of the same opinion as you. Sooner or later, we surely will experience war again – right here in our country. So we should make

73

preparations for relief work, as you and my mother and our relatives did during the Great War."

Paul gloomily nodded his head in agreement. One week before Christmas, Elizabeth and David arrived from Brussels to replace the retired woman, and they were accommodated in a two-room apartment within the compound. The entire Jeanmart family members and several friends made a special welcome ceremony for them.

CHAPTER 10
(24th December 1935 – Tuesday)

Paul and Christine's home and much of the neighborhood was in a Christmas mood. Decorations were everywhere. And nearly all the local community members had come to their house around seven p.m. to celebrate Christmas. While the children, including Jennifer, played in other rooms, Paul, Christine, John, Jane, and many other men and women were sitting around the fireplace in the living room. They, however, were not in a joyous mood. Paul started the discussion.

"Now, we know about the various laws that the National Socialists have instituted in Germany. For example, the Nuremberg Laws passed on 15th September revoke the Jews' citizenship and prohibit them from marrying or having sexual relations with persons of 'German or related blood'. These laws define a Jew as someone with three or four Jewish grandparents, including those who converted from Judaism to another religion, among them even Roman Catholic priests and nuns, Protestant ministers, and so on. On 14th November, they extended the prohibition of marriage and sexual relations between people who could produce 'racially suspect' offspring to other ethnic groups. It's widely interpreted as meaning relations between 'those of German or related blood' and Roma (Gypsies) and blacks."

Everyone was listening to Paul attentively, and they all looked anxious. Then, after a few moments, he continued. "So with the mounting intensity of conflict and violence in Germany among political parties and different sectors of society, and among major powers around the world as well, especially in Europe, a major war seems more and more likely. Until now, there's not been a single positive sign of finding a peaceful solution among the belligerent powers. Therefore, Christine and I have decided to wait for one or two more years to see how things continue to develop. If the situation worsens, we're going to spend time in America again until tensions calm down. But Jane will have to stay here and keep running our family business when and if we go."

Paul then turned to John and said, "And for you, John, we'll have to think very seriously because if a war breaks out, we Belgians will surely be its victims again. The Germans will undoubtedly come back into our country. And being black, you'll have a hard time with the race laws I've just talked about. So it might be a good idea if you go back to the States and observe the situation from there."

John expressed his opinion. "Paul, I think you're quite right with your analysis. For me, it could be a good solution. But we'll have to think seriously about Jennifer as well."

Paul agreed. "Yes. And I think she should stay here with her mother. Since she's not a full-blood black and her mother's European, she will probably have a better chance. But let's wait and see how things develop over the next few months. We should not let this ruin the Christmas mood; let's make the most of the present."

Everybody agreed with him. A Roman Catholic priest and a Methodist pastor conducted two separate worship services. The children sang four choruses and all sang Christmas songs. The last guest left at one o'clock in the morning. They all met again to greet the New Year as well. Although all the adults tried so hard to hide their melancholic mood, they did not really succeed.

(10th June 1936 – Wednesday)

"Jennifer – Jennifer? Come here for just a few minutes."

Jennifer, who was in her room, ran into the living room. "Mama, what's the matter?"

"Your opa has just called me and asked us to spend the weekend with them. I said we'd come. We'll leave the day after tomorrow and come back on either Monday or Tuesday. So make preparations, okay? We may stay longer, depending on your grandparents' mood."

"Oh, I'm already excited, Mama. I'll go and pack. Is Papa also coming with us?"

"Sure. I'll tell him when he comes home this evening."

Early on Friday morning, John, Jane, and Jennifer loaded their baggage into their car, a Ford V8. At noon, after having lunch at home, they sped off. Paul and Christine were already waiting for them at their house when they arrived. After they heartily greeted each other, Paul said, "Jennifer, go into the house. Your cousins are waiting for you there. I have to talk with your mama and papa for a while, okay?"

While they were still standing in the courtyard, Paul started the conversation. "Well, the main reason why I asked you to come here so urgently is that since the Rhineland was remilitarized by German forces on 7th March, in violation of the Treaty of Versailles, my instinct tells me that war has drawn nearer. The German defense industry is working at full speed, and the armed forces are enlarged rapidly. And the feverish diplomatic efforts of major powers are getting nowhere. There are rumors that our king might impose a stricter policy of neutrality for our country in case of a conflict between the major powers. But I don't think any major power would respect our neutrality. Jane, your mother and I are very seriously thinking about preparing for a journey to America, should the situation in Europe and elsewhere become more complicated, so that we could leave on the spur of the moment. It could be this year or next. Nobody knows. But we'll have to discuss the family business in detail."

"Yes, that's what I thought, Papa."

They all then went into the living room and started the discussion. Only Paul, Christine, Jane, and John were present. Paul began. "Jane, I told you in the courtyard briefly why I asked you to come here this weekend. You and I will have to get all the most important aspects of the family business in order and discuss in detail how you should run the business while we're away. You did so well during our last absence. Aside from that, here are some papers I've written about our experience of relief work during the Great War. Much of this we've told you already, but there are some important points that we might not have mentioned. As we intend to do relief work again, you must know the work in advance so you'll be able to avoid the mistakes we made."

"Yes, I'll read all these papers as soon as possible, Papa."

"One of the big mistakes we made was that we called our work base a relief center, so everybody believed it to be a government or religious organization. As a result, some institutions wanted to interfere with our work. In the future, therefore, we'll call it an orphanage. And we'll take care of only the elderly, the disabled, and orphans – independent of any other relief organizations. Above all else, we'll keep a very low profile."

Paul then turned to John and said, "John, it might be a little bit too early to talk about it, but I think we'll also have to begin to think seriously about what you're going to do if the political situation in Europe keeps getting worse. We need to consider when you should go back to America. It would be best if you made the necessary preparations so that you can leave at any moment. If we look at the speed at which things are deteriorating from day to day, we may not have to wait long before terrible things happen again in Europe. As for Jennifer, let's hope it won't be too bad for her since she's still young, and she's with her mother. But even if it could be dangerous for her, we don't have a better choice. She cannot go to America yet, and even if she could, she'd also suffer intense racial discrimination over there."

Paul's words moved John deeply. "Christine and Paul, thank you so much for your kindness. I think of you as my own mother and father. What you've suggested is an excellent idea. Jane and I'll think it over and let you know our decision soon. As you've just suggested, I'll begin to make preparations."

CHAPTER 11
(10th June 1936 – Wednesday)

"Jennifer and John, breakfast is ready."

Jane called Jennifer and John to join her in the dining room. They came in and greeted each other very warmly. It was around eight o'clock.

"Good morning. Jennifer, today we're going to have a very special visitor. She'll arrive around noon. So when we finish breakfast, please help me clean the rooms, okay?"

"Yes, I'll help you. Mama, who is she?"

"Sister Hanna. She lives in the convent and will drop by on her way to see her parents in Martilly, not far from here."

"Oh, Sister Hanna? I'm so glad to see her again. Didn't we meet her a few years ago in Bastogne? Mama, why didn't you tell me about it earlier?"

"I couldn't because she called only yesterday morning, and you were away. She said she did not know it in advance. It was a spontaneous decision. Yes, I think it was three years ago that we met her, but only for about twenty minutes. She was in a hurry, so we didn't have much time to talk. But she'll be with us for some hours this time, so we'll have time to talk about various things."

"Why did you say a 'very special' visitor?"

"She was one of my best friends—perhaps even my best friend—from childhood until she decided to become a Catholic nun."

"Why did she become a nun, Mama?"

"You'd better ask her yourself. We were born in the same year and went to the same school here. Later her family moved to the village where they're living now. We went to university together. I decided to study economics, and she studied literature. I'll prepare her favorite lunch."

By 11:30, they were dressed and eagerly awaiting Sister Hanna's arrival.

"Jane, why didn't you tell her that we could pick her up at the railway station?"

"I offered, but she said she preferred to walk since she wouldn't have any luggage and the station is just a few hundred meters from here. When she leaves, let's drive her to her parents' home."

They lined up in front of the house and gazed toward the road that led to the railway station— almost precisely at noon Sister Hanna headed toward them carrying a small bag. Jane and Sister Hanna ran toward each other and warmly embraced.

"Oh Hanna, how much I've missed you; it's so good to see you again!"

"Jane, I've missed you too!"

Jane introduced Jennifer. "Jennifer, this is Sister Hanna, my best friend, and Hanna, this is Jennifer. She's almost eight years old now."

"Hello, Sister Hanna, I'm happy to see you again."

"Oh Jennifer, you're all grown up now. When we met a few years ago, you were still quite small. I'm so pleased to see you, too. Your mama tells me how sweet and intelligent you are."

Jane then said to John and Sister Hanna, half-jokingly. "I hope you still recognize each other. You didn't see each other since our wedding party, I think."

Sister Hanna laughingly said as she shook John's hand, "John, do you still recognize me?"

John shot back as he was shaking her hand, also laughingly, "I'm not quite sure, Sister Hanna. Well, I'm happy to see you again."

They all were heartily laughing together.

"I'm also delighted to see you again, John. John, I used to tell Jane so often how lucky she is to have such a loving husband. Didn't I, Jane?"

"Yes, Hanna, you did that."

They all laughed again, heartily. Then John shot back, "The truth is the other way around, Sister Hanna. I'm the one who is so lucky to have met such an extraordinarily beautiful, charming, and loving wife."

They all laughed once more and then disappeared into the house and took their seats in the living room. Jane initiated the conversation. "Hanna, I told Jennifer this morning that we were going to have a 'very special' visitor, and she asked me who. When I told her, she asked me why I said you were a 'very special' visitor. I told her that you've been my best friend since childhood. And she asked me why you became a nun. I told her to ask you directly. So she'll be pleased if you tell her."

"Jennifer, do you really want to know why?"

"Yes, Sister Hanna. The first time I saw you, I asked my mama why such a beautiful woman became a nun. I thought what a great pity it was. She didn't say anything at the time."

"Thank you very much for your compliment, Jennifer. Most of the nuns at the convent are more beautiful than me. And all of them have their reasons for becoming nuns. I never dreamed of becoming a nun until I studied literature. Then another childhood friend, Michael, suddenly died in an accident, and my heart was broken. I didn't see any sense in going on living alone without him ..."

Hanna's words saddened Jennifer. "Oh, I'm so sorry to hear that, Sister Hanna. Were you in love with him when he died?"

"Yes. We were madly in love with each other, nearly all our adult life. He was also studying literature, like me. And we made all kinds of plans for our future life together – how many children we would have, where to live, what type of house we wanted, and so on. We were always so happy to be together, and we were always together. One day, when we were crossing a junction in winter, a car lost control in thick snow and hit him in the middle of the road. He died on the spot, before my eyes. I was so shocked that I had to be treated in a psychiatric hospital for months. When I recovered, my strongest desire was to meet him again in heaven when I die. And although I met many men who were interested in me, I couldn't fall in love again. As he had been an orphan raised by his adoptive parents, I started to sympathize deeply with orphans. So I decided to devote my life to the helpless people, especially mentally, in this world. That's how I became a nun."

As she was telling her story, her voice broke down, and they all started weeping. She could not continue and remained still for a very long while.

"Sister Hanna, I'm so sad to hear about that."

Several minutes later, Sister Hanna, with great effort, said, "Jennifer, the world is full of such sorrowful lives, you know. My only hope is that I'll see Michael again in heaven someday. There will be no more sorrows up there. That's true for everybody who believes in Jesus Christ and God."

"Sister Hanna, if my papa hadn't rescued Mama at the very last moment, she could have met the same fate as your boyfriend. But I believe that you've found peace of mind as a nun."

"Yes, Jennifer, I've got my peace of mind, and I'm always happy in the thought that we'll be together again forever in God's kingdom."

"Sister Hanna, how did your parents react when you decided to become a nun? Were they glad or sad?"

"My parents had started talking about grandchildren just before the incident happened. Fortunately, I have a younger brother and sister. So my becoming a nun was not that catastrophic for them; otherwise, it could have been a great dilemma for me. I mean, whether I should try to make them happy by marrying someone and making babies, or devoting my life to those in need of help, as I'm doing now. Another great relief for me was that both my parents are very religious, so in fact, they were proud that I became a nun."

"Sister Hanna, may I visit you some time at the convent?"

"Of course, Jennifer. Just tell me a week or two in advance, okay?"

"Thank you very much, Sister Hanna. Mama, may I visit Sister Hanna soon?"

"Sure, I'll take you in a couple of weeks, Jennifer."

"Sister Hanna, where exactly is your convent? Mama told me once, but I've forgotten it."

"It's the Abbey of Our Lady of Peace or Chimay Abbey."

"Thank you. Oh, Sister Hanna and Mama, I'm very excited about it. Sister Hanna, may I ask you one more question?"

"Sure, what do you want to ask me?"

"Are the other sisters also kind and nice like you?"

"Yes, they are. Many of them are even nicer than me!"

"Yes? Are there many black nuns?"

"No, only a very few. By the way, do you go to church often?"

"No, Mama doesn't go to church, but I used to go to church with my cousins now and then. But since I asked the priest a certain question during a service, they haven't wanted to go to church with me anymore. They're afraid that I might ask a similar question again. I therefore go more often to Papa's church with him."

"What was the question?"

"He was preaching about God's love for all human beings. So I asked him if God loves all human beings equally, why did he create us with different skin colors?"

"How did he answer?"

"He said God must have a reason, but there's no way for us to know it."

"Were you satisfied with his answer?"

"No, not at all. But what else can I do since I don't know what is written in the Bible?"

"Your mama and I always used to go to church together when we were young. And one day, a young black girl asked the priest exactly that same question. Your mama and I were there. The priest gave the same answer. From then on, your mama stopped going to church. But I never tried to persuade her to think like me. It's her life. Your mama told me that your papa goes to a Methodist church. Sometimes, you used to go to a Catholic church with your oma and sometimes to a Methodist church with your papa? Did you notice any great difference between the two?"

"I feel more at home in the Methodist church, mostly because I think the pastors are more open and warm, and there are fewer rituals."

"Jennifer, that's fine. God is God, no matter which church you go to. He'll have mercy on everyone who believes in him and his son, Jesus."

"Sister Hanna, to tell you the truth, I'm very doubtful about their love. I cannot understand why he created humans with black skin."

"Jennifer, thank you very much for telling me about what you're thinking deep in your heart. I understand. But if you ask such complex questions, you'll never find anyone on this earth who can give you satisfactory answers. So I don't look for answers to things that I'm not capable of discovering. Instead, I'm trying to believe in their love and the eternal life and salvation that the Bible says they will give me. My simple thought is that even if they don't exist, or they're not all-powerful, I'll lose nothing by doing good deeds while I'm alive. But it's up to every individual what he wants to believe. I cannot force someone to believe in something that I believe."

Jennifer wanted to ask Sister Hanna about a nun's life in a convent and the process of becoming a nun, but she did not have the energy to put those questions to her. Jane and John also had a lot of things they wanted to talk about with Sister Hanna. They ate lunch together, and around five o'clock in the evening, they drove Sister Hanna to her parents' home, which was about fifteen kilometers away. Her parents and brother and sister were waiting for her when they arrived.

On their way back home, Jane asked Jennifer, "Were you satisfied with Sister Hanna's answers?"

"Yes, Mama. I like the way she answered. Unlike some people, she did not try to impose her own beliefs on me. I still have many questions I'd like to ask her, but I'll do that later when she's got more time."

"Jennifer, how do you like Sister Hanna personally?"

"Oh, I like her so much. She's very kind and sincere. I'd like to see if the other nuns have also found peace of mind like her when you take me to them, Mama. Would you have any objection if I became a nun someday, Mama?"

"No, not at all. If you found peace of mind and happiness as a nun, your papa and I would be pleased. Am I right, John?"

"Sure. It's your life, and it'll be absolutely up to you to decide what you want to be, Jennifer."

"If I became a nun, Oma would also be very happy, I'm sure."

Jane and John said simultaneously, "Yes, she'd surely be so happy."

It was Saturday, 12th December 1936, and the time was two p.m. After finishing their lunch at Paul and Christine's house, Christine, Paul, Jane, and John were sitting in the living room. They all looked anxious. Paul initiated the discussion.

"John, it seems more and more likely that you'll need to leave before the end of next year. Tensions are everywhere. If a major armed conflict suddenly broke out here in our neighborhood, you might not be able to leave in time. I suggest you leave no later than the middle of next year. But how will we explain it to Jennifer? She will surely feel rather helpless and lonely without her papa."

Jane had an idea. "Papa, I think John and I could tell her that the health of her oma in America is rapidly deteriorating and that Papa has to go there urgently, which is partly true. Do you have any other ideas, John?"

"I think that's an excellent idea, Jane."

Paul said, "Okay, do that. But only a short while before your departure. She must not suffer unnecessarily for long. Let's celebrate this Christmas and New Year as happily as possible."

Jane and John left for home in the early evening. They celebrated Christmas and New Year with nearly everyone in the community and their closest friends at Christine and Paul's house. Their huge compound was nearly full.

It was now the middle of July 1937. The time was seven o'clock in the evening. Jane, Jennifer, and John were sitting in their living room. Jane initiated the conversation, carefully choosing her words.

"Jennifer, your papa and I had a discussion with your oma and opa the other day. It's about your papa. We received a telegram two days ago from your opa and oma in America, informing us that your oma is seriously ill and that she wishes to see your papa as soon as possible. Your papa will therefore have to go back to America. We've booked a cabin for him on an ocean-going ship that will sail from Antwerp on 30th September. For the first time since you were born, we'll have to celebrate Christmas and New Year without him. But we'll try to make the celebrations at your oma and opa's house as happy as possible, okay? All your cousins, aunts, uncles, close relatives and friends will be there."

The unexpected news deeply saddened Jennifer, and with tears streaming down her face, she interrupted her mother. "Oh, I'm so sad, Papa and Mama. How can I live without Papa?"

Jane answered before John could. "We all are so sad, Jennifer, but we don't have any alternative. But we're still there: your oma, opa, I and our relatives and friends. So don't be so sad, okay? There are also countless people of color elsewhere who are in the same situation. At least you have us."

"Yes. Your words have made me feel much better, Mama. So nobody knows when Papa will come back, right?"

John answered this time. "No, nobody knows yet, Jennifer. It'll depend on your oma's condition, but I'll come back as soon as she recovers. It could be sooner or longer. But I'll try to come back as soon as possible, okay? You know that everybody here loves you. You're secure here. First, I'll go to Paris to say goodbye to our friends there, and from there I'll go to Antwerp. You and your mama will spend some days with our friends in southern France meanwhile, so you won't need to come to Antwerp to see me off."

Jane then explained to Jennifer, "You and I will stay here; I'll have a lot to do with the family business. As you may have heard from your friends and cousins, the world's political situation is becoming more and more dangerous. The Great War is still fresh in everyone's mind, but it seems that we're going to experience another war very soon, and possibly here in our country. So we'll have to make some preparations in advance for how best we can avoid its hardships."

"Mama, how long will Opa and Oma stay here?"

"They want to wait at least one more year to see if the diplomatic efforts of the great powers to solve the tensions around the world might still prevent war. Let's hope that war can still be avoided – at least in our country."

Jennifer's eyes started to fill with tears again. Jane took her tenderly in her arms and asked her, "Why are you crying, darling?"

"I'm so sad, really sad. I don't know how I'll survive in such hostile surroundings without Papa and Oma and Opa." Her voice was trembling.

"But I'll be here, darling. I'll give you all the protection you need. So nobody will harm you, you know? Cheer up, darling. You've got a lot of loving cousins as well."

"Yes, Mama – you're such a loving mama. You have always been so good to me. But still – can't I go with Papa to America?"

Jane tried to comfort her. "Darling, your papa and I know very well how lonely and helpless you're feeling. But the decision had to be made urgently, so we won't be able to arrange all the necessary travel documents for you at the U.S. embassy, and we won't be able to get you a passport in such a short space of time. So let's make the best of the situation, okay? Even if we could get all the necessary papers in time and you went with your papa, we think you'd feel even worse with the intense racial discrimination in America. There'd be almost nobody there who could give you protection like here. Your oma, opa, aunt, and relatives on your papa's side experience hardship every day."

"Does that mean that if a war broke out shortly, we might not see Papa again until the end of the war?"

John answered, "Yes. And nobody knows how long a war might last. The Great War lasted four years. But we'll always be in contact, either by post or telegram or telephone. So you don't need to worry too much, okay?"

Jennifer finally gave up.

CHAPTER 12
(25th September 1937 – Saturday)

Since a few months previously, John and Jane had been making all the necessary preparations for John's return to America. And they invited about fifty people for a farewell party at their home. Among the invited were John's two American and Belgian friends with their own families and Barbara and her husband. The party began at around four p.m. The mood was somewhat downbeat, although everyone tried to hide it. As soon as they finished their dinner at seven, Jane briefly spoke to the guests.

"Hello, everybody! We're so glad that you all come to say goodbye to John. As everybody knows why he has to leave, I won't go into detail. You have all been so nice to us, especially to John and Jennifer. They are both deeply thankful for your kind-heartedness during these hard times. You've accepted them gladly as members of our society, which has been a great relief, especially for my parents, me, and our relatives. Until now, we never had the chance to express our gratitude to you, although deep in our hearts, we were always so grateful for your understanding and kindness. Now John would like to say a few words of thanks."

As John started his short farewell speech, his eyes were full of tears. "Hello everybody, I'm so glad you are here. First of all, I'd like to thank you all for being so kind to Jennifer and me over the last several years. As I have been discriminated against my whole life just because of my skin color, it was a great challenge for me in the beginning to integrate myself into a society like this. But you all have made Jennifer and me feel at home. I cannot express in words how happy and grateful I am. First of all, I was fortunate to meet such a kind-hearted woman in Jane and her parents and relatives. I sometimes wondered if I were not in a dream. My forefathers and my own family back in America are very poor, but fortunately, I had a very wise grandfather. He taught his children and grandchildren the lessons of humility, forgiveness, and friendliness. He taught us that these are the only weapons that we blacks have. With these weapons in hand, I can make the hardships of life a little bit more bearable.

"My mother is quite sick, and she wants to see me. We haven't seen each other for more than ten years. And as we all know, another war is looming closer with every passing day. If I stay on and the situation gets bad suddenly, I may not have a chance to leave in time. These are the main reasons for leaving now. As for Jennifer, I am hopeful since she's at least biracial. She most likely won't suffer the same degree of hardship as a full-blood black like me. And she's among very kind people. I'll miss you all very much, and I'll try to come back as soon as possible. I leave at twelve the day after tomorrow by train for Paris, and I'll see a few friends there. Then I'll go to Antwerp and sail on 30th September. I'll arrive in America a few weeks later. I'll miss you. Thank you so much, and may God bless us all!"

There was loud applause for several minutes. Many of the guests were trying to hold back their tears but without much success. A few of them also described how they first came to know John and how they overcame their initial racism due to his humility and friendliness. Many of the guests had brought presents for him and said goodbye at around ten o'clock. On 27th September, Jane, John, Jennifer, Christine, Paul, David, Elizabeth, and many close relatives and friends sent John off at the train station. Many of them were openly sobbing.

Jane freed herself gradually from John's embrace and handed him an envelope and said, "John, please take these blank checks with you. If you need more, you can withdraw it from our partner bank in the States."

"Honey, what I'm taking with me should be more than enough. But thank you so much anyway."

John took Jennifer, who had been crying silently, into his arms lovingly and whispered to her, "Jennifer, don't be so sad, okay? We love God, and we know that He loves us, too. He'll protect us and do the best for us. And he'll let us see each other again very soon. Darling, try to be strong, okay? I'll always love and miss you. I'll be back soon. Take care!"

They all said a prayer. The train arrived and departed punctually and finally disappeared over the horizon at noon. For the first time in several years, Christmas and New Year's were celebrated at Christine and Paul's home with Jane, Jennifer, their relatives, and close friends without John's participation. Although everybody tried so hard to observe the two feasts as joyously as possible, nobody could successfully suppress the gloomy mood. And they did not utter a single word about the possibility of war. Everybody knew that it had become just a matter of time.

CHAPTER 13
(15th March 1938 – Tuesday)

"Why are you crying, Mama?"

It was Jennifer who asked this question with a faint and broken voice. She stood silently at the door of the living room. The time was about eight o'clock in the evening. She had been there for a few minutes, silently observing her mother, who was reading a letter and shedding tears.

"Oh, come in, darling. I didn't know you were there. I'm reading a letter from your papa. The postman came this morning, and among the mail were two letters for us – one for me and one for you. But I was afraid it might be bad news and didn't dare read it immediately."

Jane handed Jennifer a letter, but Jennifer did not open it. She put it on her lap and said, "I see, Mama. What did he write?"

"I know that my crying makes you sad, but sometimes I just can't help it. I'll tell you later what he wrote."

"Mama, it's nearly a month since we received Papa's third letter. I wonder what happened to him and his mama. Hopefully, everything is okay with them. I hope I can go there someday and meet Oma and Opa and other relatives."

"Yes, that's always been my wish, too. Your oma, opa, and aunt over there must be very loving people, Jennifer. They wrote us beautiful letters. But don't worry about them. If there's anything urgent, he'll send us a telegram or give us a call. I'm afraid it might be a long time before we can go there and see them. If you read the newspapers these days, it's mostly bad news; there are tensions everywhere in Europe, not only between nations but also among different sectors of societies within every nation. The only thing that we little people can do is hope for the best. Jennifer, should I read my letter to you now, or shall we do it later? Or you may read yours now if you want to. I'm afraid you will also cry when you read it."

"Mama, why don't we do it like this: I read yours if it's not too personal, and then you read mine for me?"

"That'll be fine, darling; no, it doesn't contain anything too personal."

Jennifer took her mother's letter and started reading slowly. As she read, tears began to roll down her cheeks, and her hands shook.

My dearest Honey!

At first, I thought I'd tell you what I'm writing here on the phone, but then I got the idea that you might want to use these words someday in your novel. So I wrote them down on paper instead. Honey, I know that you'll surely be shocked when you read this letter and feel very sad. But I don't have any other choice. Therefore, I'll make my points short. I have decided to join the U.S. Army.

The white Americans don't want to use black Americans as combatants because they think we blacks are not fit enough. Therefore, blacks are usually assigned only to menial tasks such as cooking or nursing, mail clerks, file clerks, typists, supply clerks, orderlies, truck drivers, etc. I knew that several hundred thousand blacks either volunteered or were conscripted into various armed forces during the Great War. To get the actual statistics, I made many inquiries at the Defense Ministry, and I found out that more than forty thousand blacks were deployed as combatants in the Great War alone.

So what I want to say is that I want to enlist as a combatant to prove that we blacks are qualified to fight on the frontline. (Fortunately, I'm still just about within the age limit for this opportunity!) The world situation is getting worse these days, and another worldwide war seems inevitable so that I could be sent to the battlefront someday. If this happened and I either died a heroic death in battle or made my name as a distinguished soldier in another way, it'd help us gain more respect from the whites, and as a result, we blacks might face less discrimination in the future.

Honey, you're still young, and Jennifer would surely want a brother or a sister. Therefore, I'd like to tell you not to wait for our next reunion. Please try to make a new life without me. I know that you'll very easily find a new life-partner of your choice since you had sev-

eral admirers before we met. You know how much I love you, and I also know how much you love me, but we can't overcome the reality. Even if we could be together again someday, we wouldn't have the courage to have more children who would only suffer endlessly. So let's try to be realists. I'll try to find someone from my own social background as a life-partner, too, although I haven't seriously started looking for someone. I know I'll never find someone like you again, and even if I did, I know that my life would never be as happy as my life with you because I would surely always compare her with you. I'm missing you so much, every second, every minute, and every hour, and I know it's the same for you, too.

Please start a new life. I'll always respect your decision. I know more than ever now how much you mean to me. I'll still keep you informed of how things are developing on my side. As long as you're there, I'll feel confident for Jennifer. Although you don't believe in God, I will always pray for your health and safety and that you find another life-partner with whom you could have a new, fruitful, peaceful, and happy life, and I will pray that we will meet again somewhere beyond this world. Whenever I think over our short-lived togetherness, I believe I truly am one of the luckiest people in the world. Well, I could write endlessly about how much you mean to me, but please let me end here. May God bless us all!

With all my love and a big hug and millions of tender kisses!
John

While Jennifer read the letter, she became so overcome with emotion that she had to pause several times. Both of them were audibly weeping. When Jennifer finished reading, Jane took her tenderly in her arms and remained silent for a very long while. Then Jennifer broke the silence.

"Mama, would you please read mine now?"

Jane started reading John's letter to Jennifer.

Hello, my little darling,

As I told you during our last conversation on the phone, we are all fine here except for your oma. Your oma is also gradually getting better now. I hope it's the same with you over there. Jennifer, I'm so sorry that I have to write a few sorrowful lines to you, but please don't feel depressed, okay? You're a big girl now. Darling, I've decided to join the army in a few months. I want to prove that I'm brave enough to serve my country as a soldier. I believe I'm brave enough to be a distinguished fighting man. And by proving my bravery in battle, I may be able to help improve blacks' image in the future, and as a result, they might face less discrimination in society. I want to become a distinguished soldier of whom you can be very proud one day.

The world's situation has become extremely dangerous, and a big war may break out sooner or later. So in my letter to your mama, I told her to start a new life with a new partner and not wait for me. You told us a couple of times some years ago that you didn't want us to make more babies who'd only suffer like you, so even if there were no war and we could live together again, we wouldn't dare give you a brother or sister. That's why we used contraceptives in the past to avoid accidentally conceiving.

Jennifer, I love you so much, and I know how much you love me, too. But unfortunately, the world is not friendly to us. Keep on praying, okay? God will give us love and guide us in our daily life. God and Jesus Christ are the only beings in the whole universe who can still give hope to black people. I'll always keep you informed about what's happening on my side. Your oma and opa (my parents) asked me to say hello to all of you from them. I miss you so much, and I embrace you tenderly with all my love, darling!

We'll see each other again soon. Let's not give up hope. If a major war breaks out and if I'm sent to a battlefront, I'll try to be a hero so that you can be very proud to be the daughter of a hero, okay? I could even be sent to Europe, and if that happens, we might meet again during the war. Take care, and may God bless you, darling!

Your loving Papa

Jane, too, had to pause a couple of times during her reading because she could not control her voice. And both of them were sobbing and wordless for several minutes. Then Jane asked, "Darling, when would you like to reply?"

"I'll think about what I should write first. Perhaps next week. And you, Mama?"

"Me too. Let's reply to him in a week or two, all right?"

"Yes, that's fine. You could perhaps give me some advice on what I should write."

"No, Jennifer. It must all come from you. If you write what I tell you, he'll sense it. Okay?"

"Okay, Mama. How sad are you now?"

"My heart and my world are broken into pieces. Everything he wrote is logical and realistic, but at the same time, it's so sad. You know human beings always have to struggle throughout their lives with reality, illusion, logic or rationality, irrationality, and emotion."

"I don't understand what you're talking about, Mama. Could you give me some examples in plain words?"

"Okay, I'll try. Look, your papa and I love each other so much. And the color of his skin means nothing to me. But to the society in which we're living, it means a great deal. And you want us not to have more children because they would only suffer discrimination, like you. So even if he decided to come back to us, it'd be complicated for us all. He and I are still quite young, and he might very well want more children, and I too. That's the reality. But we love each other so much that it's hard to think about getting divorced and living apart. It's so painful."

"Mama, I think I understand now what you mean to some extent."

"I'm glad, darling. Okay, let's reply to him next weekend."

"Mama, I think we should inform Oma and Opa about the contents of Papa's letters; don't you agree?"

"Yes, of course, we must. But let's wait for a few days first, and then I'll speak to them. I'll let you know what they say."

A week had passed since Jane and Jennifer received the letters from John. They were sitting once again in the living room.

"Have you written your letter to Papa, Mama? I've almost finished mine."

"Yes, I've also finished mine. If you like, I can read mine aloud, and you can read yours."

"That's a good idea. May I go first, Mama?"

"Yes, go ahead!"

"Oh, Mama, by the way, have you spoken with Oma and Opa about Papa's letter?"

"Yes, we've discussed it. I even showed them his letter."

"How did they react?"

"Your opa didn't show any emotion, but your oma was so sad and cried a lot. Your papa had informed them of his decisions, so they knew about the whole situation. They said they would fully understand if I decided to start with a new life with someone, but they preferred not to give me any advice. It's entirely up to me, they said. Now, go ahead!"

My dearest Papa,

Thank you so much for your kind letter. Mama and I were crying for hours. We were so sad. But Mama gave me the courage and said we must think realistically and logically. So I gathered all the energy I could. I'm now grown up enough to understand our hopeless situation. I won't write at length; I only want to tell you that I respect you for your noble decision, and I'll always be very proud of you and admire you whatever happens to you – whether you become a war hero or just a simple soldier.

I love you and miss you so much. Since Mama, Oma, Opa, my aunts, uncles, cousins, and friends are all so loving and protective, please don't worry about me. I'll always long to see you again. Please convey my most heartfelt greetings to my oma, opa, and aunt. I love you, and I miss you, Papa. Take care! May God bless you, too!

Your little darling

She was crying as she read her letter, and Jane, too.

"Darling, your word choices are so beautiful. I know your papa will be so glad to read it."

"Thank you, Mama."

After some minutes, Jane said, "Now I'll read mine. It's not long, either."

Hello, my dearest Honey!

Thank you so much for your letter. Jennifer and I were so moved by your beautiful though sad letters that we cried for hours. I respect and admire you for your decision to join the army, although emotionally, it's so hard to be separated from you. I think your reasons are noble, and I'm sure the God in whom you trust will fulfill your wishes. Although we love each other so much, the great barrier called "skin color" prevents us from being together. I don't know if I'll be able to start a new life without you. Just like you, I know I'll never find someone like you again. And even if I did, I also know that my life would never be as happy as my life with you because I would always compare him with you. But as you said in your letter, I'll try to overcome my emotions and be realistic, although I don't know whether I'll manage it.

I was always very proud to be your wife, no matter what the world said, and I'll always be proud of you until I die, no matter what happens. Please forgive me, but I can only write this much. My heart is full of emotions. If I wrote down everything I'm feeling, I'd have to write hundreds of pages. Please give my love to your parents and younger sister. I hope I'll see them someday. Don't worry about Jennifer. We will all take care of her. I've always loved you, and I still love you, and I'll always love you, honey. I'll always be very proud of you and respect you for your noble decision, no matter whether you become a hero or remain a simple soldier.

Take care, and may God bless you.

With all my love,

Jane, your loving wife

CHAPTER 14
(1st June1938 – Wednesday)

Jane was reclining on a couch, reading a book. It was a sunny day, and the time was two o'clock in the afternoon. She was alone. The phone suddenly rang, and she picked it up.

"Hello?"

"Hello, Jane, good afternoon. It's Thomas. Do you remember me?"

"Hello Thomas, good afternoon. I'm sorry, but I have three friends called Thomas, and their voices are nearly identical."

"Thomas from Berlin, your great admirer! I found your phone number in my old address book yesterday, and I suddenly got an urge to call you. How are you?"

"Oh, I see. Yes Thomas, I recognize your voice now. I'm fine. Thanks for calling me. And you?"

"I'm fine, too. Thank you. We haven't seen each other, I think, for nearly ten years, isn't it?"

"Yes, it's a very long time. Where are you calling from?"

"I'm in Frankfurt right now. Tomorrow I'm going to visit an aunt in Antwerp, and I wondered if I could drop by either on my way to her or on my return trip to say 'hello'."

"Oh sure, I'd love to see you again. Why don't you drop by on the way back from your aunt's? You could even stay with us for a couple of days if you wanted. How long are you going to be with your aunt?"

"I think one or two weeks. I've never been there before, and I'd like to make some sightseeing trips around the region. Yes, I'd love to stay with you for a day or two. But wouldn't John have a problem with that?"

"No, he wouldn't. He's in America now. But even if he were here, he wouldn't have any problem at all. He's one of the most trusting and mature people I've ever met. Why don't you call me a few days before you leave your aunt's? By the way, will you be alone or with someone?"

"I'll be alone. I'm still looking for a life-mate, so far without any luck. Oh, I'm glad to know that John is such a person. Then your married life must be a very peaceful and happy one. When is he coming back?"

"Yes, it is. I cannot imagine how I could live with an insecure and jealous partner. Well, he may be there for another couple of years. His mother is unwell, and he wants to be with her."

"I see. By the way, I think your first child was a daughter, right? She must be grown up by now! Do you have other children?"

"Yes, she's a girl. But no, she's an only child. We once asked her if she wanted brothers and sisters; what she said saddened us so deeply that we decided not to have more children. But I won't go into it now."

"Oh, I'm so sorry to hear that, Jane."

"Thank you, Thomas, but we're quite happy with our decision because we can give her all our love and devotion. And she's happy. By the way, have you got a job? What are you doing for a living? I know that your family has a printing press."

"I'm helping my father with his printing business as a part-time employee for the time being, but it's rather boring. I don't know what to do with my degree in psychology."

"Have you become a member of the National Socialist Party?"

"No, I'm not interested at all in politics, and I'm not nationalistic. I've never gone to their rallies. And if I became a member, what could I contribute to the party or the country? I'd be just a number, a tiny cog in the giant system."

"I'm glad to know that. What I hear on the radio and from friends and what I read in newspapers about the things that are happening every day in your country, especially when it comes to the Jews, people of color, communists, socialists, et cetera, is terrifying. So is the incorporation of Austria into the German Reich in March. What do you think about all this?"

"I don't know. As I've told you, I'm not political. And even if I were, I wouldn't know how to judge since I have no means to influence things. But yes, everything that is happening in my country is very frightening. But what can I do as an ordinary man on the street? Nothing. Let's talk more about it when I see you, okay? Jane, are you alone right now?"

"Yes, why?"

"I wanted to be sure that no one else was with you. I still think of you very often, you know. I can't forget our first and last dates – and our last kisses!"

"Oh, Thomas … experience has taught me that old memories only make your life painful. So I try to forget things that I cannot enjoy anymore."

"But I don't believe that you've forgotten our blissful moments, Jane."

"Thomas, I wish you a nice trip to your aunt's and a good time there, and I'll be glad to see you again. Thank you very much for calling and goodbye for the time being."

"Goodbye. I miss you, Jane!"

The moment Jane hung up the phone, Jennifer came running into the room. She excitedly declared, "Mama, my three cousins and Auntie Clara are visiting Paris in two weeks from now, and on their way back home, they intend to drop by Sister Hanna's convent as well. May I go with them? I'd like to see Sister Hanna, too."

"Yes, you may. By the way, Jennifer, a former friend of mine has just called me unexpectedly, and we had a good conversation. He's called Thomas, and he lives in Berlin. He's going to visit his aunt in Antwerp, and he asked me if he could drop by. So I invited him to stay with us for a day or two on his way back to Berlin, and he said yes."

"How well do you know him, Mama?"

"He used to take an interest in me, and we dated a couple of times. But when I met your papa and fell in love with him, I ignored Thomas's advances. So far as I know, though, he's a very nice, warm, and humorous guy."

"Did you study together?"

"We were at the same university. He studied psychology, and I studied economics."

"I'm sure he must have been hurt to lose you to Papa."

"Perhaps, but he was very popular among women, and he flirted a lot. Although I liked him, he was too superficial for my taste."

"Does he know that Papa is in America?"

"Yes, I told him. I told him about you, too."

"Is he married?"

"He said no."

"Mama, have you thought about starting a new life with someone else?"

"Not really, not yet. The problem is that I would compare my new partner with your papa, and if he did not match your papa's qualities, neither my partner nor I would be happy."

"Perhaps Thomas might fulfill your expectations?"

"No, at the moment, I'm not thinking about it. As I've just told you, he was too superficial for me. Let's see if he has changed, though."

"What does he look like?"

"He's maybe four or five centimeters taller than me – that means about 172 or 173 centimeters, as I'm 167. He's not that handsome but is quite charming, with blond hair and gray eyes. What would you think if I fell in love with someone – perhaps with Thomas – and tried to have more children?"

"Well, since it seems that nobody knows what will happen to Papa and the rest of us in the future, I'd support you in your decision. After all, it's your life. As long as you were happy, I'd be happy, too."

"Let's see what happens, darling. I won't do anything that would make you unhappy. Oh, by the way, I met your class teacher the other day, and she told me that you'd made excellent grades. She's preparing your report. Do you have an idea of what you'd like to study at university?"

"Oh, I'm pleased to hear that. Well, perhaps medicine. I want to study something that would help the poor and the needy, Mama."

"I'm thrilled to hear that. I know that you've got a good heart, and I'm proud of you for that. By the way, when Thomas is here, we won't tell him that your papa is joining the army, okay? He said on the phone that he isn't interested in politics and what's going on in Germany, but he's also human, and people can change their minds at any moment. If that happened and if your papa was sent to a European frontline, there could be complications in our relationship. So we'll tell him that your papa is looking after his sick mother."

"Yes, Mama, that's a good idea."

It was the 14th of June, a Tuesday, 12:30 in the afternoon. The weather was fine. From the living room, Jane shouted to Jennifer, who was in her room, "Jennifer, are you ready? We'll be leaving in half an hour."

Jane and Jennifer were preparing to pick Thomas up at the railway station. They were very excited. After a few more minutes, they left for the station. When they arrived, there were already many people there, everyone eagerly looking at the clock. Then, at last, the train appeared on the horizon. Some passengers got off as Jennifer and Jane searched for Thomas among the alighting passengers. A rather tall man, dressed in casual clothes, was waving at them from a short distance and heading toward them. He shouted in a loud voice, "Hi Jane! Jane! I'm here."

Thomas took Jane into his arms, looked deeply into her eyes, and said, "Oh Jane, you haven't changed at all. You're still so beautiful, just like ten years ago."

"Thank you, Thomas. I'm flattered. You also still look youthful." Then she introduced Jennifer. "Darling, this is Thomas; Thomas, this is Jennifer."

"I'm glad to meet you, Thomas."

"I'm glad to meet you, too, Jennifer. How are you?"

"Fine, thank you, Thomas. My mama told me a little bit about you the other day."

They headed for the car and home. On the way, Jane started the conversation.

"Thomas, you told me on the phone that you had an enjoyable time at your aunt's. Did you go to see a lot of places?"

"Yes, I did. But many ruins from the War haven't been fully repaired yet. So seeing them was sad and depressing. But I was able to spend a lot of time with my aunt. She's married to a Belgian."

"Thomas, you told me on the phone that you could stay for two or three days with us. We're happy about that. We'll have lunch when we get home, and then I'll show you around the area. Let's catch up properly this evening. For dinner, I've made reservations at a local restaurant. The food is delicious there. I've already ordered exactly what we had together several years ago when we last met."

"Oh, I'll love that. It'll remind me of many good things."

In a few minutes, they arrived home, unpacked the car, and then disappeared into the house. Jane showed Thomas around. They rested for a while after lunch, and they then left the house for a sightseeing tour of the area without Jennifer. They came home at around five o'clock. Jennifer was waiting for them at the main gate, with a small suitcase and a handbag.

"Mama, I'm ready. Thomas, I'm going to Paris with three cousins and an aunt of mine. We'll spend about two weeks there. We planned to leave the day before yesterday, but we postponed until today because I wanted to meet you. I wish you a nice time here and hope to see you again soon. Why don't you stay until I come back? That'd be very nice. Mama, don't worry about me at all, okay? Goodbye."

Thomas responded, "What a pity we won't have time to get to know each other better, Jennifer. We'll surely have more time in the future, though since the political situation is quite bad now, we'll probably have to wait until things calm down a bit. Have a nice holiday, and take care! Goodbye, Jennifer."

Jane and Jennifer left the house. As they were on the way to the station, Jane suddenly said in a shocked voice, "Oh my God! Jennifer, I forgot to put your papa's letter away. I wanted to reread it, and I left it on the living room table. Hopefully, Thomas is not curious enough to read it."

"Don't worry, Mama. Even if he's found it and read it, he might think that you intentionally left it there as a hint that you're free to start a new life."

Jennifer was giggling heartily, to Jane's annoyance.

"Oh Jennifer, that would be a cheap trick, and I wouldn't do such a thing to get him. He used to be madly in love with me in any case, so I don't need such tricks."

"Mama, by the way, you told me that you spoke with Papa on the phone the other day. Did he tell you if he has met someone with whom he could start a new life? I'm very curious about what kind of a stepmother, sisters, or brothers I'd have over there."

"No, he only said that his parents wanted him to look seriously for someone. But he's not sure if he'll be able to do it. He promised that he'd let me know when and if he found someone else. That's all."

"Mama, by the way, may I tell Thomas about your writing an autobiographical romance novel when I meet him again?"

"No, I don't think you should do that."

"Why?"

"If you did, he might suspect that I'm good to him not because of my true feelings but out of some selfish motive."

"What do you mean by that, Mama?"

"He might think that I'm doing what I'm doing simply to gather dramatic episodes for my novel."

"Okay, I understand."

They arrived at the station. Jennifer's cousins and aunt were already there. Jane waited until the train departed and then drove home. When she arrived home, she discreetly looked at John's letter on the table. She suspected that Thomas may have read it because it lay now in a slightly different place. But then, she was not quite sure how she had left it lying. She did not remove it, fearing that in doing so, she might arouse Thomas's suspicion. She pretended to be unaware of it. The time now was six o'clock.

"Thomas, shall we go now?"

"Yes, I'm very excited."

"It's rather small, but it's always nearly full. Let's go on foot since it's just around the corner."

In about twenty minutes, they arrived at the small restaurant. It was a rather old building, perhaps hundreds of years old. When they entered, the waitress led them to a corner.

"Oh, Jane, how thoughtful of you – a candle-lit dinner!"

"Just to remind us of our last dinner together."

They uncorked a bottle of vintage champagne, which she ordered especially for the occasion, and they toasted their happy reunion. Thomas thanked her lavishly for this special gesture. As they dined, they talked excitedly about several topics. He took her hands into his and tenderly caressed them. She did not resist. After a long, long while, she looked at the clock on the wall and said, "Thomas, look, it's already almost ten o'clock. Let's go home."

"Thank you so much for the delicious dinner, Jane. I'll never forget it."

"I also enjoyed it very much, Thomas."

They went home, and as they entered the living room, he started to kiss her, tenderly first and then passionately. She freed herself from his embrace and disappeared into a room that adjoined her bedroom for a while, and when she came out, she said, "Thomas, I've prepared a bed for you in the guest room. I'm rather tired now, so let's go to bed."

Thomas walked over and took her in his arms and kissed her again. Again she did not resist. After a long while, he asked her, "Shall we go to your bedroom or mine?"

Thomas carried her in his arms to her bedroom. They then passionately petted each other on the bed, and he started to undress her.

"No, Thomas, not now. I don't have condoms. And we'll have to discuss a lot of things first if we're going to do this. Let's talk about the future tomorrow. Okay? I hope you're not angry with me."

She freed herself from his arms.

"No, not at all, Jane. Yes, let's talk about the future tomorrow. Good night!"

"Good night, Thomas."

Jane got up at eight o'clock and went into the bathroom for about twenty minutes, and from there, she went directly into the kitchen and prepared breakfast. In half an hour, Thomas got up and, having spent some minutes in the bathroom, came into the dining room and took a seat.

"Good morning, Thomas. Did you sleep well?"

"Good morning, Jane. Yes, I did. And you?"

"Yes, I did, too. I'm preparing breakfast now. Around noon, let's drive to the countryside and have lunch somewhere, okay?"

"That's a good idea, Jane."

After breakfast, Jane began dressing. It was sunny. At around noon, they left for their day trip. They drove through several villages, farmland, and little forests and finally came to a restaurant situated on a small hill overlooking the valley below.

"Thomas, this is my favorite restaurant. The food is not that good, but the service is excellent, and the views are fantastic. Let's have our lunch here."

"Yes, the views from here are so fantastic."

They ordered some food and leisurely enjoyed it while admiring their beautiful surroundings.

"Thomas, I hope you were not angry with me last night."

"No, Jane, not at all. Why should I be? I understand. I don't know where to start our discussion, so you start, and I'll respond since you're a bit older and more experienced than me."

As Jane was quite sure that Thomas had read John's letter, and realizing that she should take every opportunity to find a new partner, she decided to tell Thomas the truth about her life now and her plans for the future.

"Thomas, I don't know how to begin either. Sure, I'm a few years older than you, but it doesn't necessarily mean I'm any wiser. Well, my first question is: You know my family situation at the moment. Is that true?"

"Yes."

"Good. When we were studying and dating, you used to tell me that you liked me for my straightforwardness and sincerity. Well, as you already know, then, John is in America looking after his sick mother. And he wants to wait and see how the situations in the world, especially in Europe, develop before he comes back. If a major armed conflict breaks out here in Europe, you Germans will surely invade this country, and with the racial ideology of your government, John, as a black man, would face huge hardship. He therefore told me to start a new life – Jennifer might want to have at least one more, brother or sister." Jane then told Thomas what Jennifer had said about the children's likely suffering. "So what John said was that even if he came back here, we'd not be emotionally in a position to have more children – colored babies, that is."

Thomas was listening with total concentration. Jane continued, "It may not be very romantic, what I'm telling you. It may even come as a shock for you. But since the political situation is getting more serious with each passing day, we cannot afford to live with illusions. I want to see the realities. Now, my first question is: Do you think you could start a life with me if I were ready to do so, or do you want to have a few blissful moments with me while you're here? If you want to start a life with me, you'll have to consider living with Jennifer – a colored girl. It could become a big problem if she had to live at your place, given your government's frightening race laws. It would not be easy for you. But if you want to have a good time together for a few days, then I'll make some arrangements. I'm also human, flesh, and blood, not a holy angel. Am I too direct, Thomas?"

"Oh, no, no, no. Not at all. I like your directness very much. I'm still madly in love with you, Jane. I'd be so happy to be with you. And I wouldn't have any difficulty living with Jennifer."

"No, Thomas, I want you to take your time and think about it very carefully. I'm afraid you'd tell me that you'd happily start a new life with me to sleep with me. If you're only interested in sleeping with me while you're here, please tell me frankly, and I'll get some condoms, and we can have a good time. In the current situation, I don't want to bring a baby into this world. And I'd never have an abortion, on moral grounds. But if you're seriously willing to be my life-partner, we won't use condoms."

"Jane, you don't need to doubt my feelings."

"Okay, I'm glad to hear that. But now the second question: What would your parents think? Are they religious, liberal, conservative, or racist?"

"They're fairly religious. My mother might have difficulty with the marriage of her son to a not-yet-divorced woman. But that should not be a problem in the long run. She had a daughter with her boy-friend, and he left her. By the way, I have an excellent relationship with my half-sister. Her name is Heide...Then my mother met my father, and they got married. My father is very liberal. So even if he has a problem at the beginning, I think I can handle him. After all, it's my life, and I'm an adult. I don't care what my other relatives might think. So we'll be able to solve any problems that might arise. But how about your parents – I mean, to have a German son-in-law?"

"Don't worry about them, Thomas. They're completely liberal. My third question is: Do you want to have a religious marriage or a civil marriage or both? I think you're a Lutheran, yes?"

"Well, I used to belong to the Lutheran Church in the past, but I was never a church-going Lutheran. I think that civil marriage would be okay. But I'll ask my parents what they think. And how about you?"

"I don't belong to any religion. Now and then, I accompany John and Jennifer to a Methodist church, but I don't feel that I belong to it. I've told you the reason, way back when we were students. But if your parents want it to be a religious wedding, and if your Church will accept me as your bride, that's fine."

"Yes, if I remember correctly, you don't believe, for example, in the biblical God because he created human beings with different skin colors. How did you get married to John – with religious rituals, or a civil ceremony?"

"We had two ceremonies because John wanted to have it both ways, and to make him happy, I didn't oppose the idea. So please take your time and carefully think it over, and also discuss it with your parents. Whichever way you would want to do it, I won't mind fulfilling your wishes –"

"Thank you very much, Jane. I'm sorry for interrupting you, but do you have any idea how the marriage of a German and a Belgian is legally regulated?"

"Oh, sorry, I don't. I don't know anyone who has gone through that process." Jane continued, "Now, my fourth question: You know that I cannot leave this place because I'm managing our family business as my father's assistant. So how often could you come here and stay with us?"

"I'll talk with my father and propose that I come and stay with you for at least one month out of every three or four. Would that be okay with you?"

"I'd love to be with you longer and more often. But if there is no better alternative, then I'll have to live with that. Now comes my fifth and probably most important question: How long will you be able to steer clear of the National Socialist Party? Even if you don't want to join it voluntarily, there could be circumstances in which you might not be able to resist, or they might force you to join the army against your will."

"I can only assure you that I'd never voluntarily join the Party. If circumstances forced me, that would be another case. And since I'm not physically fit enough to be a soldier, I'm quite sure that they can never conscript me. I've had problems for years with one of my knees following a car accident, and I've got ample medical records to prove it."

"I'm delighted to hear that you'd not become one of them. What one hears about what's going on in your country is frightening, even though we're not Jewish. And I worry so much for Jennifer if war broke out and the Germans came into this country again. Okay Thomas, it's already nearly four o'clock. Let's go home. By the way, why don't you stay with me until Jennifer comes back?"

"Oh, that's what I was thinking, Jane. I would love to. I'll call my father this evening to see whether it would be possible. I've got to start helping him in the office quite soon. By the way, may I ask you a serious question in return? You've just said that your parents are liberal. But you told me once that you lost many of your possessions, including your brother, during the Great War. So wouldn't they have something against us, the Germans?"

"Thomas, don't worry about that. We come from a very long tradition of being pragmatic and realistic. We don't blindly blame a particular political or social or ethnic group for the wrongdoing of some people in power in such groups. We look at every act of wrongdoing that affects us without emotional bias and on an individual basis."

"Will you inform them about our relationship?"

"Yes, of course, I'll have to inform them when it becomes necessary – like if I'm pregnant."

Thomas called his father at eight p.m. and spoke with him for a while. His face lit up when his father agreed that he could stay with Jane for two weeks.

It was nine o'clock in the morning, and Jane and Thomas were still luxuriating in bed, tenderly cuddling each other.

"Jane, I got the impression that you were very tense all night and did not enjoy it fully. Does it have something to do with how I was? I'm feeling a bit insecure."

"No, don't worry about that, Thomas. It has nothing to do with you at all. I felt guilty because John has only been gone a few months, and I'm sleeping with you now. Although he's given me his approval to start a new life, I could not free myself from him emotionally yet."

"Jane, I don't think you're the only person who feels like that. I'm quite sure many other people in the same situation have the same feelings."

"I'm not sure about that. But don't worry about it. I may overcome it while you're with me. Now, let's get up and have breakfast. We'll discuss our plans for today."

"Jane, I don't want to make any grand plans at all while I'm here with you. I want to stay at home and enjoy life as much as possible. Who knows how long we'll be able to be together like this? Let's enjoy every single second, okay?"

"Okay. I'm not too optimistic about the future, if I'm candid. You've seen with your own eyes and heard with your ears the news in your country. How optimistic are you? I don't see a bright future for Europe at the moment – and perhaps for us as well."

"If I'm honest, I'm not too optimistic about the immediate future, either."

"Okay then! Let's try to enjoy every moment at hand and forget about the future."

Several days and nights passed while they stayed home and enjoyed their togetherness. Then came the day before Jennifer's return.

"Thomas, tomorrow evening, Jennifer is coming back around 8:30, and you're leaving the day after. Let's try not to be sad when we part, okay? That's what I always aim to do whenever someone I love goes away. I always try not to shed tears, even though I always feel so sad and empty in my heart. Parting is always so painful for me."

"Do you always succeed in not shedding tears?"

"Not always. But I don't want to make the other person sad by showing my sorrow. I always try to hide my true feelings."

"Jane, it'll be hard for me, too, not to shed tears when we part. I'm also a very sentimental person. But I'll try. Now, please don't talk about it anymore until the moment comes, okay?"

"All right then. Let's keep on enjoying these last few hours."

"By the way, how will Jennifer react when she knows that we've been sleeping together?"

"She'll have sensed it before she left anyway. She knows that I like you very much. I'm sure she's glad, even. I'll explain to her later about our plans for the future. You may become her surrogate father."

"I'd love to be a father figure to her if she'll accept me. She's such a lovely, intelligent little girl."

"Yes, I worry so much for her in the event of Germany starting another war."

"Let's hope the situation does not get that far. By the way, Jane, tomorrow night shall we sleep together or separately?"

"We'll sleep together. Jennifer will understand."

Jane went to the railway station to pick Jennifer up at eight o'clock the next evening. Jennifer was quite tired from the journey, so Jane asked her only a few simple questions back home. When they arrived home, Jennifer went straight to bed after greeting Thomas. As Thomas would have to leave the next morning on 29th June, at 9:30 a.m. for Berlin, he and Jane also went to bed early. =

CHAPTER 15
(29th June 1938 – Wednesday)

It was eight o'clock in the morning. Jane and Jennifer were busy preparing breakfast when Thomas came into the dining room. "Good morning, ladies."

"Good morning Thomas."

"Good morning Thomas."

"Thomas, we'll have breakfast, and then we'll take you to the station."

After breakfast, they all left for the station at nine o'clock. They did not speak much on the way, for they were sad. Jane and John affectionately embraced each other for several minutes and were fighting back their tears with an effort.

"Goodbye, Thomas. I'll miss you so much."

"Goodbye, Jane. I'll miss you so much, too. Goodbye, Jennifer. I'll think of you a lot."

"Goodbye, Thomas. I'll think of you, too."

The train arrived punctually, and Thomas boarded the train. He popped his head out of the window and waved to them. Slowly the train disappeared out of sight.

"Jennifer, we'll stay at home today, and I'll tell you what happened between Thomas and me while you were away. Okay?"

"Okay, Mama."

It was noon, and after they had had their lunch, they were both sitting in the living room.

"How was your holiday, Jennifer?"

"It was so nice. We went on several sightseeing trips, and I met a boy my age named Carlos. He was so cute. He said he was a Mayan from Guatemala, now living in Spain temporarily with some relatives. I think I'll visit him someday in Spain. But we couldn't communicate much because he could barely speak French, and as you know, I don't speak Spanish except for a few words. I'll learn Spanish as soon as possible so that we'll be able to talk to each other."

"How did you communicate, then?"

"Fortunately, we met a young Spanish girl who spoke French and Spanish, although she could say only the basics. So we just exchanged addresses. My cousins also made the acquaintance of some young boys from southern France."

"And how about your visit to Sister Hanna?"

"Oh, her convent is so lovely and calm. She showed us around. I can imagine becoming a nun myself someday. She said I could visit her at any time. She's so kind and sweet. I wish I could have stayed longer and learned more about a nun's life."

"I'm glad to hear that. Did she or any other nuns talk with you about religion?"

"No, not at all. Perhaps it was because they knew that my mama doesn't believe in God, so they didn't want to burden me with the subject."

"Yes, that could be one reason. And another could be that you tend to go to a Methodist church with your papa." Jane continued, "Jennifer, I'm sure you're curious about what happened between Thomas and me while you were away. We talked a lot about our situations and the future. I think I could start a new life with him. But we made it a condition that we would marry only if I got pregnant. Let's wait and see if I do. If not, then we'll have a relationship without getting married. What do you think about that?"

"Mama, when I arrived yesterday evening, I realized that you were so happy, and it made me very happy. If you're happy, I'm also happy. I got the impression that he must be a very warm-hearted person."

"Yes, he is, just like your papa. The one difference between them is that your papa is quieter than Thomas. Thomas is rather more talkative. That could be a bit irritating in the long term; otherwise, I don't think I'll have big problems with him. And he's not superficial anymore like he was when we were studying. What worries me most at the moment is the political situation in Europe, especially in his country. He told me that he and his parents are liberal and that they're not interested in politics. And they're not nationalistic either. I think that's a good sign. But I'll always have certain reservations."

114

"Why do you think you'll have reservations about that, Mama?"

"I mean, I won't blindly take his words to be the absolute truth. You know the human mind can change at any moment, sometimes because of some pressure from outside, which is beyond your control, and sometimes you change your mind on your own."

"Mama, why don't you try to enjoy being with him for as long as you can? You never know what'll happen next. If you worry too much about the future, you may become pessimistic and lose your chance to be happy."

"Jennifer, when did you become so philosophical?"

"This wisdom is not my own. It's from my teacher. She used to tell us words of wisdom now and then. But I'm not sure whether I'll be able to use such wisdom in my daily life because, as I'm still experiencing discrimination every day, it's not that easy for me to stay optimistic and philosophical all the time."

"I understand that, Jennifer. And now I want to tell you about our arrangement for the future. Thomas is working at his father's small printing press part-time. It's a small family business with about ten employees. So he's arranged with his father that he can stay with us for at least a month out of every three or four. They're Lutheran but not church-going. So they'll not demand that we have a religious marriage. If I'm pregnant, I'd try to visit him and his family at their home. And it'd be better if you didn't come with me. You know why?"

"Yes, I know why. I wouldn't be able to bear the racism that the people over there would throw at me. No, it'd be all right for me to stay at home."

Almost two months had passed since Thomas had left for Berlin. Now it was early September. An autumn mood was already in the air. Jane and Jennifer were sitting leisurely in the living room. It was around noon, and they had just eaten lunch.

"Darling, I think I'm pregnant. What would you like – a sister or a brother?"

"Oh, I'm so happy to hear that, Mama. If it were my choice, I'd like to have a sister, but a brother is also okay with me."

"We'll wait one more month, and if I don't get my period, I'll inform Thomas about it. I know he will be happy, too. He has called me several times already and asked me if I was pregnant yet, but I didn't want to tell him at the time. I want to make very sure first."

A few days had passed. Jane and Jennifer were in their sitting room again as usual, and Jane suddenly got an idea. "Jennifer, I've changed my mind. I'll inform Thomas right now."

"I think that's a good idea. May I ask you a question, Mama?"

"Sure."

"Have you told papa about your relationship with Thomas?"

"No, not yet, but I'll have to tell him about it soon. Is that okay, darling?"

"That's fine, Mama."

In the next moment Jane called Thomas straight away. "Hello, Thomas, good afternoon. How are you, my dear? Listen, Thomas, I'm quite sure that I've conceived …"

Thomas was so excited. "Really, Jane? I'm so glad to hear that. As you know, these days there's almost no good news around, and this is the best news I've had since I came home. How about if I come to you in the first week of next month and stay with you for a month? That would be until about mid-November."

"That timing will be good for us, too, Thomas. Listen, I don't want to disappoint you, but I've had second thoughts about getting married amid all these huge political tensions. Everybody knows war has become inevitable. It's just a matter of time. So is there any sense in getting married now? Shouldn't we postpone for a few months – or even years? A number of my relatives and friends have begun saying that we're crazy to plan a wedding now."

"I don't know, Jane. Within my family circle, many people got married recently, and many more will marry soon. So let's go ahead. Only time will tell us whether we've done the right thing or not. Okay, Jane?"

"Let me think it over for a few days, Thomas. I miss you. Good-bye."

"No, no, Jane, wait a minute! If we're to get married in a church, we'll have to do it as soon as possible, before your belly becomes too obvious. That means in the next month, or at least not later than the middle of November. If it'd be too bureaucratic to get permission for a civil marriage, let's do it in church. So could you perhaps make inquiries about that on your side? Please tell me what documents you need from me, and I'll try to send them to you immediately. What do you think?"

"Yes, that's a good idea. I'll take action in a few days and let you know. Goodbye, Thomas. I miss you."

"I miss you too, Jane. Goodbye."

The next day, he informed her that he would be with them on 7th October, a Friday, and would be returning to Berlin after a month on 7th November.

CHAPTER 16
(7th October 1938 – Friday)

The weather was fine and the sky blue. Jane and Jennifer were waiting in excitement at the local railway station for Thomas's arrival. It was three p.m. when the train appeared. He was waving very animatedly at them out of a window. He got off the train, and they greeted each other heartily. He tenderly took Jane in his arms and kissed her affectionately, and while doing so, his right hand went to her belly to check whether her pregnancy was already noticeable or not.

"Thomas, it has just begun to show, but only if you look closely. And since I'm wearing loose clothes, nobody can see it yet. Maybe in another month or two, it'll be quite visible."

"I don't have much idea about pregnancy. When do you think the baby will be born?"

"Around March or April next year."

"Jane, would you prefer to have a son or a daughter?"

"You tell me first what you'd prefer, Thomas!"

"I don't have any preference …"

"Me either. The most important thing is that the baby is healthy."

"Yes, that's what I've been thinking about, Jane."

"Thomas, actually, you've asked me all these questions, and I've also answered them on the phone…"

"Yes, I know. But I'm so excited that I wanted to repeat these questions. Please excuse me."

Thomas then turned to Jennifer. "Hello Jennifer, I think you've grown up quite a lot during the last few months. What would you prefer – a brother or a sister?"

"Hello Thomas, thank you for the compliment. We were so excited about this reunion that Mama couldn't sleep last night. I'd prefer to have a sister, but a brother would also be fine."

After a short while, they left the station for home.

"How lucky you got here safely, Thomas. How did the situation look on the way? I'm sure there's a lot of political activity everywhere in Germany."

"Yes, I saw a lot of troop movements on a large scale in several places. But let's hope that they're just harmless maneuvers. Let's talk about happier things. As I told you on the phone, I'll be able to stay with you for a month. So we'll have a lot of time together."

"I'm so glad to be with you again, Thomas. But thirty days are too short for me. We'll have to make every second as meaningful as possible. I'm going to prepare a special dinner, and then let's make plans for the next thirty days, okay?"

"Excellent idea. Oh, heartfelt greetings to you both from my parents and sister. When I told them about your life, they were very excited and hoped to get to know their soon-to-be-daughter-in-law personally as soon as possible. And, of course, their future granddaughter as well."

Thomas's words moved Jennifer to tears. "Thomas, do you mean it? If it's true, I'd also be most pleased to meet them. But are they racists?"

"So far as I know, they're not racists. But they seldom mix with foreigners, even Europeans."

Jennifer was a bit sad and asked Thomas, "We hear almost every day what's happening in your country with the Jews and the coloreds. The news is so frightening to me. Why do some Germans hate such people so much? What have they done to you?"

"Jennifer, I don't know about it in detail either. It's a very complex subject. I think it has to do with politics, theology, economics, finance, ethnicity, social and racial ideology, and so on. And it's partly the result of anti-Semitism, which goes back several centuries. But there are also a great many Germans who don't support these views. So you don't need to feel threatened, okay?"

"What is anti-Semitism, Thomas?"

"According to the dictionary, it's discrimination or prejudice against, or hostility toward, Jews."

"And what role does theology play?"

"For example, most – or probably even all – Christians blame the Jews for the death of Jesus. Many Christians hate them for this reason alone."

"But didn't the Christians themselves make wars against each other in God's name?"

Jane and Thomas were quite surprised by Jennifer's question, and they exchanged worried glances. "How do you know that, Jennifer?"

"My teacher told us about it some weeks ago in class."

"Yes, that's true. But it's a very complex subject. So I don't think I'm qualified to explain in detail. The next question, please, if you have one?"

"Thank you very much. And what is racial ideology?"

"The simplest explanation is that those who rule the country now are making the public believe that Germanic people are superior to all non-Germanic peoples around the world."

"By 'those who rule the country', do you mean the Nazis?"

"Exactly, the Nazis."

"I see. And what do you think about that?"

"Until now, my close relatives nor I have been influenced by this ideology, Jennifer. And there are a great number of Germans who don't accept it either, at least openly. Although what these people really think deep in their hearts, I don't know."

After they had finished their dinner, they gathered in the living room and relaxed as usual. Jane started the conversation.

"Thomas, here's what I think we can do for the next thirty days. Mostly we should stay at home; I would like to spend every moment possible with you. And now and then, we could invite some of our friends and relatives over. What do you think?"

"Good idea, Jane." Thomas continued, "Jane, we've talked about having a church wedding on the phone, and I've brought some documents that we might need. As I've told you, my parents, especially my mother and sister, are happy that we're going to have a church wedding. You said that you'd also make some arrangements. What have you managed?"

Jennifer interrupted, "Mama, but you're still married to Papa!"

"Yes, you're right, Jennifer. I've thought about that and made some preparations to solve the problem. I called your papa and asked him to send me a legal document stating that he permits me to file for divorce because a reunion is not possible in the foreseeable future due to impossible circumstances. And I asked John's Methodist pastor if he could dissolve our marriage, and he said he would do it for us if need be. I also spoke with the civil marriage officials last week; they would do it as fast as possible upon my request. But because of the political situation, they were very skeptical if it could be so urgently arranged. And I applied last month for a divorce, so I'll be legally divorced from your papa on the 12th of this month. And our religious union will be dissolved on the 16th, in the church where we got married. That's a Sunday. Our marriage, Thomas, will occur in the local Lutheran church on the 23rd of October, also a Sunday. Since it might not be possible to have a civil marriage soon under the present political circumstances, we'll have a religious wedding first so that we can be together openly. Then, when the situation in Europe has stabilized, we'll have a civil wedding."

"You're smart, Mama," Jennifer said.

Thomas was overjoyed at the news and cried out, "Oh, honey, you're so lovely. I love you so much. Have you already arranged all this? Incredible! I admire your efficiency dearly."

"Thomas and Jennifer, I think we should invite only our relatives and very close friends on both sides for the wedding ceremony and make it as simple as possible. But what shall we do about your parents and relatives?"

"Jane, I agree. Concerning my parents and relatives, we can formally invite them, but I'm sure none of them will be able to come here on such short notice."

"Mama, by the way, I'm curious to know how a religious marriage is dissolved."

"I didn't know much about it either, so I asked your papa's pastor about it, and he told me that it'd be very simple. He said there is no instruction in the Bible, but I must appear in the church with two witnesses, and we all sign the divorce paper, which is prepared by the church, and a copy of it will be kept in the church's archives. Before or after the signing, the pastor will say a prayer asking God to accept our divorce. Living together as wife and husband is no longer possible under the present circumstances, which are beyond our influence. Neither of us is responsible or something like that. That's all."

"I see, Mama."

Thomas asked Jane about her parents. "Jane, I forgot to ask you one significant thing. I'm quite sure your parents are already informed about our plans. What's their opinion?"

"Yes, they're up to date – and many heartfelt greetings from them, by the way. At the moment, they're in Italy, on holiday. They won't attend the wedding ceremony either, since they won't be back till late February. They've got only one big concern with our relationship. It's about the timing since war could break out at any moment. But they'll support us in every possible way to help make our marriage happy and successful. They said they're looking forward to seeing their future son-in-law as soon as possible."

"Oh, I'm so glad to hear that, Jane."

Jane and Thomas stayed at home almost every day. Now and then, her cousins and friends made short visits. Jennifer was rarely at home. She was mostly with her cousins or friends or going to school. Jane's divorce proceedings ran smoothly, and the religious marriage took place as planned on the 23rd of October in the local Lutheran church. They celebrated it joyously at Jane's house with fifty close friends and relatives. Among the guests were Barbara and her husband Leo, and Heide, Thomas' half-siter, and her husband Richard. Thoma's parents also wanted to come, but they could not at the last moment. Jane and Thomas had received a very beautiful wedding card fom John a few days earlier wishing them a happy and long-lasting married life. During the ceremony, Christine and Paul made a long-call from Italy where they spent their holiday and heartily congratulated them. Jane and Thomas promised their guests that they would hold a grand wedding party again in Berlin as soon as Germany and Belgium's situation calmed down, and they could do the civil marriage. And Thomas told the guests that he would come back within a few months. The ceremony started at three p.m. and the last guests left at eleven o'clock.

Jane and Thomas made preparations as the day for Thomas's return to Germany was approaching. On the 4th of November, just three days before he planned to leave for home, there was a surprise call from his father telling him that he could stay with his family until the 8th of January – the New Year of 1939. The joy in the family was overwhelming. So from that moment on, they began to plan in detail how they would spend Christmas and New Year. Then, to the great shock of people around Europe, thousands of Jewish shops were destroyed on the night of the 19th of November, and hundreds of synagogues burned down in Germany and Austria. Around one hundred Jews were murdered. The root cause was the murder of a German embassy staff member in Paris by a seventeen-year-old Jew in retaliation for his father and his family's poor treatment at the Nazis' hands. The shock waves spread across the world, especially among the Jewish communities in Europe. The incident later became known as *Kristallnacht,* or the Night of Broken Glass. It was a great shock for Jane, Jennifer, and Thomas. When they heard the news, they and a few of Jane's relatives and close friends were at a mutual friend's birthday party.

Jane turned to Thomas. "It's so shocking. Thomas, what shall we do? I mean you, Jennifer, and me."

Thomas replied, "Yes, it's really shocking, but I think there's nothing we can do at the moment. We can only wait for a few days and see how things develop."

Jane agreed. He continued, "Tomorrow I'll call my father and some friends and relatives and ask them about the situation. Then let's decide what steps we need to take."

Jane and Thomas left the party at eleven o'clock. The next morning at eight, Thomas called his father and a couple of relatives and friends. They all told him that there was nothing he could do if he came back early. His father told him that the family printing business was very quiet anyway because of the political upheaval and the upcoming Christmas season, so he should stay with his family until the New Year. The whole community was busy decorating their houses for Christmas despite the bad news that was filtering in from all corners of Europe. Everybody tried to make the best out of the crisis.

It was the 24th of December. Jane, Jennifer, and Thomas arrived at Peter and his wife Josephine's house at eight o'clock. Peter and Josephine were among Jane's best friends. The couple had invited some seventy people for the celebration of Christmas. The house was quite large, but the place was nearly bursting at the seams. Peter discreetly took Jane into a corner and whispered to her, "Jane, I've so arranged that nobody will talk about the political situation in Germany while Thomas is here. And we'll not discuss any sensitive political topics either. Only joyous subjects. Okay?"

"That's a perfect idea indeed, Peter."

It was now half-past eight o'clock. Peter began his announcement, and everybody turned to him and listened attentively. "Hello, good evening once again. May I, on behalf of my family, heartily welcome you once again to our humble home. Thank you very much for coming and spending this auspicious Christmas with us. As everybody knows, we have invited our close relatives and friends and those who don't have relatives or friends and would otherwise have a lonely Christmas. We've done this for three or four generations. All of us are fully aware that tensions are running very high in the countries around us. Nobody knows what destiny awaits us in the coming days, months, or years. We don't know whether we'll be able to spend next Christmas again like this or not. Therefore, I'd like you to forget all your worries this evening, forget about the dangers that are looming around us. At midnight Father Jacob and the Reverend Daniel will lead a service with prayers. We'll depart at around one or two a.m., but many of us will see each other again here when we celebrate the New Year. I hope you have all received our invitation for the next big event. If there's anyone who hasn't, I beg you to come again. Meanwhile, we wish you a Merry Christmas! May God bless us all!"

Young children sang some carols. All the adults visibly tried to dampen their worries for the future, and the Christmas celebration ended with joy. The last guest left at one a.m. Nearly all the same people celebrated the New Year at Peter and Josephine's house until one o'clock in the morning. At ten o'clock in the morning on the 8th of January, many of those who celebrated the Christmas and New Year parties together went to the railway station to say goodbye to Thomas. They all were overcome with sorrow, for nobody knew what would happen until they met again.

CHAPTER 17
(25th January 1939 – Wednesday)

Christine and Paul had initially planned to get back from their holiday in Italy in late February, but they had to come back earlier for some urgent reasons. So Paul asked Jane to come to them punctually. It was two p.m. when she arrived and was heartily greeted in the courtyard by her parents and four elders of the clan who usually came together whenever something critical had happened or was going to happen. So Jane immediately sensed the urgency of the meeting. When she got out of the car, her pregnant belly was quite noticeable. After greeting each other warmly, they entered the house and took seats in the living room. Then Paul initiated the discussion.

"Jane, seeing us all together like this, you may have sensed that something important is taking place. Initially, I thought we could meet a few days later, but two of your uncles have to leave unexpectedly for somewhere this evening; therefore, I asked you to come here urgently. So let me get directly to the reasons why we're here today. We've lately been observing political and military affairs in Europe, especially among our powerful neighbors. Let's have a look at five major events that took place in the last year as examples of what I mean. One: Adolf Hitler replaced Werner von Blomberg as commander of the German army on 4th February; Two: He ordered the German army into Austria on 12th March. On the 13th, Germany declared it a part of the German Reich; Three: On 12th August, he ordered the mobilization of the German army; Four: On 1st October the German army occupied the Sudetenland; Five: On 9th November, Dr. Goebbels organized the Night of Broken Glass. Tensions are rapidly escalating now among the major powers around us so that the overall situation is getting out of control. We no longer doubt that a major war is no longer just a possibility but has become unavoidable. So your mama and I have decided to leave for America as soon as possible – probably not later than July or early August of this year. We'll make our departure as low-key as possible. I've already made a detailed plan for the relief work you will undertake for the sick, the elderly, and orphans, at two locations, based on our experience of giving aid during the Great War. Have you read all the papers that I gave you on the subject?"

"Yes, Papa, I've read them, but not thoroughly yet, since the situation until recently still seemed avoidable. I think you gave me those papers on our visit here in June 1936 – about two and a half years ago."

"Okay. But the plan I've prepared now is much more complete than the plans I sketched out in those papers. I'll tell you a few of the critical points. We had had only one center during the last war, here in Florenville, but you'll prepare to run two centers-cum-orphanages this time. As war is imminent, we'll have to speed up the preparations for these orphanages in the coming months. I'm very seriously thinking about moving our head office to St. Vith in the next few months. The reason is, as Florenville is too close to France, it could become a battlefield. If we move to St. Vith, we'll set up an orphanage there and another in Waimes. The distance between them is only some twenty kilometers, whereas the distance between here and St. Vith is more than a hundred. That's a long distance in case of an emergency. You may want to ask me why two centers and not just one? One of the simple reasons is for the safety of the residents in case of aerial bombing. Another reason is that it might be easier to manage them separately. Take this outline with you and read it carefully. Since your pregnancy will limit your activities, we'll have to rely heavily on your cousins and friends and some hired help – doctors and nurses and psychologists, for instance. We should have at least two to three doctors and six to ten nurses at each center. We could also invite a few volunteers. When you've read the outline, we'll discuss the plans in detail with your cousins and a few other people who will be engaged in the projects. Jane, should I go on, or would you prefer to read it first?"

"Please go on, Papa, so I'll have a rough picture of what you've planned."

"Okay. First, you'll stay put, since, in a big war, the conflicts spread very quickly everywhere anyway; otherwise, you would only be wasting your energy, time, and resources. Second, you cannot be too emotional, too generous, or too compassionate to all those in need – that would be very hard psychologically for you to bear. Since nobody knows how long the war will last, you'll need to stick strictly to the iron-clad rules that you set down at the beginning. You must prepare yourself to encounter many heartbreaking experiences. We had certain occasions during the last war that your mother and I haven't dared to tell you about until now. I think you must strictly limit the number of those your care; a hundred and fifty people at each center at the most would be ideal. Otherwise, your financial resources could very quickly deplete, especially if the war drags on. Third, you must never give the impression that you've got enough financial resources at your disposal. Fourth, you'll need to store essential foodstuffs and materials, sufficient for a few months, in various hiding places, for example, in cellars in many villages.

"You'll have access to the necessary finances from our Swiss bank accounts. It's good that we've managed to move a large portion of our fortune to this account in time. There are some useful tips concerning this in the outline. And from now on, you should start recruiting trustworthy people for the relief work. And one thing that you should give the highest priority to is acquiring two or three pianos for each orphanage. We've got one here, and there's another at your home. The rest you may borrow from our relatives or buy. During the last war, we realized too late the piano's tremendous benefits for those in our care – piano music can soothe people's sorrow and loneliness and take their fears away in times of great danger. That also means you must recruit a few people who can play and teach the piano. I think this is enough for the time being, Jane."

"Thank you very much for this information, Papa. By the way, how much money might I have at my disposal?"

"Let's suppose the war lasts six years. We should prepare to spend an average of a couple of six-figure sums on both orphanages annually. Your mother and I think we should give away at least half of our fortune on these centers, which could amount to a few million Swiss francs."

"Yes, I think we could manage that."

"Jane, as you know, we have a long tradition of generously helping those in dire need, and people admire us for it. But we've never done these things to be admired; it comes from the very bottom of our hearts. We also owe a great deal to countless people for our well-being down the generations. And I nearly forgot to tell you one important thing: You must try to retain your independence as much as you can; you should not allow other institutions or organizations to interfere in your planning and performance. That means we absolutely must not give the impression that we're doing our good works for any reward, either in this world or the next. It would be best if you, therefore, keep a low profile. Do you have anything else to say now, Jane?"

"Papa, thank you very much. These are excellent ideas. I think this will be enough for the time being. I'll start polishing my piano skills. And I'll carefully read the outline, and when I finish it, I'll let you know, and then we can discuss it in more detail."

"By the way, when is Thomas coming back, Jane?"

"He wanted to come back around late April or early May, but some of their employees were conscripted to join the army very recently, so he could not leave as he had planned. As soon as they find someone to fill the vacancies, he will come."

"Hopefully, he'll come back while we're still here. Your mother and I and our relatives and friends would like to know him more intimately. It's a real pity that our two meetings with him were too fleeting."

They went on discussing several critical matters thoroughly until six o'clock. Jane returned home at seven o'clock after having dinner with the four elders and her parents.

CHAPTER 18
(10th April 1939 – Monday)

The time was around ten a.m. Jane and Jennifer were sitting together in the living room, as usual. Jennifer had become quite stout for her age and was a charming little girl. She studied her mother discreetly from her chair. Jane tried to exude joy, but Jennifer sensed that it was not genuine. Jane could barely hide her real feelings. Jennifer started the conversation with a question.

"Mama, you said you wanted to tell me something important. Hopefully, it's not bad news."

"Jennifer, I wish I could give you good news, but I must tell you something very sad. Earlier this month, I was urgently summoned by your oma and opa to have a discussion. Four elders of the clan were also present. They all believe that a major war is inevitable. It could break out at any moment, anywhere. So your oma and opa decided to go to America and stay there until Europe's situation becomes normal again. They asked me to tell you …"

On hearing these words, Jennifer's eyes were suddenly filled with tears, but she did not cry audibly. Then she asked her mother, her voice distorted by sorrow, "Oh, how sorrowful it is, Mama. When are they leaving?"

"Yes, it's so sad. But it's also the nature of human existence. We'll have to try to be realistic and try to be strong, darling."

"Yes, Mama. I've lately become more realistic and more philosophical."

"Jennifer, I've noticed that, and I feel somewhat relieved. Tentatively, they plan to leave in the first week of August. We'll make a farewell party, and only our relatives and friends and we will know it, also about their departure time. They said you could stay with them until they leave if you'd like to."

"Yes, I'll do that, perhaps from June onwards. I want to stay with you too, Mama, for as long as possible since nobody knows how long we can be together if war breaks out."

"You can move as freely as you like between their place and here."

"Have you heard any news from Papa lately, Mama? Have you talked with him on the phone? The last time we heard from him was, I think, two weeks ago, wasn't it?"

"Yes, I called him yesterday, and we talked for about thirty minutes. He's fine, and his parents and sister, too. He sent heartfelt greetings to you from one and all. He said that he had joined the 333rd Field Artillery Battalion, which is made up entirely of blacks. The battalion was officially formed in 1917. It served in France during the Great War but did not see action. He said that he hoped to be sent to the frontlines if war broke out again."

"Oh, that's great. He will surely have a chance to prove to the white people how brave he is so that they'll have more respect for blacks in the future. Do you believe he's brave enough to do that, Mama?"

"I've no doubts about it. We've had big car accidents three times, and every time he was so calm. He was always in full control of himself. For that reason alone, I've total confidence in his courage."

"Mama, I'm very pleased to hear that."

At that moment, the doorbell rang. It was the postman, bringing many letters. Jane frantically checked them and found a letter from Thomas. She opened it immediately with great excitement and began to read. As she turned the pages, her hands began to shake, and tears began to roll down her cheeks.

Jennifer worriedly looked at her mother and asked, "Why are you crying, Mama?"

Jane did not answer for a long while and kept crying silently. Jennifer tenderly took her mother into her arms and asked her the same question. Jennifer herself began now to weep. And with a trembling voice, she asked her mother the same question once again.

"Mama, Mama, why are you crying?"

Jane gathered herself and reluctantly replied in a sorrowful tone, "Thomas has joined the National Socialist Party. Not only that, but he's got an important position in the Propaganda Department ..."

"What is that, Mama?"

"Wait, I'll look in the dictionary for the exact definition of propaganda." Jane got up and took a dictionary down from a bookshelf and searched for the word. "Listen: 'Propaganda is information, often false information, which a political party or organization publishes or broadcasts to influence the opinions or beliefs of people.' I knew that its meaning must be negative, but I never cared to find out its exact meaning until now."

As the conversation progressed, Jane shed no more tears. Her voice became stable again.

"But Mama, Thomas is a very nice and intelligent person. How could he do that?"

"Jennifer, if you look at world history, most of the worst crimes in politics and religion, for instance, have been initiated or committed by intelligent or super-intelligent people. Uneducated or ignorant people are not capable of it."

"Mama, please don't feel so sad, okay? Did you never sense that he could do that someday?"

"He always told me that he was not interested in politics, especially in the Nazi ideology, and that he'd never become one of them. So I accepted his word. On the other hand, human beings are emotional animals. Jennifer, let's not talk about it anymore, okay?"

"Did he mention why he joined the party?"

"Yes. He said that he listened to a speech given by Dr. Goebbels, the head of the Propaganda Ministry, and he was so impressed by the speech that he spontaneously decided to join. And with the help of a very influential relative in the Ministry, he got an important position."

"When was Hitler born, by the way?"

"I think it was on 20th April 1889."

"What might his job be, Mama?"

"He did not mention it, but with his degree in psychology, he could be very useful to the Party. He was extremely bright in class."

"Mama, don't you want to find out what Dr. Goebbels said in his speech?"

"What's the use, since I won't be able to change his opinion anyway? I heard somewhere that Dr. Goebbels had made several speeches since the founding of the Party."

"Did he mention my name or ask you to give me greetings from him?"

"No … That's another reason why I'm sad. He only wrote that I'd never forgive him and that I'd hate him my whole life for this. But he'd not beg for my forgiveness. He's ready to accept the blame, though. If you want to read his letter, you can. There's nothing personal in it."

"That's so strange. No, I don't want to read it. What shall we do now, Mama? Will you reply?"

"I don't think I'll reply, no."

"Did he mention anything about the baby?"

"He only said I had the sole right to decide about it."

"It's a great pity that my new newborn brother or sister won't have a chance to see its father."

"He asked me if I'd allow him to see his son or daughter when the baby is born. But I won't inform him about the birth, nor will I invite him to come. If he gets the news from somewhere and comes, then fine, but I won't inform him."

"Oma and Opa will surely be very sad, too, when they hear this. When are you going to tell them?"

"I'll have to tell them soon, but I don't think they'll be that sad. They've gone through several heartbreaking phases in their own lives, especially during the Great War, so they're very philosophical about the nature of human beings."

"Mama, do you think he will come?"

"I don't know. But if he does, he probably won't feel comfortable among us since so many scary things are happening in his country and elsewhere because of the Party."

"Mama, do you hate him?"

"No. I can understand his situation. Anything can happen to anyone in his circle under the present circumstances. But I'll have to distance myself from him emotionally as quickly as possible."

"Mama, did you ever discuss names for the baby with Thomas?"

"Yes, we agreed that if it's a boy, he'll choose, and if it's a daughter, I will."

"If it's a boy, will you still let him choose the name now?"

"If it's a boy, I'll name him after my late brother. But if it's a girl, I'll let you choose."

Jennifer thought for a long moment. "Oh, I'd love to, Mama. Perhaps I'll name her Julia or Sarah or Karin or Judith or Magdalena or Miriam. And which family name will you give him or her?"

"Since we intended to have a civil marriage as well, I'll use Thomas's family name: Mueller. But I may at some point try to change it to our family name."

"I see, Mama. But how would you do that since he's not here?"

"I've no idea. I'll have to ask the civil marriage office. If it's not possible or the process is complicated, I'll use our family name."

"I see Mama. By the way, would you promise me something?"

"Sure, just tell me what it is."

"That you won't cry anymore."

"No, I can promise you only one thing, Jennifer – that I won't cry anymore because of *Thomas*. As we women cry very often for different reasons, and even for no reason at all, I cannot promise you that I won't cry. Is that okay?"

"Yes, that's okay. But whenever I see you crying, I'm so sad, Mama."

"I love you so much, darling. You always give me strength, the will to go on living. Whenever I see or hear of colored people being unfairly treated just because of the color of their skin, you and your papa come into my mind, and it breaks my heart."

They embraced tightly and wept together for several moments. The next day, Jane informed her parents about Thomas's letter. They reacted philosophically, as Jane had expected. They encouraged her to be strong and accept her fate as a natural part of life. Christine promised to say prayers on her behalf and for the soon-to-be-born baby. Jane's pregnancy was already in the final stages, and she could barely move now.

(15th April 1939 – Saturday)

The time was eleven a.m., and the place: Jane's house. Christine, Jennifer, Jane's aunts, cousins, and Elizabeth had gathered at her home since early in the morning, waiting for the new baby. At almost precisely eleven o'clock, Jane gave birth to a big and healthy daughter, to the great joy of everybody present. After Jane had stilled, washed, and dressed the baby, all the women took her lovingly in their laps one after another. Jennifer decided to name her Sarah, as Jane had promised to let her choose the name if it was a girl. They made a big celebration in the evening, with even more people joining in, until nine p.m.

It was the evening of 29th July, a Saturday, and about fifty relatives and close friends of Christine and Paul's gathered for their farewell party at Jane's house. Christine and Paul would leave for the United States on 31st July by ship from Antwerp. Everyone could barely hide their melancholy, for the tensions in Europe and worldwide continued to escalate rapidly. But they did not utter a single word about the situation; no one wanted to spoil the gathering's mood. A Catholic priest and a Protestant pastor held a worship service. The celebration finally ended at around ten o'clock. Some of Jennifer's aunts and cousins decided to spend the night at the house. On the day of Christine and Paul's departure, all those at the farewell party went to the railway station to say goodbye. They all could barely manage to fight back their tears.

CHAPTER 19
(1st October 1939 – Sunday)

Germany invaded Poland on 1st September; France, Great Britain, Australia and New Zealand declared war on Germany on 3rd September; the British forces moved to the Belgian border on 3rd September, anticipating a German invasion. Canada declared war on Germany on 10th September; Russia invaded Poland on 17th September; Warsaw surrendered on 27th September. The Polish government went into exile. Poland was divided between the Germans and the Soviets on 29th September.

It was nine o'clock on Saturday morning. Jane was preparing breakfast in the kitchen and Sarah was playing in the kitchen with her toys. When Jane had breakfast ready, she called, "Jennifer … Jennifer? Come. Breakfast is ready."

There was no sign of Jennifer. Jane called a bit louder. "Jennifer … Jennifer. Come. Breakfast is ready!"

Still no response, so Jane went to Jennifer's bedroom and knocked on the door. There was no reply. Jane slowly opened the door and looked inside. Everything in the room was in order, but as there was no sign of Jennifer, Jane began to worry. She entered the room and nervously checked every corner. The bed was cold. She then saw an envelope on the table and frantically picked it up. On it was written clearly in large letters: "For My Beloved Mama!" She quickly opened it, and as she read it her hands began to shake and she was overcome with shock and sorrow.

My dearest Mama,

When you find this letter, I might not be in this world anymore. So please don't try to look for me. As you know my situation so well, I won't write at length. I've always pretended to be strong for you, Papa, Oma and Opa and our other relatives because I didn't want to make you sad. But deep in my heart, I was always so sad and so lonely. There were many occasions when I thought I could no longer go on living, but because all of you were so kind and loving I didn't want to make you sad by departing from you so soon. For this reason alone, I tried to go on living.

When my papa left us, my world broke into pieces. And then, when I began to regain the will to live, my oma and opa left us. I can imagine how sad you'll be when you read this letter. I wish I could be with you and say, "Mama, please don't cry!" I can foresee how much I'd suffer when the war comes to us – and it'll surely come very soon. I've therefore decided to disappear from this world before I'm forced to leave it anyway.

Please convey my deepest gratitude and most heartfelt greetings to Papa, his parents and sister, Oma, Opa, Sarah, Auntie Elizabeth, Uncle David, my cousins, and all our relatives and friends. Please tell them how thankful I always was. If not for their love and care, I'd have left this world a long time ago. Mama, I know that you don't believe in the biblical God, and I fully understand your feelings. I deeply respect you for your noble thinking. I know how lucky I was to have been born among such loving, caring, and protective people as you, Papa, Oma, Opa, other relatives, and friends. But the outside world is cold and heartless and hostile to me.

Please forgive me for making you so sad now. Even if I stayed on till the war came to us, you'd suffer anyway with the hardship I'd have to go through. Mama, I was suffering for myself, for Papa and all black people. And whenever I saw how much you were suffering for us, too, my own suffering became unbearable. So please try to console yourself. I'll be waiting for you in a place where there's no more sorrow and death. We'll meet again there. Please don't cry, Mama! I love you so much, and I'll always love you!

May God bless you until we meet again. Goodbye, Mama!

P.S. Would you please kindly allow me to make a last supplication to you, Mama? Since it'd be of no use to blame the biblical God for having created different skin colors and different levels of intelligence and physical features, would you please think about Jesus' message of love and forgiveness in the four Gospels? As you've long been fas-

cinated by Buddhism, I know that you may become a Buddhist some day and seek your peace of mind in that. But if you did, and if Buddhism doesn't forbid you to believe in Jesus at the same time, would you also try to find solace in him as well? You wouldn't lose anything by doing it. I want to see you again in God's kingdom. But the decision is absolutely up to you, Mama.

As she read the letter, Jane could not control herself any longer and burst into torrential tears. It took hours to calm herself down. Then she began calling Jennifer's cousins and friends one after another, asking them if they knew Jennifer's whereabouts, but nobody knew where she might be. A shockwave spread rapidly among Jane's relatives, friends, and the immediate neighboring communities. Several relatives and friends came to comfort her. Jane then asked her aunts, uncles, and friends for their advice. Some of them advised her to inform the police, but others said she should wait a few days to see whether Jennifer contacted her. So Jane decided to wait for two days before she went to the police. Everyone wondered whether Jennifer had run away or had taken her own life.

Some of Jane's relatives told her that they would look in the local newspapers for any clues. The whole community was in great shock and filled with sorrow. People flocked to Jane's home to comfort her. Catholic priests and Protestant pastors visited her and prayed for her. But she could not find peace of mind. She could not sleep or eat.

As there was no sign of Jennifer after two days, Jane and her relatives decided to inform the police. The police asked Jane various questions about their lives and Jennifer's psychological state, and so on. They wanted to know if Jennifer had ever had a boyfriend and whether any of her clothes or other belongings were missing, and if she had left any addresses or letters other than the one to Jane. Jane told them that a few clothes were missing but she had not found any addresses or letters or notes. She told the police about the young Guatemalan boy whom Jennifer had met on holiday in Paris some years ago and liked very much.

The police wanted to know whether Jennifer and the Guatemalan boy had ever written to each other. Jane told them that so far as she knew, they had written a couple of times, but since Jennifer could not speak Spanish, she had conducted the correspondence through a friend, who had told Jane that there was nothing romantic in the letters.

The police then wanted to know if Jennifer had ever tried to learn Spanish. Jane replied yes, and that she had a French/Spanish dictionary in which Jennifer had made some notes. The police wanted to know if Jane had any idea how to discover the boy's identity. Jane said no. The police suggested that she come back to them the next day at the same time. They would conduct inquiries within Belgium and then make an analysis.

Jane and a couple of her relatives went back to the police the next day at the same time. The police informed them that there was no further information about Jennifer. They believed that she had most likely not committed suicide but had run away to an unknown destination. Where it could be, they had no idea. They suggested that Jane try to find the Guatemalan boy. On their way home from the police station, one of Jane's female relatives suggested she contact Sister Hanna. The idea struck Jane like a lightning bolt.

"Yes, good idea. It didn't occur to me. I'll call her right away when we get home. Thank you very much."

As soon as they arrived home, Jane rang the number of Sister Hanna's convent, and a female voice came on the other end.

"Hello, good afternoon. I'm Ms. Jeanmart, calling from Florenville. May I speak to Sister Hanna sometime today?"

"Good afternoon. I'm Sister Maria. You're fortunate, Ms. Jeanmart. Sister Hanna is coincidentally right here. I'll pass her the phone."

"Hello, good afternoon, Hanna. It's me, Jane. How are you?"

"Hello, Jane, good afternoon. I'm fine. I suppose you're calling me because of Jennifer?"

Jane was surprised by the question. "Yes, Hanna. How did you know?"

"She wrote me a sorrowful farewell letter and told me that she had also left a similar letter for you."

"Ah, I see. She visited you twice recently, didn't she? Did she give you any hint about what she was going to do?"

"I knew that she was suffering very much psychologically. But she didn't give me any sign at all that she would disappear like this."

"I've been to the police, and the police psychologists thought Jennifer most likely did not take her own life but went away somewhere. Do you have any idea where she might have gone?"

"I'm so sorry, I don't have any idea. Jennifer mentioned a young boy by the name of Carlos from Spain or somewhere in Latin America a couple of times. That's all."

"Hanna, what shall I do now? I'm so sad, it's burning me up. I feel so helpless. I don't know what to do. If she had died in a traffic accident or from a disease, I don't think I would be suffering this much. The police suggested that I try to find out the identity of the boy, but I don't know how I can do that."

"Jane, since you don't believe in the biblical God, and I know that you're rather fascinated by Buddhism, I can only give you this advice. A couple of days ago, I heard that the Congress of Freethinkers in Brussels had invited a Buddhist monk from Ceylon, who visited England recently on the Buddhist Society's invitation in London, to come to Brussels for a few weeks to give some lectures. I don't know if he's already here or if he'll even come, given the situation in Europe. But I know the person who organized the event well. I'll call him and tell him about your predicament. He might be able to arrange a personal audience with the monk. I'll let you know when I've spoken with my friend, okay?"

"Hanna, that's an excellent idea. Thank you so much. I'll be waiting to hear. And I wish you all the best, meanwhile."

Two hours later, Hanna was on the phone again. "Hello Jane, I've just spoken to the man I mentioned. His name is Professor Matthew Fleming; he's a member of the internationally known Belgian School of Buddhist Studies and the Congress of Freethinkers. He's an amiable guy, about forty years of age, still relatively young, but he and his wife are not yet Buddhists because they can't decide which school would be most suitable for them. So they're still studying the concepts of all the large Buddhist schools. You'll like him immediately. He told me that the monk is temporarily stranded in Belgium due to the sudden outbreak of war. He also said the famous Indologist Professor Etienne Lamotte of the Catholic University of Louvain, who has authored several books on Buddhism, may again come to Brussels in a few days. And he said he'd be able to arrange a personal audience for you with the monk or the Indologist or both. If you would like an audience with the monk, he can set it up for ten o'clock in the morning until eight in the evening the day after tomorrow at his home, where the monk is staying. They had planned for him to give a lecture that evening at the house, but when I told him about you, he changed the plan so that the monk could devote the whole day to you. And those who had planned to attend his evening lecture will go to Matthew's house anyway to listen to your discussion with the monk instead. But if you'd prefer to meet with the Indologist, Matthew will make an appointment for you at a later date."

"Oh Hanna, how kind of you. I have to go to Brussels tomorrow anyway, so it'll be perfect. I'd prefer to meet with the monk since I've never met a Buddhist monk before. I have nothing against the Indologist, but a person who has spent nearly his entire adult life as a monk will probably see things differently from a pure scholar like Professor Lamotte. I'll never forget this favor, and I'll tell you in detail about our discussion. Hopefully, you won't convert to Buddhism if what the monk tells me is enlightening! I'm just joking, Hanna. May God bless you. We'll talk again soon."

"Jane, I've also read many books on Buddhism, but I'm convinced that what I believe in now is right for me. I'm glad that I could do this little thing for you. You can always call me at any time if you need me. And please keep in mind that I share your sorrow. You know that Jennifer was like a daughter to me. Although you aren't religious, I'll always remember you in my prayers. Hopefully, the monk will be able to give you the peace of mind that you so badly need now. I wish you the best of luck and may God bless you, Jane!"

"Thank you so much once again, Hanna, I wish you the same. Goodbye."

Jane immediately called Matthew to make arrangements for the meeting. He asked her if she would mind if fifty or sixty people also participated in the discussion. He told her that about half of them would be members of the Belgian School of Buddhist Studies, and the rest would be members of the Congress of Freethinkers. Jane replied that the presence of other participants would enhance the occasion. She was visibly relieved and started making preparations right away for the trip to Brussels.

The next morning, she took Sarah to one of her cousins, and then she and her cousin and secretary, Victoria, took a train to Brussels, where they would stay with her aunt Maria. The next day, they arrived at the professor's house punctually at 9:45 a.m. Matthew and his charming wife, Natalie, were waiting for them at the front door. After they all had introduced themselves warmly, Matthew and Natalie escorted them into a spacious room where the monk and about sixty people waited for them. The monk was in his mid-sixties and very friendly.

After Matthew had introduced Jane and the monk to each other, he introduced her to the others in the room; about half were men and the other half women. He told Jane that she should feel completely free to be with the monk without any time pressure and ask him whatever she wanted. They all agreed that the discussion would be very informal. She thanked Matthew and the monk profusely for the great favor. The monk's name was Balangoda Ananda Maitre Thera. Matthew told her that since the monk's name was very long and difficult to remember, she could address him as "Your Venerable." They took their seats opposite each other.

The monk began the conversation. He spoke English very fluently. "I'm happy to meet you, Mrs..."

Seeing that the monk had difficulty recalling her family name, she quickly came to his aid.

"Your Venerable, you can just call me by my first name: Jane."

"Oh, thank you, Jane. When one is no longer young, the memory does not function very well anymore."

They all laughed heartily together. The monk then continued, "Jane, we can simply address each other as 'you' and 'I'. Whenever I come into contact with non-Buddhists, I always tell them to address each other thus, because the informality makes the atmosphere more relaxed. But when I speak with Buddhist audiences, I cannot let them address me simply as 'you,' not because I crave their respect, but because they've been used to addressing all monks as 'Your Venerable' for generations. That's why I urged Professor Fleming to use the more informal form of address with me from our first meeting. Please don't be surprised if I call him by his first name, too, during our discussion. Well, Jane, I feel so honored that you want to talk to me. But I must tell you from the outset that you should not expect words of great wisdom from me. Of course, I'll try my best to answer your questions as well as I can."

The monk then turned to the audience and said, "Before we start our discussion, I'd like to make a humble request of you all. First, I'd like to remind you once again that I'm just an ordinary monk, so I don't represent the Sangha's views in my country. I wasn't officially invited here in the name of the Congress of Freethinkers; I was approached by Matthew and his colleagues from the organization to give some lectures. I know that some of you are devoted Buddhists and belong to a couple of different schools, and some are interested in learning more about Buddhism in general. I don't know what kind of questions Jane will raise, but I'll try to answer her questions freely, which means many of my answers will be my personal opinions or my personal interpretations, based loosely on the teachings of the school to which I belong – namely, Theravada. In other words, many of my opinions will not necessarily reflect the beliefs or concepts of some of the other major Buddhist schools. So some of you may even be rather disappointed by my opinions. Therefore, I'd like to beg you for your understanding if any of my thoughts seem to contradict what

143

you've understood about Buddhism. Since an established Buddhist society did not invite me, I understand that I can freely express my personal views on the topics Jane will raise or anything I deem to be interesting to you."

All the participants expressed their understanding and signaled him to go ahead, so the monk continued after thanking them for their approval and understanding.

"Jane, Matthew told me very briefly about your life and your present agonies. How would you like to begin our discussion?"

"Thank you very much, Your Venerable. First of all, before we start, may I make a humble request? I started writing an autobiographical romance novel more than ten years ago. And I feel that I should share what you say today with as many people as possible. So I wonder if you'd allow me to use this material in my book?"

Her words aroused all the participants' curiosity, and the monk asked her, "You're writing a romance? Very interesting. I hope I'll be able to read it. And I have no objection at all. When will it be published?"

"Thank you very much. I don't know when I'll publish it. I may have to collect some more life experiences first, so it could even take some decades. But I can assure you that you'll be among the first to read it. If you don't mind, Victoria, my cousin and my secretary, will write down our discussion in shorthand, and in the end she'll read it back – or if time is tight I can send it to you, and you can check it. You'll then have the chance to add to or delete any parts you may wish. I'd be very grateful if you could give me written permission to use it in my book. I promise that I'll donate a certain amount of what I earn in royalties from the sales of the book to you personally or to any organizations according to your wishes."

"I agree with your proposals, Jane. I don't expect any donations from the sales of the book. And if you decide to donate anyway, I won't take anything for myself. From the moment I entered monkhood, I lost my attachment to all things material. I'll name two orphanages and a religious organization to which you may donate, though; they have an excellent reputation for their integrity."

"Thank you very much. But isn't it against your religion for a monk to read novels? It contains some intimate passages."

"So far as I know, there is not a single regulation regarding this. It could be because, in Buddha's time, there were no novels yet …"

He was suddenly interrupted by hearty laughter from the whole audience. He continued with a broad smile, "That was just a joke. But every monk can decide freely for himself what is appropriate and what is not. And I will be careful not to let any romantic scenes in the novel distract me from my spiritual endeavors."

"Thank you very much, Your Venerable. Now, I've got so many questions to ask you, which I've listed on these sheets. But I'm worried that I might overburden you."

Jane produced a couple of sheets of paper and showed them to the monk.

"Jane, you don't need to worry about that. I'm only afraid that I might not have enough wisdom to give you satisfactory answers."

"Thank you very much. I want to ask you to be patient with me since my questions are not listed systematically. I didn't have enough time to do that. So I'll have to jump around between different topics."

"That's okay, Jane. Don't worry about that."

Before Jane could say more, the monk had an idea. He turned to her and said, "Jane, wait a minute. An idea suddenly popped up, and I think I should tell you what it is. Since you want to integrate our discussion into your novel, shouldn't we ask Matthew to tell us something about the Congress of Freethinkers? I'm sure the readers of your novel will be very interested to know about it."

"Your Venerable, that's an excellent idea. Matthew, would you please tell us about your organization? Everybody here, and my readers, will be very grateful, I'm sure."

Matthew was delighted by the monk's and Jane's words and stood up. "Thank you very much for giving me this opportunity to tell you briefly about it. Well, Belgium's well-known status as a seat of international associations and venue for international meetings in the decades preceding the First World War applies in the case of the Freethinkers and Freemasons. The foundation in 1880 of the International Federation of Freethinkers (IFF) took place at a conference in Brussels and preceded the creation of a national federation for Belgium. Although the Belgians had difficulty starting their own federation, they were key actors in free thought internationally, and Belgian leaders remained its core group for a long time. The series of Free-thinkers' conferences that followed was significant in creating an extended network of international links between organizations and individuals—with Brussels as the center, where all the threads came together.

"Since the National Congress adopted its constitution on 7th February 1831, freedom of religion has been guaranteed by supreme law, which means that no one can be banned from, or forced to respect, a religion in Belgium. This constitution was considered the most liberal and progressive of its day; in addition to freedom of religion, it also guarantees freedom of education, association, and the press. This long tradition of toleration in religious and philosophical matters has recently been highlighted by the International Humanist and Ethical Union (IHEU), an umbrella organization bringing together humanist, atheist, rationalist, secular, and skeptical free-thinking associations. A few words now about why we invited His Venerable: He is quite well known among religious and secular scholars in his country and especially in England for his unusual points of view on various topics. And we're very fortunate that he could come here amid the great battles that are being fought right now among our neighboring countries. I think this is enough for the time being. Thank you very much, everybody."

The whole audience was grateful. After thanking Matthew profusely, the monk asked Jane to tell him her story.

"Thank you very much, Your Venerable. As you've heard, I'm suffering terribly with the loss of my daughter, so I'm looking for someone or something that can give me peace of mind. It's burning me up inside. Many Christian clerics have tried to comfort me by citing biblical verses and saying prayers for me, but they haven't given me the slightest relief. I've also read some books and articles on Buddhism in the past few years, and I think your religion might give me peace of mind. I'd be very grateful if you'd tell me about the fundamental teachings of Buddhism. Unfortunately, all the books I've read so far were rather difficult to understand, so I couldn't get a clear picture."

"Jane, let's talk first about your present suffering since you're full of sorrow right now. A long discourse on Buddhism wouldn't help you through your suffering and give you peace of mind. Shall we?"

"Yes, Your Venerable."

"Just address me as 'You,' Jane. Matthew told me that your daughter was brilliant and calm. And that she rarely did anything impulsive. And was kind and helpful, and also quite courageous and religious. Are all these traits accurate?"

"Yes, everything you say is true. But may I address you anyway as 'Your Venerable'? I'd feel more comfortable with that."

"Well, if you feel like that, that's okay, Jane. You may also use both interchangeably if you like. Jane, would you mind reading your daughter's farewell letter for all of us to hear, if you have it with you? But if it'd worsen your sorrow, you don't need to feel obliged."

Jane was a bit reluctant. Every participant was observing her. At last, though, she took Jennifer's letter out of her handbag and began to read. As she slowly read, her voice was distorted by sorrow and her hands began to shake. But she made a great effort and read it through to the end. Everybody's eyes, including the monk's, were filled with tears. There was a long pause. Then the monk broke the silence.

"Thank you very much for reading it for us. As you see, we are all moved to tears by Jennifer's words. Jane, you should stop worrying about her. If she's alive, rest assured that she has done what she wanted to do. And if she's no longer alive, she has surely found her peace of mind. I know that this is easily said, and it will be challenging for you to accept it at the moment."

"I don't understand what you mean, Your Venerable."

"It's evident that she planned what she has done a long time ago.

And she will have considered every possible risk. So if she's still alive somewhere in the world, she'll undoubtedly have her peace. And if she's no longer on this earth, she'll have found eternal peace – perhaps in heaven where the biblical God may dwell. Either way, she's found her peace. And as she says in her letter, if she had stayed until the war came and the enemy mistreated her, you would suffer terribly – there would probably be nothing you could do to help her. You're fortunate that she left a letter for you. Just look at the countless wars around the world since recorded history began, in which millions of people vanished without a trace. If she had not left the letter, your suffering would be much worse."

"Thank you very much, Your Venerable. I understand now what you mean, to some extent. These few words of wisdom alone have lessened my suffering already."

"You might not yet fully understand everything I say because you're under such great stress. But think it over and you'll see the truth in it with time, and your suffering will further recede. I know that it takes a person an average of three years to detach himself from his emotional attachment to a lost loved one. In my case, it took me much longer than that to live without thinking all the time about all the family I lost. What is very important for you to understand is that no matter how much you're suffering, you cannot change what has happened."

"Oh, you lost your whole family? I'm so sorry to hear that. And thank you so much for what you just said. I also feel guilty about her suffering, being a white person."

"Yes, I lost my whole family in a flood. I was the only survivor. But let me tell you more about that later."

Everybody expressed their deep sympathy for him. The monk continued, "Everybody, thank you so much. But Jane, it's not your fault that you were born white. It was not your choice. You should only feel guilty about something you did consciously. Matthew tells me that you're a very loving, warm-hearted and protective mother. In this, you've fulfilled your duty. Nothing will live forever on this

148

earth. Everything that came into existence in this universe will leave it again sooner or later. That is the laws of nature. If you can accept this reality, it'll be much easier for you to endure hardship, pain, and sorrow."

"The laws of nature? What's that?"

"I'll explain what the laws of nature mean according to Buddhism: If you tell a Buddhist about the death of a loved one, he'll most likely say, 'Oh, I'm so sorry to hear that. But don't be so sad. It happened according to the laws of nature.' Buddhists have no illusions about the precarious existence of all beings in this world. So they can much more easily overcome their sorrows about the loss of their loved ones than, let's say, Christians."

"All this is new to me. I'll need some time to digest it. But Christians believe in an eternal existence somewhere in the universe with the biblical God. What would you say about that?"

"I can only talk about these things from a Buddhist's point of view."

"You've mentioned different schools of Buddhism. How many schools are there, and are their opinions on these matters uniform?"

"There are many of them, but three are most prominent: Theravada, Mahayana, and Vajrayana, also known as Tibetan Buddhism. Their opinions are more or less the same on these matters."

"Different schools mean there must be different doctrines or beliefs among them, though. Is that true?"

"Yes, that's true. But let's talk about some of those beliefs later, Jane."

"And there's also another religion called Jainism, I suppose."

"Yes, there is. But its adherents are quite a few compared to those of Hinduism and Buddhism. We wouldn't have enough time to discuss it."

"Okay, then. Now, my next question is: Have you ever read the Jewish and Christian Bibles? If so, I'm curious to find out how a Buddhist sees them."

"You mean the Old Testament or Hebrew Bible and the New Testament? I've never studied any Christian theology systematically, but I've read these Bibles several times from beginning to end, and quite a lot of Christian literature and the doctrines of many Churches as well. Not only that, but I've had several discussions with some leading Christian theologians and clergymen. Unfortunately, I haven't studied much about Judaism, partly because the population that professes it is relatively small compared to other great religions' adherents. Its impact on humankind is also less significant, I think. Another important reason I'm interested in Christianity is that it has shaped a large portion of humankind's destiny in either a positive or negative way since its birth."

"I'm glad to know that you've read these Bibles and other Christian literature, and that you've had serious discussions with theologians and clergymen. I'd therefore like to ask you some questions concerning Christianity, too."

"Well, I've always avoided openly speaking about Christianity until now – in either a positive or a negative way. But I'll tell you frankly today what I think about it. So I'd like to tell you something in advance: I'll use the word Bible in plural form when your questions and my answers are directly relevant to both religions, but if an issue is relevant only to Judaism, I'll say 'the Old Testament' or 'the Hebrew Bible' In like manner, if it's an issue of Christianity alone, I'll use the phrase 'New Testament.' And another important point I'd like to make in advance is that as I look at Christian theology from an independent observer's perspective, many of my opinions may seem quite radically different from the established theological concepts in colonialist countries. Therefore, I'd like to beg you for your understanding and tolerance in advance."

"That'd be even more fascinating, and I can imagine that your points of view certainly would be very refreshing for me and for many people in the West."

"May I ask you a question before I continue?"

"Of course, Your Venerable."

"Thank you. You said a while ago that you might even need a few decades to collect all the material for your novel. How long could it be – two, three, four decades?"

"As I cannot foresee how long I'll live or what'll happen to me in the future, I cannot give you a precise answer. But I'd like to take as long as possible before I publish it because as I'm financially secure, I wouldn't need to publish to make a living out of it. But at least two to three decades, I suppose."

"Thank you very much, Jane. The reason I ask you this question is that some of the opinions I'll express could make many powerful state, religious and political institutions and their leaders in the Christian West very uncomfortable. Therefore, I'd like to suggest that you integrate the ones that could be too controversial only into your final draft when it's ready for publication; otherwise, some unexpected problems could arise prematurely and unnecessarily. That means you won't integrate controversial ideas into the drafts you may make for distribution among your friends. Hopefully, the powerful institutions and personalities in question will become more liberal and tolerant of new ideas thirty or forty years from now."

"Thank you. I understand and fully agree. My next question is: Despite your deep knowledge of Christianity, you remain a Buddhist monk. Does that mean that you feel Buddhism is superior to Christianity?"

"In my opinion, every religion is unique in its own ways. I'll never use the word 'superior' in this context. The simple reason is that as there are various conflicting doctrines among the several branches of Judaism and Christianity, there are also different concepts, interpretations and rituals among the Buddhist schools."

"Thank you very much. May I put my question differently, then: Are you sure that what you believe in is the 'absolute truth'?"

"It's not easy to talk about absolute truth or reality, or truths or realities for everybody, while we're living in this world as human beings. In my opinion, we can talk about truth or reality only in certain contexts. For example, you're a woman and I'm a man. That's an absolute truth. Before you die, you're still alive. Once you're dead, you're no longer alive. These are absolute truths. But the question of whether or not, or in what form or in what way, our soul or consciousness might exist beyond this human existence is pure speculation."

"But don't Buddhists believe in birth and rebirth? Isn't that an absolute truth?"

"Yes, it should be an absolute truth. Most Buddhists believe it to be so. But the problem is that nobody has ever seen a human soul, or consciousness, that has been reincarnated. There are several people in my country and elsewhere in Asia who may have been reincarnated. Many of them were born with inexplicable birthmarks and could recall their past lives when they were still young – say, until they were four or five years old – or, for example, how they died. When these people get older, they slowly begin to forget their early memories. And none of them can recall how the process happened. For example, the Tibetan Lamas claim to be able to steer where they want to be reborn. But even then their disciples or fellow monks have to consult mediums, astrology and other methods to learn about their reincarnations and prove or disprove whether the reincarnations are genuine or not. An interesting book on the subject, the *Tibetan Book of the Dead* by Evans-Wentz, was published in 1927 by the Oxford University Press. A layperson may have difficulty understanding its contents. Among Asian societies where reincarnations are said to be common, it's generally believed that those who died by violence are more often reborn. That's why nearly all of them have birthmarks. But there's a big, big question mark. Countless people have died in wars from their wounds, so theoretically, many of them – if not all – should have been reincarnated. But why don't all of those reincarnated have birthmarks? Another question is, if only those who die by violence reincarnate, how could the Tibetan Lamas, who die peacefully, be reborn? Then the next question is: Who or what decides who should or should not be born again? Most Buddhists would simply say that it happens according to one's karma, or one's karma will decide. But what is karma? Is it a living force or a divine being? Nobody knows for sure. Countless questions don't have answers for non-initiates – or even perhaps for initiates as well – in many cases. You can, of course, easily repeat what is written about it in scripture, but that doesn't solve the essential nature of it."

"It's so fascinating, Your Venerable. You mentioned the soul and consciousness. Could you explain?"

"Well, some people believe that it is the soul that keeps on reincarnating, while some others believe it to be the consciousness. And some people believe the two to be the same thing. But I don't burden myself too much with this abstract question because I know that I'll never find a satisfactory answer in this life, and even if I did find it, I wouldn't know what to do with the knowledge."

"Still, would you please kindly tell me what the human soul, according to Buddhism, *is*?"

"I think I need to explain first the different concepts of it in Hinduism and Buddhism. According to Hinduism or Hindu philosophy, the soul is called *Atman*; the Hindus believe every living being has a soul. It's a person's 'true self,' which keeps on reincarnating. It is indestructible; it is unchanging; it is eternal – ageless. But the Buddha rejected this concept. This is a major point of difference with the Buddhist doctrine of *Anatta*, which holds that there is no soul or self. The Buddhist concept of reincarnation is that a 'stream of consciousness' links life with life. The process of change from one life to the next is called *punarbhava* (Sanskrit) or *punabbhava* (Pāli), literally 'becoming again,' or more briefly *bhava*, 'becoming.'"

"Since you're a Buddhist, you surely believe in the Buddhist concept?"

"If I'm to be honest, I think the Hindu concept is more acceptable in this case."

Everybody was surprised by the monk's words.

"But you remain a Buddhist, nevertheless?"

"There are many reasons why I remain a Buddhist, despite this 'heresy,' but we won't have enough time to discuss them in detail."

"Could you please mention at least one or two reasons anyway?"

"I'll mention just two: the caste system of Hinduism and its concept of God. Hindus worship one Supreme Being called Brahman, though by different names. This Supreme God has innumerable divine powers. When God is formless, He is referred to by the term Brahman. When God has form, He is referred to by the term Paramatma. So the three forms of an Almighty God are Brahma – the creator, Vishnu – the sustainer, and Shiva – the destroyer. Hinduism's unique understanding is that God is not far away and living in a remote heaven, but is inside every soul, in the heart and consciousness, waiting to be discovered. And the goal of Hinduism is knowing God in this intimate experiential way."

"Could you perhaps tell me what you think about these definitions?"

"I must honestly admit that these definitions are too abstract for me."

"Isn't it dangerous to propound such a heresy in Buddhism? If you were a Christian in the Middle Ages and openly expressed an idea that did not conform with your Church's doctrine, you'd surely be tortured to death or burned alive at the stake."

"In Buddhism, nobody can impose upon you any belief. That's the very good side of my religion. Everything is voluntary. I alone am responsible for my actions and their consequences. And I'd like to tell you an intellectual curiosity of mine concerning the concept of endless rebirth: Humans are developing more and more sophisticated and powerful weapons, so nobody can rule out that someday somebody might develop weapons capable of destroying this planet and all the living beings on it. So imagine what would happen to this concept if there were no more human beings on earth. It's perhaps just a crazy thought. By the way, you might find it interesting to know that Buddhists regard their religion as 'the middle way.'"

"Thank you very much. It's so fascinating. And the human consciousness, according to Buddhism?"

"The explanations are again very abstract. Numerous Buddhist scholars have tried to explain it, but there's not a single clear-cut answer that can be easily understood. It's no wonder that, like the great scientists and philosophers, Buddhist scholars cannot agree upon any concrete definitions. They can only speculate."

"You must surely have given it some thought, though. And if so, would you please let me know what you think about it?"

"I'll tell you something you might find interesting, but it's my own speculation, and it has nothing to do with Buddha's teachings. Although I've told you that I find the Hindu concept of 'soul' more acceptable for me, I think one cannot completely rule out that what reincarnates could be consciousness, since humans can reincarnate as animals, too. If what reincarnates is the soul, it might have difficulty retaining its 'form' when it reincarnates as an animal. But this is just an intellectual curiosity. I hope I've not baffled you too much. I don't think any living human being will ever find out the truth about the soul and consciousness."

The audience's reaction was a mixture of confusion and fascination. The next moment, the monk continued, "Now I'll tell you a little bit more about this topic. Like the scientists, philosophers and psychologists, I don't know whether consciousness comes from the brain or the mind or the soul, or from all of them, or what the mind itself is. I've never, therefore, burdened myself with this puzzle very profoundly. However, I find consciousness itself very interesting for several reasons. Buddhism, of course, has a theory about it. According to this theory, there are nine levels of consciousness. But these levels are probably difficult even for highly qualified Buddhist scholars to fully understand. Of course, one can repeat what is written about it in scripture without genuinely understanding its deep meanings. So I'll try to explain it in a simple way. In general, we all know that people have five senses. But in reality, I think there must be several other kinds of consciousness, with many different levels or degrees. Among them could be love, hatred, jealousy, anxiety, happiness, sorrow, pleasure, loneliness, gratitude, compassion, and so on. Some people may have more and some less. Generally speaking, people have different interests. Some are interested in politics, some in religion, some in music, some in sports, some in literature, some in the military, some in science, some in the arts, and some in several subjects simultaneously, et cetera. And they try to develop their skills or deepen their knowledge in their fields of interest. As a result, their consciousness in areas in which they're not interested may be less developed."

"Do you think some animals might also have some sort of consciousness?"

"It's said that animals have only instinct – the survival instinct. But I think some animals may have some basic consciousness as well. When a baby – either human or animal – is born, it immediately knows where to find milk. That's instinct. Just have a look at several species of birds that build very sophisticated nests without being taught by their parents – and they also know automatically when they should start building their nests. That's instinct. All animals know how to mate with each other without having been taught. That's instinct. But if you put an animal on one edge of a deep gorge and food on the other edge, it might take the risk and jump into the gorge in the hope that it will survive and get the food, since if it didn't do that it'd die a slow death anyway. Or it might decide to starve itself to death instead of trying to get the food by jumping into the gorge. The capacity to make such a calculation, I think, is consciousness. Therefore, I assume that animals also must have some basic consciousness. I don't have any idea how psychologists and philosophers would interpret it. But how can one prove if an animal has a high level of consciousness? My simple criteria are whether an animal can feel sorrow, happiness, thankfulness, loneliness, and whether it has highly developed memories, et cetera. In my opinion, only dogs fulfill these criteria. So the level or levels of a dog's consciousness must be rather high – even higher than in some people. Their only problem, perhaps, is that they cannot express their feelings verbally like humans. Some human beings are not capable of being thankful or happy or sad. It may sound arrogant of me, but I often wonder whether many of the people I've observed closely were fully conscious or even aware at all of their own lives and their surroundings. So I ask myself very often if such people's consciousness might only be slightly higher than the basic survival instinct of the animals."

"I know that compassion is one of the most important elements of Buddhism. Would you tell me what it means?"

"Yes, it is indeed one of the most important elements, and is called *karuna*. But instead of telling you what it is according to Buddhist scripture, I'll tell you how I interpret it. I think it takes many different forms. But since we don't know how long our discussion will last, let us deal with them – and consciousnesses as well – in the most simple way. You may have compassion only for certain types of people and under certain conditions – for instance, you cannot be compassionate with someone you know is bad or ungrateful. And it's very easy to manipulate it through religious, racial, or political ideologies. Just look at the present German racial ideology or the Hindu caste system, to name but two examples. In my opinion, compassion is a fickle thing – you may most likely have a higher degree of compassion for your own family, friends, someone from your ethnic group or your religious or political circles, than for those from outside these circles. In other words, all types of compassion are subject to different conditions. So it's not easy to preach and persuade everybody to cultivate and practice it toward everybody else. And some people are born with a certain degree of compassion, whereas in some people it may be absent. It may be possible to persuade some people to develop and practice it, but it wouldn't work with others. Just look at sadistic people who experience satisfaction by causing or seeing innocent people's or animals' suffering. It might be possible to teach some people who lack compassion in their lives to cultivate it through, say, some form of religious concept; or they might develop it alone in the course of their lives through their experiences. Some may never even be aware of its existence. There are a lot of people in this world who cannot understand why some people feel compassion toward animals."

"Could there be any connection between compassion and higher levels of consciousness in any field?"

"That depends, I think. And I think it's too complex to go into detail. If you look at world history, countless brutalities against innumerable innocent people have been either initiated or even personally committed by people who must have had high levels of consciousness in certain fields of their interest."

"So you mean consciousness and compassion are different things?"

"Yes, in my opinion, they are two completely different things, dependent on several factors. If they were not two different things, the rich would share their wealth with the poor, and as a result, there would be no communism in the first place. And there would probably be no colonialists at all, or even if there were some, they would be much more humane than what they are today. And there would surely be much fewer wars in the world and less suffering as a result."

The audience liked the monk's explanation.

"Do you think there could be any connection between the level of consciousness and the degree of intelligence?"

"Yes, there could be, I suppose. But that would also depend on the type or types of consciousness."

"And could there be any connection between levels of intelligence and compassion?"

"If you look at world history – and what is now happening around the world – I'm very doubtful about that because of the countless disgusting acts that have been – and are still being – committed or caused by super-intelligent people. I think intelligence and compassion are also two completely different things. In everyday life, we can see how unintelligent people often do good things for their fellow human beings and how intelligent people often do bad things. Intelligent people are not automatically kindhearted. Perhaps you had better ask psychologists for more appropriate answers to this question."

"And what about the role of religions in the development and uplifting of the levels or degrees of consciousness?"

"I think they surely play some important roles, but I cannot precisely pinpoint how. It may partly depend on the type or types of consciousness. Just one example: I don't think you can raise a Buddhist's level of consciousness in *his* religion by teaching him Christianity, or vice versa. In like manner, you'll never be able to raise a true atheist's levels of consciousness in religion through any religious teachings. If I'm to be honest, Buddhism may be the only major religion through which you could raise levels of consciousness in other fields."

"Why only through Buddhism and not, say, Christianity or Judaism?"

"In Buddhism, you have to strive for nirvana and your enlightenment. As Buddhism is a philosophy, you cannot expect a higher being to arrange for your salvation on your behalf. But so far as I know, in Christianity, the only thing you need to do to attain salvation and eternal life is to observe the moral teachings of God and Jesus."

"How about through Hinduism?"

"Without doubt, most Hindu priests are well versed in their numerous holy scriptures, and as a result their levels of consciousness in many fields that are related to their religion must be very high. Just look at the super-fine architecture and sculpture in many ancient Hindu temples. But whether you'd be able to raise an average Hindu's general consciousness in non-religious fields or not, I am not sure."

"What about self-consciousness or self-awareness?"

"I don't know how psychologists and philosophers define them, but for me, both of them are the same thing. For me, they are equally important as other types of consciousness – or perhaps even more important than all the others in some cases. In this, I want to say that nearly all human beings can see the weaknesses or strengths of other people, but there are very few who know themselves or who want to try to know themselves. And there are even fewer people who can appreciate criticism from other people, even when the criticism is constructive."

"Thank you very much. Your Venerable, here's my next question: I'm not quite sure about this, but I think I've heard that some Buddhists believe they can escape endless rebirth through the grace or blessing of monks without personally striving for it – or by lavishly helping those in need in every possible way."

"That could be true in some circles, I suppose, because, as in every religion, some Buddhist monks could misinterpret Buddha's teachings – or interpret them differently. As a result, there are many schools with different doctrines. I think it's the same with many Christians believing that their religious leaders' blessings could help them attain eternal life."

"But why do Buddhists worship Buddha if he exists no more?"

"Let's discuss this in more detail later, Jane."

"What about the major religions' influence on compassion in general?"

"In the case of Christianity, compassion may well influence a large percentage of its ordinary adherents on an individual basis, but I don't think it has any significant influence on the powerful Christian institutions and their leading personalities. Just look at what the various Churches have been doing against each other for the past 2,000 years. Another vivid example is colonialism. Buddhism may have a rather stronger influence on its adherents, one of the simple proofs being that Buddhists don't justify their wrongdoing in the name of the teachings of the Buddha. However, some exceptions might be interesting to you: I know many Buddhists who cannot feel compassion for some people's misery. Their simple argument is that such people don't deserve compassion, for they're reaping now what they had done in their past lives."

All the participants were deeply absorbed in the discussion.

"But isn't compassion also one of Jesus' moral teachings?"

"That's true. The big problem here is: How could those who claim to be true believers and worshippers of the biblical God and Jesus so badly manipulate their moral teachings and cause so much suffering for each other and other countless non-Christians in those deities' names?"

"Thank you very much. You know why I can't believe in the biblical God?"

"… Why a loving God created human beings with different-colored skins. Isn't that it?"

"Yes. Not only that, but why did God create us with different physical features and different levels of intelligence?"

"We Buddhists don't have these problems because in Buddhism there's no Creator God."

"Many people have told me – and I have read some literature on this, too – that no one has ever made war in the name of Buddhism. Is that true, and if yes, how would you explain it?"

"Yes, that's true, so far as I know. The reason is simple: because we don't believe in an all-powerful God. Even the Buddha didn't claim to be God. So everybody is responsible for the consequences of his own actions and also for his spiritual liberation, or nirvana. This idea is absolutely in contrast to the concept of the biblical God. But suppose Buddha had claimed to be a loving, forgiving and all-powerful god existing eternally somewhere in the universe and making divine judgments on human beings. In that case, it's likely that several of his worshippers would also have committed some awful acts in his name, like the Christians. Nor do we Buddhists have an evil being called Lucifer or Satan as a scapegoat whom we can blame for all the evil deeds that we commit."

"Do Buddhists not believe in the existence of evil spirits? I'm just curious."

"So far as I know, many Buddhists do believe in the existence of good and evil spirits, partly because elements of superstition still linger in their minds. These evil spirits are called 'demons.'. It may come as a surprise to those who equate Buddhism solely with its intellectual and mystical traditions to learn that demons, too, are a central aspect of its history."

"Thank you. But I think I've heard a couple of times that Buddhists also have a being who is quite similar to Satan."

"I think you mean 'MARA.' The Pali Buddhist texts record episodes in which Mara urges Gotama to become a universal king and establish a great empire of peace. But he (Mara) and the other evils and monsters of Buddhism are utterly different from the Christians' Satan and the fallen angels. We don't believe that these monsters and evils tempt humans to commit evil deeds."

"Thank you. Do you think Buddhists are in general more moral and humane than Christians?"

"I'm not sure whether Buddhists are more moral than Christians since there are many different criteria for moral uprightness. Here's an example to show you what I mean. Some people have high sexual morals – that is, they are faithful to their life-partners – but are not reluctant to do disgusting things to certain innocent people. Some are the reverse. But I'll answer your question in this way: If we look back at world history, especially what the Christian colonial powers have done in their colonies, justifying their acts in the name of their religion, and also how the Christians treated each other during innumerable religious and secular wars, one is inclined to conclude that the average Buddhist is indeed more moral and humane than the average Christian in most instances. At least, Buddhists don't torture and kill each other in Buddha's name, even though there are many different Buddhist schools. There may have been some incidents at a local level somewhere which I don't know about, but it wouldn't be possible to attach such acts to the name of Buddha or his teachings."

"But as you hinted a while ago, most Christians claim to be the best observers of a loving and all-powerful God's laws. Is there an explanation for this?"

"I think the strongest points of the Christian religion are also its weakest points at the same time, ironically."

"What do you mean?"

"Their God is said to be a loving, forgiving, all-powerful God, so they believe that he will forgive them their crimes or sins if they pray to him and beg for his forgiveness. And for their evil deeds they can blame Satan and the fallen angels."

"Could you briefly tell me how you became a Buddhist monk?"

"My native village was located on a riverbank. During one rainy season, the river flooded and destroyed many houses. Among them

162

was our house. So I lost my parents, two sisters and two brothers. I was the only survivor. All our other close relatives were also gone. My life was so hopeless that I tried to commit suicide twice. I was six years old. Fortunately, I found a childless couple from a neighboring village who wanted to adopt me. As I had been born a Buddhist, I regularly went to worship at the village monastery. There, the abbot told me the following story. Thanks to this story, I slowly overcame my grief and found the will to go on living. This famous story is generally known as the *Kisa Gotami and the Parable of the Mustard Seed*. You can find it in the fundamental texts of Theravada Buddhism. The story goes like this: Kisa's only child, a son, died. Unwilling to accept her son's death, she carried him from village to village and begged for medicine to bring him back to life. The villagers advised her to go to Buddha, who had attained enlightenment and meditated nearby. She found Buddha and pleaded with him to bring her son back to life. Buddha told her to go back to her own and neighboring villages and gather mustard seeds from the households of those who had never been touched by death. He would make medicine with these seeds to bring her son back to life. She went around, but she got not a single grain because every household had experienced death. She thus became enlightened and found her peace of mind. This story also gave me peace of mind and a form of enlightenment, in reminding me of the precarious existence of all living beings on earth. And it taught me to be humble."

"I'm so sorry to hear about your family's tragic fate, Your Venerable."

Everybody else also expressed their sympathy for him.

"When did you decide to become a monk?"

"It was quite late on. I graduated from Colombo University, in English, with distinction; my reason for majoring in English was that I wanted to read books on religion and philosophy as deeply as possible; not many books on these disciplines were translated into our language. So when I decided to wear the monk's robe, I was about twenty-seven years old."

163

"You told me that you've read the Old and New Testaments and that you've had discussions with many leading Christian theologians. Why did you do all this?"

"There were three main reasons. One, I wanted to find out why Christians should wage wars against each other in the names of their *common* God and his alleged son Jesus, whom they all claimed to be worshipping and whose teachings they claimed to be observing. Two, I wanted to find out if other religions could offer a safer spiritual haven for my soul than Buddhism. Three, I wanted to find out who Satan (or Lucifer) and the fallen angels, who are believed by Christians to be the main culprits for all the miseries in this world, really were or are."

"What did you find out in the end?"

"Well, as I've already said, Christianity's strongest points are, ironically, its greatest weaknesses as well. When I was studying at Colombo University, I was fascinated for a long time by the concept of eternal life. But later I became rather disappointed with Christianity for the following reasons: First, after long and careful observation I found out that Buddhists can much more easily overcome their grief at the loss of loved ones than those who believe in eternal life in the biblical God's realm; in my opinion it should be the other way around; second, heavenly beings – or angels – are supposed to be so holy, but according to the Bible, Lucifer/Satan and a great number of angels rebelled against God in his own kingdom; third, if you read world history you'll find that Christians have made countless merciless wars either against each other or non-Christians, so I could not imagine how their souls would be able to live peacefully together with God in his kingdom; fourth, another great puzzle that keeps me wondering is why they continue to study theology to this day while waging wars against each other in the names of God and Jesus; fifth, even though they feel empowered to wage wars on their behalf, they're still endlessly debating the definition of God; and sixth: the strangest thing of all is that a large number of them are even still endlessly debating his existence or non-existence."

164

"Are these the main reasons you became a Buddhist monk?"

"I'd say yes."

"And what did you find out about Satan or Lucifer?"

"Let's discuss him later. Anyway, a long time after I became a monk, I met an unconventional theologian whose ideas on these questions seemed to be reasonable."

"What were they?"

"He said he also was always thinking about the factors I was talking about, yet he remained a Christian because the fact that a heavenly being called Jesus came into this world 2,000 years ago could indeed mean that God existed, at least until then. And he did not let himself be blinded by what other Christians had been doing to each other for centuries. He said he put his faith only in the words that Jesus had spoken according to the four Gospels. And he said he remained a Christian in the hope that Jesus would indeed come back a second time and that, although Christianity had many weaknesses, he had found not a single other religion that could give him more satisfaction and hope."

"If Jesus reappeared today somewhere, could you imagine converting to Christianity?"

"He doesn't need to reappear in person. If all, or at least, say, two-thirds of Christians worldwide, could live in harmony in my lifetime, I could become a Christian. But I know that will never happen."

"Why should you wish that at least two-thirds of Christians were able to live together in harmony for you to convert to Christianity, Your Venerable?"

"Because my soul wouldn't want to live among ever-quarreling souls in God's kingdom. My soul would need its peace of mind up there; otherwise, God might drive us out of heaven as he did with Lucifer and his angel followers."

The room echoed with the laughter of all the participants. The monk continued in the next moment, "If I understand the Bible correctly, only those who are sinless will enter God's kingdom. But I've got the impression that most Christians seem to believe that their souls will become sinless or holy *once they are in* heaven."

Another wave of hearty laughter broke out.

"What are the main obstacles to Christians' unity, then?"

"I think one of the main obstacles is the institutionalization of the Churches. Even Jesus himself wouldn't be able to unify them all now. And with time, the disunity of the Churches will get even worse."

"Could you tell me any other reasons?"

"Here's just one: I'm very doubtful as to whether even God himself would be able to unify them all if he came down to this world. He had more than enough problems with the Jews in ancient times that were quite similar to the Christians' problems. Another major obstacle is the personal rivalries of leading members of the Churches. Every one of them seems to think that he alone is the most outstanding biblical expert or the sole rightful person to represent him."

"What's wrong with the institutionalization of the Churches?"

"The simple answer is that institutions don't have life and soul."

"Could you elaborate on this?"

"If I understand the Bible correctly, it's the human soul – not the building that houses a Church or the writings on which Churches are founded – that will get salvation or eternal life. In other words, a lifeless religious institution won't be able to give you salvation or eternal life. Religious institutions are created by man, not the other way around. That means if there were no human beings, none of these institutions would exist."

"Talking of the institutionalization of religion, isn't Buddhism also institutionalized?"

"Yes. But in Buddhism you've got to take care of your salvation or nirvana. No institution or deity can do it for you. But if I'm honest, I'm very much annoyed by Buddhism's institutionalization in many Asian countries. For instance, monks have to pass examinations that are organized by state institutions. In other words, Buddhist clergy and some state institutions work very closely together. In my opinion, the state and religion should be strictly separated. But since I'm only interested in my own spiritual liberation, I don't care that much."

"Nearly all Christians from the different Churches accuse each other of being Satan incarnate. So could the lack of unity among them be the work of Satan? And what about his role in biblical times – that is, before Jesus appeared?"

"A fascinating question indeed: So far as I know, the Jews disobeyed God's laws endlessly in biblical times, but he did not explicitly blame Satan for their acts. Of course, his name is mentioned a couple of times, but not as the main culprit of all the sins that the Jews committed. And there are some verses that foretell the downfall of a powerful evil being. But if I understand it correctly, the role of Satan and his fallen followers began to be emphasized only after Jesus' appearance."

"What do you think of Satan or Lucifer and his fallen angels tempting human beings to do evil things, as all Christians believe?"

"As a non-Christian, it's a great challenge for me to accept this idea. The simple reason is that, so far as I know, nobody has ever seen a 'fallen angel' with his own eyes, and nobody knows how many of them were expelled from heaven or whether they're still around today. If they were the main culprits of all the evils that have been committed by humans around the world for thousands of years, there must be several hundred million of them working feverishly round the clock in every corner of the world. Otherwise, they wouldn't be able to do their dastardly work. The world's population at present is a few hundred million. To be able to tempt everyone to commit evil deeds, and at the same time monitor all their activities, there must at least be three times more fallen angels than human beings. But nobody knows if they're also endlessly reproducing or aging like us. Or if they even die. A few verses in Genesis say that humans were so attractive to the angels that the angels transformed themselves into humans and married them, and God was not happy with those angels. So one can assume that the fallen angels might indeed be reproducing endlessly, just like us – if they still exist, that is."

"If these fallen angels are not responsible for the sins of mankind, who or what could be responsible?"

"I think Christians should also think about the following puzzle:

How is it possible that there are countless good people in numerous non-Christian societies around the world? Even among animists, who are afraid of evil spirits and therefore worship them, there are many good people. Some of these animistic societies have never even had the concept of a god. In other words, who or what should be blamed for the wrongdoings of non-Christians? We know that some humans are bad by nature, and some are good from birth, even before any religious or moral teachings ever influence them. I'll give you a vivid example to substantiate my point. A couple of times, I visited various animistic tribes in northeast India, who had been conquered by the British. Those primitive tribes believe that evil spirits can cause all kinds of disease, so they make animal sacrifices to appease the evil spirits. But I've never heard that those evil spirits ever killed even a single animist with guns, as the British soldiers had done. And the simple modern medicines that the Christian missionaries introduced to them proved to be much more effective and powerful than the evil spirits they were very much afraid of and therefore offered all kinds of sacrifices to. And animists are not necessarily more evil than Christians."

"So you don't believe that the fallen angels are responsible for the evil in human beings?"

"One cannot completely rule out the idea that Satan and his fallen angels could be partly responsible. But the problem is that God or Jesus did not clearly differentiate between crimes or sins caused by the fallen angels and purely human evils. It's also possible that Jesus did define the differences clearly, but the authors of the Gospels failed to record them."

"Where did Christians get the idea in the first place that Satan and his evil followers are always tempting humans to commit evil deeds?"

"They got this idea from two of the Gospels: Matthew and Luke – and the Book of Revelation, I think. There are a few verses in these two books about Satan's tempting of Jesus in the wilderness for forty days, and also in Jerusalem. And Jesus himself warned his believers not to let Satan tempt them."

"I see. Well, in that case, it's no wonder that Christians blame Satan all the time for their wrongdoing –"

The monk hastily interrupted, "If I were a Christian, I wouldn't blame him all the time for all my weaknesses. Otherwise, he might intentionally tempt me out of spite to commit some major crimes or sins so that God could punish me severely."

A peal of loud laughter suddenly broke out in the room. The monk continued in the next moment, "Jane, talking of Satan and the fallen angels and Christian disunity, there's a fascinating point to think about: Even when God was always in contact with the Jews through prophets, and his presence and power were thus evident, they endlessly rebelled against him. Just look at the numerous miracles in the Exodus story in the Hebrew Bible, for example. So it's no wonder that there are so many rival denominations among Christians today, since the only sources of their knowledge of the existence of God and heavenly beings are the Bibles that are more than 2,000 years old."

"Very fascinating indeed, Your Venerable. But the main problem, I think, with Christianity is that you wouldn't be able to convince a single Christian with these radical ideas of yours."

"You're right, Jane. But it's not my duty to persuade them to accept these ideas. What they should also consider is, if angels are not everywhere twenty-four hours a day to monitor all Christians' activities, who – or what – would record their activities in the Book of Life? According to the Bible, God will judge humans according to what is recorded in that book."

The whole audience liked the monk's ideas.

"Thank you very much. But may I repeat my question once again: If the fallen angels are not responsible for humans' evil deeds, who or what could be responsible?"

"As I've said, you cannot rule out that the fallen ones are not responsible, for Jesus himself implied that. But we know that human characteristics such as greed, pride, ignorance, anger, hatred of all kinds, et cetera, are among the main roots of human wrongdoing, regardless of their religious beliefs or cultural backgrounds. There is, of course, an exception: If anybody can convincingly prove that all these negative traits are the works of Satan, then you may be able to accept that humans' evil deeds are his works. And another two crucial questions that Christians should ask are: one, since angels are said to be much more powerful than the fallen angels, why couldn't they prevent the fallen angels from tempting humans to commit evil deeds? I think the leading personalities of the Churches owe their followers a convincing explanation. Two, why haven't all the non-Christians eliminated each other a long, long time ago if Satan is responsible for all evil things that happen in the world?"

"Slowly, I get the impression that all the Christianity's fundamental theological concepts might need to be completely revised then."

"I don't think you can ever do that even if you wanted to. The simple solution, perhaps, is that the Christians should stop blaming Satan for all their shortcomings. They should try to take responsibility for at least some of their actions, if not for all."

"Talking about Jesus, what do you think of what is known as the Second Coming and the so-called Last Judgment?"

"Honestly, I'm quite confused about the two prophecies describing the Second Coming. Some biblical verses seem to suggest that he will come back incognito, like a thief. The other version is that he will come back in great glory upon the clouds, in the company of angels. And about the Last Judgment: If I understand the Bible correctly, there seem to be *two* judgments – the first upon Jesus' Second Coming and another by God in heaven. What I can't understand is how Jesus would be able to judge powerful wrongdoers – for instance, by accusing them of being Satan incarnate – if he came back incognito like a thief. Suppose he said something like that against the rich and powerful. In that case, they'd most likely either lock him up in a psychiatric hospital or throw him in prison for life – or perhaps even crucify him again. And if he came back to judge the poor, that would be a breach of his 2,000-year-old moral teachings. And he wouldn't need to come back to judge them in the first place, for he could do it very easily with their souls when they die. He might have fewer problems passing judgment upon the rich and powerful if he came back in great glory on the clouds, in the company of angels. And there could be another big problem if he came back incognito like a thief: His worshippers might accuse him of being an impostor *pretending* to be Jesus. If he performed the sorts of wonderful miracles that he performed on his first coming, almost all Christians would say that he was using some sort of black magic to mislead them. Or they might even accuse him of being Satan and crucify him again. Moreover, many powerful Christian institutions and individuals worldwide are profiting tremendously from his name, so they wouldn't sincerely wish for his Second Coming, even though they all claim to be eagerly awaiting his return. And suppose he repeated exactly what he said and did on his first coming. In that case, he'd most likely be crucified again by those powerful institutions and people anyway, for they'd feel that he was a threat to their well-being."

"Thank you very much. Now, my next question is: Do you think the school of Buddhism to which you belong is the best among all the schools?"

"Jane, I think you've already asked me a similar question."

"Oh, have I? I'm so sorry, Your Venerable. I'm much younger than you, but my memory is not that good anymore, either!"

Everyone was amused. The monk then thought for a short while and shook his head slightly and said, "I'm so sorry, Jane. You haven't raised this question yet."

They were all roaring with laughter once again. Then the monk continued, "Jane, I'll answer your question in this way: No, I don't claim that the school I belong to is better than all the others. How you judge a certain school depends on many factors, like where you were born and where you live; what kind of education you received; what kind of cultural and religious background you have; what kind of life experiences you have; which era you live in; what kind of social background you come from; what kind of religious teachers you have, and so on. I need to tell you a bit more here, though, otherwise, you might not get my point. Theravada Buddhism is practiced in India, Ceylon, Burma, Thailand, Cambodia, and Laos. And Mahayana Buddhism is practiced in China, Japan, Korea, and Vietnam. Vajrayana Buddhism is practiced in Tibet and Mongolia."

"And there's also Zen Buddhism, I think."

"Yes, that's a branch or school of Mahayana Buddhism; it's a mixture of Mahayana Buddhism and Taoism. But since our time is rather tight and you're just starting your search, I think you could study this later if you're interested in it."

"Are you sure that the doctrines of all the Buddhist schools are free from superstition?"

"I know that some Buddhists in some countries are not entirely free from superstition because their societies were originally animistic, and you can still see many elements of animism in them, like the belief in good and evil spirits."

"How dangerous is it to be superstitious within Buddhism? In other words, not to be free from the influence of certain elements of animism?"

"I think it's desirable at least for the leading monks to be free from such things. But you cannot tell the ordinary believers to cast aside these beliefs. Talking of superstition, some years ago I made a pilgrimage to several pagodas in Burma. There are thousands of beautiful pagodas and temples, old and new, and nearly all laypeople believe some of the pagodas are more powerful than others. So they try to make pilgrimages to the pagodas they believe to be most powerful. But so long as the believers are content in their beliefs, I don't see any negative effect."

"Many Western scholars and missionaries in the past regarded Buddhism as a religion of idolatry and animism. Could the facts you've just mentioned be the reasons?"

"Yes, I think so. In many Buddhist temples and monasteries in Asia, figures of spiritual beings – supposedly both good and evil ones – are abundantly painted. And I see nothing wrong with them so long as the average believer can draw inspiration from them. I strongly believe that using such figures and other animistic elements is much less harmful than the Christians' religious wars against each other. So those who branded Buddhism a religion of idolatry were either ignorant or arrogant."

"Would you recommend that I follow a certain Buddhist school?"

"No, I won't do that. You and you alone are responsible for yourself. Therefore, you must try to find out for yourself which school is best for you. I think every intellectually capable person should search for his spiritual liberation independently, even though a high degree of intellect doesn't automatically enable you to see things more clearly than a person with a lesser intellect. You surely know that some Christian Churches accused hundreds of thousands of people of being witches and tortured and burned them at stakes in the Middle Ages. And yet millions of the world's brightest minds still follow these Churches. So I'd recommend that you study all the major schools before you decide to become a Buddhist."

"I used to hear that in many Buddhist schools there are various levels of examination for monks. And many monks are holders of doctorates in Buddhist theology. Is that true?"

"Yes, that is true, at least in my school. But in my opinion it's absurd, because I don't think that a doctorate in Buddhism is a guarantee of enlightenment and nirvana. Of course, it's necessary if you aim to reach a higher position in the hierarchy, or if you aim for a teaching post at a religious institution. But as I did not become a monk to earn the respect of the laypeople or to achieve a higher position in the hierarchy, I did only some basic examinations. Only the spiritual aspect is important to me."

"Somebody once told me that there are more learned Buddhist monks who are well versed in Buddhism than Hindu priests who fully grasp their religion. What would you say about that?"

"I'd say that it's much easier for the average person or monk to understand the fundamentals of Buddhism than those of Hinduism. One of the simple reasons is that Hinduism has so many holy scriptures. But even among the Buddhist monks, I doubt very much if all of them fully grasp it. I know that many of my fellow monks accept what they read or hear to be absolute truths without deeply and critically analyzing the whole of Buddhist scripture. They pass on wholesale what they've learned. The Buddhist scriptures are in Pali, a complicated ancient language. That's another reason why it's difficult for laypeople to grasp Buddhism fully. But I have nothing to say about the Hindu priests."

"What do you think of Islam?"

"I'm sorry, I haven't had enough time to read the Qur'an. And even if I did, I probably wouldn't study it. The reason is that, like Christianity and Judaism, Islam has several different branches and I wouldn't know which branch's doctrine I should study. I've got enough problems with the Hebrew Bible and the New Testament. And as the various branches of Judaism have problems among themselves, all the Christian Churches also have more than enough irreconcilable theological differences. So concerning Islam, I can only tell you an interesting true story. One of my best friends, a lifelong Muslim, and some of his Muslim friends surprised me a few months ago by suddenly converting to Christianity just because of a single sura that they read in the newly published Qur'an in English. The author was Abdullah Yusuf Ali, an Indian Islamic scholar born in 1872. It has rapidly become one of the most widely known translations used in the English-speaking world since its publication in 1938 by Sheikh Muhammad Ashraf in Lahore, Pakistan."

"Which sura is it?"

"I won't tell you, although I know it. It's in the beginning parts of the Qur'an."

"Why don't you want to tell me?"

"Since I don't have any ideas about all the remaining suras, I don't want to cause a controversy unnecessarily by naming it. Some Muslims might think I want to promote Christianity. So if it's so important for you to know it, why don't you ask some Islamic theologians which sura it is and how the various branches of Islam interpret it?"

"Okay. To which Church did your Muslim friend convert?"

174

"I'm sorry, Jane. I can't tell you that."

"Do you know anything else about him – I mean Abdullah Yusuf Ali?"

"Yes, a little. I'll read just a few lines about him from his book: Abdullah Yusuf Ali, CBE, MA, LLM, FRSA, FRSL, was born on 14th April 1872 in Bombay, British India, and died in London on 10th December 1953. He studied English literature and studied at several European universities; he spoke both Arabic and English fluently. He could even recite the entire Qur'an from memory …"

The monk continued, "And another reason why I did not pursue this religion further was that, since the Muslims also expect the return of Jesus, I decided to concentrate my study on what is written about him, what he personally said, and what he taught in the four Gospels and the Book of Revelation."

"Thank you very much. I think the Muslims believe him to be only a prophet, like Muhammad, not God's son. How much do you know about that?"

"I also know only that much."

"Thank you. And a great puzzle that has been troubling me for years, Your Venerable, is: Christianity should be much more attractive than, say, Buddhism or Hinduism for the simple reason that, in opposition to the beliefs of Buddhism and Hinduism, it promises eternal life. But hundreds of millions of people have yet to convert to it. Do you have any answer to this puzzle?"

"Well, it would sound arrogant to claim to have found the answer to this. I think the following factors could be some of the reasons, though. First of all, the human mind is so mysterious; once it has accepted something as true, it's difficult to change that opinion. Another reason could be that most of the 2,000-year history of Christianity is not peaceful because it's divided into various denominations with conflicting doctrines, so people get confused. With the concept of an all-powerful God and eternal life, Christian missionaries of the first generation must have believed that they would be able to convert Hindus, animists and Buddhists en masse to Christianity. That is the

175

opinion of many leading theologians and clergymen with whom I've had serious discussions.

"So they must have been disappointed with what happened in reality. They could only convert mainly the animists. Hence, some of my discussion partners expressed their great pity for – in their words – the 'lost souls.' I told them that they should be glad that there are far fewer rival Churches today because of that. They were not amused. And take another example: Look at the 'untouchables' or Dalits in India. Theoretically, one would be inclined to speculate that Buddhism or Christianity would seem much more attractive to them than Hinduism, for there's no caste system in either of these religions. But in reality, there are very few converts in terms of their number as a whole."

"Very interesting. Do you have any other ideas why that is so – I mean, in this particular case?"

"As I said earlier, Hinduism has millions of gods and goddesses – and several holy scriptures. The original Buddhism is void of supernatural elements – except, of course, its various legends; it's purely philosophical by nature. But I think most human beings are by nature more fascinated and more easily influenced by supernatural things than by pure logic. So sometimes I wonder if this factor might not play an important role in this case."

"Did you have your discussions with those leading theologians and clergymen before you became a monk, or after?"

"Many of my discussions were before I became a monk, and I also had some afterwards."

"Talking of religion and philosophy, I used to hear that Buddhism is more of a philosophy than a religion. What is your opinion on that?"

"I think it depends entirely on the beholder – I mean, how you define religion. As we don't have the right to define what religion is for another person, nobody can define what religion is for us either. My definition of religion is very simple indeed: If you believe in a stone or a tree or a mountain and thus worship it, it's religion for you. In ancient times, the sun and the moon were also worshipped in many societies around the world. I used to discuss this subject with many learned people, and most of them believe that 'true' religion should have a God or gods and good and evil spirits and holy scripture, and the concept of existence beyond this human world, and so on. So far as I know, Confucianism and Taoism, for instance, were also originally philosophies. But people turned them into religions, with temples and rituals and rites and priesthoods. Therefore, my simple conclusion is that it doesn't matter whether something is a religion or a philosophy so long as it gives you satisfaction, hope, and peace of mind. You don't need to be bothered by other people's definitions. Simple as that. What is disgusting is if you harm innocent people in the name of religion."

"Another question, if I may: How can I become a Buddhist?"

"Every school has its rituals and rites. But in my personal opinion, such rites and rituals are not necessary for one's spiritual enlightenment. If you recognize the realities – I mean the generally accepted realities from the average Buddhist's point of view – you're already automatically a Buddhist."

"What do you mean by the 'generally accepted realities?'"

"Well, although there are several different schools, all of them accept what is called The Three Universal Truths: 1. Nothing is lost in the universe; 2. Everything changes; 3. The Law of Cause and Effect. And also the Four Noble Truths and the Eightfold Path to Enlightenment. The Four Noble Truths are: Life is suffering or Dukkha; Dukkha arises from craving; Dukkha can be eliminated or overcome; the way to eliminate or overcome Dukkha is the Eightfold Path. The Eightfold Path is as follows: Right View/Understanding; Right Intention/Thought; Right Speech; Right Action; Right Livelihood; Right Effort; Right Mindfulness; and Right Concentration."

"I know that Buddhists make pilgrimages to pagodas and temples and worship monks so as to be blessed by them. What are their real purposes in doing that?"

"I think it's quite natural that most religious human beings, regardless of their religion, prefer to worship in such places, with rituals and rites, under the guidance of priests and monks. In such places, they can concentrate their minds more fully on their spiritual affairs. Christians can worship their God anywhere and at any hour of the day, but Buddhists need monks to guide them in their worship."

"What roles do the robes of a monk play in Buddhism?"

"A monk's robe doesn't make him holier; that's for sure. All other religions' spiritual leaders also wear certain robes that identify them as spiritual guides. In the Bible, though, I've never seen a single verse that demands that its religious leaders wear priests' robes or anything like that. Jesus even spoke in the New Testament *against* priests wearing such robes. According to Buddhist scripture, Buddhists are supposed to worship the robe, which symbolizes the Buddhahood, not the person inside it. But in reality, most of them understand the opposite. You cannot blame them, for it's the person in the robe who speaks, not the robe itself. The advantage of the monk's robe – at least in Buddhism – is that it emits a positive aura to the laypeople that no non-religious garment can. I could give sermons in normal daily clothes, too, but nobody would take my words seriously if I did. I think it's the same with many Christian Churches, and many other religions as well."

"Talking of enlightenment, could you tell me what enlightenment is in Buddhism?"

"Originally, it came from the Sanskrit and Pali word 'Bodhi', which means 'to awaken' or 'to understand.' I'd interpret it as 'the awakening from illusions' or 'the realization of the truth or truths' for a layperson like you. For instance, when you fully accept that this human existence is not permanent, that's a kind of awakening from an illusion. Another example is that many people do bad things that hurt innocent people in one way or another, but they don't realize that what they're doing is terrible. But if they one day realize that they're actually doing bad things and thus refrain from them, that's also an awakening. The problem with the term is that it cannot apply to everyone because what one person perceives to be an illusion could be reality for another person, and vice versa – at least in religious matters. Here's an example: The Buddhist concepts of impermanence and endless rebirth may be illusory to a Christian who believes in eternal life in God's realm, and vice versa. So I'd suggest that you try to find something *you* believe to be reality, or the truth, instead of blindly accepting – or forcing yourself to accept – other people's perceived truths. You might be surprised and even disappointed if I told you that different Buddhist schools interpret the concept of enlightenment differently. The means to achieve it are also different in each case. Even prominent Buddhist scholars still argue about the exact interpretation of *Bodhi*. I hope I've not confused you, Jane."

"No, not at all. The opposite is true. I'm even more fascinated now. But I'll need a lot of time to think about and digest what you're telling me. I'm quite positive that you must have attained at least some sort of enlightenment."

"I won't answer this question, for many reasons."

"Why not? Is it too sensitive a subject for you?"

"Not because it's too sensitive … Okay, let me answer it abstractly. If I say yes, it could mean I'm not yet fully enlightened. On the other hand, if I say no, it could be a naked lie. Does that make sense?"

All the people in the room broke into laughter. Jane then put this question to the monk: "If you're so sure about your enlightenment, why shouldn't you frankly admit it, Your Venerable?"

"Well, Jane, even if I did believe that I was already fully enlightened, it could just be self-deception. And if I believe that I'm not yet fully enlightened, in reality I might have already attained it."

More laughter.

"Your Venerable, I don't get what you mean."

"Jane, the problem with the human mind is that people are attracted to, and fascinated by, abstract things. Most people tend not to be interested in the subject you're talking about if you say it in a simple way. But I'm not trying to be abstract now to pique your curiosity. The topic we're discussing itself is quite abstract, so my explanation

179

also may seem to be abstract. Both the problem and the advantage of enlightenment is that there's no universal yardstick to measure what it is. And nobody has patented it yet, so anybody can claim that he's already enlightened, regardless of his religion.

"You cannot tell someone that what he perceives to be enlightenment is just an illusion. The only thing you can do is accept his claim unconditionally, or laugh at him. I'll tell you a few exciting experiences I've had concerning how people interpret enlightenment in different ways. I was shocked to find out that three or four fellow monks who had been wearing the robes for several years left monkhood to convert to Christianity. When I asked them why, their answers were all in unison – that is, they had attained enlightenment, meaning they had found the ultimate truth: the eternal existence that is supposedly conferred by the biblical God and Jesus. Then I met some Buddhist monks who had unexpectedly converted to Buddhism *from* Christianity. They also claimed that they were enlightened because they'd found the ultimate truth – namely, the impermanence of things material – and identified some of Christianity's fundamental weaknesses. So I think one should try to find out what is most satisfactory for oneself. Here's another simple example of the issues surrounding enlightenment: If people hear or read what I've said today, some of them may feel that I am at least partly enlightened, whereas others might think my words are nonsense."

The whole audience was highly amused again.

"That means enlightenment doesn't belong to Buddhism alone. Is that right?"

"I think it's not even necessary to be religious. It can be relevant to every aspect of all human societies. Just have a look at the 'Age of Enlightenment' or the 'Age of Reason' – the intellectual and philosophical movement that took place in Europe during the 18th century – as an example. Jane, I'd like to tell you one more thing before we proceed: Since you might ask me more questions on the subject of enlightenment, I'll try to answer as if I am already fully enlightened and know all the answers to your questions."

180

The monk ended with a broad smile. The audience found his words hilarious.

"Okay, I agree. Would you please tell me, then, what methods Buddhists use to achieve the Buddhist version of enlightenment?"

"Meditation is one of the main methods. Others involve listening to hours of discourse delivered by learned priests and monks. But I think many other simple methods can also awaken you from your illusions. One example is the *Kisa Gotami and the Parable of the Mustard Seed*. If Buddha had preached long and abstract discourses at her, she might not have understood them, and as a result her suffering most likely would have had no end. In like manner, if a loved one of yours loses his life unexpectedly in a violent incident, for instance, it'd shock you so deeply that you'd most likely question the nature of life. As a result, you might develop the desire to search for the *meaning* of life. This desire, then, could also give you some kind of enlightenment – the realization that nothing is permanent, for instance. With this realization, some people may try to find consolation in Buddhism, whereas some may prefer to seek consolation in the Christian concept of eternal life."

"Should I also start with meditation to find peace of mind?"

"There's nothing to lose by starting with meditation, if you can find someone who can give you the right guidance. But if I were you, I wouldn't do that yet. It would be best if you first tried to become fully aware of your suffering's tap root. I won't say that meditation is the best way for you in your present situation, although many meditation experts might disagree with me. When your mind is empty of illusions, peace of mind will be within you and you may not even need meditation to sustain that peace of mind. On the other hand, as long as your mind is still full of illusions, the peace of mind you would get through meditation would be short-lived. As soon as you stopped meditating, your sorrow and pain would come back. So to attain peace of mind and enlightenment, you must also be in an economically stable position. If you worry about daily subsistence, you won't be able to fully concentrate on what you're aiming to achieve, and probably wouldn't be able to pursue it in the first place. Of course, one solution would be to become a monk or nun so that you wouldn't need to worry about your daily affairs. Furthermore, in some cases, I think simple logic can also bring you to a state of awakening. The *Kisa Gotami* story was the beginning of my serious search for spiritual liberation because my family's loss in the flood kept torturing me through all my waking hours for several years. A simple method of achieving some enlightenment in politics or religion or social issues is through cartoons and caricatures. Sometimes, a biting, enlightening cartoon can be much more effective in conveying a particular message than hours of lectures or thousands of words of explanation."

"You said, 'When your mind is empty of illusions, peace of mind will be within you …' Could you tell me more about this? It's too abstract for me."

"I'd classify illusions into two categories: constructive or harmless ones and destructive, harmful ones. When it comes to constructive illusions, I mean, for instance, beautiful fairy tales. And in Buddhism, there are several legends. Some creative souls may have invented many of them to educate ordinary believers. Yet most believers believe them to be true stories and get inspiration and energy from them to endure the hardships in their lives. Many lay Buddhists believe in supernatural beings and that they themselves will become such a being when they die. I'd define such belief as an illusion, but since it doesn't harm anybody else and gives the believers happiness or at least some kind of hope in this heartless world, I regard it to be a constructive illusion. In like manner, although believing in eternal life could be interpreted by non-Christians as an illusion, I'd define it as positive since it gives its believers happiness and hope. One of the most dangerous types of destructive illusion is, for instance, the waging of religious wars by Christians against their fellow Christians on *their common God's behalf*, in the belief that they're serving him in the best way. It's crucially important that you can differentiate between constructive and destructive illusions and that you get rid of the harmful ones."

"Talking of 'empty mind' or 'emptiness' in Buddhism, could you explain it more in detail?"

"In Buddhism, what is generally understood by non-Buddhists to be 'empty' is not empty at all from a learned Buddhist's or a martial artist's point of view. We won't go deeply into that now, for it could be too abstract for you, and it'll take up a lot of our time. But I'll tell you what it is very briefly. 'Emptiness' or 'voidness' is one of the most important doors to liberation in both the Theravada and Mahayana schools. But if I try to explain it to you according to Buddhist philosophy, it won't make sense. Have you ever heard about how Asian martial artists can break stones or several layers of bricks with their bare hands without getting hurt? A few moments before they strike the rocks or bricks, those martial artists *empty* their mind – that means there is nothing in their mind that can distract their concentration. But this 'empty space' is full of energy in reality, and enables the martial artists to break the stones or bricks without their hands getting harmed. That energy is understood to be 'life energy' or 'life force.' But to do such things, one needs to reach a certain level of meditation and have a lot of practice. The simplest way to explain to a layperson what it is, is the power of the mind. It's a strong indication that Buddhists understand the nature of the mind rather well and master it despite its mysteries, and thus know how to use it to their advantage."

"Why doesn't the mind play an important role in Christianity and Judaism?"

"Because the members of these religions only need to believe in their deities and observe their morals to attain eternal life or salvation. Whereas, as I've said, Buddhists have to strive for their own liberation. As a result, they need to use their mind."

The whole audience was deeply fascinated by the ideas the monk had just expressed.

"Thank you very much, Your Venerable. Could you tell me now about some other methods to attain enlightenment?"

"Jane, at the beginning of our discussion, you asked me to give you a discourse on the fundamentals of Buddhism, in the hope that they might give you the peace of mind that you so badly need. But instead of explaining these fundamentals right away, I tried to ease your suffering by asking you a couple of questions about your daughter and yourself. From your answers, I guided you to see some of the realities of your situation. And you have admitted that you feel that you are suffering less as a result, in contrast to the minimal effects of biblical verses and Christian clerics' prayers. So I'd interpret your latest experience as a form of enlightenment. If you were a Christian, the recitation of biblical verses and prayers might have helped ease your suffering to the same extent, but you're not a Christian, so they were ineffective."

"Now I'm beginning to understand to some extent. Even so, my previous question once again: Could you discuss some more methods?"

"I don't believe in the effectiveness of pure meditation for the attainment of the Buddhist concept of enlightenment. Since Buddha's appearance 2,500 years ago, the world has gone through so many great changes and developments. During his lifetime, there were probably no major wars in India and Nepal. And there were no world wars. Life was rural and simple. There were only Hinduism, Jainism, and Buddhism, and most likely various kinds of animism. But nowadays, we see all kinds of great changes in different sectors of society around the world. So we can no longer isolate ourselves totally from outside influences. Therefore, I keep myself well-informed about the world and local events and the changes in social, religious and economic sectors worldwide. I don't want to believe blindly in anything – religious or secular –"

"Are you interested in politics, too?"

"Sure. Without politics, we might not still exist. Or in other words, since we humans may not survive without it, you cannot ignore it. But several fellow monks of mine completely ignore it…"

"But politics is understood by all humans to be corrupt and dirty."

"Yes, that's true. But we cannot live without it. We don't have any other better systems. And we cannot rule ourselves with religious morals alone, partly because all the religions' religious morals are not uniform. Not only that, even within each religion, the various branches interpret them quite differently. And millions of people have been killing each other for centuries in the name of religion."

"In that case, you probably don't have peace of mind because you know too much about the problems in the world?"

"But all these changes and developments also fascinate me. Since I don't have dreams that I cannot fulfill, I can live with the human species' brutal realities quite peacefully. I regard myself as a realist. Then again, seeing the world's realities as they are can drive you to insanity if you aren't mentally strong enough or deeply philosophical. The realities are so brutal that many of my fellow monks prefer to ignore them and retreat into their world and concentrate only on spiritual matters. So I wouldn't recommend that everyone follow my ways. On the other hand, if you can use the brutal realities to your advantage, they can help you toward the attainment of some form of enlightenment, I think."

"Very interesting words. Perhaps a little more explanation on this topic?"

"Sure, I'll tell you two short stories – but you may find them confusing."

"Please, go ahead."

"One of them goes like this: Once, a young monk, who aimed to attain enlightenment by meditation, asked the monk who was supervising one of the meditation sessions in which the novice took part about the meaning of reality: 'Many people say that there's no reality; what we humans perceive to be reality is just an illusion ...' At that very moment, the meditation master struck him hard on his back with the cane in his hand. (During meditation sessions in many monasteries in some countries, meditation masters carried canes to wake somebody up if he fell asleep while meditating.) The novice cried out, for it was painful. The meditation master asked him what or who had cried out if there was no such thing as reality. At that moment, the novice attained enlightenment. His enlightenment was that his existence was real."

A roar of laughter broke out. The monk continued, "If the meditation master had tried to explain to the novice what reality was through lengthy discourse, it might have taken him years to attain the same degree of enlightenment, or he might never have attained it at all."

Jane was amused and begged the monk to tell the next story.

"Have you ever read or heard about the abstractness of Taoism?"

"No, never."

"Here's a very popular explanation of it: 'If someone asks another person what the Tao is, and if the one being asked tries to explain what it is, it means neither of them understands the true nature of the Tao.' Enlightenment could be explained in this way, too."

"Excuse me, Your Venerable, but that sounds so crazy!"

"Yes Jane, you're right. Many religious ideas seem crazy to the non-believer. But to the believer, they appear quite normal, or even enlightening. It all depends on the point of view from which you look at each religious concept. What you think sounds crazy the first time you hear it could help you look at things from a new perspective. Let me explain further. As far as I know, reincarnation was unknown in the West until Hinduism and Buddhism came here. Even now, it seems an impossible idea for the great majority of Christians, because they believe that the human soul goes to heaven or hell when a person dies, or that our souls wait in purgatory for the Last Judgment. In like manner, certain Christian beliefs would also sound crazy to many Buddhists."

"Why is Taoism so abstract?"

"It's generally understood as 'the Way.' It is interpreted in various ways by different people but eludes precise definition. An abstract description of it is: if you think you can define it, it's not the true Tao. If you've got some free time, I recommend that you read up on this topic; there are many books on the subject. You might start with these first: *101 Zen Stories*, published this year by Rider and Company,

186

London, and David McKay Company, Philadelphia. These stories recount the actual experiences of Chinese and Japanese Zen teachers over more than five centuries. Then there's *The Gateless Gate*, published by John Murray, Los Angeles, in 1934. It is a collection of problems, called *koan*, that Zen teachers use in guiding their students toward release, first recorded by a Chinese master in 1228. *10 Bulls* was published in 1935 by De Voss and Company, Los Angeles. It is a translation from the Chinese of a famous twelfth-century commentary upon the stages of awareness leading to enlightenment. The stories in all these books are concise and easy to read. You'll find many of them pretty crazy for a while, but over time it's possible that many – if not all – turn out to be enlightening. Or they could at least enable you to look at things from an unconventional perspective and give you some food for thought about life. But it's also possible that many of them will seem to be nonsense for your whole life."

"Could you please briefly tell me about Confucianism and Taoism?"

"Confucianism is often characterized as a social and ethical philosophy system rather than a religion per se. It was built on an ancient religious foundation to establish the social values, institutions, and transcendent ideals of traditional Chinese society. In some places, though, Confucianism is treated as a religion, and there are Confucian temples and rituals. Chinese scholars honored Confucius as a great teacher and sage but did not worship him as a god. Nor did he ever claim divinity. The system is practiced mainly in Asian countries such as Korea, Japan, Vietnam, and China. Five centuries before Christ, Confucius set down his Golden Rule: 'Do not impose on others what you do not wish for yourself.' Taoism does not have a God in the way that the Abrahamic religions do. There is no omnipotent being who created and controls the universe. In Taoism, the universe springs from the Tao – the 'road,' 'path,' or 'way.' There are Taoist temples, monasteries and priests, rituals and ceremonies, and a host of gods and goddesses for believers to worship."

"Thank you very much. I'm sure I'll read the books that you mentioned some day. My next question is: So far as I know, *nirvana* is the ultimate goal of all Buddhists. How might you explain it to me in the simplest possible way?"

"Its literal meaning is 'blowing out' – the cessation or liberation from circles of rebirth. But there are two different versions of it. For Theravada Buddhists, it's their ultimate spiritual goal. For Mahayana Buddhists, their highest goal is to attain Buddhahood – whereby a Buddha continues to be reborn into the world to help liberate other beings from rebirth by teaching the Buddhist path."

"Your Venerable, I'm even more confused now. Which version do you believe?"

"I'm a Theravada Buddhist, so I believe the first version."

"I always thought that the fundamentals of Buddhism were uniform."

"I can understand why you're confused by my words. Please wait until we finish our discussion. What we discuss later might help you to see things a bit more clearly. What I ought to say is that so far as I know, there are contradictions within every religion. So it would be best if you stuck to the ones that you find best suited to your own life. An example: Christianity promises you eternal life. That's the gist of this religion. But if you read all the different doctrines of the various Churches, you won't be sure anymore about which ones you should believe. You'll be confused. Your search for a single truth – or the absolute truth – will never end. Or you may give up your search for it in frustration. Nearly every Church is said to have been founded by people who regard themselves as biblical experts. But the big problem is that there are tens of thousands of verses in the Bibles, and everybody can interpret them to suit his own interests.

"A most vivid example is: God forbids murder unconditionally, but what have the Christians been doing to each other for centuries? And if you try to find the one great truth in Buddhism, you'll also get confused because different schools have different interpretations of it. Like the Christian Churches, the various Buddhist schools were founded by those who could recite the entire Buddhist scripture by heart. There's probably not a single perfect religion for the whole of humankind, or there is one, but different people interpret it so differently that its true nature – if there is such a thing – has been lost. My simple solution to this puzzle is: The religion that gives you the most satisfaction in this life is the best one for you, no matter how other people see or interpret it. If you start asking questions, you'll most likely find some deficiencies in every religion."

Nearly everyone was quite delighted, if a little confused.

"Your Venerable, I like your explanation, but could you tell me a bit more in plain words?"

"Jane, I think I should not tell you too much now. Take your time, take some months, or even years, to digest what I say today. You may find some of the topics that sound pretty confusing today could turn out sometime in the future to be enlightening. Equally, what you think is enlightening today might turn out to be just some kind of illusion – depending on many factors, like your changing outlook on religious matters and your life experiences."

"Thank you very much. Yes, I'll take my time, then. Talking of conflicting doctrines in the Christian Churches, have you ever thought which Church's doctrines, rites and rituals might be the best way toward the attainment of the eternal life that God is supposed to offer us?"

"I'm sorry, I cannot answer this question. The simple reason is that, so far as I understand what Jesus himself says in the four Gospels, you don't need any special doctrine or ritual or rite for the attainment of eternal life."

After a short pause, Jane continued, "Thank you. Okay, now my next question: What roles do the chants and the chanting of mantras play in Buddhism?"

"In Theravada Buddhism, Pali is used in most chanting, sometimes with vernacular translations interspersed. Among the most popular Theravada chants is the Buddhabhivadana or Preliminary Reverence for the Buddha. Mantras are sacred utterances (syllables, words, or verses) considered to possess mystical or spiritual efficacy. Like other rites and rituals, the chants and the chanting of mantras are indispensable parts of Buddhist worship. Many Christian Churches also have their liturgies and rites and rituals. But I don't think chants and the chanting of mantras play any crucial role toward attaining enlightenment – at least for me personally, although a large proportion of Buddhists may disagree with me. I prefer meditation in complete silence. But if I lead a traditional worship service, I naturally have to lead chants and mantras that are thousands of years old. And if you observe Tibetan Lamas, for instance, you'll see that they chant mantras endlessly for hours nearly every day. These mantras are part of a centuries-old tradition. So you cannot stop a believer from chanting them. And there's nothing wrong with them. They even enhance the worship.

"There's one big difference between Buddhism and Christianity in this regard, however. In Christianity, you can worship the biblical God anywhere and at any time of the day. All you need to do is to say prayers as the situation demands. But in Buddhism, you cannot perform a worshipful service without chants or chanting mantras. You may, of course, be able to chant some mantras that you deem to be suitable for the circumstance you're in, if you can recite such mantras by heart, that is. And while Christians believe that their prayers are heard and answered by angels or God himself, pure Buddhists cannot hope for the same. However, in every Buddhist's home there's an altar, with statues of Buddha, before which prayers are said many times daily in the form of chanting standardized mantras. So far as I know, most of the mantras are in Pali, and the great majority of laypeople don't even know their meaning. They chant them by rote. But I won't make any further comment on this."

"If there are no supernatural elements in Buddhism and chanting mantras doesn't play an important role in the attainment of enlightenment as you've just said, what is the real essence of mantras, then?"

"I can tell you about it only from my perspective. I've just said that you cannot do a Buddhist worship service without chanting mantras. Christians sing religious songs in worship services, and some Churches also chant standardized liturgies and say prayers. But Buddhists don't have similar songs. So the only thing they can do is chant mantras and conduct rituals and rites, depending on the occasion. Just one example of the importance of mantras: When someone, especially a Lama, dies, Lamas chant different mantras for days on end for the soul of the dead, guiding the soul to the right place. Another important thing that you should know is that there are not many people who can devote their entire life to attaining the Buddhist version of enlightenment compared to the whole Buddhist population around the world.

"There are a significant number of ordinary and even highly qualified Buddhist scholars and monks who believe that there are invisible, powerful spirits that hear their mantras and thus protect and bless them. As a result, they hope to become better human beings or attain a higher social status in their next lives in this world or in spiritual worlds through their good deeds and the blessings of monks and those imagined powerful spirits. The laypeople, therefore, give alms lavishly to the Buddhist clergy and also to people in need. So when you look at Buddhism, you need to look at two different things: the learned man's and the layperson's perspectives, although these perspectives may, in most cases, be blurred. Personally, I don't believe that one can attain either nirvana or enlightenment or both by worshipping at pagodas and temples and chanting mantras or through a monk's blessings. But if I told a religious Buddhist this, he'd feel very offended and wouldn't agree at all. I think there are many Christian Churches in which the clerics also bless laypeople in God's and Jesus' names. I've got nothing against such practices, since such blessings give laypeople peace of mind and hope and happiness on this earth. As I said earlier, Buddhist schools have different concepts for the attainment of enlightenment. There are some schools, for instance, that believe it can be instantly attained through specific methods and practices, whereas other schools think you can achieve it only through long years of meditation and worship. In like manner, all

Christian Churches have different ideas about how to gain salvation and eternal life, even though, unlike in Buddhism, Jesus himself clearly described in simple words how to attain these ends in the four Gospels.

"Last but not least on mantras: Their most important role, I think, like the Christians' prayers, is to give the chanters some spiritual security and a strong sense of being united with some unknown, invisible, supernatural beings or forces. The positive psychological effect on chanters is what is important. Therefore, I think mantras and prayers are more like placebos than actual 'medicine.' Jane, I'm telling you all this because I wish you to make a decision freely that's right for you, without the influence of the religious concepts of particular religions."

"Thank you very much, Your Venerable. Do you think we need beautiful, elegant church buildings, pagodas or temples for our spiritual liberation?"

The monk suddenly had a second thought and continued. "Wait, Jane, I'm so sorry, I forgot to tell you about the role of mantras in Tibetan Buddhism: As I mentioned, Tibetan monks use mantras to guide the soul of the dead to the right place. These mantras, therefore, are indispensable to them for the process of preparing for their reincarnation. Now I come back to your question: In general, nearly all religious people – regardless of their religion – are fascinated and spiritually inspired by such buildings. And you'll never be able to stop somebody from constructing such things. Such elegant buildings also enhance the look of a village, a town, a city or a landscape. But if I were a Christian, the most beautiful church or church building would be my own heart and mind."

"What do you think of the prayers and rituals and rites of the various Christian Churches?"

"The different Churches have their own liturgies, rituals, rites, and ways of saying prayers. But if I correctly recall, Jesus is said to have taught his followers not to say long prayers, like hypocrites. So if one were to pray exactly as he teaches in the Bible, it wouldn't last more than two or three minutes at a time. However, the prayers of most Christians last considerably longer. And during a normal service that lasts for about two hours, several people say prayers either individually or collectively again and again. In short, people cannot worship their God or gods without rituals and rites and long prayers. Through such practices, they feel they're in accord with God, Jesus, or other heavenly beings. If you consider what Jesus teaches about saying prayers, though, you can be pretty sure that he most likely did not use rituals and rites when he was on this earth. You may find it interesting what I used to ask my Christian discussion partners from the West: Why don't you give your poverty-stricken followers something to eat every day, instead of begging God on their behalf, since anybody can say prayers anyway? They were not very amused."

"Could Christian prayers perhaps help someone to achieve some kind of enlightenment?"

"What kind of enlightenment do you have in mind? There are several different interpretations of enlightenment, as we've discussed, depending on how you define them."

"Let's say, to find a true Church with the right doctrine in God's eyes."

"Let me answer your question as I understand it: Since all the Churches' members believe theirs to be the only true Church and all other Churches are false, I don't know what kind of enlightenment one should pray for. Otherwise, they would all have belonged to a single Church for the past 2,000 years."

"Thank you. Fascinating thoughts indeed. A little more explanation, perhaps?"

"Christians say prayers for all kinds of things, and they believe many of their prayers are heard and either partly or even fully answered by God. But what one should also bear in mind is that the lives of countless non-Christians are not necessarily worse than those of Christians who often pray and believe that God answered their prayers. Right now, a great war is being fought around us – mainly by Christians against Christians. I'm sure that Christians on the winning side believe God is answering their prayers, whereas those on the losing side also pray to God to free them from their conquerors as fast as possible and punish them harshly. So how can you know on whose side God stands? I think it's purely a matter of personal interpretation or belief. However, whatever the truth is, the positive side of prayer is that every Christian – from the poorest to the richest or mightiest – believes God is on his side. This belief at least gives the poor and the helpless some hope and energy to go on struggling for survival."

"Thank you. Here's my next question: Can a Buddhist be a Christian at the same time and attain the Christian version of eternal life?"

"That's no problem at all from Buddhism's point of view because, unlike the words of the biblical God, in Buddhist scripture there's isn't a single commandment that forbids its adherents to worship other gods. The problems would surely arise only from Christianity's side. All Christians point out that the biblical God forbids the worship of other gods, citing one of the Ten Commandments."

"What kind of counter-arguments would you use in this case?"

"My answer to this question could be extremely controversial among Christians of all Churches. Therefore, I'll answer it in this way. The two Bibles say that everything in this universe is God's creation and that Jesus is a loving and forgiving deity. So I don't see why a moral Buddhist shouldn't also get eternal life, if even those who wage religious wars against each other in God's name still expect to get it. At least we Buddhists don't abuse his name for any reason."

"But they would say Buddhists worship Buddha and monks ..."

"Jane, Buddhists are not supposed to worship lifeless statues; instead, they should merely inspire themselves through such statues, which are supposed to symbolize the Buddhahood. In like manner, a Buddhist is supposed to worship the monk's robe, which also symbolizes the Buddhahood, but not the person in the robe. But with time, the average Buddhist often misunderstands these essentials. So he worships the person in the robe. In short, then, I don't think you need to worship either a pagoda or a statue of Buddha or a monk to become a good Buddhist and attain enlightenment or nirvana."

"But maybe most Christians would still argue that only those who believe in God and Jesus will get salvation and eternal life. Many of them even believe that one can get eternal life only through faith and God's grace, not through good deeds or work. What do you have to say about that?"

"I won't make any further comment on this matter. I'll leave that decision to Jesus and his Father, since they alone could bestow it. But I wonder if it'd be enough to believe in Jesus. If that is the only requirement, he would not have taught his followers the dos and don'ts. He would not have needed to preach against the Jewish clergy of his day at the risk of losing his life. He would only have needed to say, *'In order to gain salvation and eternal life in my father's kingdom, you only need to believe in me. That's all. Nothing more.'* Or something like that. But he preached against the teachings and practices of Judaism. That's my interpretation as an independent observer of Christianity.

"Concerning the Commandment you invoked, I'd like to say this: Sometimes I wonder if a large number of Christians are not, in reality, worshipping their fellow human beings in high office, who they themselves have elected and pay, instead of worshipping God directly. In other words, I often get the impression that many Christians prefer to observe the moral codes that were concocted by their leaders in God and Jesus' names rather than directly observing the morals of the two deities as written in the two Bibles. In case someone might feel offended by the opinions I've just expressed, I'd entreat them to read the Ten Commandments, Matthew 23:1-37, and the Sermon on the Mount, carefully once again. And he'd have to tell me if there was any living human being who was powerful enough to change any of these biblical verses. Your next question, please, Jane."

Many people in the audience liked what the monk was saying, but at the same time a few of them seemed uneasy.

"Why do you think God strictly forbids his believers to worship other gods?"

"Let me explain to you in this simple – but also perhaps in an abstract - way: If you want to enter and live in another land, you'll have to obey its laws; you cannot enter and live in it with the laws of your own making. Does it make sense to you?"

"Thank you," Jane said. "And some people claim that there are similarities between Buddhism and Christianity by referring to their moral teachings. What do you think of that?"

"Yes, it's true that the moral teachings of both are quite similar. The emphasis on sexual morality, for instance, is one example. And a few biblical verses in the Hebrew Bible and New Testament seem to suggest that the concept of reincarnation existed in biblical times. Once, Jesus asked his disciples who the people thought him to be. They answered that they thought he could be either the prophet Elijah or Jeremiah. On another occasion, Jesus asked the Pharisees what they thought of him, and they answered that he could be the son of David. He then asked them how he could be the son of David since David himself called him 'Lord.' So if these stories are true, then people in that period must have known about reincarnation since they certainly must have known that Jesus did not come down on the clouds from heaven. Apart from such similarities, though, the origins and final goals of both religions are entirely different. The concepts of creationism and eternal life in Christianity, for instance, are totally different from Buddhism."

"Thank you very much. Could you tell me where I can find the son of David in the Bibles?"

"Psalm 110:1. The text reads: *'The LORD said unto my Lord, Sit thou at my right hand, until I make thine enemies thy footstool.'* What I cannot understand is, if Jesus had really identified himself with the 'Lord' in this verse (and one can read up to 7), there will be some critical questions: King David appeared 1,000 years before Jesus, so how could the Pharisees say that he could be the son of David? Could someone have invented this verse? So far as I know, there are only some sketchy mentions of the royal lineages starting from David in the Gospels of Luke and Matthew. And the next critical question is: Did Jesus believe that he was among his enemies? We know that his

196

only 'enemies' were the Jewish law experts and priests of his day, against whom he made several negative statements. One could speculate that Jesus implied that the Romans were his enemies. But since he was only preaching about love, compassion, forgiveness, humility, eternal life and peace, the Romans may have had no reason to fear him. It was the Jewish priests who were responsible for his death, not the Romans."

"Thank you. It's too complicated for me to follow, although it sounds quite interesting, Your Venerable. Do the Buddhists believe in evolutionary theory, then?"

"Here's the simplest way to answer your question: In Buddhism, there's no beginning and no end. Buddhists believe that the world is constantly being recreated millions of times every second and will always continue to be. As no major principles of Buddhism contradict evolution, many Buddhists tacitly accept it. In other words, the final ending of a Buddhist's life would take place when and if he attains nirvana – at least according to the beliefs of the Theravada school."

"Could you tell me what you personally think about creationism and evolutionary theory?"

"If I'm honest, I think the theory of creationism is more plausible, despite its many weaknesses, than evolutionary theory as it stands."

Many people in the audience were quite surprised and yet delighted, but some were visibly perplexed. The monk continued, "But since evolutionary theory is still in its infancy, we'll have to wait a few more decades – or even perhaps centuries – to see how scientists further prove the theory. My standpoint is that there are so many mysteries in the world which science cannot yet explain – reincarnation, for instance, and how such extremely sophisticated beings could have emerged out of nothing. Suppose evolutionary theory should prove at the end to be true. In that case, scientists will then have to try to find out what 'nature' itself is – something that is responsible for the birth of all living beings and inert matter in the universe. Theoretically, it must have super-consciousness and the ability to cause living beings and inanimate matter to emerge out of nothingness. And another im-

197

portant point is that if living beings and inanimate things are the products of pure evolution, it should not be possible for us humans to make predictions about our future. Or did everything in the universe come into existence purely by chance? If yes, what is that thing called 'chance' itself? You could ask such crazy-sounding questions endlessly and never find satisfactory answers."

The audience's reaction was a mixture of curiosity, excitement and bewilderment. In the next few moments, Jane asked the monk this question in an amused tone: "Your Venerable, that is what my father used to say. Do you have any points to substantiate your opinion?"

"Actually, I could tell you a lot more, but I'll make only three points for the time being. In my opinion as a layman, I don't think you need complex instruments and calculations to see that it's easier to accept creationism than evolution. I don't think scientists will ever be able to find out whether the chicken or the egg or the male or female of any living creature came first into being."

Jane delightedly interrupted him again. "This is also what my father used to say, Your Venerable. And the second point?"

"It's clear enough. If living beings are purely the products of evolution, why should nearly all living creatures have two eyes to see, two ears to hear, legs to run upon, and two hands with fingers, in the case of us humans? Theoretically, they should all be just like worms. And why are there so many different species, not only one or two? I'll give you another example - the anteater that feeds on ants. Did the ant or the anteater exist earlier? Theoretically, we can assume that the ant must have existed first, for it could exist alone, but the anteater might not survive without the ant. So the great question or mystery is: Why should the anteater come into existence if there were no creation? What is the purpose of its existence? It's just an example of countless other similar mysteries of our existence."

The audience was impressed and deeply absorbed in the discussion.

"Your Venerable, that's so fascinating. And the third point?"

"I believe even ordinary people on the street may have thought about what I've just said. These ideas are surely not new. But what

I'm going to tell you now will most likely sound crazy. It'll be a great shock for many of you."

Half the audience exchanged worried glances.

The monk continued, "I'll have to refer to the Hebrew Bible and New Testament, especially the Book of Revelation, to substantiate my hypothesis on why it would be easier to deem creationism more plausible. First, I assume that the greater part of the stories in the Old Testament and the four Gospels and the Book of Revelation are true, and as a result of this assumption, I find a few things that strike me as very interesting. According to a few verses in Genesis, human beings were so attractive that heavenly beings, or angels, transformed themselves into human form and married them; this angered God very much. And if Satan and one third of the angels could rebel against God in his own kingdom, one would naturally conclude that angels are not completely free from the desires that are supposedly associated with earthly beings. Is this already too confusing for you, or may I continue? I ask every one of you."

All begged him to continue, for they found it fascinating.

"Thank you. So if a person named Jesus had not appeared 2,000 years ago in Israel, you would never be able to find out if the biblical God and heavenly beings really existed –"

Jane impatiently interrupted him. "So your conclusion is …?"

"My simple conclusion is: If Jesus was a heavenly being and the angels transformed themselves into humans to marry them, then the biblical version of creationism is highly plausible. As the Bible does not specifically mention the number of angels who did that, some of us could even be the descendants of those angels. Therefore, it's conceivable that the seeds of all living species originated in heaven. But you should not be too shocked by my words. I'm just talking as a freethinker, in line with the policy of the Congress of Freethinkers."

Many in the audience liked the idea. Jane said to the monk, "I think your opinions are fascinating and radical, Your Venerable."

"The fact that a heavenly being by the name of Jesus came down to this world in human form means heavenly beings must be immortal. And the angels in the Book of Revelation looked, talked, thought and behaved exactly like us humans. That means they must have existed up there long before people appeared on the earth. They were surely not the reincarnations of human beings. And if we're not closely related to them somehow, they wouldn't need to care for us and care about what happens in the world. But according to the Bibles, God and Jesus made every effort to correct our wrongdoing and save us from self-destruction. Jesus even came down to this world and sacrificed his life for our salvation from eternal damnation."

"Now, how could you prove that the seeds of other living beings also originated in heaven, Your Venerable?"

"It is written in the Book of Revelation that around God's throne in heaven there were four living creatures: the first looked like a lion, the second like an ox, the third like a man, and the fourth like a flying eagle. It sounds strange that such creatures existed in heaven. But we can assume with absolute certainty that these creatures also were not the reincarnations of the same animals on earth."

The audience reacted differently to this. Jane tried to formulate a question, with apparent effort. "Your Venerable, if you think we could have come from heaven, and many of us could even be the descendants of angels, have you ever speculated how the biblical God, Jesus, the angels and heaven could have come into existence in the first place?"

"If we don't even know how *we* came into existence, I think there's absolutely no possibility of knowing how heavenly beings could. We can only make wild speculations. So we may have to accept that they were always there, eternally. I don't think we can do any more than that. And this realization teaches me humility, Jane."

"Not long ago, I met someone who seemed to be quite well versed in Christian theology, who told me that the biblical God could have created Jesus himself. Could you tell me the verses that he referred to, or what would you say about that?"

"He probably meant some of the verses in Proverbs Chapter 8. But I won't comment on it."

"So far as I know, there are a large number of so-called creationists who believe that God must have created this world and all living creatures in it just a few thousands of years ago – and in just six days! Would you also accept this theory?"

"We don't need sophisticated scientific instruments or formulas to test how old the universe might be, and we know all too well how long we humans have taken to reach our present level of civilization. Therefore, I don't think I need to answer this question."

"And what about the six days of creation?"

"We can discuss it later under the topic of time units."

"Okay, I'm curious what you have to say about it. Won't you have problems with your religious organization – the Sangha – after expressing such radical ideas freely?"

"A very good thing about Buddhism, as I've said before, is that you'll not be tortured or burned alive for deviating from the teachings of your school! And you don't need to fear divine judgment either. Buddha himself said that one should not blindly accept his teachings. But of course, I would not express such liberal ideas before a devoted Buddhist audience. By the way, Jane, have you ever discussed with your father the greatest mysteries of the universe?"

"I've never spoken with him about them in depth, and I've never thought about them very seriously either, until now."

"In my opinion, the first greatest mystery is that we – every living being and also inanimate objects – exist. And the second greatest mystery is we're incapable of knowing how we came into existence in the first place. The third greatest mystery is we don't know what will happen to us when we die, even though our knowledge in science is advanced and our general knowledge in the different branches of occultism is also far-reaching."

The whole audience was delighted. Jane was itching to shoot another question at the monk. "Your Venerable, talking of creationism, what do the Hindus think about it? I'm curious."

"Very interestingly, the Hindus also believe in creationism. But their version is completely different from that of Christianity and Ju-

201

daism. Hinduism includes a range of viewpoints about the origin of life and evolution. Due to its dynamic diversity, there is no single story of creation, and these are derived from various scriptures, like Vedas, Brahmanas, Puranas, and philosophical concepts, et cetera."

Jane's next question was, "Could it be that God is powerful in certain ways, but not perfect, as some people believe?"

"I also think that's a possibility. Just look at the existence of different skin colors as an example: Did he intentionally create them, or did they happen accidentally? We'll never find out the answer or answers, if there are any answers at all."

"Talking of skin color, what do you personally think about the discrimination that arises out of the differences?"

"Discrimination as a result of different skin colors is not an exception. All forms of discrimination have been everywhere throughout human history. And they'll always be there so long as human beings exist in this world."

"Could humans be taught or persuaded not to discriminate – say, with some religious concepts?"

"I doubt it very much. Out of compassion or out of one's own life experience, individuals could perhaps change their mind in the course of their lives."

"Thank you. May I ask you now what you think of the emphasis on sexual morality in Christianity and Buddhism?"

"I don't have a clear-cut answer to this either. I can tell you only my own theory. I think it's so because, in many human societies, including even primitive and animistic ones that don't have the concept of godship, it's a generally accepted morality. So the founders of Buddhism and Christianity were perhaps afraid that if they didn't say something about it in their teachings, their adherents might interpret the subject's absence as condoning free sex. I cannot say anything more than that on this matter. By the way, talking of sexuality, there's one thing that has been troubling me for my whole adult life concerning the human psyche. All living beings come into existence because of – or thanks to – sex. But a great many people, regardless of their religious beliefs or social or cultural background, look down on prostitutes, who earn their living by selling their body, instead of having empathy for them and lending them a helping hand. And someone who commits adultery may also be looked down on and condemned, even shunned, by people in his community. Yet those same people are very much fascinated by such acts. In contrast to this, numerous people who cause great suffering to countless people may be hated, but they are probably not looked down on like prostitutes or adulterers. And while criminals are also looked down on and shunned, people are fascinated by tales of criminality at the same time. Just look at how popular detective stories – or stories of crime – are everywhere, regardless of different religious and cultural backgrounds. So the human psyche is very complex and hard to understand. I don't think it'd be possible to change the innate, shared mentality of humankind, regardless of differences in ethnicity or religious belief or cultural background."

"Talking of sexual morality, the 'sinfulness' of same-sex relationships, for instance, is very much emphasized in Christianity. What does Buddhism say about that?"

"In Buddhism, only 'immoral sexual conduct' is to be avoided. I think it is differently interpreted by the major schools. Some leading Buddhists have interpreted it to include same-sex relationships. And adultery is one form of conduct that is quite openly discouraged. So far as I know, the emphasis on sexual acts in Christianity is partly man-made. And these are just a few out of several biblical morals."

"What do you mean by man-made?"

"Instead of directly answering your question, let me speak about this issue in a different way: Why don't the leading personalities of the established Churches concentrate their energy and time and resources more on the solution to hunger and armed conflict, instead of imposing all kinds of morals upon their starving followers? I don't think any kind of sex-related act could be more sinful than the waging of war or the causing of suffering to countless innocent people in God's own name. But if so, God will make the judgment, not we mortals. We know about the existence of God, Jesus, heaven, angels, Satan, evil spirits, and hell only through the Bibles, and everybody can buy these books freely in bookshops. Nobody knows about these things further than what is written in these books."

"So you seem to imply that sexuality is everybody's private business?"

"Exactly. Look, countless people come into this world in poverty. The only thing that can give them brief moments of happiness, regardless of skin color, social class, ethnicity, religious beliefs, cultural background, gender, et cetera, is SEX. So what right do you have to burden those whose lives you don't even know about with a morality of your own making? I can't understand it. What I wonder quite often is: How many of those who have waged religious wars against each other in the names of their two deities would dare to be crucified like Jesus? Perhaps just a handful at the most – or none at all. And if I were a Christian, I wouldn't care for the moral teachings of a fellow being who had never given me a single meal or a cup of water and who doesn't even know about my existence."

"Many Christian Churches strictly forbid divorce or the remarriage of divorced persons. What do you think about that?"

"This is one of the man-made morals I was talking about. There are many reasons why married couples can no longer live together as husband and wife and therefore need to get divorced. I'll tell you just one example: In most societies around the world, marriages are arranged. And there are no schools or seminars where you can learn the dos and don'ts of making a marriage successful. So suppose I were a leading personality of any of these Churches. I'd give some basic lessons to the would-be married couples on how to make their marriage successful – one of these lessons could be sexuality, for instance. I'll tell you a true story. I once saved the marriage of a Christian couple that was about to be broken, with simple methods. Both of them were among my best friends. But their Church leaders didn't allow them to divorce each other. When I inquired discreetly, I found out that it was the woman who wanted to divorce. The reasons were very simple: He did not care about cleanliness and had horrible bad breath that she could no longer bear. But she did not dare to tell him lest he feel offended. So I had to give him this message diplomatically. Their Church leaders might have even believed that Satan and his evil followers had tempted her. I'm quite sure there must be numerous similar cases worldwide. In my opinion, nobody has the right to impose such man-made morals on someone else on behalf of God, because nobody has seen God with his own eyes. So suppose I were a Christian and could not live any longer with my wife as husband and wife, and my Church forbade us to divorce on religious grounds. In that case, I'd demand from them a document that was personally produced by God or Jesus himself. If they could not produce it, I wouldn't care about their authority. As simple as that."

"But not everybody is courageous enough. So don't you perhaps have any ideas that could be used by ordinary believers?"

"How can I have an idea for millions of people?"

"Thank you very much. Now, I'll jump to the next question: Would you say that one doesn't need to be holy to get eternal life?"

"Well, talking about holiness, I've got the impression that a great number of people around the world seem to interpret abstinence from any sexual activity as holiness. I think the words 'holy' and 'holiness' can be very dangerous. We know that a large number of 'holy men' have abused their 'holiness' so badly throughout history."

"How would you personally define holiness in religion, then?"

"My criterion is very simple indeed, and it doesn't necessarily have to do with religion. For me, anybody who doesn't directly or indirectly cause any suffering and loss – be it mental or physical or material – to any innocent human being and is selflessly compassionate is holy, regardless of his religious beliefs. He could even be an atheist."

"So far as I know, many people have got the impression that Buddhist monks, in general, emit an aura of holiness and wisdom. What would you say about that?"

"I cannot speak for my fellow monks in general, but I know that I don't have the wisdom of my own. I regard myself only as a simple middleman between Buddha and some less fortunate laypeople, who, for whatever reason, don't have the opportunity to learn his teachings firsthand like me. I'm only passing on his wisdom to them in a more understandable way. Nothing more than that."

"In most Christian Churches, men monopolize the leading positions on the simple grounds that all Jesus' disciples were male. What would you say about that?"

"But his disciples did not kill each other and initiate any religious wars in the name of their Lord."

The whole audience was very much delighted.

"Thank you, Your Venerable. I've heard a couple of times that all the leading Buddhist personalities in many Sanghas are also male. What did Buddha say about the roles of women?"

"If you read the Anguttara Nikaya (5:33) in Buddhist scripture, for instance, Buddha tells women to be submissive to their husbands, and he describes the seven types of wife: the destructive wife, the thievish wife, the mistress wife, the motherly wife, the sisterly wife, the friend wife, and the slave wife. I know that for this reason alone some people interpret Buddhism as a gender-biased religion. But the 'monopoly' of leading positions in Buddhism by monks doesn't disturb me at all. The simple reason is that, unlike the adherents of Judaism and Christianity who endlessly worry whether their soul will still retain their gender when they enter the realm of the biblical God, we Buddhists don't have this problem. Our only worries are whether we'll ever attain enlightenment and nirvana or not. You might find it interesting to know that Gautama Buddha first ordained women as nuns five years after his enlightenment and five years after ordaining men into the Sangha. The first Buddhist nun was his aunt and foster-mother, Mahapajapati Gotami."

The monk's words made a deep impression on the audience.

"Thank you very much, Your Venerable, I've got food for a lot of new thoughts. Could you tell me now more about compassion and happiness from Buddhism's point of view?"

"We've already talked about compassion, but I'll add a few more thoughts in the following way. I prefer to tell you my thoughts from my own life experience, instead of citing the Buddhist texts. Monks and priests have been preaching compassion and urging their followers to cultivate and apply it to their fellow man for thousands of years. But in real life there are not very many people who can truly implement it. One vivid exception, for instance, is you yourself. If I understand correctly, you fully sympathized with people of color's suffering even before meeting your American husband. Your empathy for these people was not the result of any religious teaching – in other words, you did not develop this attitude in the expectation of some reward from a deity. It came naturally out of your own humane feeling, your understanding of the world. But the degree of your sympathy for these people after you met your husband and then the sorrowful experience that you've gone through because of him and your daughter may be greater. Another example: In the past, you may have sympathized with those whose loved ones had disappeared without a trace, but the degree of your sympathy for such people may once again be greater now. To be able to fully understand compassion and apply it in one's daily life, one needs to go through certain personal experiences. Matthew told me that you're setting up two orphanages where you're going to take care of orphans and the elderly and sick during the war. I cannot express the admiration and respect I have for you, your parents and relatives for your selflessness and compassion in this regard."

"Thank you very much. Now, about happiness?"

"I think it's a very complex subject, although it sounds simple. If I recited what's written in the Buddhist texts, it might be too theoretical for you, for we'd have to start with the Four Noble Truths and the Eightfold Path. So I'll try to put my explanation more simply. First of all, I don't think you can formulate any general guidelines for every human being because people are different, and the reasons for either their happiness or unhappiness are also different. For instance, if you asked me to give you a formula for happiness, how could I do so without first knowing the nature and root of your present agony? Namely, that you're separated from your husband, your daughter has disappeared, and a major war is raging around us.

"Generally speaking, different people achieve happiness through various means – some through religious belief, like me; some through wealth; some through love; some through good health; some through friendships; and so on. For example, a Christian may be happy at the thought of seeing the biblical God and living with him forever in his kingdom. In contrast, a Buddhist like me would be blissfully happy at the thought of not reincarnating anymore – or reincarnating again as a better-situated human being. And several other factors also play equally crucial roles; for example, the era in which you are born; the country in which you are born and live – whether democratic principles or some dictatorship governs it – and the economic system it uses; your cultural and social background; your religious beliefs; the ethnic makeup of the country in which you live; the color of your skin; your physical features – whether you're attractive or not; your financial situation and that of the country in which you live; your family background – whether you've got loving or bad parents, brothers and sisters, or whether you're an orphan; your gender – whether you're male or female; your education; your characteristics: whether by nature you're an optimistic or pessimistic person, a friendly or unfriendly person; whether you're kind or selfish or generous or stingy or compassionate or egoistic or aggressive; whether you're healthy or not, and so on. The factors that play essential roles in making humans happy or unhappy are endless if you start looking at them. And many people's basic characteristics could be shaped further, for better or worse, by changes in their outlook on religion and their experiences at many stages in their life.

"And don't forget that one person's happiness could be another's misery, and vice versa. Have a look at all the brutal dictators in human history! They all achieved their happiness through the suffering of those under their rule. And also think about the people in colonialist countries and their colonies. While most people in colonialist countries are enjoying life thanks to colonialism, the majority of people in their colonies are experiencing all kinds of hardship. So whenever someone asks me for some guidelines for happiness, I try first to learn the key factors relevant to him or her. Only after having considered all these factors can I give any useful advice on individual basis.

"A few more suggestions on this subject ... We'll need to consider two more crucial factors as well: the internal and the external. By 'internal factors' I mean the happiness or unhappiness that originated in inherited characteristics that one can change or improve. As I've already said, I think these internal factors have something to do with self-consciousness or self-awareness. In brief, if you know your weak points and want to change them and succeed in doing so, you can attain happiness through your efforts. But if you don't know your weak points, you won't be able to change them in the first place. People with such problems blame others, or fate, all the time for their misery, instead of making a self-analysis and trying to find practical solutions. The problem with many people is that they're not capable of self-criticism. But this is not a problem for individuals alone. If you look at powerful nations, they all have this problem, too. They only see what other countries have done to them, but they don't want to know about or can't see their own victims' suffering. It's perhaps human nature. One thing that can prevent someone from achieving happiness is too much self-pity. It's a common human characteristic that most people cannot bear even constructive criticism from others, but what one should do is ask one's best friends to frankly point out one's strengths and weaknesses.

"By 'external factors,' I mean things that influence your life but you're not in a position to change or control them – like the war that is being fought right now around us, or the economic situation of the country in which you live, et cetera. It's therefore impossible to give somebody a formula for happiness amid a war. Last but not least, people's Sun Signs and certain mystical numbers are also not to be underestimated. And there is also short-, medium- and long-term happiness. But we won't have time to go into detail on this subject today."

Everybody was quite satisfied with the monk's lengthy explanation. And he continued thus: "Can you guess who the happiest person in the world might very well be, by the way? I think it's the person who is not interested in any religion. In other words, the one who doesn't care about the possibility of existence in some other form beyond this human life."

Many people in the audience were surprised. They looked at each other in disbelief. Jane quickly asked the monk, "I hope you're not joking, Your Venerable."

The monk was quite amused.

"No, I'm very serious. Look, Christians claim to be very happy at the thought of living eternally in God's kingdom, yet they keep studying theology and even arguing endlessly about the existence or non-existence of *their* God. All learned Buddhist monks claim to feel blissful at the thought of attaining nirvana, yet they also keep studying Buddhist scripture and the doctrines of the schools to which they belong. But you cannot see what they think inside their mind. In brief, the simplest and most effective formula for happiness is contentment. It's most important that you're content with what you have and who you are. Thus, he who doesn't believe in any religious concepts can fully enjoy his life, provided, of course, that the other crucial factors I've just mentioned are in his favor. He doesn't care about what will happen to him after his death. I wish to be such a person. Please excuse me if I've disappointed you with this sincere and honest statement."

Some of the participants were dismayed, while a few were quite delighted. Jane then spoke up. "I admire you greatly for your honesty, Your Venerable, but I'm quite sure there must be many Buddhists and Christians who are truly happy in their religious lives."

"Without a doubt. Such people accept the religious ideas and concepts that others preach, without making further inquiries. And for plenty of reasons, not everybody can do further research. Your problem begins if you want to know more than what your religious leaders tell you and begin to study more deeply. In most cases, the more you study and the more you think you know, the more mysterious things become. And then you come to a point where you don't know anymore how to proceed with your search. Or, in other words, you come to a dead end."

"So I don't think you would suggest that I read books to deepen my understanding of Buddhism?"

"I wouldn't do that if I were you – at least for the time being; although you could perhaps start with the books I mentioned a while ago. Besides, so far as I know, the existing books on Buddhism in European languages are mainly academic, so they're very hard for the ordinary man and woman on the street to understand."

"When do you think would be the right time for me to become a Buddhist?"

"I think now is not yet the right time. Right now, you're in great distress. So you're vulnerable to any new idea that you think might give you what you so badly need – that is, peace of mind and tranquility. If you did something impulsive now, you might regret the decision some day. Take your time and think over what I've told you. After a few years, you'll be able to think clearly about what you want in life – I mean spiritually. If you're still interested in the fundamentals of Buddhism, then explore the different concepts of the various schools. At the end of your search, you'll probably find something you like – or you may lose your faith in Buddhism and find another religion instead. Or you could become a person without any religious beliefs at all. Anything is possible. You could even become a devoted Christian again."

"Thank you so much, Your Venerable. Would you receive some divine reward if you converted somebody to Buddhism?"

"No."

"Can a Buddhist leave his religion freely?"

"So far as I know, there's no restriction at all. It's up to you. You'll not be punished in your next existence for that. It's completely voluntary."

Just at the point when Jane thought she had asked him enough and had decided to bring the discussion to an end, she suddenly thought of some more questions. The wall clock struck six times. It was already six o'clock. They all looked at it.

"Your Venerable, I thought I'd already asked you enough questions, but some new ideas are still popping up. I know our time is running out, though."

"Don't worry about the time, Jane. Matthew and Natalie are very patient people …"

The monk turned to Matthew and his wife, Natalie. They both smiled and Natalie said, "Yes, don't worry about the time, Jane. Just go ahead with your questions."

"Your Venerable, Matthew and Natalie, thank you so much. Judaism and Christianity are said to be religions of prophecy. Since you've read the Bibles quite thoroughly, what do you think of this idea? Did it have any impact on your study of Christianity?"

"The prophecies in the two Bibles are fascinating indeed. But since nearly all those who regard themselves as biblical experts decipher the prophecies quite differently, I don't pay much attention to them. I don't give them much attention because many of these misinterpreted prophecies were the main roots of countless religious wars amongst the Christians themselves. Many more will probably be waged somewhere in the future due to the self-proclaimed experts' interpretations of the prophecies. So in my opinion, it's perilous to take the prophecies seriously. Of course, I've got my own interpretations, but I won't confide in anybody about them. For me, prophecies are, like dreams and visions, too mysterious to decipher fully and accurately. And one of the main problems with biblical prophecies is that they are scattered across several chapters in the Bibles over a time-span of thousands of years. So if you want to go deeper into them, you'll need to know a huge amount of world history. And I don't have the time or patience to study that in depth. So it's an almost impossible task to interpret them accurately. Hence, they can be very easily manipulated by anybody to serve their interests. Above all else, I think one should be very cautious, for nearly all the interpretations in the past have turned out to be completely wrong."

"What would you say about the prophecies in the Book of Revelation?"

"I won't make any comment on them publicly, but I won't rule out making one or two comments later, if the necessity arises."

"Yes, that's what my father says. Are there any similar prophecies in Buddhism – like Jesus' Second Coming, for example?"

"So far as I know, there's only one important prophecy in Theravada Buddhism, namely that the fifth Buddha, Maitreya, will appear. The present Buddha, who appeared 2,500 years ago, is the fourth and is called Buddha Shakyamuni. But the Mahayana Buddhists recognize many bodhisattvas as Buddhas. A bodhisattva is a person who has attained enlightenment, but postpones nirvana to help others attain enlightenment."

"How about the Hindus?"

"They're expecting the coming of Kalki, an avatar, descending on a horse and wielding a sword. An avatar is a deity in the form of a physical entity like a human being. And they're also expecting the coming of a Golden Age. In the *Brahmavaiverta Purana*, Lord Krishna tells Ganga Devi that a Golden Age will come in the Kali Yuga – one of the four stages of development that the world goes through as part of the cycle of eras, as described in Hindu scriptures. Lord Krishna predicted that this Golden Age will start 5,000 years after the beginning of the Kali Yuga and will last 10,000 years. The Hindu Kali Yuga calendar began on 18 February 3,102 BC. So many Hindus believe the Golden Age will arrive very soon – probably in the next century."

"Thank you very much … And how would you explain what is called 'karma?' If I understand it correctly, it's a crucial element of Buddhism."

"Its definition is 'causality.' If you do a good thing, you get a good result in return. If you do bad things, the consequences are harmful. But in my personal opinion, this is probably applicable only beyond this human existence, perhaps in your next reincarnations, not in your present life. Hence, countless bad people do terrible things and yet prosper. And innumerable good people suffer. So I think karma explains that people will be rewarded or punished in their *next* human life, or in their existence in a spiritual world. There's a widespread saying among Buddhists when something bad or good happens to a person: They say 'that's his karma' – meaning that he's reaping the fruits or being punished in his present life for what he did in his previous incarnations."

"Do you accept that theory?"

"I can make many counter-arguments against it, but we won't have enough time to go into detail, and these arguments wouldn't be beneficial for you."

"Could you tell me at least one or two of these counter-arguments?"

"Okay, I'll tell you just one: In the recorded history of humankind, millions of innocent people have lost their lives in countless wars. In the present war alone, at least tens of millions of people will surely lose their lives. My simple argument is that not all of them could have committed disgusting crimes in their past lives. So it'd be senseless to say that they're paying now for the sins of their past lives."

"Thank you very much. I wonder if Sister Hanna has told Matthew about my father and whether Matthew has informed you about him or not. He doesn't conform to any particular religion, but he's not an atheist. He's deeply absorbed in various types of occultism or mysteries, such as palmistry, numerology, different kinds of astrology, different divination methods, and so on. But the Christian Churches regard them as the work of Satan or some other 'dark force.' How does Buddhism see them?"

"Well, if they're the works of Satan or some other 'dark force,' then nearly all Buddhists and Hindus must be followers of him or that other so-called dark force. Buddhists and Hindus have been using different forms of divination in Asia for thousands of years. Without these methods, I don't think they could have even survived. Here, I'd like to ask a counter-question to those who oppose the use of such divination methods on religious grounds: Why aren't those who don't use such methods more moral and better people than those who use them? For example, in Burma, when a child is born, a local astrologer makes a horoscope for him on palm leaves, and the child keeps it for his whole life. The fascinating thing is that although the great majority of Buddhists believe in and rely on various kinds of divination, there are also a large number who don't believe in multiple types of occultism at all."

"Do you believe in them?"

"I'm not obsessed with any one of them, but out of curiosity I've studied quite a number."

"Talking of numerology, my father is fascinated by the mystical numbers from the Bible, such as 7, 12, 40, 49, 70, et cetera. Do you have any explanation for them?"

"I'm also quite interested in these numbers, but they're so mysterious that I haven't found the reasons why they are so important. The number 7, for instance, is quite an important number in other major religions, too. In the Bibles, this number alone is said to be mentioned more than 700 times. But I don't know why it is so. Of course, I could repeat what I've read about these numbers, but the knowledge won't benefit you. By the way, in case you're curious why the number 49 (7 times 7), for example, is important, you can read Leviticus 25."

"Are you also interested in Nadi or Palm Leaf astrology? My father is."

"Yes. But one has to be very careful with it. It's crucial to find the right palm leaf reader and the right leaves. There are some dishonest readers in the trade."

"It sounds as if you have consulted one or more yourself?"

"Yes. But I won't say any more than that. What I can tell you is that most of what was written on those palm leaves came true in my life."

"Very interesting indeed to know about all these things. Could you please tell me a bit more about it? My father used to tell me about it, but I never concentrated very well."

The monk asked the audience if they were also interested. They begged him to tell them more. Nearly all of them admitted that they had never even heard of it before. So he started. "Good, I'll tell you very briefly. It's said that the *Nadishastra* was written down by the seven rishis, or sages, about the destinies of souls that go through the cycle of reincarnation, through yogic and intuitive powers gained through severe penance. It reveals man's fate, past, present, and future, using the thumb's impression, and comprehensive details about one's life are read in the palm leaves. It is practiced in Tamil Nadu and adjacent regions in India. These ancient records of providence were made famous by practitioners around the Vaitheeswaran Temple in Tamil Nadu. Nadi readers say that the seekers would come of their own accord in search of the leaves at a predetermined time. Thumb prints are taken (the right thumb for males and the left for females). The seers classify 108 categories of thumb impressions. To find the right leaf for a seeker, he is asked to answer a set of questions – yes or no – based on the leaf's verses. Nadi leaves are also classified accordingly, based on the different thumb impressions.

"The right leaf tells the names of the seeker, his parents, spouse, and so on. Each leaf has a different answer for a seeker. And only those who are predestined to seek this form of divination seek it. Very strangely, the leaf also mentions at what time the seeker will appear to have his reading. It is divine in essence. The accuracy of the prediction depends mainly on identifying the right leaf and how proficient the reader is in interpreting the verses on the Nadi leaves. I think this much is enough for the time being. If you're interested to know more about it, you may make further inquiries on your own."

Everybody was fascinated and thanked the monk lavishly for his brief exposition. Jane continued after a few moments. "And a couple more subjects that also fascinate my father are the concepts of determinism, or predestination, and *free will* in Christian theology. Since you've studied a lot of Christian literature and discussed it with leading theologians and clergymen, I'm curious to know your opinions on these subjects."

"Well, so far as I know, the concept of predestination in Christian theology arose in the 1st century AD. It is the doctrine that the biblical God has willed all events. The concept of determinism had already been introduced in the 7th and 6th centuries BC by the pre-Socratic philosophers Heraclitus and Leucippus. It was later dealt with by several prominent philosophers, theologians, and scientists. I can only give you my personal opinions on them in the following way. Suppose one believes in the biblical prophecies or other forms of foretelling. In that case, one is naturally inclined to believe in the theory of predestination or determinism – call it what you want ..."

Jane abruptly interrupted him. "I learned that for that very reason, some philosophers and Christian theologians doubt if we humans have free will at all. What is your opinion on that?"

"My interpretation of free will is perhaps different from that of any established religion or philosophy. Theoretically, I believe every individual can make decisions freely, depending on several factors or conditions that I mentioned when speaking about happiness. But I'll add a few more factors now: The nature of the decision one has to make – whether it's for a group of people or an individual, a political party or a nation, for instance; whether one is brave or not, if the making of a certain decision demands such a quality, that is; the timing of when a decision has to be made, and how important the decision is, et cetera. What I find very irritating about some philosophers' concepts is the indiscriminate use of 'we, we, we' – implying that the whole of humankind sees and does things in the same way, regardless of the factors I've mentioned. But look at the present situation: Nations are waging a brutal war around us, so most people don't have the chance to use their own free will anymore, or the possibility of making their own decisions has been radically limited. They all have to do things collectively against their will. And whether a god or gods predestined this war, or if it's happening at random, there's no way for us to know for sure. We can only speculate. In conclusion, I'd like to tell you my thoughts on this subject. If we look at world history, it's possible that the fates or destinies of all ethnic groups or nations – and humankind as a whole – could have indeed been preprogrammed or predestined. We've just discussed Nadi astrology, which could also prove the existence of predestination or determinism. But if that is the case, the question of who or what was responsible for it would arise. We humans may never find the answer. It's even possible that there are no answers to these mysteries at all. Or if there are, they may be beyond our comprehension. We often speak of luck, ill luck, destiny, fate – but nobody knows what they really are. We can only speculate wildly that they're unknown forces that govern us from some dimension we don't know about."

"By the way, talking of luck and ill luck, I used to hear that not only humans but even animals like dogs can have good luck or ill luck. What do you think about that?"

The monk answered with a broad smile, "I think that's true. Lucky dogs are owned by kind, rich owners and are well treated and well fed; unlucky ones are owned by cruel or poor people and badly treated or poorly fed. But I don't have much time to think about such things in detail."

The whole audience was amused. Jane continued, "You've just told us that you've made your own interpretations of the biblical prophecies. Is the present war perhaps among those prophecies?"

"I'm sorry, I won't answer this question, for various reasons."

"How do you see the Germans' racial ideology, which is one of the main causes and driving forces of this war?"

"I won't make any comment."

"You know that nearly all Christians around the world accuse the Jews of having murdered Jesus, and use this as an excuse to hate them. What would you say about that?"

"Yes, it's a real pity that they've blamed the Jews for centuries when those who were responsible for his death numbered no more than just a handful. But what those Christians forget is that they themselves justify their own wrongdoing in his name, like waging religious wars against each other. And they belong to various rival

Churches, yet they all believe at the same time to be observing his moral teachings."

The audience liked the monk's words very much.

"Thank you very much," Jane answered, "this is all food for thought indeed. Many of these ideas are very similar to my father's, Your Venerable."

"Thank you, Jane. It's terrific to know that. If you start seriously thinking about Judaic and Christian theologies, it's mind-boggling, especially the concept of predestination, for example. If you're going to believe that the biblical God preprogrammed all the events in the universe, then the first question for both the Jews and Christians would be: Did he plan for Satan and his follower-angels to rebel against him in the first place? If you read the Hebrew Bible, you learn that the ancient Israelites rebelled countless times against his laws, and he was furious with them. So the next question again would be: If he had planned all the events in the universe, why was he so angry with them every time they disobeyed his laws? He should have known these things in advance. But Jane, if you struggle to find answers to such great mysteries, you'll only exhaust yourself and waste your time."

"That means we should blindly worship him?"

"I don't think you have to worship him blindly. My understanding is that Jesus' teachings are sufficient to attain the Christian version of salvation and eternal life. So I'll try to answer your question from the standpoint of an independent observer of this religion. If you try to find answers to the many great theological puzzles in the two Bibles, I don't think you'll get anywhere. I'll tell you about just three of the most mysterious puzzles as examples to prove my point. First, why did Jesus emphasize the danger of Satan's temptation of humans, since he could have foreseen that it would be used later by his believers in their religious wars against each other? Second, I'll quote a few verses from Genesis 6:1-3: '1 *And it came to pass, when men began to multiply on the face of the earth, and daughters were born unto them. 2 That the sons of God saw that the daughters of men were fair; and they took them wives of which they chose. 3 And the LORD said, "My spirit shall not always strive with men, for that he also is flesh: yet his days shall be an hundred and twenty years ..."'* Third, Genesis 6:5-7: '*5 And God saw that the wickedness of man was great in the earth, and that every imagination of the thoughts of his heart was only evil continually. 6 And it repented the LORD that he had made man on the earth, and it grieved him at his heart. 7 And the LORD said, "I will destroy man whom I have created from the face of the earth; both man, and beast, and the creeping things, and the fowls of the air; for it repenteth me that I have made them."'* You can endlessly raise questions or theorize about these great puzzles, but I don't think any mortal being will ever find any satisfactory answers."

"Would you please name a few questions that could be raised?"

"With regard to Jesus' emphasis on Satan's temptation of humans, I don't know what kind of questions could be raised, but I'll name just three potential questions concerning the biblical verses from Genesis. One: Are the angels exclusively male? Two: Since God is omnipotent according to the Bible, didn't he know long before he created humans that they would one day become so wicked? Three: When he spoke of the destruction of humankind and the world, did he mean the great biblical flood mentioned in Genesis or another form of destruction in the future? Another crucial question, apart from the three I've just mentioned, is: Did God send Jesus as a last-ditch attempt to save humans and his other creations from their aforementioned total destruction?"

"That means ..."

"If I were a Christian, I'd concentrate my attention on Jesus and the four Gospels and the Book of Revelation."

"But it's said that there are many contradictions in these four books."

"Yes, they do contain some contradictions. One version, for instance, says that those who were with him would not experience death before his Second Coming, but in another version he says his teachings must be spread first to the ends of the world. But the dos and don'ts in them are almost the same."

"Could you explain why people should concentrate their attention on these elements alone?"

"I'll give you three reasons. First, Jesus spoke with authority, full of self-confidence. All the prophets before him were only intermediaries between the Jews and God, so they always said, 'The Lord said …', but Jesus said and did things without referring to God all the time. Second, the various visions of heaven and heavenly beings in the Old Testament are not as vivid as the visions of heaven and the angelic beings in the Book of Revelation. I don't know how significant these differences are to the various Churches, but if I were a Christian they would mean a great deal to me in terms of my attempt to get a full picture of both Judaism and Christianity. If Jesus were not a historical person and a powerful heavenly being, there would never have been a Book of Revelation. Or if there were one, the visions of God, celestial beings and heaven would most likely be exact copies of the Hebrew Bible's equivalent visions. But the visions in Revelation are radically different from those in the Hebrew Bible. I think one can use them as concrete proof of the authenticity of Jesus' claim to be a powerful heavenly being. Third, even if you're puzzled by such mysteries, you don't have any mechanisms to decipher them. You don't have any better alternatives. The exception, of course, would be if you decided to follow a non-monotheistic religion like Buddhism or Taoism."

"Thank you very much. A crucial point, which has been disturbing me for years, is: If God truly loves us all, why doesn't he appear to us in person? If he did that, we would surely have fewer problems."

"According to the Old Testament, he did that once, when the Israelites came out of Egypt. But they were so frightened by his appearance that they pleaded to Moses to beg God to communicate with them only through him, Moses. However, soon after this happened, the Israelites began to disobey God's commandments again. We can ask ourselves why, but I don't think we'll ever get a convincing answer."

"At the beginning of our discussion, you said that every religion has its own unique aspects. What kind of unique aspects do you see in Christianity?"

"I think one of the most salient aspects of Christianity is the relationship between humans and spiritual beings. These are not just legends or fairy tales from a distant past, but a reality that may be proved through the appearance of Jesus, who became a human just 2,000 years ago. There is no doubt about his historicity anymore. The next unique thing is his teachings. If human beings – I mean those who claim to believe in him and his teachings – strictly observed them, Christianity would, like Buddhism, be a fully peaceful and compassionate religion. Just have a look at Jesus' Sermon on the Mount, for example. He only teaches the virtues of love, forgiveness, peace, compassion and humility. He does not preach that people should make wars against each other in his or his Father's name, or fight against Satan and his fallen angels on their behalf."

"But there are millions of people who still doubt his historicity."

"Well, even if he were not a historical person, even if he were fictional, one must at least admit that the teachings attributed to him are still radically unique. So these teachings truly deserve great respect and admiration. And for countless people around the world, his name alone gives hope and the will to bear all kinds of hardship on earth. This fact alone means a great deal to a large part of humankind…"

Jane impatiently interrupted him again. "Please excuse me for interrupting you, Your Venerable, but on the other hand, countless people around the world in the past 2,000 years have been suffering at the hands of powerful institutions and personalities who used his name for their own interests."

"That's exactly what I was going to say if you hadn't interrupted me, Jane."

"Does Judaism also have its unique aspects?"

"Its uniqueness, like that of Christianity, lies in the relationship between the Jewish people and a spiritual being called God, and the fact that the stories in the Hebrew Bible or Old Testament took place just a few thousand years ago. If the stories in this book were just a handful of people's experiences, you could easily say that they were invented. But that's not the case. These stories are about the collective history of an entire people. (According to the Exodus story, those who followed Moses were more than 600,000.) So even though several prominent historians and biblical scholars are skeptical about this number, one can still conservatively assume that they must have numbered at least tens of thousands. So you cannot say that they are just a collection of fairy tales dreamed up by a small group of people. Another fundamental fact here is that, so far as I know, there are no other pieces of contemporary literature comparable to the contents of the Old Testament."

"What are the main differences between Judaism and Christianity, in your opinion?"

"There are several. But three of the most important, in my opinion, are the physical appearance of a powerful heavenly being in human form, namely Jesus; the concept of salvation and eternal life in Christianity; and the different accounts of God and heavenly beings in the Old Testament and the Book of Revelation."

"Would you please elaborate?"

"If you read the 1906 *Jewish Encyclopedia* under the entry 'Immortality of the Soul,' according to Judaism, the human soul is not immortal. The author of this entry emphasizes this point by citing several verses from the Hebrew Bible. According to these verses, eternal life was ascribed exclusively to God and celestial beings, who ate from the tree of life. So eternal life is a completely new concept with the appearance of Jesus."

"But most Jews haven't accepted Jesus as their long-awaited Messiah. The greatest blasphemy for the Jews is his claim to be the son of God. What would you say about that?"

"I won't comment on that, for it's an extremely sensitive issue for the Jews – and also for most Christians. You had better ask them directly."

"Please kindly make at least some comment, Your Venerable!"

"No, I just can't. The reason is that even different branches of Judaism have their own interpretations; in other words, their interpretations are not uniform."

"Couldn't you at least give us some hint about what you think about it?"

"No, I can't do that. But I'll tell you something else which could indirectly be relevant to your question. From Abraham's time to Jesus' appearance, many major and minor prophets appeared whose main duty was to act as an intermediary between God and the Jews. But from Jesus' appearance to this day, not a single prophet of his caliber has appeared again. Through Christian and Jewish literature, and through my discussions with many prominent Christian theologians and clerics, I've tried to find out why that is so. I still haven't come across any convincing explanations. I'd very much appreciate it if somebody could offer me one. Purely out of curiosity."

"You just said 'from Jesus' appearance to this day, not a single prophet of his caliber has appeared again.' But how about Muhammad? The Muslims might say that he is of the same caliber as Jesus."

"The difference between them, I think, is the Muslims themselves believe Jesus will come back, but not Muhammad. So in my opinion, even if Jesus were just a prophet and not the son of God, he must be a prophet with special status."

"I've heard that there were some among the Jews who claimed to be their long-awaited Messiah and that there have also been some people who claimed to be Jesus or a prophet."

"I've also heard such stories, but I've never made further inquiries, nor am I interested in such claims. By the way, speaking of prophets, do you know what prophets were called in biblical times?"

"No."

"They were called *seers*. An occult term. There are some biblical verses in which this term is used."

"Really? Very interesting. Could you tell me which ones?"

"No, I'm sorry. I won't do that. But you could ask some Christian theologians."

"What are the characteristics of a true prophet, then?"

"According to some biblical verses, one of the characteristics of a true prophet is whether the prophecies that such a person makes in the name of God turn out to be fulfilled or not. Many Christians have claimed to have had direct personal communications with God and prophesied the end of the world soon after Jesus' death. But the world still exists today."

"Any other traits of a true prophet?"

"Speaking out fearlessly against the injustices that are being perpetrated by the rulers of his time is another characteristic of a true prophet. What I'm going to say now might not fit into the immediate context, but ironically, the Jews who cannot accept Jesus as their Messiah can at least find great consolation in the fact that, unlike the Christians who waged religious wars against each other in the name of their proclaimed Messiah, they – the Jews – didn't start any wars against each other – or against any other people – in the name of *their* God."

"Supposing you were a Christian, would the Hebrew Bible still be relevant for you?"

"Absolutely."

"In that case, which parts could still be relevant for Christians today?"

"I'd say mainly the prophecies about the coming of 'the son of man,' which has been interpreted by many Christian theologians and clergymen to be Jesus or another prophet. Jesus is said to have identified himself as such. And the prophet Ezekiel is also addressed thus in the book named after him. Also, the prophecies concerning the entire humankind's destiny seem to be so important that they cannot be ignored. But please don't ask me to name all these verses, because Jewish religious leaders and theologians interpret them differently."

"Do you think Jesus will come back?"

"If the person in the New Testament is Jesus, I think he'll come back. If he could come into this world once as a human being, he can surely come back. This I believe, provided, of course, that he's still alive."

"Do you have any idea when he might come back?"

"I've got my ideas about it, but I won't say."

"Tomorrow, next year, a decade or a century from now?"

"I won't say when. But I'm positive that he will. There are some concrete signs for his return – or the appearance of a powerful person – prophesied in many verses in the Hebrew Bible and the Book of Revelation. But I won't say which verses they are."

"Are some or all of these signs already here in the word now?"

"I won't comment."

"What are the unique aspects of Buddhism?"

"I'd say its peacefulness and tolerance, its cosmology, its units of time, and its analysis of the nature of the human mind. If I understand it correctly, Christianity and Judaism don't have the units of time, and they don't analyze the human mind."

"What could be the reason why Christianity and Judaism don't have units of time? The only units of time that are mentioned in the Bibles are one hour, one day, six days, seven days, and one thousand years, for instance."

"The simple reason, I think, is that these time units are celestial or heavenly – not earthly. That's one reason why all Christians have problems interpreting them: They think about these time units in earthly terms. The six days of creation is an example. If you live in a place where there are only days and no nights and no time-measuring instruments of the kind we use on earth – and if you exist for eternity – you wouldn't have the same sense of time as we human beings have. Therefore, a celestial day could be equal to several million or even billions of earth years. Nobody knows."

"And the reason behind the lack of analysis of the human mind in these religions?"

"I think we've spoken about it to some extent. Unlike in Buddhism and Hinduism, in Christianity and Judaism you don't need intellect for the attainment of eternal life. Your faith and the observation of God's and Jesus' morals alone are sufficient for your salvation. So you don't need to think much about it, for the human mind plays no significant role at all."

226

"What are Buddhism's greatest contributions to the world – to humankind?"

"Buddhism brought wisdom, peacefulness, tolerance, civilization, the concept of enlightenment, and a consciousness of compassion to every corner of Asia. If there were no Buddhism, large parts of Asia would most likely still have been animistic when Christianity arrived. And as a result, there would be no progress …"

Jane interrupted, "Your Venerable, you used the word 'peacefulness,' but didn't Buddhist countries also wage war against each other?"

"Yes, of course. But they didn't fight each other in the name of Buddha. Fortunately, Christianity did not arrive in Asia before the Age of Enlightenment had taken root in Europe – in other words, before secularism got the upper hand in Europe. If Christianity had reached Asia a few centuries earlier, countless people would have converted to various rival Churches. As a result, there would also have been a number of merciless religious wars fought between them, as happened in the West. That's one of Buddhism's greatest contributions to humankind – at least in Asia. The dark side of Buddhism is that some more martial religions took advantage of its peacefulness and tolerance."

"If there were no Buddhism, do you think Hinduism could have spread throughout Asia as Buddhism did?"

"That's a possibility. It had spread quite widely already, at least in Southeast Asia. You can see many Hindu temples in the region. But I don't know whether it could have spread as widely as Buddhism. Its caste system could have been a hindrance in many Asian societies, I suppose."

"What are Hinduism's greatest contributions to the world – or at least to the people in Asia?"

"I think they're almost the same as those of Buddhism."

"And how about Islam's unique aspects?"

"I'm sorry, but I have very little knowledge of it."

"And its contributions to mankind?"

"As far as I know, the Islamic world has made great contributions in science, astronomy, mathematics, arts, medicine, literature, and more."

"By the way, I'm curious how Buddhists and Hindus see Jesus."

"Well, I'm not aware of the existence of any official view, but so far as I know, most Buddhists regard him to be an enlightened person, though not God or God's son. The Hindus believe him to be one of many great and holy men. Many of them believe that he was a good teacher and perhaps one of their millions of avatars."

"You were talking about the Age of Enlightenment in the West. How much does it influence your thought?"

"A great deal, I'd say."

"The different Christian Churches around the world impose many commandments of their own making upon their adherents. What would be your ideal Church?"

"My ideal Church would be one without doctrine. If I were to found a Church, I'd make a long list of the dos and don'ts that were delivered personally by Jesus himself and hang it somewhere inside a church building. And I'd give every member of the Church complete freedom to observe the items on the list – voluntarily. Nobody would be threatened with eternal damnation in a place called 'hell.' And no one would be judged, for Jesus himself said, 'You shall not judge!' I'd preach only the virtues of Jesus' moral teachings – that is, love, peace, forgiveness, compassion, humility, et cetera. Everybody would be able to observe these values voluntarily. Above all else, I'd emphasize that heaven is not a dumping ground for the souls of wrongdoers on this earth, and God doesn't need cheap laborers in His kingdom. Unlike the methods and concepts of the different schools of Buddhism that you have to choose for the attainment of the Buddhist version of enlightenment or nirvana, you don't need any special knowledge or qualification in Christianity to achieve the eternal life that Jesus and his Father are believed to give. Hence, I see no reason for creating a doctrine."

"With your fresh and radical religious ideas, I'm quite sure you could get many followers if you founded a Church."

"No, I don't think that's entirely true. So far as I've ever observed, a large number of people prefer to be told or commanded by someone with authority, but I'll never do that because heaven and hell don't belong to me, and I don't even know if these two places and God and Jesus and the angels really do exist. So what right do I have to counsel someone with a doctrine of my own making? I'd never do that. Above all else, I'm a very individualistic person, and peace of mind is extremely important to me. There are already more than enough rival Churches with conflicting doctrines around the world. So I don't need to create more problems by founding a new Church."

"Thank you. My next question is: Why is our existence in this world and our existence or non-existence after our death so elusive and mysterious?"

"I think I've already expressed indirectly what I think about that, and I don't think I've got a concrete answer. I can only speculate. Certainly, we cannot deny the existence of other dimensions or realities or laws that we're not capable of truly knowing but which govern us directly or indirectly, whether we like it or not. Many Christians would naturally incline to call such mysterious forces the work of either God and the heavenly beings, who are believed by Christians to supervise our daily affairs, or some dark forces that belong to Satan and the fallen angels. Just look at this: Human beings are divided into twelve Sun Signs in astrology, and each Sun Sign has its own characteristics. And in the Bibles, the numbers 7, 12, 40, 49, and 70 play crucial roles in the relationship between the Jews and God. These are just a handful of the great mysteries for which we have no answers, despite thousands of years of theological study and significant advances in science."

"That's exactly what my father says."

"I wish I could meet him one day so that we could exchange ideas, Jane. I'm sure he must be an exceptional person."

"Yes, he is, in many ways. I'll tell him in detail what we've been discussing today. He and my mother are in America. They'll come back as soon as the war is over. Then we could arrange a meeting. He'll be extremely pleased to meet you, too."

"I appreciate your curiosity very much, and have enjoyed our conversation tremendously. I'm surprised and delighted by your hunger for spiritual knowledge."

"Thank you. I'm glad to hear that. I often used to talk with my father about some of the topics we've discussed today. But this is the first time I've ever discussed them with a Buddhist monk. And I know that if I discussed them with a scholar of Buddhism, the results would surely be quite different. My father has been researching some of them for years, but he's still walking in the dark. By the way, may I ask you once again why the Sun Signs play crucial roles for us?"

"I'm afraid I might have to disappoint you, Jane. I can only tell you a joke which I found quite amusing. I've discussed this topic several times with many prominent scholars, both religious and secular. A fellow senior monk of mine, who is also well versed in Christian theology, said this, half-jokingly: 'Human beings multiplied so rapidly that God and the angels alone could no longer manage their daily affairs, so he created the Sun Signs and some mystical numbers to take charge of humans' daily affairs on their behalf.'"

The room echoed with thunderous laughter.

"A while ago, you said that we might have free will to some extent. But couldn't it also be that what we perceive to be our free will is either directly or indirectly – and partly or wholly – influenced by the invisible forces we're talking about?"

"We cannot rule that out. But I don't think we have the mechanisms to prove or disprove whether what you suggest is true or not. I'll tell you a fascinating thing about astrology; it might help you see our actions from a different perspective, although it might make the issue more complicated. If you go to a real expert astrologer in my country or in India to consult him on particular issues, you don't need to tell him what those issues are. After having calculated various data like the time (if possible, to the nearest hour, minute and second), the date, the day of the week, the month, the year, the place of your birth and the time of your arrival at his place, he'll tell you exactly why you have gone to see him."

"Oh? How fascinating!"

"It's true. I've told you this story because we can never really rule out whether the said forces might influence our decisions or not, at least to some extent. But we can be quite sure that these unknown forces don't have any influence on our trivial daily decisions, like what we eat or what we drink, for instance."

Jane apologized to the monk. "It's already seven o'clock, and I'm afraid you're tired, but may I ask you a few more questions, Your Venerable? They'll be brief."

"Don't worry. I'm still enjoying our discussion."

"Thank you very much. How do you think the majority of Christians would react to what you've said today? Wouldn't they accuse you of interfering in their religious beliefs?"

"I don't know how they would interpret what I've said or how they would react. But since God and Jesus and the Bibles are nobody's private possessions, I'd hope they would all be kind enough to forgive me if I offended anyone. And since everybody can buy the Bibles in bookshops anyway, I don't think anybody has the right to make any accusations against me. But there's one thing I'd like to add: In my adult life, I've come across a large number of Christians, and they always gave me the very strong impression that they felt as if God, Jesus, the heavenly beings and heaven belonged to them alone and therefore they alone had the sole right to interpret the Bibles as they wished. And that their interpretations alone were legitimate. But as their actions around the world have had both positive and negative consequences throughout history, I believe everyone has the right to say anything they like about Christianity and its adherents. If they don't want non-Christians to say anything bad about them, they should try to observe Jesus' moral teachings strictly. It's as simple as that."

"Thank you. Does our existence have any sense? I mean, from Christianity's point of view."

"There must be sense in the world for those who believe; otherwise, they wouldn't become Christians. But if you look at it from a logical point of view, many questions need to be answered. For you, for instance, your existence could make sense because you're white and a privileged person with all the facilities that enable you to lead a very comfortable life. And you've got two loving parents, and you are all healthy. But for the great majority of black people, who encounter discrimination in their daily life, or for those who are starving to death, or for those who are suffering from disease, their existence could even be interpreted as a curse. So I think one has to differentiate case by case."

"What a pity it is that so many people are born just to suffer endlessly."

"Suppose some unavoidable natural catastrophes cause your suffering. In that case, it's still bearable, but what is so heartbreaking, especially for countless Christians around the world for centuries, is that their fellow Christians are the main culprits of their miseries in the very names of God and Jesus. That's a reason, I think, why millions of poverty-stricken religious Christians wonder why their God doesn't come to their rescue. But Buddhists, for example, can afford to be philosophical about their suffering by simply blaming their karmas; and they try to find consolation in Buddha's teachings and strive for the attainment of nirvana."

Everybody liked the monk's words. He continued in the next moment, "I think the only hope for Christians could be what is written in chapters 21 and 22 of the Book of Revelation. At least there's still hope for them, according to these biblical verses."

"And also in Buddhism, as you've just said?"

"Yes. Just think of the former Christians who converted to Buddhism. I know many former Christians who got fed up with the factionalism and hypocrisy among several established Christian Churches and their thousands of years of bloody history."

"Why did you refer especially to the last two chapters of Revelation?"

"Because they relate to how the true believers – that is, those who truly believe in and thus strictly observe Jesus' teachings – will be rewarded. And a new heaven and new earth are also mentioned."

"Why not the rest of the chapters of the book?"

"The rest of the chapters are, of course, important, too, but I won't elaborate on them here. I'll keep my interpretations for myself alone."

"There are some references to the Whore of Babylon in Revelation. How would you interpret that?"

"I won't comment."

"I know that most Christians talk quite a lot about another number: 666 – the 'number of the Beast.' How do you interpret it? For them, this number seems very important."

"I won't comment."

"With your vast knowledge on Christianity, I'm wondering if you might not convert to Christianity someday?"

"Anything is possible, Jane. Or I may secretly already be a Christian … No, I'm just joking."

"Is it still possible for you to leave the monkhood?"

"That's absolutely up to me. Unlike what is commonly practiced in some Christian Churches, nobody and no institution can prevent me from doing that. And there's nothing that can punish me for doing so."

"Did you ever want to study Christian theology before you became a monk?"

"No, never. And I'm glad I didn't."

"Why? If you had, your opinions might be different."

"Yes, you're probably right, but most likely not in a positive way. If I had done that, I'd perhaps be locked up in a box, and as a result I wouldn't be able to see any theological issues from a critical, detached perspective."

Jane formed her next question to him. "What do you think of studying Christian theology in general, then?"

"I cannot answer your question precisely. So let me put it in this simple way: If you're already powerful enough to wage religious wars against each other in your God's name, what's the point of studying theology? According to the New Testament, he even sent his only son to this world to save human beings from self-destruction and eternal damnation."

The entire audience was highly delighted. The monk then continued, "Of course, the exception would be if you wanted to study it as a purely academic discipline. But even then, unlike any secular academic disciplines, I don't think you could ever become an expert or master of Judaic or Christian theology. The simple reason is that both theologies deal mainly with the relationships between the visible and invisible beings and prophecies – prophecies that have so far only been misinterpreted or misused and thus caused the loss of countless innocent people's lives for nothing."

"But I don't think you can forbid someone to study it."

"You're right. But if you can't even observe the Ten Commandments and the moral teachings of the Sermon on the Mount, how can you master the several thousand verses in the Bibles? It's simply impossible. We all know that nearly all the religious wars between Christians were not initiated by some illiterate fools but by those who regarded themselves as having mastered the Bibles. And since every Church strictly teaches theology based on its own fixed doctrine, how can you study it without bias?"

The monk's words made a deep impression on the audience.

"But Your Venerable, I don't think most Christians would want to be led by someone who hadn't studied theology."

"So far as I know, Jesus himself did not study theology."

A burst of hearty laughter broke out. The monk then continued, "Well, everybody will have to decide for himself how he prefers to practice his religious beliefs."

"But although Jesus did not study theology, he is said to have performed many miracles, and above all else, was resurrected. These are the reasons why Christians believe in his divinity."

"Very interesting points indeed, Jane. But I think it's also interesting to do some thinking about what those who claim to believe in him do themselves. I've never heard that any Christian in history has ever performed similar miracles, yet countless numbers of them have tortured and killed each other in his name."

The monk's words deeply moved everybody. He continued in the next few moments, "Another fact I find very disturbing is that several theologians have written books that contradict some or many parts of their mother Churches' existing doctrines, yet they remain in their Churches anyway. In my opinion, if you believe in the doctrine of a Church and join it, you must be able to obediently accept its doctrine."

"Do Christians still need clergymen, then?"

"Sure. They need somebody to lead worship and wedding and funeral services."

"Thank you very much. Despite your far-reaching knowledge of Christianity, you remain a devoted Buddhist monk. So may I ask you a very personal question? I'm afraid you might interpret it as an insult, though."

"Ask me any question you like. Even the worst insult can give you some sort of enlightenment, or can let you see things from a different perspective."

"Thank you very much. Do you perhaps remain a Buddhist partly because you enjoy your privileged position?"

To the great surprise of the audience, the monk burst into hearty laughter.

"Well, you may not believe it, but I've got no privileges, and I don't have any worldly possessions except what I need for my daily subsistence. I did inherit a small tea plantation from my adoptive parents, but I keep only what I need for my daily subsistence out of my plantation earnings. The rest I donate to needy people. When this war is over, you can visit me at my monastery and check it out yourself. There are, of course, some monks who are quite well off materially, but not me."

Many participants, including Jane, expressed their deep respect and admiration for the monk's kindheartedness. After a few moments, Jane said to him, "Thank you. Your Venerable, if I'm to tell you the truth, I'm curious what you think deep in your heart – I mean about Christianity and Buddhism."

"Jane, you can fully trust my words. There are no secrets inside my heart. I've openly spoken today about what is in my heart. I didn't want to influence your thoughts on religious concepts with my own ideas. Take your time and think carefully about what I've said today. I've talked about the negative and the positive sides of both religions. It's up to you to decide how you want to use these new ideas in your life."

"Thank you so much, Your Venerable. I have no doubt about your honesty and sincerity. As a gesture of my gratitude, I'd like to make a small donation to you, although you don't need it, as you've just said. Would you accept it?"

"Jane, a donation is not necessary, as I said. I'm enjoying our discussion tremendously. But if you want to, you may donate to the Maha Bodhi Society of Ceylon and the two orphanages I mentioned at the beginning of our conversation. The Maha Bodhi Society strictly uses donations for the spreading of Buddhist studies. They have a good reputation for their integrity. Well, Jane, I'll be very pleased to meet you again someday soon in peace. Do you have any more questions?"

"Thank you. Yes, I'll be looking forward to seeing you again someday in peace, Your Venerable. I don't think I have any more questions. I'm feeling much better now."

The monk thought for a short while and then said, to the surprise of Jane and the rest of the participants, "Jane, by the way, I think you've perhaps forgotten to ask me about one or two things that could be interesting to you: for instance, about the Buddhist version of hell. Or did you intentionally avoid this subject?"

Jane's face lit up. "Exactly. This was among the most important questions that I originally wanted to ask you, but I forgot about it. My father used to talk about it sometimes. Thank you so much for reminding me."

"Okay then. I'll tell you very briefly about it. It's called *Naraka* in Buddhist cosmology. But it's different from the Christian hell. There are eight cold Narakas and eight hot Narakas. Human souls are not sent to them as a divine punishment, but people are born into a Naraka due to their accumulated actions and karma. The length of a soul's stay in a Naraka is extremely long – hundreds of millions, even trillions, of earthly years."

"Do you believe in the Narakas? And are you afraid of being sent to or being born in any of them?"

"As I've never heard that someone has come back from any of these hells, I'm not interested in them. And since I've never caused someone to shed a single tear or drop of blood in my whole life, I don't need to be afraid of any divine judgment or bad karma. So I don't take them seriously. And such numbers are beyond my comprehension. Even 100 earthly years are already quite long enough for me – and perhaps for a large number of other people as well, especially if you have to struggle very hard for your daily survival, or if there's no peace around you."

"But couldn't you be punished for not taking such things seriously?"

"The marvelous thing about Buddhism, as I've repeatedly said, is that you have the right to be skeptical about Buddha's teachings. You don't need to fear divine judgment."

"If Buddha himself is no longer alive and there's no divine judgment, and there are no supernatural beings who monitor people's daily activities, who or what decides who is to be reborn and who should go to hell? In Christianity, as you know, angels are believed to monitor humans' activities round the clock, and they'll be judged accordingly by God on the day of the so-called Last Judgment, when the souls of the sinners will be eternally condemned to hell."

"I think we've already partly discussed your first question. But I'll repeat my answer again briefly in a slightly different way. That's a great mystery for me, too. But I wouldn't downplay the possibility of divine judgment before a religious audience because the fear of such a divine judgment might indeed have prevented a large number of Buddhists from committing evil deeds during the past 2,500 years. My answer to your second question is: I don't think I have the right to say how Christians should regard them. But if I were a Christian, I wouldn't care about them for the following reasons. The first reason is that all the existing Churches define them quite differently. The second reason is the leading members of those Churches themselves are not afraid of them. If they're really afraid of them, why don't they all belong to a single Church and worship together in harmony? The third reason is they even dared to wage ruthless religious wars against each other. Yet, they still expect to get eternal life. The fourth reason is they don't know about hell and the Last Judgment beyond what is written in the Bibles. The fifth reason is countless people around the world who don't have the concept of divine judgment are not necessarily more evil than those who always claim to be very much afraid of hell and the Last Judgment. There is, of course, one exception: If someone could show me a place called 'hell' and also a written document signed by either God or Jesus authorizing him to speak and act on their behalf, then I'd believe him and obey whatever he commanded. I know very well through the Bibles what kind of divine judgment could be awaiting me, so nobody needs to tell me or threaten me with his own self-conferred power. Above all else, the Bibles do not belong to any particular ethnic groups, organizations, institutions or persons. They belong to the whole of humankind."

The whole audience was deeply moved by the monk's ideas.

"Since you're from a British colony, do you think colonialism has at least some kind of positive side?"

"Instead of directly answering your question, let me put it in this way. I can tell you only about how I personally look at it. In general, I look at it from three perspectives: legal point of view, biblical point of view, and political point of view. If you use the legal systems that the colonialists practiced in their countries as the yardsticks, they breach their own legal codes. And from the biblical point of view, the colonialists' acts are one hundred percent against God's and Jesus' moral teachings since they (the colonialists) themselves are Christian. If they were not Christian, you could not use these biblical morals as yardsticks against them. But, then, if you look at it from a political point of view, the outcome would be completely different. For instance, well-established kingdoms and empires that lost their kingdoms and empires through colonialism would, without doubt, believe that it doesn't have any positive side for them at all. In contrast, for those who got their freedom or identity back and also for numerous ethnic peoples who got a chance to establish their existence in the form of independent states, colonialism could be a blessing in disguise. And it has brought to several primitive societies such crucial things for survival in modern times as civilization, writing, and knowledge in numerous fields. So for such people, too, it could be a blessing. But as there are different types of colonialism and colonies, I don't think you can generalize and put them all in a single category. We would therefore need to analyze case by case. But I must add that it's not my duty as a monk to pass judgment on this sensitive and complex subject. And no matter whether there's a positive side to it or not, we cannot reverse what has been happening."

"Your Venerable, you said colonialism is against God's and Jesus' moral teachings, but I think various Churches justify colonialism by arguing that it brought the concepts of salvation and eternal life to the people of their colonies."

"Sure. As there are always winners and losers in any system – be it religious or political or social or economic – how you judge a system will depend on whose point of view you look at it from – either the winners' or the losers'. We can endlessly debate this topic's pros and cons, but it's not our business to do so right now."

"Would the world situation today be much better if there were no colonialism?"

"I've never thought about that, but let me put it in this way just out of intellectual curiosity: without it, the world situation might not necessarily be better than today. But it'd most likely be completely different, and the winners and the losers as well. But I don't think anybody would benefit from such wild speculation. So it'll remain just an intellectual curiosity."

"Thank you. But could all these events have probably been pre-programmed or predestined as we've discussed earlier?"

"It'd be much easier for those who believe in the biblical God and the biblical version of creationism to accept this theory, but how would you persuade Buddhists, for instance, who don't believe in a creator God but only in their karmas, to accept this theory? The main gist of the problem here is what the purpose of our existence should be. Every individual perceives and defines it based on his religious belief or philosophical outlook. So I don't think we can make a single conclusion that can be accepted by all human beings."

"Thank you. What do you think of the so-called 'end of the world?' It's very much feared, especially by Christians. Aren't you afraid of it?"

"Why should I be afraid of it? For me personally, the world ends when I die. It's as simple as that."

Many people liked the idea. Then Jane commented: "Thank you. In the past, I've discussed many topics that we're discussing today with theologians and clergymen. They all expressed opinions that were based solely on the doctrinal lines of their specific Churches. So I was disappointed and frustrated every time. But from you, as a neutral source, I've learned quite a lot of new things about both Christianity and Buddhism. But aren't you afraid that there could be certain people who might want to make a new religion or a new theological doctrine out of what you've said about Christianity?"

"I don't think the ideas I've expressed today are really new or particularly unique. They must have been thought through by countless people in the past 2,000 years. However, powerful religious and political institutions and their leading personalities may have forcefully suppressed them – separately or in coordination – because such ideas could be dangerous for them. I don't think my ideas on Christianity deviate radically from the gist of existing concepts, especially those in the four Gospels – namely, love, peace (or peacefulness), compassion, humility and forgiveness. I really can't understand why so many people want to make the Bible – in this case I mean the four Gospels – so complicated for the ordinary man on the street to understand. Just look at the Ten Commandments, the Sermon of the Mount, and Matthew 23: 1-37! They're written in a straightforward form so that anyone who can barely read and write can easily understand them. And these verses are the real gist of the two Bibles!"

"But many Christians would find some of your opinions radically different from all the mainstream doctrines, I think."

"Which ones do you mean?"

"Your downplaying of the role of Satan in leading humans to commit evil deeds – and the danger of being punished in a place called 'hell,' for instance."

"Well, I can give you a very clear answer to this. I've never come across a single verse in which God or Jesus says, 'You shall wage war against Satan and his evil followers on our behalf by accusing each other of being Satan's followers, and then kill each other.' So far as I know, that is not the duty of us human beings, who don't even know whether God or Jesus exists or not, or if we have souls in the first place. If God and Jesus have to make war against Satan, they will do it in their own way. And I've never come across a single biblical verse that says God created the universe to destroy it all someday or to let human beings destroy each other in his name. God and Jesus only urged us to love each other and make peace, not war."

"Talking of Satan, may I ask you once again a very critical question in a slightly different way concerning his alleged temptations. Nearly every Christian believes that all the conducts that their Churches define as "sins" are his and his evil followers' works. So do you perhaps have some good ideas to reverse this perception?"

"Let me ask the leaders of those Churches a counter-question: If the commitment of some sexual acts, for instance, is defined as Satan's temptations, how would they explain the waging of ruthless religious wars by Christians against Christians, or colonialism, or the causing of or the neglecting of the suffering of countless innocent people? Couldn't such acts also be the work of Satan?"

"And what do you think about the idea of the Antichrist?"

241

"If the information I've collected so far is correct, it was one of the most commonly used mechanisms to justify the religious wars that have been waged by Christians against Christians – accusing each other of being either Antichrists or Satan incarnate. To my knowledge, the simple definition of 'Antichrist' is someone who does things that are the opposite of Jesus' moral teachings. The communists and the Muslims were - and still are - among those who have been branded Antichrists. And the fact that the members of every Church believe theirs to be the only true Church implies that they regard all other Churches as Antichrists, although they may not openly say that. Otherwise, they all would belong to a single Church. So if I were someone who wanted to accuse another person of being an Antichrist or Satan incarnate, I'd check first to see whether I myself was genuinely observing his teachings or not before I did so. The best solution to this problem would be to ask God and Jesus directly who the real Antichrists were, instead of blindly accusing each other of being Antichrists and killing each other. Or, if it's impossible to ask them (God and Jesus), they could or should at least let neutral, secular legal experts define the characteristics of an Antichrist.

"Most of the Christians who accuse communists and Muslims of being Antichrists seem to have forgotten that the members of some Churches made religious wars against each other long before Islam came into existence and the communist ideology appeared on the world scene. So one can assume with some certainty that if even all the Muslims and communists disappeared from this earth some day, Christians wouldn't stop accusing each other of being Antichrists. And certainly, people of all colonies could also regard the politicians in colonialist countries and their colonial troops as Antichrists, since the killing of humans is against God and Jesus' morals."

"Talking of communists, what do you think of communism?"

"I've never seriously thought about it. What I will say is this: If the wealthy and powerful Christians in the West had strictly observed Jesus' messages during the last 2,000 years, communism might never have come into existence in the first place."

Jane thought she had asked the monk everything she wanted to, but at the very last moment she realized that she must ask him some more questions.

"It seems we'll have to go on discussing things all night! No, I'm just joking. This is one of my very last questions, so please don't worry."

"That's okay, Jane. I'm enjoying expressing my opinions tremendously because I've never had quite this sort of opportunity to do so. And since I've no intention of putting all these ideas and opinions in a book myself, I'm glad to be able to share them with my fellow human beings through your book. So tell me what your question is."

"Thank you. Do you think there could be any discrimination in heaven against blacks or colored people?"

"I don't think so."

"Is that pure speculation?"

"My reasoning is simple. If Jesus really was a historical person and was crucified and then resurrected, and if the descriptions of the events that followed his resurrection in the Gospels are true, my sense of it can't be pure speculation. Look, his disciples didn't recognize him immediately after his resurrection, and there are countless interpretations of why that was so. Some say that they did not recognize him because of the distance between him and them. Some even say that God veiled their eyes so that they would not recognize him. It's written that Mary Magdalene, the only known woman disciple of Jesus and someone he loved very much, did not recognize him; she mistook him for the gardener. But my interpretation is that he did not retain his physical features. It's entirely different from the other existing theories. Had he still possessed at least some of his former features, like his voice, height, skin color, gestures, et cetera, his disciples surely would have recognized him regardless of the distance between them or the time of the day. In my opinion, the contradictions could ironically prove the authenticity of the resurrection story. If people had invented the stories about his resurrection, one would assume that all his disciples would have recognized him immediately.

Considering all these factors, I think that human souls lose all their earthly physical features. That means it's very likely that there's no discrimination in heaven in any form, including on the grounds of skin color – there will most likely be no different skin colors – or differences in physical features. And talking of the color of one's skin, one should not forget that all the biblical events took place in the Middle East, where colored people have been living for millennia."

"Thank you very much," Jane said. "Fascinating ideas indeed. But there seems to be a hierarchy in heaven among the angels. Doesn't that mean discrimination?"

"I'm sorry. My intellect is not great enough to give you an answer to this question."

Hearty laughter broke out.

"Your Venerable, did the concept of resurrection begin with Jesus?"

"No. There are a few resurrection stories in the Old Testament."

"Really? Where?"

"In 2 Kings, for example."

"Does Buddhism have this concept?"

"No."

"A couple of times, you used the phrase 'spiritual liberation.' What do you mean by that?"

"I very often use this term unconsciously; it simply means one's liberation from our obsession with things material. Most people are not content with the material world in which we're living, so they search for some spirituality, hoping that they might be able to continue to exist somewhere beyond this human world in some form. I think it's enough to use a single word: *spirituality*."

"And you quite often use the word 'salvation,' too. What exactly do you mean by that?"

"It's a term used by all Christians. So far as I know, this word's meaning is similar to 'deliverance' or 'redemption' – the 'saving of human beings from death through the death and resurrection of Jesus.'"

"Thank you. For the time being, I've got no more questions. Or am I forgetting something important?"

"You might also want to ask me how I perceive the so-called 'original sin,' I suppose, which is one of the most critical elements in Judaic and Christian theology."

Jane and many people in the audience were excited to hear the monk's words.

"Oh, yes! Thank you so much. I'd be so grateful if you could tell us how you interpret that."

"I haven't got much to say about it because it's too mysterious if you're to believe every word that describes it. If the story behind it were true, we might find its essence in predestination or determinism. If you compare it to the kinds of laws that we use on earth, it's simply too brutal – that is, countless generations of their offspring must pay the price of the sin or sins of just two persons, Adam and Eve. The question here is: Why didn't God appear *before* Adam committed the original sin and command him not to believe Satan's words? God must have known what Satan and Adam would do in advance, so why didn't He prevent it before it was too late? Some people might argue that God gave Adam – and all of us – the free will to choose between good and bad, and therefore he did not intervene. But the big problem is that not everybody knows what is good or what is bad. And even if they can differentiate between them, not everybody is capable of choosing the right one, depending on many conditions."

"Does that mean we have to accept everything meekly?"

"I think those who believe in Jesus have one solution: his teachings. Before his time, the Jews had to observe numerous laws and rituals and rites that were said to have been handed down directly by God through prophets. But Jesus replaced them with his moral teachings: love, peace or peacefulness, forgiveness, compassion, and so on. The most important question now is whether he was a historical person and was resurrected or not. If his resurrection is real, then he must be powerful enough to change the concept of original sin. In this context, I'd like to add one of my favorite passages from Matthew 22:34-40. A Pharisee expert in law asked Jesus which was the greatest commandment in the law; Jesus replied that the first and greatest commandment is to love God with one's heart and soul and mind. The second greatest commandment is to love one's neighbor as oneself. On another occasion, he preached, 'So in everything, do to others what you would have them do to you, for this sums up the law and the prophets.' Five centuries before Christ, Confucius had also set forth his own Golden Rule: 'Do not impose on others what you do not wish for yourself.' What disturbs me very much about original sin is that all Christians say Jesus freed them from its consequences with his blood on the cross at Calvary, but at the same time a large number of them use his name to justify their wrongdoing. And if I'm not wrong, several Churches still instill a feeling of guilt in their followers with it - that is, the original sin. I'm sorry, but I can say only this much on the subject, Jane."

"And Jesus' coming into this world and his death through the betrayal of Judas – this happened according to predestination or determinism as well?"

"I think one can only speculate."

"Some people believe that it happened according to God's will – that God intentionally led Judas to betray Jesus so that he could be killed and resurrected. But many others blame Satan for Judas' betrayal of his master."

"I think these are also pure speculations."

"You have a strong opinion of your own, though?"

"Yes, I do. In my opinion, those who wanted to arrest Jesus would not have needed someone to betray him by kissing him, since Jesus had a lot of followers. He was a well-known personality. I don't know about the Roman laws of 2,000 years ago, but I think it was probably just a formality. Even in our time, all legal systems require someone to file a lawsuit against somebody who has allegedly committed a crime. But whatever the case is – whether it happened because of Satan or God's will – Judas was fully rehabilitated anyway."

"How can you prove that?"

"There are various ways, but the most concrete proof is that his name was written along with Jesus' other disciples on the twelve foundations of the New Jerusalem in the Book of Revelation. If he had not been rehabilitated, his name would not be there."

"Thank you very much. What a pity it is that there are more and more Churches with conflicting doctrines, and, as a result, less and less love and harmony among Christians."

"Yes, it's deplorable, but since they cannot even agree on a definition of God, what can we do? I think there is a solution, though, to reverse that trend in case Jesus doesn't come back."

The monk's latest words aroused everybody's excitement and curiosity, and Jane asked him, "What's that, please?"

"A number of the world's best legal experts and historians should form a commission to examine the contents of the Bibles and world history thoroughly, to discover the legal system that God would use in heaven to decide the fate of human souls on Judgment Day. Those experts would also check the biblical prophecies that have been fulfilled, and determine when those that haven't yet been fulfilled will be in due course. Since the world doesn't belong to Christian theologians and clergymen alone, the whole of humankind's fate should not be put in their hands alone. Everybody knows that innumerable innocent people around the world have lost their lives due to misinterpretations of the Bibles."

"Thank you very much. A very radical idea indeed. Here's one of my very last questions: There are several different versions of the Bibles; so which ones should I use if I want to study Judaism and Christianity?"

"I don't care much about them. I'm only interested in the Ten Commandments, the Sermon on the Mount, the words that are said to have been personally spoken by Jesus, and the Book of Revelation. No matter how different the various Bibles are, at least on these few important episodes they're almost the same."

"I used to hear quite often that although God commands, for instance, that one must not kill, he commanded the Israelites to annihilate the entire populations of many ethnic groups on their way to the Promised Land – that is, Israel. So those who don't believe in Christianity argue that he is a merciless, warmongering God. What would you say about this?"

"Yes, I've quite often heard that opinion from non-Christians, and I think they're right to some extent – that is, if Jesus and his teachings had not been there. A big problem here is, God claimed to be the creator of the whole universe, so if you look at it from us human beings' point of view, it seems quite natural that he should feel he can do whatever he wants with his creations. But in my opinion, the fact that Jesus is said to have replaced God's laws with more humane ones is a big consolation. We only need to find out if Jesus really is a powerful heavenly being as he claims to be so."

"When I hear this, I get the impression that Christianity and Buddhism might need to be reformed radically."

"No, I wouldn't go that far. Regarding Buddhism, you should perhaps look into the doctrines of all the schools. You might find one that is acceptable to you. Who knows how many Buddhist monks and scholars or how many Christian theologians and clergymen think like me? There may be quite a lot. But should Christianity be radically reformed? No, I don't believe that its entirety can ever be reformed because there are so many powerful institutions and individuals who profit tremendously from it. What is more important for me personally is my own spiritual liberation. I think it's the same for many other people, too. And why should I burden myself with the idea of reforming both religions since I myself am still searching for answers to many mysteries? Everybody should decide for himself what is good and what is bad for him. For example, despite my many negative opinions on Christian theological issues, on a personal level I find Christianity much more lively and attractive than Buddhism. Before I became a monk, I often joined my Christian friends at various religious festivals. I enjoyed carol singings very much at Christmas times."

"Your Venerable, you said a couple of times that everybody should decide for himself how he prefers to practice his religious beliefs, and what is good and what is bad for him. But not everybody is capable of reading and understanding the Bibles fully. So how can they decide how best to practice their religious beliefs, and what is good or bad for them?"

"Well, I don't think you need to read the entirety of the Bibles to get eternal life. If you can genuinely observe the Ten Commandments and the moral teachings of the Sermon on the Mount, you'll surely get salvation. That's what I understand about Christianity."

"Thank you very much. What do you think of the miracles in the Bibles, especially the ones in the New Testament that are said to have been performed by Jesus? Do you believe in them?"

"I'd answer your question from an independent person's point of view who has not yet been influenced by any particular Christian doctrine. The first and greatest miracle is the appearance of a heavenly being called Jesus in human form. The second greatest miracle is his teachings. The third greatest miracle is that not a single prophet of his caliber and stature has appeared again in the world in the last 2,000 years – in either Judaic or Christian communities. The rest of the miracles that he is said to have performed in the four Gospels would be secondary for me."

"I'm sure you're aware of the existence of people who claim, by citing some verses from the four Gospels, that Jesus himself is God. What do you think about that?"

"There are indeed some verses in the Bibles that seem to imply that point strongly. One among them is Revelation 22:12-13. But despite all the verses that seem to contradict each other, you can be quite sure that – based on several other verses and factors – God and Jesus are two separate beings. I think the best way to prove this is the visions in the Book of Revelation, despite the two verses that I've just quoted."

"Can Jesus also give eternal life?"

"He claims to do so in many verses."

"We're now deep in the midst of a second world war. Everybody is talking about world peace. All the world's religions are praying for it. Do you think we will ever have worldwide peace?"

"No. I don't believe there will ever be world peace because there are so many potential conflicts in every corner of the world – political, racial, religious, economic, et cetera. Just look at the powerful nations around the world. They blame each other endlessly for what they have been doing to each other in the past and present, but none of them has ever thought of what they have done with the poor, small, helpless ethnic groups and nations. The world is full of hatred. And the arms industries earn great fortunes at the cost of the blood and tears of countless innocent people. Such powerful industrialists would never want to promote peace. And those who are supposed to bring love, harmony and peace are endlessly quarreling among themselves and sowing ill will among their followers. I doubt very much if God himself could bring global peace if he came down personally. So the only thing you can do is try to stay away from major conflict. That's my advice to you, Jane."

"Your Venerable, that's what we've been doing for at least four generations. I mean, all my close relatives. When you read my novel, you'll get to know more about us."

"I'm delighted to hear that. I really must learn more about your family. I'm dying to read your novel. Would you give me a copy of what you've written up to now? I'll be here for a few weeks."

"Okay. Up to now I've written eighteen chapters. What has happened since the disappearance of my daughter and our discussion today will become Chapter 19. At the beginning of our discussion, I thought Victoria would read the whole transcript back at the end of our talk and you would edit it on the spot, but since our time is running out I'll send you a copy, with Chapter 19, in a couple of days instead. Then you'll be able to edit it as you wish, Your Venerable."

"Oh, that'll be great. Thank you so much in advance, Jane."

"Your Venerable, could you give us a brief conclusion about both religions?"

"No, that's impossible. Even if I could, I wouldn't do it for many

250

reasons. But I hope I haven't sounded more like a politician or a Christian theologian than a Buddhist monk."

Everybody laughed heartily. The monk thought seriously now and asked Jane a question. "Jane, I thought you'd ask me this question, but you haven't. You and perhaps other participants in our discussion might want to know how I see the description of the Israelites as the 'Children of God' or the 'Chosen People.'"

All of them were surprised and highly pleased by the question, and begged him to tell them his opinion.

"Please don't expect a satisfactory answer to this great puzzle. I know that there are countless ideas on the subject. In my opinion, the strangest thing of all is, although they were chosen by God to be 'His Children' or the 'Chosen People,' he did not promise them eternal life. They suffered so much throughout their history because they disobeyed his laws. So in my opinion, if Jesus with his concepts of salvation and eternal life had not appeared, it'd almost be impossible to understand the real essence of being God's 'Chosen Children.'"

"You said there are several existing ideas. Could you perhaps tell me some?"

"Yes, I'll tell you one. A quite common thesis is that God wanted to use his relationship with the Jews as an example to all Gentiles, or non-Jews."

"Do you perhaps want to say that the Jews should accept Jesus as their long-awaited Messiah?"

"No, I wouldn't go that far. And I know that I don't have any right to tell them what to believe. It's just my intellectual curiosity. Look, as I said a while ago, the different branches of Judaism have their different definitions and interpretations. And their versions of the Messiah and the timing of his appearance are also not uniform."

The audience liked his explanation. The monk then got another idea and asked all the participants if anyone had any questions, or found his opinions disturbing, or were disappointed with them. Except for a woman who may have been in her seventies or early eighties, all the participants expressed their satisfaction and gratitude for his open-mindedness and liberal views. They all said his ideas enabled them to look at many aspects of Buddhism and Christianity from different perspectives.

The woman then stood up and said, "Your Venerable, may I ask you how you define God?"

"Well, as I have never seriously given it any thought, I don't know what the appropriate definition should be. I think it's everybody's private business to form a definition for himself. I, for example, bow before the statues of Buddha as a gesture of respect for him as a great philosopher and a great teacher, but not as a God."

"But there are many people who openly or indirectly act as if they *were* God."

"In my opinion, the word 'God' itself escapes a precise definition. I'll give you just a few examples. For many Buddhists who don't have any ideas about the Bibles – or the gist of Christianity, to be more precise - the biblical God is only a warmongering God because of the Christians' centuries of bloody history. In like manner, the Buddha means nothing for non-Buddhists who don't have any ideas about Buddhism. Therefore, you have no right to force somebody to accept your own definition of God. I think it's one's own business.

"And so far as I know, there's no universal law that forbids you to claim to be God. You'd only need to heed two things if you want to claim to be God: First, be careful that people wouldn't lock you up in a psychiatric hospital for life, and secondly, you'd have to find someone to worship you voluntarily. Several societies worldwide even worshipped the sun and the moon in ancient times."

The woman and all the other participants were highly satisfied with the monk's answers. Jane then asked him her next question.

"Your Venerable, here is the first of a few last questions."

Many participants seemed a little bit irritated. Jane herself felt a bit uneasy.

"Yes, please go ahead, Jane."

"May I know what your Sun Sign is?"

"I'm a typical Aquarius – why?"

"Perhaps that's why you're so liberal."

The audience was quite amused.

"And yours?"

"I'm a typical Cancer."

"When we meet again, let's talk about various kinds of astrology, okay?"

"I'm already excited about it. I'll try to visit you at your monastery as soon as possible. I'd like to have my Nadi leaf read by a well-known reader, too; I hope you can recommend me one."

"I'd be most happy to see you again at my place. I'm sure I can recommend someone with an excellent reputation."

"Oh, I'd love that. Is there anything you'd like to tell me – and perhaps the other people in this room as well - before we end our discussion, Your Venerable?"

"Thank you very much for asking me this question. I want to say that the universe is full of great mysteries that science cannot explain. No one knows how these mysteries and ancient pearls of wisdom arose. I think some people believe them to have come from dimensions that are beyond our imagination. Many people believe that humanity's problems could be solved through science, but right now we're witnessing how dangerous scientific developments can be. Each of us becomes human only once – except, of course, for the very few who know that they're reincarnations – so I wish you long-lasting peace of mind and success in your search for the meaning of your existence in this world and beyond."

"Thank you very much, Your Venerable..."

To the surprise and irritation of many participants, the monk unexpectedly asked her this question: "May I give you my very last message?"

Jane deeply appreciated it and asked him to go ahead.

"Thank you, Jane. It's a short and simple message: If the leaders of powerful Churches would allow their poverty-stricken followers to directly worship *the* God, who would forgive the wrongdoings of the rich and the powerful and give them eternal life, all the problems of

Christianity would automatically disappear overnight. It's as simple as that."

Everybody, especially Jane, was happy with the monk's message. "Thank you, Your Venerable. If you had said that at the early part of our discussion, we might not have needed a day-long discussion on this religion. I think your final message contains the gist of all the topics we were discussing on Christianity today. And I'd like to tell you all that my pain and sorrow have become remarkably much more bearable. Thank you so much once again, Your Venerable."

"I'm happy to hear that, Jane. I've got a strong feeling that you and your daughter will meet each other again someday - say when the war is over, but I cannot tell you how I got this feeling. She might have fled to a place where the war will not reach. So she'd most likely contact you again when she feels safe."

"Thank you, Your Venerable. Such kind words of yours mean a great deal for me."

Just before the discussion ended at half past eight, all the participants also thanked the monk, Matthew, Natalie, and the leading members of the Congress of Freethinkers that were among them. During the discussion, they had taken a one-hour break for lunch and two thirty-minute breaks for tea and cakes and snacks, which Natalie and a few of the women participants had served. Jane handed four checks to the monk: one for the Maha Bodhi Society of Ceylon, two for the two orphanages in Ceylon, and another one for the monk himself; he declined to accept this one. But Jane insisted that he take it because he could donate it to another organization if he wished, and she handed Matthew one for the Congress of Freethinkers, too. Each was for $10,000. She promised to donate more to the orphanages and the Bodhi Society of Ceylon in the future, if her novel became a success.

Matthew, his wife and a number of the participants accompanied Jane, Maria and Victoria to the main gate and bade them goodbye. Before they left, Matthew took Jane into a corner and asked her if she was really satisfied with the discussion. She said she was so happy, and that it would be a milestone in her life. In turn, she asked Matthew what he thought of the monk's words and which school he found to be his ideal school, since he had already studied the most well-known schools' doctrines. He replied that much of what the monk had said was new to him and his wife and that they would need a lot of time to digest it all. As to her second question, he told her that they had not found their ideal school yet.

On their way home, Jane asked Maria and Victoria what they thought about the discussion. Maria said that she was somewhat confused, for she had never been seriously interested in any religion. Still, she had nevertheless found it very absorbing. It was the same for Victoria. Jane and Victoria stayed one night with Maria and then headed home the next day at one p.m. by train.

Throughout their journey home, Jane pondered the discussion. When they arrived home, many of her relatives were waiting for them at her house, and she warmly greeted them. They were relieved to find that Jane was in a very relaxed mood. She told them briefly about her conversation with the monk.

The next day, she wrote a letter to Sister Hanna, in which she briefly described the day's events. She wrote that the discussion had given her a lot of food for thought and that she had already begun to look at many things from different perspectives. She promised Sister Hanna that she would send her the full text as soon as the transcript had been typed up.

Sister Hanna received the transcript three weeks later and replied to Jane the following week. She wrote that she found the discussion quite refreshing, and she was pleased that Jane had found peace of mind through her time with the monk. Jane sent the monk a copy of her novel, including Chapter 19, three days after the discussion. A few days later, she received a thank-you letter from him, remarking that he liked it very much and that the content needed no editing from his side; he further mentioned that he had become quite emotional a couple of times while reading it.

(4th November 1939. Jane's home. 2 p.m.)

Jane held an emergency meeting in the living room of her home. Present were a number of her cousins and also some unfamiliar faces. Altogether there were about thirty attendees. Jane started the discussion.

"As we all know, the preparations for our two orphanages are nearly finished, as we had sped them up since the Night of Broken Glass on 9th November last year. Every sign indicates that the Germans are on the warpath and are escalating military maneuvers in every direction. So it's just a matter of time before they come into our country. It could be tomorrow, the day after tomorrow, or in a few weeks. Therefore, we'll have to go on accelerating the rest of our preparations.

"I'd like to suggest that we wait a few more months to see how things develop, especially in neighboring countries. We'll have to meet together here much more often from now on, since the situation could change drastically from hour to hour. Do any of you have anything to add? If you don't, we'll discuss everything in more detail in the coming weeks."

The meeting went on for about two hours and was closed.

(24th December 1939 - Sunday)

On Christmas Eve, several people from the community in which Jane and her close relatives lived gathered together to celebrate Christmas at the Community House. It was quite large and could accommodate about one hundred. Even though battles were raging in several European countries, they made every effort to make the event as joyous as possible. Among the crowd were a Catholic priest and a Protestant pastor. After dinner, Jane stood up and made a short speech.

"Good evening, everybody. Merry Christmas to you all! Thank you so much for coming to celebrate Christmas with us. We're all aware of the conditions we're living under at the moment. New battles are being fought in several countries right now. It's a great pity that many people in these countries cannot celebrate this normally joyous event. We must appreciate how lucky we are. But nobody knows what our destiny will be in the coming days, weeks and months, and none of us knows whether we'll be able to celebrate together again here next year – or further into the future. History shows that major armed conflicts between nations last an average of five to seven years, so we'll have to prepare for the worst and hope for the best, not only for ourselves but for all humankind. So let's try to make this Christmas as joyous as possible. Since anything could happen at any moment, we'll not stay here until midnight and go to church as we usually do. And since we belong to different denominations, I've invited Father Martin and Pastor Adam to lead worship for us at about eleven o'clock. That will be the end of the evening. And if no major changes take place in our country in the next few days, I'd like to invite you all here once again to celebrate the New Year. May God bless us all!"

Young children sang three or four Christmas carols and the adults joined them at the end, also singing Christmas songs. They avoided discussing the latest battle news. At eleven o'clock, the evening's program ended and everybody quietly went home. As no significant dramatic events took place in Belgium between Christmas and 30th December, almost all the same people who had celebrated Christmas together gathered again at the same place and celebrated the New Year. Everyone tried to make the best of the situation. The celebration ended on 1st January 1940 at one a.m.

Chapter 20
(12 May 1940 – Sunday)

The German invasion of Luxembourg, Belgium, the Netherlands, and France began on 10th May 1940. At 5:30 in the morning, General Guderian's XIX Armored Corps (XIX Panzer Corps) crossed the border into Luxembourg. By 10 a.m., the leading German units had crossed the German and Belgium border. To the north, Army Group B was advancing with its tanks and airborne troops. The Allies believed the main thrust was coming from the north and sent their forces to counter it. Meanwhile, the real main thrust was making its way through the thick Ardennes Forest, filling the roads with vehicles. At the same time, overhead Luftwaffe fighters raced forward to keep back enemy reconnaissance or attack planes.

The shock waves of the invasion spread throughout Europe like wildfire. The invasion had long been expected for months, but nobody knew when it would take place. There were conflicting information and rumors for weeks before the invasion, as there were large German forces' movements along the German and Luxembourgish and German and Belgian borders. Paul and Jane wanted to move their main office in Florenville to St. Vith more than a year before, but they could not do so due to several unexpected obstacles. Thus, some months before the German invasion, they set up two temporary orphanages – one in Florenville, named Orphanage South or OS, and another one in St. Vith, named Orphanage North or ON; the distance between the two orphanages was one hundred kilometers. Jane personally supervised the OS with the assistance of some of her cousins from both sides of her family. The ON was put under Karin's supervision, also one of Jane's cousins. She, too, was assisted by some cousins and friends. Karin was in her mid-twenties.

A few months before the invasion, the staff and personnel at the two orphanages had started making lists of those from several surrounding communities who would need help the most in case of emergency. A few weeks before the invasion, several people on the lists had already been accommodated at both orphanages in some empty buildings that were used previously as storehouses. Among them were the elderly, handicapped, and orphans. In the early afternoon of 10th May, the orphanages began to be overcrowded as several people who were not on the lists also sought refuge there. Altogether, there were about three hundred at each orphanage, although they had initially planned to take only about one hundred and fifty at the most. Emergency meetings were held at four p.m. at both orphanages on the same day to discuss how best to cope with the unexpected chaos. So at the end of the meeting, they agreed to wait for a few more days before taking some practical steps; it was impossible to make some clear-cut arrangements on such short notice as the situation became more and more out of control. There were the sounds of heavy guns, airplanes, and bombs in every direction.

Near the town of Bazeilles in France, the engineers and assault infantry of the 10th Panzer Division gathered to prepare ninety-six rubber boats to cross the Meuse River at Wadelincourt. However, an artillery barrage from the French positions destroyed eighty-one of the boats. The attack plan had included an assault by the 69th Infantry Regiment, but the loss of so many boats meant only the 86th Infantry Regiment could conduct the crossing. Therefore, the 69th Infantry Regiment was kept in reserve to follow the 86th Infantry Regiment as reinforcements. And the German Army Medical Service unit, which was attached to the 69th Infantry Regiment, and the command post of the 10th Panzer Division, were temporarily set up close to the OS. The station had to treat a large number of wounded soldiers.

At about seven p.m. on the 12th, amid the distant sounds of gunfire, another sound, that of classical music played on a piano, suddenly floated from a large building in the middle of the OS. The piece was *Ballade No. 1 in G Minor, Op. 23*, one of Friedrich Chopin's best compositions. A group of German soldiers, mostly from the Army Medical Service, were quite surprised to hear the music amidst the battle and wondered who the piano player could be. They headed for the huge hall from which the music emanated. When they entered it, they saw Jane playing the piano in the center of the hall. Until recently, the hall was used as a storeroom for construction materials and equipment and agricultural produces. But just before the invasion, it was then urgently converted into an empty hall where those at the orphanage could mingle and relax together during the day and sleep at night. Now, it was full of German soldiers and those who sought temporary refuge there.

When the piano music first came out of the building, General Ferdinand Schaal, commander of the 10th Panzer Division, was at the medical station inspecting the wounded soldiers. He asked the medical officer in charge of the station about the orphanage, but the medical officer did not know much about it. Then the music stopped all of a sudden. The general was surprised and wanted to find out who the musician was and why she or he had suddenly stopped playing. So the general and the medical officer went to the hall in the company of the general's bodyguards. As they entered the hall, which was nearly full of German soldiers and those who sought temporary refuge, everyone stood up; fear was written on several people's faces. After having greeted the crowd friendly and signaled them to sit down, the general went to Jane, sitting at the piano. He extended his hand to her and introduced himself in fluent English. He could be in his late forties or early fifties, with a sympathetic look.

"Good evening, Ms. …? I'm Schaal, Ferdinand Schaal, the commander of the 10th Panzer Division."

Jane stood up and shook hands with the general and answered, "Good evening, Mr. General. I'm Jeanmart, Jane Jeanmart."

"Ms. Jeanmart, I'm happy to meet you. Was that you playing the piano? It's one of my favorite compositions. It's wonderful, and you play it very well. Why did you stop?"

"I'm also very pleased to meet you, Mr. General. Thank you very much for your kind compliment …"

She hesitated to answer the general's last question and worriedly turned her head toward a German officer standing nearby. The officer interrupted Jane before she could continue. "General, it was I who asked her to stop playing."

"Colonel, why did you do that?"

"I told Ms. Jeanmart that we've just come from our Poland campaign and we don't want to hear any music that was composed by a Polish composer. I asked her to play anything of Wagner's, our Führer's favorite composer, or any piece by other composers. But she said she had only recently learned to play and could play only Chopin."

The general understood the situation now. He took the colonel into a corner, and they talked in whispers for a few minutes. Nobody could hear what they were saying.

"Colonel, tell me your real reason for doing that, please."

"General, I was afraid that if we allow her to go on playing Chopin, we might have problems with the Party. That's why I stopped her. I think it could even be a provocation."

"I see. But I don't think we should do that. We're here illegally. And it's a neutral country. So I'll tell her to go on playing. If there's a problem with the Party, I'll take full responsibility."

"All right, General, but would you be kind enough to tell her what you're telling me now?"

"You're worried that I might retract my statement if I haven't made it public, and the Party wants to make trouble with us. Is that true?"

"I'm so sorry, General, but it is. It's not that I doubt your honesty. Please forgive me if I've offended you."

"Don't worry about that. I understand your concern."

The general and the colonel went back to Jane. "Ms. Jeanmart, I'm so sorry that this happened. This is Colonel Nehring, my Chief of Staff. He was worried that if we allow you to play Chopin's compositions, we might have problems with the Party. First of all, it's your country, and we're uninvited guests here. So go on playing as you like. I believe that all those present will be glad to hear such beautiful, soothing music amid all this sorrow and fear. It's a great relief for all of us."

Everybody was much relieved now. General Schaal then continued, "Ms. Jeanmart, it's really a great surprise to hear such music amid the fighting. Where did you get such an excellent idea?"

"Mr. General, it was my father's idea. My mother and father also did relief work during the last war. They discovered how beautiful music could take the fear, sorrow, and loneliness away in times of great danger. We've set up two centers – we call them orphanages; one is in the north, in St. Vith, and this is the other. We're taking care of orphans and elderly and sick people at our own cost – I mean cost to my family. We've got three pianos here and another three in the north. We'll teach the orphans and the adults in our care piano playing, and we'll have piano concerts now and then, for the residents and also for those in the neighboring communities."

"Oh, what wonderful people you are, Ms. Jeanmart. I admire and respect you for your noble deeds. I wish you all the best in your work. I look forward to listening to more beautiful pieces played by you under happier circumstances soon."

Jane thanked him profusely and started playing the piece again. It lasted for about ten minutes. The general was given a seat, and he enjoyed the music tremendously. When the music ended, there was loud applause, and the audience gave a standing ovation. Jane then invited the German soldiers to play. But except for Lieutenant Vogt, the medical officer, no one else was a pianist.

Lieutenant Vogt, who had accompanied the general from the medical station to the hall and stood for the whole time beside the general, said in a barely audible voice, in relatively good English, "I can play only a few classical pieces but not any of Chopin's. I'll play Pachelbel's *Canon in D Major* if you don't have any objection. But I'm just a beginner."

Jane gave him a sign to come to her. They shook hands, and Lieutenant Vogt introduced himself. He was much taller than Jane, serious-looking yet with intriguing traces of charm, and in his mid-twenties. He had blond hair and blue eyes. Everybody was excited. He started playing his selection, which lasted only some four minutes. He played rather well. Jane, who was standing opposite him, discreetly exchanged a few flirtatious glances with him while he was playing. The general keenly observed them both and, judging by their body language, sensed that they liked each other. As the music came to an end, there was a roar of applause and a standing ovation. The general stood up and signaled Lieutenant Vogt to follow him to a corner. General Schaal then spoke to him in a very low voice amid the distant sounds of big guns.

"Daniel, I didn't know that you played the piano so well. It's another of my favorite pieces, and I enjoyed it very much. I get the impression that you and Jane rather like each other. Both of you may want to talk a bit. I'll give you exactly fifty minutes, but after that, you'll have to go back to your station immediately. Okay?"

"Yes, General, thank you so much for your understanding. That's what I also sensed."

The general went back to Jane and said to her, quite loudly so that the audience could clearly hear it, "Ms. Jeanmart, I've told Lieutenant Vogt to give you some medical advice, in case you need it, for your orphanages. But he's got only fifty minutes. After that, he'll have to go back to his post. I wish you all the best, and may God bless you, Ms. Jeanmart. I look forward to meeting you again. Hopefully, soon and in peace. Goodbye!"

"That's very kind of you, Mr. General. As the doctors who will be in charge of this center could not arrive on time due to the sudden outbreak of the war, Lieutenant Vogt could be very helpful. Yes, let's hope to see each other again in happier times. Good luck and goodbye, Mr. General."

Many people heard their conversation. The general then ordered all the soldiers in the hall to leave within fifty minutes, for the situation could change at any moment. Jane asked one of her cousins to play some other Chopin compositions, and then she left the hall with the lieutenant. She started the dialogue while they were standing in the courtyard.

"Lieutenant Vogt, you played well. How long have you been playing the piano? That piece is one of my favorites, too."

"Thank you very much for the compliment. But you played much better than me, Ms. Jeanmart."

"What do you prefer to be called – Lieutenant or Doctor?"

"Call me by my first name, Daniel. And may I do the same, Jane?"

"Yes, do. Daniel, the fact that the general called you by your first name means you know each other rather well, I suppose."

"Yes, that's true. He had an accident in Poland, and I was responsible for his treatment. He's a very warm-hearted and understanding person. You know what he told me just now?"

"I'm very curious."

"He said, 'I get the impression that you and Jane like each other. I'll give you fifty minutes to be together.'"

"Really? Oh, how nice he is. Would you please briefly tell me about yourself?"

"Yes, he is. I'd worked for just over a year in a hospital when I was conscripted to serve in the Army Medical Service."

Both of them were very nervous now because their time was running out quickly. They often looked at their watches.

"I see, Daniel. Could you tell me a little bit more?"

Lieutenant Vogt was even more nervous now. Reluctantly, he said, "Jane, did you realize that I liked you the moment I saw you?"

"Yes, of course, I noticed it immediately, Daniel. You may also have noticed that I liked you too. If I'm to be honest, I've only ever had three or four boyfriends, including my husband, and I've never experienced what is called 'love at first sight.' I hope I haven't surprised and shocked you too much with my directness. But we're in a hopeless situation for romance, Daniel."

"Yes, you're right. Under these circumstances, we cannot afford to be romantic. Well, I'm from a small village called Olbersdorf near Zittau in the Görlitz district on the German-Czechoslovakian-Polish border. My father was a farmer. He and my younger sister died during the last war. Now I live with my mother. I'm twenty-six years old. Jane, if I asked you an intimate question, would you be angry? If you don't want to answer, it's all right. I'll understand."

She suddenly wondered if she should tell him about her brother who had died in the last war, too, but at the last moment, she decided she should not burden him with that sorrowful incident.

"No, I won't be angry. Please go ahead."

"You've just mentioned your husband. Are you still married? If not, I'd like to ask you a great favor."

For a moment, Jane did not know how to answer. But then she realized she might as well tell him her story.

"I'm recently divorced. I have two daughters. What kind of favor can I do for you?"

"Thank you so much. If you don't like what I tell you, please don't get angry, okay?"

She nodded her head in agreement.

"Thank you. If I don't survive this war, my family line will end. And we don't have any close relatives anymore. So ..."

He could not go on. He was extremely nervous.

"I think I understand what you're trying to say. Okay, let's go into that building over there. It's my office and also a storehouse."

As she listened to his story, she immediately deeply sympathized, for his life was quite similar to her own. She had also been feeling lonely since Thomas had left her. They disappeared into the building for about thirty minutes. When they came out, Daniel hurriedly wrote on a piece of paper and handed it to Jane, saying, "Jane, this is my Service Number and home address. We're not rich, but we've got some farms and a forest. A large part of them will belong to you and the child. I'll inform my mother about what happened between us just now. I'll always love you and miss you so much, Jane. May God bless you. Goodbye."

"Daniel, I'm not interested at all in worldly belongings. I've got more than I need. If I'm pregnant, I promise you that I'll try to find your mother, and the baby will get my love and protection in full. I'll always love and miss you, too. Take care. May God bless you. Goodbye!"

They embraced each other affectionately, but did not kiss, for some German soldiers and residents of the center were still in view. As they parted, they were fighting back their tears. Jane longingly watched him as he hurried back to the medical station. They waved to each other once again just before he disappeared into a tent. Tears streamed down her face. Nobody knew what had happened between them. During the night, there were the distant sounds of heavy guns and bombs in every direction. Jane could not sleep the whole night as she was thinking about him. Since Thomas left her, she felt that she would try not to get emotionally involved again with anyone and believed she would manage it. But what had happened between her and Lieutenant Vogt was so fast that she lost her self-control.

As she could not sleep, she got up at five o'clock and went to the medical station in the hope of saying goodbye to Daniel once more. But the station was no longer there. Someone at the site told her that all the Army Medical Service personnel had moved out together with the troops in the direction of Sedan in the early morning. Dejected, she went back to her home. She was heartbroken.

CHAPTER 21
(10th July 1940 – Wednesday)

It was a Wednesday, and the time was two p.m. The place was Jane's office at Orphanage South. Jane was holding a confidential meeting with Julie, Karin, and Alice.

"I'll start with the main point. You all remember the night of 12th May when we were in the hall playing the piano. General Schaal and his entourage and some medical personnel of the 69th Infantry Regiment of the 10th Panzer Division joined us. To cut a long story short, I secretly had a brief 'encounter' with the medical officer who played Pachelbel's *Canon*. Do you remember that the general told him quite loudly in front of everyone to give me any medical advice I might need? Well, we had a brief conversation first in the court-yard. I asked Lieutenant Vogt, the medical officer, to tell me briefly about himself and his family background, and when I heard his story, I deeply sympathized with him immediately. A few minutes later, he very nervously asked me for a favor, so I agreed to fulfill his wishes ..."

Julie interrupted her. "I watched both of you from the very begin-ning and sensed right away that you were interested in each other, Jane."

"Oh, you were observing us, Julie? That's what the general told the officer later in a corner after the officer had finished playing the piano."

Julie continued, "Karin and Alice were also watching you. We also noticed how the general signaled him into the corner and whispered with him for a few minutes. What did the general tell the officer? I'm curious to hear."

"The general said, 'I've been discreetly observing you both, and I sense that you like each other, so you may want to talk together. I'll give you fifty minutes. After that, you must go back to your station."

Julie, Karin, and Alice could not believe their ears. Alice said, "What a wonderful man! It's unbelievable – a German general with a human heart. The general and the medical officer must know each other well, I suppose. Did the officer tell you about his relationship with the general?"

"He told me that the general knew him well because the general had had an accident in Poland and he was responsible for the general's treatment. He said the general was an amiable and understanding person."

Alice then spoke. "Now I see why the general told him in front of everyone to give you any medical advice you might need – so that people wouldn't suspect you of having an intimate moment together."

They all giggled. Jane agreed with Alice. Then Karin asked, "Did you really like each other, or was it just a physical attraction – to put it diplomatically? In my eyes, he's quite a good-looking man, but not handsome. He's got a strong and attractive body. Hasn't he?"

Jane thought seriously for a moment and answered, "I must admit that it was love at first sight for me. I've only had three or four boyfriends in the past, excluding John and Thomas, and I've never experienced the same feelings as when I first saw him. He told me it was the same for him, too. I'm missing him a lot."

Karin spoke. "Jane, I'm not a psychologist, but it could be that since John and Thomas and Jennifer left you, you're feeling so lonely deep in your heart that you simply need someone to love and someone who loves you."

"Karin, I think that's a possibility. As you all know, I was afraid to get emotionally attached again, and I thought I was doing quite well. A couple of handsome men had approached me recently, and I could prevent myself from falling in love with them. But this time, it seems I was not strong enough."

Karin spoke again. "Jane, excuse me, but let's get directly to the most exciting part: What happened next? And what did he tell you about himself?"

"He told me that his father was a simple farmer and that his father and his sister – Daniel's younger sister – died during the last war. He now lives with his mother, and if he doesn't survive this war, his family line will end. So he very politely and shyly asked me if I'd bear a child for him."

"That means …"

"Yes, it seems that I've conceived. I have missed periods. So I need your advice on how to handle this sensitive matter, as it will become visible soon."

They all thought for a while, and then Alice asked Jane, "Do you have other details about him? Like his unit, his Service Number – every soldier has one. Or his home address and so on?"

"As we came out of the building, he jotted all that information on a piece of paper. But I can't find the paper; I've been searching for it for several days."

"That's not good. But you might find it again someday. Don't worry about it too much. Even if you don't find it, it should not be difficult to trace him since he was not just an ordinary soldier. Did he tell you where he came from, at least?"

"I think a village called Olbersdorf or something like that, on the German-Polish-Czechoslovakian border."

"I think that's good enough, Jane. Write it down while you remember it."

"Thank you, Alice, for your advice. I will."

Alice then continued, "You cannot admit the truth. If you did that, you'd become an outcast for sleeping with the enemy. We can make up a story that you made the baby with a former boyfriend who was killed in action, or you were raped."

Jane thought for a long moment and then gave her opinion. "That would only be a short-term solution. In that case, it would have to be someone who did not have any family; otherwise, his relatives might want to know about my relationship with him and claim the baby someday. And I wouldn't want to say that I had been raped. If I did that, the situation could get even more complicated."

Julie made a suggestion. "No, let's keep it as simple as possible. You simply say that the baby is from a former boyfriend from somewhere in France. It's no use worrying too much about the future now.

We'll monitor any rumors that might spread among the residents when your belly can no longer be hidden. You will surely have to make it public at some point."

All of them agreed. Before the meeting ended, Alice had a few extra thoughts and asked, "Jane, if the baby's father survives the war and comes back to claim the child, what will you do?"

"Alice, I don't want to think about it yet. But I would let him have his son or daughter. I don't want to have any emotional bonds anymore – either with the living or the dead."

"But if he doesn't survive the war …?"

"Then I'll keep the baby as my own."

Julie wanted to say something but was visibly reluctant to speak out. Jane noticed and asked her to go ahead.

"Jane, I've been weighing for a long time if I should confide in you about something. A handful of the residents have been murmuring behind your back …"

"Tell me, please. I don't mind."

"When you were in the storage building with him, someone else was also there, and he saw you making love in a standing position. According to this story, you both came three times during your brief encounter."

Jane was shocked and nervous.

"Oh really? Did someone see us? Yes, perhaps I moaned a bit too loud. Under such extremely unusual circumstances, I couldn't control myself. Well, we're only human. How serious do you think this rumor is? Could it have consequences for the orphanages or me?"

Karin and Alice said they were not aware of the rumor.

Julie went on, "I heard the rumor only a few days ago. So it's no wonder that you haven't heard. I heard it from Lara. It was Martin who saw you. He told me that it had been shared among only three or four people and would not spread further. The other persons are Miriam and Sandra. They all are brilliant, kind, and quiet persons. We can trust them."

Julie continued, "Jane, everybody here loves and respects you. You've become a mama to all the children and a daughter or sister to the older residents. So I'm sure they will all understand. I don't see why this rumor should have negative repercussions. I suggest you pretend that you're not aware of it."

Jane concluded the meeting. They all agreed with Julie's analysis.

"I thank you all; your words have made me feel much better."

It was early September, and Jane's belly was now quite conspicuous. Since she had openly said that she was with a former boyfriend of hers from France, no one at the orphanages paid undue attention to her pregnancy. The rumor had not spread among the residents. Only Sarah once asked her mother in front of many of the residents who the father was. Jane calmly replied that his name was Philippe and that he could not come to them just now because of the war.

On 1st February 1941, Jane gave birth to a healthy son. It was a great, joyous event for all the orphanages' residents and Jane's relatives and friends. Several people made a special celebration two days later. Sarah was so happy to have a brother, whom Jane named Victor, after her late brother. In the middle of July, the Orphanage South and the main office were moved to St. Vith and the Orphanage North, which was initially set up in St. Vith until then, was moved to Waimes, twenty kilometers away.

The two centers started giving the orphans and some adult residents piano lessons back in August 1940. Since then, piano competitions for the residents and people from the neighboring communities were held on every Christmas and New Year. These were the only joyous events that those people had during the war. Classical music's soothing sound served as a hugely effective means to alleviate fear, melancholy, boredom, and loneliness. Many people thus got their first piano lessons at the orphanages.

CHAPTER 22
(1st April 1944 – Saturday)

An emergency meeting was held in Jane's office at Orphanage North at one p.m. All the leading staff of Orphanage South also participated - Jane, Karin, Veronika, Silvia, Alice, Julie, Adam, Alexander, and Simon. Since January, Jane headed the ON with Veronika, Silvia, and Adam as her assistants. Karin, who was in charge of ON until the end of December 1943, was now responsible for Orphanage South. Alice, Julie, and Alexander assisted her. Because of the seriousness of the topic they had to discuss, they held the meeting in utmost secrecy. Jane started the discussion.

"Around eight p.m. the day before yesterday, a stranger came here and handed me this letter without telling me who he was, where he got it, or who the sender was. He immediately disappeared into the darkness of the night after he had handed it to me. It's so strange. The letter says there are rumors that we've been hiding some fifty Jews in two or three secret places since late 1942 or early 1943 when the Jews from this country were rounded up and deported, and that if it's true, we should get rid of any trace of their presence within one week from now, before a search is made. I've been thinking about it since I got the letter and have concluded that there must be an informer or informers among our staff. And even stranger, though, is that there must be someone high up in the German Military Administration who sympathizes with us; otherwise, we wouldn't have been warned of the danger. The stranger emphasized that no one else must know of this letter's existence and that it must be destroyed immediately. What's your opinion?"

Karin began, "I agree with your assessment, Jane. The word 'rumors' is very interesting. It's possible that the person who sent us this letter did not want to make the accusation concrete. So what shall we do?"

Jane spoke up again. "We've always thought that our stringent regulations, which many people have even seen as heartless, would save us from any suspicion of harboring Jews. On many occasions, we refused to give even temporary shelter to Jews as they were being rounded up and deported to Poland and elsewhere. In this way, we protected our orphanages from being searched or controlled by the military or the Gestapo. But now we have no option: We move them to the other safe places as fast as possible and meticulously get rid of any trace of human presence where they are now. Then we'll have to wait and see what happens in the coming days and weeks. We must be extremely cautious about the selection of those who will do the job."

They went on to discuss in detail how the task should be carried out and by whom.

Exactly seven days later – on 8th April, a Saturday, at nine p.m. – many military vehicles pulled up in a small village not far from ON and in another village in the neighborhood of OS. Those in the cars were Gestapo personnel, some in uniform, some in civilian clothing. They entered a couple of large old houses and did thorough searches for any trace of occupancy. But they did not find what they were looking for. Disappointed, they disappeared from the scenes. There was a great relief at the two orphanages.

Then, on 15th April, a Gestapo officer and sundry Gestapo personnel came to the ON and handed Jane a letter. It was about nine a.m. Jane was shocked at the sight of the Gestapo officer and his entourage but tried to hide it from them. She opened the letter and read it. There were only a few lines, politely requesting her to appear at the temporary office of the Gestapo. The officer offered her a ride and said that they would bring her back, but she refused the offer and asked the officer if she could travel in her car and bring two friends with her. The officer agreed. Jane talked frantically with Veronika and Silvia, and they all prepared to go with the Gestapo men. Everyone at the orphanage was anxious. After driving for about thirty kilometers, they arrived at an unmarked building on the outskirts of Eupin. The Gestapo officer politely ushered them into a spacious waiting room and told them that they would be called in an hour.

They nervously counted the minutes. Almost exactly an hour after their arrival, a man who appeared to be around the same age as Jane came into the room and introduced himself to the three women, very politely and friendly.

"Good morning, Ms. Jeanmart. I'm glad to see you. I am Becker, the chief of this region. Thank you very much for coming here; I must apologize for any inconvenience that we may have caused you."

He shook hands with Silvia and Veronika, then said to Jane, "Ms. Jeanmart, would you please come with me? It'll be just an informal chat between you and me, and it won't last more than half an hour." He then turned to Silvia and Veronika, who looked worried, and said to them in a low voice, "Please don't worry at all. Although we have a rather negative image in some quarters, several of us still have human hearts."

On hearing Becker's words, the two women felt much relieved. He and Jane disappeared farther into the building. They entered a spacious room, and he offered her a seat and coffee. Jane was unsure about what would happen next and was quite nervous. They were alone. He took a seat beside her and said in a low voice, "Ms. Jeanmart, since we don't have much time, I'll tell you what I have to tell you as briefly as possible. You may be perplexed about what has been happening in the last few days. I sent you the letter warning you to remove the fugitive Jews from their hiding places. You personally and your two orphanages have been under surveillance since we entered your country. Still, we haven't had any reason to suspect that you're working for any organizations hostile to us until now. And we know that you've had two children with two German men. So you have special consideration from our side ..."

Jane was confused. "Yes, when I got the warning letter, I immediately thought that someone with authority must sympathize with us, but I couldn't work out who it might be. So I thought that it could even be a trap. I've very often wondered whether those in your department are human beings at all. You have a rather negative image, too; you're rather feared and disliked by many people in this region.

Thank you so much for your help, however…but why did you do it, Mr. Becker?"

"Before I tell you why, I'd like to explain briefly about the functionaries in my department. We roughly fall into three types. Those of the first type are fanatical zealots who act like zombies and abuse their power; those of the second type are simple obedient bureaucrats who perform their duties. Like me, those of the last type try to perform our duties but as humanely as possible. I'm feared and disliked, perhaps partly because of my department's negative image. Actually, I've always tried to do my duties as humanely as possible. Now let me tell you why I'm doing what I'm doing. Your husband, Thomas, and I are best friends since our childhood. I owe him a lot for the position I now hold and some other things. So when I came here two years ago, he asked me to protect you and your relatives as far as I could."

"I see. Where is he now, and how is he? I've never tried to contact him to find out what he's doing and what happened to him since he joined the Party and got an important job in Dr. Goebbels' ministry."

"He reached a very high position in the Psychological Warfare Department. But then his Jewish girlfriend was discovered in her hideout. She was alone. She had no parents, no sisters, brothers, no relatives, and only a few friends. And just before she was to be sent to a concentration camp, she asked Thomas to intervene. So he did everything to save her, but he failed. From that time on, he became depressed and began to drink heavily. The Party branded him a potential traitor, and he was removed from his position and given a menial clerk's job in the ministry. He even tried to commit suicide once by hanging himself but was found before it was too late. He is, I'm afraid, a broken man now."

"Oh, I'm so sorry to hear all this. We were in love for just a short time before we got married. When we were studying, we dated a couple of times, too, but I didn't know him intimately enough. I know he was quite popular with many beautiful women."

"Since the race law was introduced in 1935, everybody in his family and friend circles discouraged him from continuing the relationship."

"He always told me when we were in love that he and his parents were not interested at all in politics and especially the National Socialist ideology. So when he suddenly joined the Party and got employment in Dr. Goebbels' ministry, it was a great shock for me, my family, my relatives, and all our friends."

"What he told you was true. It was a surprise for me, too. I, on the other hand, joined the Party quite early on, out of political conviction."

"How much did he tell you about our love life and family life, Mr. Becker?"

"Quite often, he told me how charming and good-hearted you are, for instance. And I find you very charming indeed, Ms. Jeanmart. It's a pity the circumstances didn't allow you to lead a long and happy life together. I'm sure he loved and still loves you."

"Did he tell you all this, Mr. Becker? Thank you very much for your kind remarks. If it isn't too personal, may I ask you a question?"

"You may ask me any question you want – the only exception is about my job."

"Thank you very much. You must have a family of your own, too, I suppose."

"Yes, I had a family … But my wife and our two teenage children were killed in Hamburg on 18th March when the British air force dropped thousands of tons of bombs."

Mr. Becker said this without any trace of emotion.

"I'm so sorry to hear that, Mr. Becker …"

Mr. Becker interrupted her. "Thank you very much for your sympathy, Ms. Jeanmart, but since we've also been causing misery to so many people, it'd not be reasonable to pity ourselves too much."

Jane was much surprised by Mr. Becker's candid words. He looked at the clock on the wall and continued, "My wife and I were childhood sweethearts. I never had another woman in my life. Our children were brilliant and lovely. We had great dreams for our future. But when they died, I began to look at the world and my existence from a completely different perspective. Since then, I began to develop more compassion for people who are suffering injustice. Deep in my heart, I'm a broken man, and I've even begun to drink. Although I don't show it to the outside world."

"I'm so sorry to hear that, Mr. Becker. It's so sad. You're still quite young –"

Jane began to sympathize with Thomas and Mr. Becker. Mr. Becker glanced up at the clock on the wall again and interrupted her. "Thank you very much for your kind words, Ms. Jeanmart, but I'm sorry to say that I'll have to come quickly to the conclusion since I've got plenty of other work to do. I can talk with you without the presence of anyone else from my department only because your records are clean, and you've had children with two German men; otherwise, at least one other person from my department would have had to be present. Do you want to know what I mean by your records being clean? It means that neither you nor anyone at the orphanages does any intelligence work for our enemies – that's the Allied forces. But I'll have to write a report on our meeting. I'll say that I asked you how much you know about the Allied forces' movements and that you've agreed to inform us if there are any unusual Allied activities in the region. You'll have to sign, but only for formality's sake. You've got nothing to worry about, so long as my assistant Mr. Schneider and I are responsible for this region. Is this okay with you?"

"Yes, I understand all that you've told me to some extent, but what will you say that I told you about the Allied forces' movements?"

"I'll write that you don't know any more than anybody else knows. Is that okay?"

"That's okay, and I agree to comply. Thank you so much for your help, Mr. Becker. By the way, I'd like to make a brief statement concerning our clean record. From the moment we decided to set up the orphanages, we were very strict about recruiting our staff. Judging by what you've told me, we've succeeded in that regard. But one thing

I'm curious about is that you seem to be very well-informed about the orphanages."

"Yes – the residents of your orphanages are rather well-fed, despite the stringent rationing of food in the country. Most of the population has lost weight as a result – could it be that you have some secret food sources? We also know that you've got a few million francs at your disposal for your relief work. My colleagues and I decided to ignore this information – but yes, we are well-informed. Oh, there's no informer among your staff or residents; we have our ways of collecting information. I'll give you an example. We know that some weeks before the first batch of Jews were due to be rounded up, you got information about it in advance. You made a list of those who had no family, and then you bribed certain police personnel to delete their names from the police lists so that their absence went unnoticed. But you don't need to suspect anyone who works for you, and you don't need to be alarmed."

"What else do you know about me, Mr. Becker?"

"We know quite a lot. I'll tell you one thing: We know you've got German blood on both sides of your family, going back a few generations."

"Really? Even I didn't know that."

"Ms. Jeanmart, you've nothing to worry about as long as Mr. Schneider and I are in charge of this region, and even if we move on, you won't need to be concerned. Avoid working with our enemies in any way. That's all. As I've told you, your record is clean. When and if either Mr. Schneider or I have to move, I'll inform you. Oh, and by the way, have you received any news of Lieutenant Vogt lately?"

"No. When the 10th Panzer Division came back from Russia and was on its way to France two years ago, I made inquiries about him but was told that he was either killed in action or had gone missing in the Battle of Moscow or the Winter Campaign. That's all that I know."

"I'm very sorry to hear that, Ms. Jeanmart. I wish you and your daughters, your son, and your orphanages all the best. Take care and goodbye!"

"Thank you so much for everything you've done for me, Mr. Becker. I'm much relieved. But I'm still very curious how you knew about the Jews in our care."

"I'm sorry, Ms. Jeanmart, I cannot betray our sources. Just don't worry about it. The Jews in your care are either too old or too sick to be deported anyway."

At that moment, the phone rang, and Mr. Becker snatched it up. He spoke with a male voice on the phone for a minute or two, and then he turned to Jane.

"Ms. Jeanmart, someone who is supposed to be here now will arrive some twenty minutes late. So if you want to say something more, we have about ten or fifteen minutes."

"I'm glad, Mr. Becker. Would you please convey my gratitude to Thomas for his concern for our safety if you speak with him? Please tell him also that our daughter is fine and very bright. And please tell him that I'm so sorry about the loss of his girlfriend and his present precarious situation."

"I'll do that, Ms. Jeanmart. By the way, don't you hate him – and us all – as nearly the whole world hates us for what we're doing? I promise you that I won't harm you if you tell the truth."

"Mr. Becker, what benefit would I reap from hating you? I'm just a woman, and I'm not interested in politics, ideology, or religion. As Buddhist philosophy influences me deeply, I'm very philosophical about everything that is happening to me and the world as a whole."

"But I'm sure you've got some opinion of us deep in your heart."

"Sure I have. But the brutality we're witnessing today is unexceptional. Countless people have committed similar acts against countless other people since the beginning of history. Just look at the unfortunate people in the numerous colonies of the white colonial powers! Excuse me if I'm a bit too preachy, Mr. Becker."

"You're right, Ms. Jeanmart … I'm sorry, but we'll have to end our meeting now. It's good to know you, Ms. Jeanmart."

Mr. Becker thought for a moment and then shot the last question at Jane. "Ms. Jeanmart, could you imagine living with Thomas again as husband and wife when the war is over?"

"Mr. Becker, if I'm to be honest, I've never thought about it since he left us. As I've gone through so many sorrowful experiences in my life, I don't think about the future at all. Emotional attachments are too painful for me. According to what you told me, he seems to be a new person, and I sympathize with him for what happened to him. I might have second thoughts sometime in the future. Who knows? The human mind is a fickle thing. By the way, would you please convey my heartfelt greetings to Mr. Schneider? I know I might not have a chance to meet him."

"I'll do that, Ms. Jeanmart."

Mr. Becker told Jane that if she trusted him with what he planned to write in the report, she could sign a blank sheet of paper, and he would write the report later; but if she was doubtful about his honesty, he could quickly prepare the report now so that she could sign it right away. Jane said that she trusted him and signed a blank sheet and prepared to leave. Mr. Becker promised to inform her if any important news could affect her and the orphanages. He accompanied her back to the two waiting women. Seeing Jane's relaxed mood, Veronika and Silvia felt immediately much better. They warmly shook hands with Mr. Becker and headed back to the orphanage. Silvia and Veronika could hardly wait to hear what Jane had to tell them about the meeting. She assured them that she would tell them in detail when they got home. None of them uttered a single word throughout the journey. Jane was thinking of Thomas.

When they got back to the orphanage, they found all the residents anxiously waiting for them. Jane told them that everything was okay and that they didn't need to worry at all. Everybody was much relieved.

CHAPTER 23
(1st November 1944 – Wednesday)

Under the command of General Courtney Hodges, the First U.S. Army captured large areas of Belgium in early September 1944 and moved into the Ardennes. The U.S. troops were spread very thinly from south of Liege through the Ardennes and into Luxembourg. Between September and mid-December, the Ardennes Forest was used by the Americans to rest battle-fatigued troops. However, during this time, what was later to be known as the most prolonged battle on German ground was fiercely fought in the Hürtgen Forest on the Belgian-German border.

Jane was in the dimly lit living room of her house at ON, sitting and reading a letter on a sofa by the fireplace. It was eight p.m. The sounds of big guns could be heard from a great distance while someone was playing Chopin's *Nocturne No. 1 in B Flat Minor, Op.9 No. 1* on the piano in a neighboring room. About thirty children in the orphanage's care were silently tiptoeing toward the place where Jane was sitting.

Jane noticed their presence and turned her head in their direction and told them to come in. About half the children were small girls and the rest boys, ranging from about seven to fifteen. They knelt on the carpet around Jane. When they were at her side, they realized that she was silently crying. They spontaneously asked her, as if they had orchestrated it, "Why are you crying, Mama?"

The children's unexpected question suddenly caused her to sob a bit louder. So she could not reply immediately. After a few moments, she tried to explain to them – with great effort – in a choked voice why she was crying. "Well, my children, before I tell you why I'm crying, I'd like to tell you why your question, 'Why are you crying, Mama?' made me so sad. My daughter used to ask me that question whenever she saw me crying. I very often cried whenever she and my husband were badly treated simply because of the color of their skin."

The children's eyes also began to swell with tears. Jane continued again with effort, "It's a long, long story. I'm writing an autobiographical novel; when I finish it, you'll be able to read it. Then you'll see more clearly why your question makes me so sad."

A young girl of about twelve apologized on behalf of them all. "We're so sorry to have asked you that question, Mama. We didn't know about its history. And you're writing a novel, Mama? Very interesting. When will you finish it? I'd love to read it."

"It's all right, my children. If I were you, I'd have done the same thing. I've written up to Chapter 22. It's still the first draft – but any of you who are twelve or older may read it. There are some intimate scenes in it that younger ones should not read yet..."

A little girl who might be six or seven years old interrupted her. "Mama, what is its title?"

"Oh, I haven't decided yet. I might not decide until just before it's published. But I'm thinking about three titles: *Why Are You Crying, Mama?* That's the question that my daughter asked me the most. And the other thing she said often was: *Whenever I See You Crying, I Am So Sad, Mama.* The third possibility is simply *Jane.* Which do you like most?"

Nearly all of them said that all the titles were equally good. Jane continued, "Now, I'll tell you why I'm crying. A few hours ago, someone from a neighboring village brought me a letter from one of my best friends, a Catholic nun by the name of Sister Hanna. She lost her childhood boyfriend in a car accident just before they were to be married. They had planned to get married and have a big family. His sudden death so saddened her that she decided to become a nun to meet with him again in heaven one day. From the moment I began to read her letter, I could not stop crying. Some or all of you may know about parts of my personal life. But if there's anyone who had not yet heard about it, I'll tell you very briefly. About sixteen years ago, on Christmas Eve, I was saved from a fatal motor car accident by a black American named John in Bastogne. If he had not been there, I'd most likely have been killed on the spot or handicapped for my whole life. Then we got married, and we had a daughter, called Jennifer. She was so intelligent and full of kindness. Then, four years ago – it was on 1st October 1940 – she disappeared without a trace. She was just about eleven years old. I didn't know if she was alive or if she had taken her own life. She left a farewell letter for me. John, my husband, had left for America in late 1937 to see his ailing mother. He wanted to come back, but the situation worldwide, especially here in Europe, was rapidly deteriorating, and then the war broke out that and he could not come back. As it was no longer possible for us to be together, we got divorced, and after the divorce, I got married again to a former boyfriend of mine, and Sarah was born. And just before the war started, my husband – Sarah's father - was forced to work for the German government. Since that time, we have not been able to live together. John joined the U.S. Army. I haven't heard from him since the beginning of the war. He could even be somewhere in Europe now.

"So I've had two daughters now and a son with three different men. The person who brought me the letter told me that Sister Hanna has been lying in a coma at the Sisters' House at Bütgenbach for a few months. It's a village some eight kilometers from here. The sisters found the letter mixed up with a lot of her other papers. Until a few months ago, we still had contacted now and then, and we wanted to meet. Sister Hanna said she would try to drop by if she came to this neighborhood, but as you know, I was always so busy with my work that I didn't have the time to arrange it. I'll read her letter out so that you will know a little more."

The children were attentively listening to what she was telling them. Their eyes were full of tears.

My dearest Jane,

I don't know whether you'll ever see this letter or not. And if you do, I don't know whether it'll make you happy or sad – most probably both at the same time. I'll write down very briefly what could be most important for you. Jennifer is still alive and doing well. Before she disappeared, she came to me for help. She said she could not go on living in this world anymore. 'If you can't help me find a safe place to live, I'll take my own life.' At first, I did not believe that she would dare do it, but please don't ask me what happened next.

So, as I didn't have any other choice, I arranged that she stay with a maternal aunt of mine at small village on the French-Spanish border. But I heard that they had moved to Madrid two months ago. So I haven't got their new address yet. I'll give it to you when I know it, or you can get it from my mother. My aunt is full of love and kindness. She and her husband are childless. I heard from my aunt lately that Jennifer feels well and that her boyfriend, Carlos, a Guatemalan, whom she met in Paris during her holiday with her aunt and cousins some years ago, visited her quite often. Both of them are now in high school, and they always get excellent grades. They're planning to study medicine so that they will be able to help the poor in his native country who cannot afford medical care.

Please forgive me for hiding the truth from you for so long. I know how much you were and still are suffering from the loss of her. But she was suffering more than all of us. And I have been doubly suffering on behalf of both of you, too. I know you don't believe in God, Jane, but please pray to Him on my behalf to forgive me for what I've done. I hope He'll be merciful enough to do so. I intentionally haven't dated this letter. I keep it with me all the time wherever I am so that if something unpredictable happens to me, those who find it will be able to get it to you. I love you and will always love you, Jane. I haven't given up my hope that you'll also find God someday and that we'll meet each other again at His place.

May God bless you always, Jane!

Your loving friend, Hanna

P.S. By the way, I read the latest chapter – Chapter 22 – of your novel in August or September, and I liked it very much. I think Why Are You Crying, Mama? *could be most suitable for its title. Just a feeling. But the other two are also equally good. And Jane, I asked my parents to tell you about Jennifer's whereabouts in case I was not in a situation to tell you myself. So, even in case you don't get this letter, they'll inform you anyway.*

As she read the letter, Jane had to pause a couple of times because she could not stop crying. The children were also silently weeping. There was a long pause. Then a little girl's question broke the long silence.

"Mama, Sister Hanna wrote that you don't believe in God. Is that true, and if it's true, why is that?"

Everybody turned to the little girl, who might have been six or seven years old. Jane lovingly took her to her side and, in a tender voice, said, "I was a very religious person when I was young. Then I began to wonder why He created human beings with different colored skins if He truly loves us all as the Bible says. According to the Bible, He is powerful enough to create everything in the universe. But recently, I've found some reasons to believe in Him again. When we have more time, I'll tell you more about it, okay?"

"Yes, Mama. Thank you very much."

In fact, it was not true. She just wanted to comfort the little girl and the other children who might also have been disappointed. Then she went on, "My children, I'll go to see Sister Hanna early tomorrow morning at about six or seven o'clock with my cousin Silvia. The Germans and the Americans most likely control the road to the Sisters' House so that it could be extremely dangerous. During my absence, Veronika and Adam will take care of you. We'll try to come back as soon as possible because a battle could break out at any moment. But don't worry about us. God will protect us all, and everything will be all right. Now, please go to bed and sleep well. Good night children."

"Good night, Mama. We love you so much. We'll pray for your safe return."

"I also love you all. I'll pray for you, too."

As soon as the children left the room, Jane had an urgent discussion with her cousins Silvia, Veronika, and Adam. They made some arrangements. What they did not know was that the children also had an urgent discussion among themselves and agreed upon something.

Jane and Silvia woke up the next morning at half-past five, and, having finished their ablutions in the bathroom, they grabbed their rucksacks and went out. To their great surprise, nearly all the children, the elderly, and the staff were waiting for them in the courtyard.

Several children greeted them and simultaneously said, "Good morning, Mama. We've decided to come with you."

"Good morning, my children. Oh no! I appreciate the thought, but the journey is too dangerous."

Carmen, who was the oldest girl among them, spoke on behalf of the rest. "No, Mama, we're coming with you. If the soldiers see you with us, they might not start fighting each other until we're safely back here. Look, we've even prepared a white flag. We'll wave it while we march."

Jane could not control her tears - tears of gratitude. She again tried to persuade the children not to come with her, but without success. Then she said that only those who were older than ten could go with them because it would be a 16-kilometer march and too dangerous. So those who could go with her were twenty. Jane suggested that they should have their breakfast as fast as possible and take some lunch provisions on the way. Jane, Silvia and the children started marching at about half-past seven. A big boy held the stick with the white flag and marched ahead of the group. The snow was heavily falling and covered the whole landscape along the way. Until they had traveled about two kilometers, all was quiet. Then, as they approached a hidden military checkpoint, a soldier's loud voice ordered them to stop.

"Stop! Who are you, and where are you going?"

They stopped, and Jane shouted back, "We're from Waimes, and we're going to a village called Bütgenbach to see a dying nun there. It's about six kilometers from here."

The soldier shouted back, "Please come forward!"

The group slowly moved forward and stopped at the checkpoint, where there were many American soldiers. One came out and spoke with Jane.

"Good morning, madam. Don't you know that the situation right now is extremely dangerous? Why do you want to risk your lives?"

"Yes, we know how dangerous the situation is. But my best friend, Sister Hanna, is lying in a coma and could die at any moment. I want to see her before it's too late. The village is only about six kilometers from here."

"Who are these children?"

"They are orphans from the orphanage I run. When they knew that my sister Silvia and I were going to see Sister Hanna, they insisted on coming with us in the hope that the opposing forces might not start fighting until we're safely back home."

The soldier went back inside the bunker and discussed Jane's words with an officer. The officer spoke with someone on the telephone. Then he came out and talked to Jane.

"I understand. But please try to come back as soon as possible – within four or five hours if possible, because fighting could break out at any time. We know that the Germans are not far from here. If you meet any Germans on the way, please don't tell them that we're here. Okay? May God bless you."

Jane thanked the officer and soldiers, and the group marched on. When they had marched for about another three kilometers, near the village of Oberweywertz, someone in a very loud voice ordered them to stop, in German.

"Stop where you are now!"

The man who gave them the order seemed to be an officer, and he told them to approach the checkpoint. Then, he greeted them, "Good morning. Who are you, and where are you going?"

Jane replied politely, "I'm the head of the orphanage in Waimes. These children are orphans. We're going to make a short visit to Sister Hanna, a Catholic nun, who is lying in bed in a coma. She's in the next village, Bütgenbach."

The soldier shook his head in bewilderment. "Ma'am, don't you know how dangerous this area right now is? Is it important enough to risk your life and the lives of these children? Why didn't you and the other woman go alone? It's irresponsible of you to travel with these children." He went on, "Have you seen any Americans on your way?"

"No, we saw none. I'm fully aware of the danger, but Sister Hanna is my best friend, and she may die at any moment. In fact, we wanted to come alone, but the children insisted on coming with us, saying that if the Americans and the Germans saw us, they wouldn't fight each other until we're safely back."

The Germans laughed. "We're a hundred percent sure that they are not very far from here."

A little girl who could barely be ten years old spoke up to the surprise and shock of one and all. "Yes, it's true. The Americans warned us not to tell you."

All the German soldiers laughed heartily. "That's okay. If I were in your position, I also would do as you're doing now. Well, I cannot permit you to proceed myself; I'll have to report to my superiors first."

He went inside the bunker and discussed the situation with a couple of officers. Then they spoke with someone on the telephone. Meanwhile, the older boys and girls tried to scold the little girl who spoke out, but Jane persuaded them not to do. After about ten minutes, the officer came out and talked to Jane.

"I'm sorry to tell you that my superiors won't let you proceed because it'd be too dangerous for you. This war has cost thousands of lives every day, so we cannot postpone the fighting just for the sake of a handful of people like you. Therefore, please go home as quickly as possible."

The news struck the group like a clap of thunder. Some of the children even began to cry. Jane pleaded with the officer in a trembling voice, almost crying.

"Please let us proceed. We've come such a long way. Bütgenbach is only two or three kilometers from here. As soon as we've seen her, we'll come back. Please!"

Before the officer could say anything, a small, tearful girl spoke up again to everybody in the group's great shock. "Jane had a charming daughter with a Negro from America, and she disappeared recently. Sister Hanna was very kind to Jane and her daughter. So Jane wants to see Sister Hanna before she dies."

Jane and the other children were shocked and filled with fear. The officer threw a quick glance at Jane and said in a stern tone, "Aha, Jane was married to a Negro, and they have a daughter? Very interesting."

Carmen, the girl who had spoken on the children's behalf before they began their march, quickly intervened. She communicated with the officer in fluent German. "No, officer. Jane's husband was not an African-American. He was a South American from Argentina with very thick lips and curly hair like a typical black, so his friends gave him the nickname 'Negro'."

The officer replied, "I see. But he might have black blood. What's his name?"

"Gustavo Schumann from Buenos Aires. He's of German descent."

The officer then spoke to Carmen in broken Spanish. She replied rather well in the same tongue.

"How do you know about all this?"

"Jane told me about him. My mother was also an Argentinian. My father was a German soldier who fought bravely on your side before he was killed in action at the outbreak of this war. My mother also died not long ago. Since then, I've sought refuge in Frau Jeanmart's two orphanages together with the other children here. Since we're at the orphanage, she has become our surrogate mother, and we lovingly call her Mama."

"I see. My name is Christian. May I know yours?"

"Carmen. Carmen Wagner."

The officer thought for a short moment and then went back inside the bunker and consulted with his fellow officers again. Meanwhile, the girls and boys tried again to scold the young girl, but Jane persuaded them again not to do it; although Jane did not explicitly say her reason, everybody knew that the two girls were mentally disabled. The officer seemed to be satisfied with Carmen's explanation.

She was very friendly and calm and never raised her voice when she spoke with him. While they were talking, the incessant sounds of big guns and airplanes could be heard in the distance. Then, to the great relief of the whole group, he permitted them to proceed. The officer said to Carmen, "Carmen, we're making an exception in your case, but under four conditions: first, you must not tell the Americans about our presence; second, if fighting breaks out in this area, we won't take any responsibility for your safety; third, we cannot postpone the fighting for you; and four, you must come back within five hours. If you can accept these four conditions, you may go ahead."

Greatly relieved, Jane said, "That's all right with us. Thank you so much. May God bless you all."

Everybody in the group breathed a sigh of relief. After they had moved away from the soldiers, Jane thanked Carmen lavishly.

"Oh Carmen, you saved us. I didn't know that you spoke Spanish so fluently or that you've lived in Argentina."

"I'm glad I had the chance to do it. My mother was indeed Argentinian, and we lived in Argentina until I was ten years old. The rest I just made up."

"Carmen, you're so quick-witted. I admire you. Thank you so much. We owe you a great deal."

"Mama, you don't need to thank me. I also owe you a great deal. The German soldiers must have sympathized with us because of the well-known German surnames."

They soon arrived at the village and the Sisters' House. They were guided to it by a young woman whom they met on the edge of the village. It was a large, two-story building in which ten Sisters were living. Two residents of the House heartily greeted the group at the House entrance and led it to the room where Sister Hanna lay. Jane spoke her name and went straight to her bed. She took Sister Hanna's hands and embraced her tenderly.

"Hanna, it's me, Jane. Can you hear me?"

Sister Hanna nodded her head ever so slightly and tears were streaming down her face. Jane and the children were also weeping.

"Hanna, Hanna, I received your letter yesterday evening. I cried for the whole night. I don't know how to repay you for what you've done for us. I forgive you completely, and I know God will also forgive you. I've come here with twenty children from the orphanage in Waimes. The German soldiers ordered us to come back as quickly as possible, so we must leave in a few minutes. A battle could break out at any moment; my responsibility for these children is too heavy. In fact, my cousin sister Silvia and I wanted to come alone, but the children wanted to accompany us in the hope that the Americans and the Germans might not start fighting each other until we're safely back at the orphanage. I could not persuade them not to come with us. But I'll come back to see you as soon as possible, okay? I'm sure you'll fully recover soon. The doctors are full of hope. So please don't give up, okay? When we meet again, we'll talk about everything – everything. And I'll begin my search for Jennifer in the meantime, wherever she is. She'll also be happy to see you again. Hanna, time is running out for us. We must go. I am beginning to believe in God again now. We all will live together eternally at his place someday. I'll tell you about it in detail when you recover and we meet again, okay? I love you, and I thank you so much for everything you've done for us, Hanna. I'll miss you so much. Goodbye, and may God bless us all."

Hanna nodded her head slightly again in agreement. Her tears kept flowing. Jane, Silvia, and all the children were still silently weeping. As they were leaving, Jane spoke with the other nine sisters, inquiring about the cause of Hanna's coma. They told her that the doctors suspected it to be either food poisoning or low blood sugar, although a thorough medical check-up was impossible at the moment. Jane also learned that Sister Hanna's parents, sister, and brother had visited her a few days before and had temporarily moved to a village nearby so that they could see her more often without risking their lives. It was a great relief for Jane.

On their return journey, nobody uttered a single word. The Germans were no longer there, and the Americans did not ask them any questions. So when they safely arrived back at the orphanage in the early afternoon, all the residents were much relieved. They all had been anxiously waiting for the group's return.

Some weeks after Jane visited Sister Hanna, two of the nuns from the Sisters' House came to the ON one late afternoon. They were visibly sad. The children discussed this among themselves and decided that the two nuns must have come to deliver a tragic message to Jane. They discreetly approached Jane's living room. The door was ajar, and Jane was holding a letter in her right hand and crying. She sensed the presence of the children, and without turning toward them, she invited them in. "Did you see the two nuns who were here?"

"Yes, we saw them arrive and then leave again soon after."

"Yes, they came here to inform me about Sister Hanna's death, and they brought me all her correspondence with Jennifer. Sister Hanna and Jennifer had regular correspondence, which I didn't know about."

The children also began to sob.

"We're so sad to hear about that, Mama. But please stop crying."

As Jane continued to sob, a girl of about ten tried to comfort her. "Mama, instead of crying, why aren't you glad for Sister Hanna? She must be so happy now to see her boyfriend again, and God."

Everybody, including Jane, turned to the small girl, and Jane said, "Oh Julia, you're absolutely right. Yes, I'll stop crying. Thank you so much for pointing this out." She went on, "But you know, Julia, I'm so sad that I could not thank her properly for taking care of Jennifer."

Julia spoke again. "Mama, why is that? You'll be able to thank her endlessly when you see her again in heaven."

Jane told Julia to come closer, and she tenderly embraced the girl. "Thank you so much, Julia, for your wise words. You're right. From now on, I'll look forward to the day when we meet again in heaven. Then, as you point out, I'll thank her endlessly."

Everybody slowly overcame their sorrow. Jane was so relieved that she had managed to see Sister Hanna before she died. She told the children that what happened between her receipt of Sister Hanna's letter and her conversation with Julia would become Chapter 23 of her novel. In the next few days, Jane was seriously thinking about her behavior during the last few days and realized that she could not yet master her emotions, for which she was regretful and sad.

CHAPTER 24
(10th December 1944 – Sunday)

The place was Orphanage North in Waimes at one p.m. The snow was falling heavily, and the cold was biting. A platoon of about thirty black American GIs from the 333rd Field Artillery Battalion was passing by Waimes on its way to Andler, where the Americans had been stationed since October. The platoon was under the command of a white officer, as usual. The soldiers took temporary shelter in a large, empty brick house close to the ON compound. Five of them came to the ON compound and asked for Jane. Several residents came out and greeted them warmly. Jane was in her office when she was told that the GIs wanted to see her. She came out immediately. Then she heard someone calling her name.

"Hi Jane, it's me – John."

John, who was standing at a distance of only ten meters from her office building, ran to her and took her in his arms. She was utterly taken aback, totally bewildered. Before she could say anything, John said, "Jane, it's me. Don't you recognize me?"

"John, I didn't recognize you with your long beard. And you look so tired."

Many of the residents of the orphanage who stood nearby were surprised and baffled by the scene. Then Jane freed herself from John's embrace and looked deeply into his eyes.

"John, why didn't you inform me about your coming here?"

"I couldn't. It's not allowed. It was impossible."

"Where have you come from, and where are you heading?"

"I can't tell you. The only thing I can tell you is that we're only passing through. We're taking a rest at this place for only a few hours."

"You'll be staying here for only a few hours?"

"Yes, we're only pausing briefly. We're so tired from our long march that we're taking a little shelter in a nearby building. Actually, I should not have been allowed to come here, but I asked my commander to do me a very special favor to let me see you. He allowed me only three hours' leave because the situation could change at any moment."

"I see. You must all be hungry, too."

"Yes, we're living on minimal rations."

"How many of you are there?"

"About thirty."

Jane asked those in charge of food and drinks at the orphanage to quickly feed the soldiers. Within an hour, the soldiers were fed. As soon as he had finished eating, John said to Jane, "Honey, if you're alone, could we meet alone somewhere?"

"Yes, I'm alone. Let's go to my office. Won't the others object?"

"I've already told them briefly about our story. So it's okay."

They disappeared into Jane's office. Inside, they immediately started embracing and passionately kissing each other. They then sat down on a sofa, holding hands.

"Jane, I can't describe how happy I am to see you again."

"It's the same for me, John. John, since our time is so limited, we'll have to make some decisions. Tell me what we should do in this hour or two, John."

"Since you informed me about Jennifer's disappearance, I've been thinking of her constantly. Did you get any more information about her?"

"You remember Sister Hanna? I met her a month ago, and she told me that Jennifer went to Spain to stay with one of Hanna's aunts and that she has a boyfriend from Guatemala, who loves her very much. They both got excellent grades in school, and they want to study medicine so that they will be able to help the poor people of his country who cannot afford medical care."

"Oh, what good news. I'm so glad to hear that. I'll write a letter to Jennifer before we leave. Where is Sister Hanna now, and how is she getting on?"

Jane almost told him that she had died, but then decided not to, because John would be so sad.

"Oh, she's living in the convent, and she's well. I'll tell her when we meet again about our extraordinary reunion today."

John added, "Give her my heartfelt greetings and my deepest gratitude to her for taking care of Jennifer. Will you contact Jennifer when the war is over?"

"She knows where her mother and father are, so I'll wait on her decision. If she doesn't contact me, I don't think I'll take the initiative because it's so painful when you lose a loved one, and we've experienced that enough in our lives. But when the war is over, we can discuss it again, and in more detail."

"Darling, I fully understand your feelings, and I completely agree about Jennifer. Jane, by the way, I couldn't tell you where we're heading in the presence of so many people. I can tell you now, though, that we've come from Mont Rigi, and we're heading for Andler, where other American troops have been stationed since October this year. Today we marched about fourteen kilometers to get here, and we want to spend one night at a village called Crope, about four kilometers away from here. Tomorrow, we'll have to march another twenty kilometers to reach Andler. Have you heard about any German troop movements in that vicinity in the last few days?"

"I've heard nothing. But it's no secret that many are hiding in that area."

"Yes, we do know that a large number of German troops are in the region. Couldn't you be in danger if they later find out that we took a rest here, and you fed us?"

"That's possible, but I don't care. If the Germans themselves were here, we'd have to do the same thing for them. John, how did you find out that I was here?"

"It was easy. A couple of people told me some days ago. Everybody in the whole region knows about your family's humanitarian works and what you're doing for the orphans, the sick, and the elderly. I admire and respect you and your parents for this noble work. And by the way, some people also told me that Auntie Elizabeth and

Uncle David were killed in an aerial bombing not far from here a few days ago. Is that true?"

"Yes, that's true. We buried them in our family cemetery. They were exceptional people. They appreciated deeply every little favor we did for them. Nearly all the women and girls cried, including me. They all loved them. It's a great relief for us that they died on the spot without suffering."

"I was so sad when I heard the news. But they led fulfilled lives, thanks to you and your family."

Looking at the insignia on John's sleeves, Jane inquired, "John, what's your rank now? I don't have much idea about military ranks."

"We fought several battles on our way here after landing in continental Europe. I'll tell you briefly about how we got here. We landed on 12th February last year. My battalion subsequently served in Normandy, Brittany, participated in the siege of Brest, and fought our way across northern France before we arrived in the Ardennes sector as part of the artillery of the U.S. VIII Corps. I lost several good comrades along the way. But yes, my superiors were so impressed by my performance that I was promoted to Staff Sergeant recently. I'm now second in charge of a platoon. As usual, my commander is white with African combat units, but my relationship with him is excellent."

"Congratulations, John. I'm so glad to hear that. I'm very proud of you. Jennifer will be, too. Did you find a partner before you were sent to the European frontline?"

"Yes, I found one. She's a very nice woman, but she's still just a girlfriend; she'll never replace you, Jane. I still love and miss you so much. And how about you?"

"I'm happy that you've found someone to love. My parents told me that they had informed you about my life with Thomas and what happened to him ..."

"Yes, they told me. I'm so sorry about that. Your daughter must be charming, like you."

"Yes, she is lovely. And very intelligent, too, like Jennifer. She has often told me that she would like to meet you."

"Really? I'm glad to hear that. Where is she now?"

"She's at Orphanage South right now."

"Does she know what her father is doing?"

"No, she's still too young to know about such things."

"How's his situation? Has he ever tried to contact you?"

"No. And I have no idea."

Jane did not want to tell John what had happened to Thomas in detail, not least because their time together was too limited.

"Did you find somebody else to start a new life with after Thomas left you?"

Suddenly Jane wondered whether she should tell him about her brief encounter with Lieutenant Vogt and their child. But she realized that it would only sadden him and make him suffer for no reason.

"I didn't try to find someone else. Emotional attachment to someone is so painful for me that I've decided to live alone."

"Soon after Jennifer's disappearance four years ago, you wrote to me about what you discussed with the Buddhist monk. How's your opinion on religion now, Jane?"

"I still think about that discussion all the time, but I haven't yet come to a clear-cut conclusion. I'm still torn between Buddhism and Christianity. I deeply admire the Buddhists for their ability to accept what they call 'the laws of nature.' At the same time, I began to think very seriously about the concept of eternal life. And one of the most important changes in my thinking about the biblical God is that I don't lay all the blame on Him anymore."

"I'm glad to hear that, honey. I still dream about eternal togetherness with you in God's kingdom someday."

"John, I promise to let you know if and when I feel that I can fully accept him."

"Thank you. Honey, would you do me a favor?"

"Just tell me. I'll do anything for you, John."

"Thank you very much. Well, I slept with my girlfriend a couple of times in the last few days before I was sent here, and she may be pregnant. So if I don't survive the war, would you please look after her and the child, and my sister and my mother as well? I heard some weeks ago that my father had passed away peacefully in bed."

Jane's eyes were suddenly filled with tears; with effort, she spoke in a broken voice. "I'm so sorry to hear that, John. I always wanted to meet them. But what happened to him happened according to the laws of nature. All living things will leave this world sooner or later."

"Jane, my dad had a fulfilled life thanks to you and your parents. One of his strongest wishes was to see you and Jennifer and thank you in person, although he and my mother and sister were so happy that I'd met such a special person like you. I'm not that sad because I believe I'll meet him again in heaven. My only wish, for the time being, is to survive the war. But at the same time, I'm quite ready to die for my country."

"John, you'll survive. When the war is over, you and your family can move here, and we'll be a close-knit circle, okay? We will all be very happy then. Let's not give up hope."

"Thank you very much, Jane, for inspiring me to be optimistic again. But if I don't survive …?"

"Please don't worry, John. I'll look after them as if they were my own mother, sisters, and children."

"I believe you, Jane. Thank you so much. They won't need material help since, with the money I took with me when I went back to the States and what I withdrew while I was there, they can survive for their whole lives. They're very frugal. But psychologically, your care will be precious to them."

"I give you my promise to take care of them all – if necessary, financially as well."

John then took a worried glance at his watch, and they realized that they had only one hour left.

"Honey, may I ask you for another favor?"

"Just tell me, John."

"Do you remember the first and the last time we made love?"

"Yes, very vividly. I will never forget those moments."

"Could we try to repeat that experience now?"

"But John, you're going to get married to your girlfriend soon, aren't you?"

"No. We agreed that we'd get married when and if she got pregnant and when and if I came back from the war."

"Okay … just a moment, please. I'll check if I still have one or two condoms."

She got up and looked in the chest of drawers near her bed. She found two condoms, and she asked him to come in. They quickly undressed, and she warned him not to make a sound. In about twenty minutes, they both came twice.

"Honey, it's as blissful as it was the first and the last time. I'll never forget this."

"John, I feel exactly the same."

They dressed hurriedly and took their seats as before. John then took a blank sheet of paper from Jane's desk and wrote a few lines to Jennifer.

My dearest Darling,

I'm back in this place and have met with your mama. When she told me that you're alive and doing well, I didn't know how to express my happiness. And I'm so glad to know that you and your boyfriend always get excellent grades and that both of you are going to study medicine so that you'll be able to do good things for the poor in his country. As I suggested in my letters before you left, I've become a soldier and have proved my courage on the battlefield since we landed here in Europe more than a year ago. Since I don't have time to write a long letter, I'll write only this much for now. We'll surely meet again when the war is over. You'll be very proud to be the daughter of a war hero. Take care. May God bless us all. I'm thinking of you all the time.

Your beloved Papa.

As John handed it to Jane, her asked her, "Honey, by the way, are you still writing your novel?"

"Yes. I've written twenty-three chapters, and what happened today will be Chapter 24."

"That's very good. I'm happy to hear it. I'm dying to read it. As soon as the war is over, I will."

In the next moment, they hurriedly left the office building and headed toward the soldiers and the residents who were gathering in the courtyard. John introduced Jane to Lieutenant Robert, the platoon commander. He seemed to be the same age as or even younger than John and with a smiling face.

"Jane, this is Lieutenant Robert, our commander, and this is my former wife, Jane."

As they shook hands, Lt. Robert said, "Hello Jane, it's a great pleasure for me to meet you. John has told me many times about how beautiful, generous, and kindhearted you are and about your marriage. And he let me read your autobiographical novel; I think the last chapter in it was the 18th. When I read your novel, and whenever he told me about the beautiful and heartbreaking parts of your lives, I could not control my tears. I'm sure it'll become a bestseller, Jane. It's a great pity that we cannot stay here a bit longer. But I'm sure we'll meet again soon. John is a great soldier. He's so brave that he will surely become a hero and an officer soon. And I'm also confident that his heroic performance in this war will surely help eliminate the prejudices that we have toward
blacks."

"I'm also glad to meet you, Robert, and thank you very much for your kind comments. I've written up to chapter 23, and what is happening today will become Chapter 24."

"Really? I wish I could read what you've written up to now."

"I'm glad to hear that. You can read it when the war is over. By the way, would it be too personal if I ask you a bit about yourself, Robert?"

"No, it's okay. My life also is rather similar to yours – quite heartbreaking. My girlfriend is black, a childhood friend, and she was pregnant when I left her. I got news recently that she gave birth to a healthy girl. That's all I know. She also has to struggle against all kinds of hardship her whole life. So I can fully understand your situation and feelings, Jane."

At hearing Robert's words, Jane's eyes suddenly began to swell with tears, and she said with a choked voice, "Oh, please forgive me for asking you this stupid question. I'm so sad to hear this heartbreaking news about you, Robert."

"It's okay, Jane. If I were you, I'd have surely done the same."

With an effort, Jane said to Robert, "John told me that your relationship with him is excellent, so it's a great relief for me. I hope to see you again soon as soon as the war is over. And my best wishes for you and your family."

In the next moment, Jane got an idea and said to Robert, "Would you please give me your wife's name and address so that when and if they ever need financial help for any reason, I could help them."

Robert was quite surprised by Jane's kind words and thanked her profusely for her generosity. He quickly jotted down his wife's address on a piece of paper and gave it to her. His eyes were full of tears. Then he said to Jane, "I don't know how to express my gratitude, Jane. My wife and I have only our mothers, and we have to struggle hard. I cannot tell you how much I admire you for the great humanitarian works you're currently undertaking in this war. Jane, I feel much relieved now for my family. I'm so sorry, but we'll have to leave in a few minutes. Goodbye, and may God bless us all."

Jane bade all the soldiers goodbye in a voice distorted by sorrow. Everybody was fighting back their tears. Before the soldiers left, Jane hurriedly introduced John to a few ON residents, telling them that he was Jennifer's father. She realized that it could be their last time together, but she said to herself in her mind that everything would be all right with them both and that they would meet again as soon as the war was over.

The pair took some photos together alone and with the other soldiers and some of the orphanage residents. Then the soldiers left the compound precisely four hours after their arrival.

A few days later, Jane heard that the soldiers had arrived safely at the small village of Andler. But then, on 16th December at 5:30 a.m., the Germans launched their final offensive, later to be known as the Ardennes Offensive or the Battle of the Bulge, on the Western Front in the Ardennes. The Allied forces were completely caught off guard. It was a great shock for all the people of the Ardennes, too. German soldiers and tanks were everywhere. One could hear the sound of heavy gunfire incessantly throughout the day and the following night. German soldiers came to the ON and searched for any trace of Allied troops. But none of the residents was harmed.

As communications between villages in the region were completely cut off, Jane could not get any information about John and his comrades. She always worried about what might have happened to him. On 17th and 18th December, she got the news that many American soldiers had been killed in action – or massacred - in small hamlets called Wereth and Malmedy. These places were not very far from ON. But there was no way to find out if John was among the dead.

Then, only a few weeks after the Allied victory in the region on 28th January 1945, information came out about John and his comrades' last hours from his platoon and battalion. According to this information, some of the units of the 333rd FAB were partly overrun by the Germans during the onset of the Battle of the Bulge on 17th December. At this point, John and his comrades were some twenty kilometers behind the frontline, laying down covering fire for the retreating 106th Infantry Division. John, Lieutenant Robert, and many of his comrades were killed in one of the battles that day, after having defended their positions so fearlessly that the German advance was delayed for four hours.

It was a great relief for Jane to know that his battalion commander planned to recommend John, Lieutenant Robert, and their comrades in the unit, for the Bronze Star Medal with a "V" device - the fourth highest military decoration for valor. A "V" device was a metal 1/4-inch (6.4mm) letter "V" with serifs – an award for heroism or valor in combat.

CHAPTER 25
(7th February 1945 – Wednesday)

The place: ON. The time: two p.m. All the leading members of both orphanages were holding a meeting. The atmosphere was joyous. Jane opened the meeting with this short message:

"As we know, our country was officially freed from the Germans three days ago. But since the war is still being fought on several fronts worldwide, we shall not yet hold a grand celebration. We'll wait until all the guns have fallen silent all over the world. Meanwhile, we'll hold two small provisional celebrations at both orphanages on the 7th of April, a Saturday. So we'll start with the preparations for it in the coming days. I had a long phone call with my parents in America yesterday, and they asked me to convey the good news to all the residents of the two centers who have been with us for the last four or five years. My father dictated this short message to be conveyed to all the orphanages' residents on the 7th of April. The message reads:

Heartfelt greetings from us, Christine and Paul, to all the residents of the two orphanages! You will provisionally celebrate the ending of the war in our country on the 7th of April. We're so sorry that we won't be able to participate this time. But we'll come back as soon as all the guns have fallen silent around the world, and we'll make a grand celebration together, either at ON or OS. We're so sad that we could not protect all the needy people in the past few years, but we're happy that we could give at least a few hundred of you some protection and care.

Although the war is over in our country, none of you need to worry about your immediate future. Since the state will be in a dire situation financially in the coming few years, we'll go on taking care until we find some humane solutions for you all. We'll soon have to think over how we should solve the problems we'll face in the most humane ways within our financial capacity. We'll have thorough discussions with all the state and other institutions relevant to our situation and with all of you as well to determine the best solutions. We'll make every effort to ensure that you, the orphans, may find kind and loving people to adopt you. We'll use rigorous criteria in selecting your potential adoptive parents. Those who haven't found the right people to adopt you can remain at the two orphanages until you do. For the adult residents, we'll try to find solutions so that you can lead your new life with dignity. Suppose there's anyone who cannot begin a dignified existence somewhere else. We'll continue taking care of you as long as it's necessary and as much as our financial capacity allows. We'll force nobody out of these places at any time.

Even when you leave, we'll maintain a close and warm bond of friendship between us so that you can come back at any time, as you would come back to your own home. And we'll hold a reunion every three or four years, depending on our financial situation. We'll try to come back next summer – provided, of course, that the guns all over the world have fallen silent. So let's hold the real celebration together at a single place then. We wish you good health, and we're eagerly looking forward to seeing you all in person soon – hopefully next year! May God bless you! May God bless us all. Christine and Paul.

The meeting went on until late in the evening. And then on the 7th of April, joyous celebrations were held at the two orphanages from two p.m. to ten p.m. among the residents and hundreds of people from neighboring communities. Among them were also the Jews who had been sheltered by the orphanages. Christine and Paul's message was read out. All the residents were much relieved and delighted to hear it, and many of them openly wept in gratitude. Priests, pastors, and rabbis held Catholic, Protestant, and Jewish prayer services.

CHAPTER 26
(30th November 1945 – Friday)

It was about nine o'clock in the morning. Jane was sitting alone in her living room, reading a book. Suddenly the doorbell rang, and she went to the door. It was the postman bringing letters. She immediately checked them one after another. And one attracted her attention most because the stamps were Spanish. There was no sender's address on the envelope. She frantically opened it and started to read it.

My dearest Mama,

It's me, Jennifer. As I don't know if you'll ever want to read this letter, I'll write only a few lines. I don't know whether it'll make you sad or happy. First of all, I hope you and Sarah and Opa and Oma are fine. Dorotea, my adoptive mother, and I are fine, physically. Mama, as I don't know how much you've changed in terms of how you look at this world and in your attitude toward me, I dared not call you on the phone. So I'm writing these few lines instead. As the Germans did not come to the village where we were living, I'm still alive, and we're now living in Madrid. I cannot tell you how glad I was when the Germans finally surrendered on 8th May this year.

Just before she went into a coma, Sister Hanna sent me a copy of your novel that you sent to her. The last chapter was 20. In this chapter, you mentioned your brief but intimate encounter with Lt. Vogt. Did you get pregnant and have a baby? I'm happy at the thought of having a new sister or brother. I've read it again and again, and every time I read it, I cry a lot. And your day-long discussion with the Buddhist monk from Ceylon on various religious concepts is so fascinating and enlightening for me that those ideas have enabled me to look at my religious thoughts from different perspectives. I wonder if you've become a devoted Buddhist now? I'm quite sure that you've found your peace of mind after your discussion with the monk. Sister Hanna once wrote in one of her letters that you don't want to have any new emotional attachments. (I got the book and her letter in mid-

September this year - that means, with a delay of four or five years. As you know, we could not contact each other during the war.)

If you still want to see me again, please write to me. We don't have a telephone. But if you prefer to have your peace of mind, I won't disturb you again, and I'll fully respect your decision. I still love you and miss you so much, Mama. And please convey my most heartfelt greetings to Sarah, Oma, Opa, and Uncle David and Auntie Elizabeth as well.

Have you heard any news about Papa? If I correctly remember, you mentioned in your novel that he expected to be sent to some battlefronts. I wrote to him, his parents, and sister twice soon after the war was over, but they apparently didn't get the letters. They didn't write back. Hopefully, he survived the war and perhaps even became a hero. Would you please inform him about this letter? He will surely be pleased to know about it.

May God bless you, Mama.

Your beloved daughter

The letter came as a shock to Jane. She did not know whether to feel happy or sad. So she wanted to take some time to decide what to do about it. When Jane had learned about Jennifer through Sister Hanna's letter, she had thought she would make contact with Jennifer as soon as the war ended. But she was now no longer sure whether she wanted to meet her again. She still thought about her daughter sometimes, but not as often as before she met the Buddhist monk. Her cousins had advised her to wait and see if Jennifer would take the initiative and contact her first. She had followed their advice.

So it took Jane nearly one month to make a decision. It was torture for her. Then, at last, on 30th December, she decided to write a long letter to Jennifer.

My dearest little darling,

If I'm to admit it honestly, I did not know – as you hinted in your letter – how to feel when I got your letter. I was glad and sad at the same time. When I learned that you were still alive and living in Spain from the letter Sister Hanna wrote just before she went into a coma, I was so overcome with joy that I decided to contact you as soon as the war ended. (I visited her in the Sisters' House, where she was lying in a coma. Although she was in a coma, she was still fully aware of things happening around her.)

I've indeed become very much influenced by Buddhist philosophy since your disappearance. At the time, I tried to find peace of mind in it, and it was tremendously helpful. But I haven't become a truly devoted Buddhist. Everyone who knew me before the war tells me that I've become detached and cold and that they're sad and uncomfortable being with me. So you may be disappointed, too, if I no longer seem to be as warm as before. But even if I'm not able to show you the warmth I once had for you, it won't mean that your presence saddens me. I've lost so many good people I liked and loved so much in my life, especially during the last war, that I've decided not to make any new friendships. It's simply too painful to part from your loved ones.

Sister Hanna wrote to say that you had a boyfriend and that you both loved each other very much and that you both had excellent grades in school and that you intended to study medicine to work for the poverty-stricken people in his country. This noble intention deeply moved me; you can always expect full financial support from me. You can also expect moral and financial help from me for any other humanitarian projects you may have.

Darling, whether you want to come home again or not is entirely up to you. I'm only afraid that I might not be able to show you the warmth that I used to have for you. At least you can always let me know if and when you need financial help. If you decide to come, Opa and Oma will return from America next summer, tentatively in July, and we're planning to hold a big celebration with them and the residents of the two orphanages, as well as our relatives and friends from the neighboring communities. I'm sure everybody would be so happy to see you again. I've told a few people among our circle about our correspondence, and they are happy about it. I haven't told more people because I'm not sure whether you'll come back or not.

Darling, I'm afraid I have some very sorrowful news. Your papa came here some months before the end of the war, and we met for just a couple of hours. I told him what I knew of about you from Sister Hanna's letter. He was so pleased to hear about you, and he left a note for you. But he was killed in action not far from here. We can at least be very proud that his battalion commander recommended him for the Bronze Star Medal; it's the fourth highest military decoration for valor. That means he died a hero.

Your paternal oma and aunt in America are still alive and okay. But unfortunately, your paternal opa also passed away, soon after your papa left for the European frontline. And I'm sorry to tell you that your Uncle David and Auntie Elizabeth were killed in a battle during the Ardennes Counter-offensive late last year. They got caught in the middle of a battle not very far from here. At least we could bury them in our family cemetery. And the other big consolation for us is that they died on the spot without suffering.

If you decide to come home, will you bring your boyfriend and Dorotea with you? Sister Hanna did not mention her name or details about her in her last letter, but I got to know quite a lot about her from Sister Hanna's mother. I want to thank her profusely for taking care of you for all those years. Darling, I'll write only this much for the time being. Loving greetings to you from your sister Sarah, too. My heartfelt greetings to Dorotea and Carlos as well.

Take care, and May God bless you.

Your loving Mama.

P.S. One thing you should be aware of with Dorotea is that she might worry and be sad deep down in her heart that she might lose you to me if you come back home. So try to assure her that you'll not leave her alone. And I'm glad to tell you that I'm still writing my novel. Everybody who has read it has liked it very much. They all cried a lot. Your first letter to me to our last letters before our reunion will most likely become Chapter 26. If you decide not to come back, I'll send you the chapters I write as they come. You've got a lovely brother. I named him Victor after my late brother. He's about five years old and very energetic and lively. But I have no news about his father, Lt. Vogt. He was either killed in action or went missing around Moscow in Russia.

Jane posted the letter and wondered how Jennifer would react. She deliberately did not give her her unlisted telephone number. There was no news from Jennifer until 30th March 1946. It was early afternoon, and Jane sat on a couch in the living room, reading her letter, which the postman had brought early in the morning.

My dearest Mama,

Please forgive me for replying to your letter very late. It was because I could not decide how to react. On the one hand, I'd like to see all of you again very much – you, Sarah, Opa, Oma, my friends, our relatives – but at the same time, I don't want to burden you emotionally.

I was so sad and yet glad at the same time to learn about Papa. I always hoped to see him again in this life, of course. But since that's no longer possible, at least I can be very proud of being the daughter of a war hero. That's a great comfort to me. With the thought of seeing him and Opa again in heaven someday, I can overcome my sorrow. Could you please send me Papa's letter, when it's convenient for you, Mama?

I'm so happy to know that I've got a brother. I'd like to see him, too. When I heard that Uncle David and Auntie Elizabeth were no longer with us, I was so sad and cried a lot. One of my strongest wishes has always been to see them again one day on this earth. They were so nice to me all the time. When I see them again in heaven, I'll tell them again and again how much I appreciated their love and care and how much I love them.

I'm so sorry that I did not mention Sister Hanna's aunt, Dorotea, my adoptive mama, in my first letter. She is full of love and kindness, like you. She's only one or two years younger than you. Although she's physically not that attractive, she's one of the most beautiful people to me. Do you remember what you used to tell me when I was very young, and I asked you why you were crying? You very often said to me that the most beautiful or handsome person in the world is the one who loves and cares for you the most. I will never forget those wise words. My life up to now has proved that those wise words are true.

She inherited a small fortune from her late husband, so our life is quite comfortable. And what you learned about me and my boyfriend from Hanna's letter is true. We're going to study medicine and become doctors. We're planning to move to his country when we graduate and work for the poor there. Before we go, we'll probably work in a hospital here to get experience. His own life and the plight of the people of his country are heartbreaking. I won't say more than that. I'm very grateful that you offered us financial and moral support for our future humanitarian projects. I've told my boyfriend, and he could not describe how thankful he is. But we would like to do our work in a very humble way. Mama, I'm quite sure now that I've inherited from you and Opa and Oma great compassion for those who are in need.

Carlos, Dorotea, and I will try to come home around the time Opa and Oma come back. We hear now and then what's happening on your side from Dorotea's relatives back in Belgium after Sister Hanna's death. (Dorotea has two or three distant relatives in Namur and Brussels, by the way.) When she heard that you'd like to repay her for taking care of me, she was so glad. She used to tell me very often that she wanted to meet you, but since I knew that you didn't want to form new friendships, I didn't dare to ask you if you'd care to meet her.

Thank you so much, Mama, for giving me that tip about Dorotea's feelings. I didn't think of that. Since you mentioned it, I've tried in many ways to reassure her of my love and loyalty, and now she doesn't have any doubts anymore. She's so thankful to you for this.

When we meet again, the first thing I want to do is to read your novel, although I know that I'll cry a lot. I'm dying to read it. Please convey all my loving greetings to Oma, Opa, Sarah, Victor, my cousins, friends, and relatives.

I love and miss you so much, Mama. May God bless you!

Your beloved daughter

Jane, silently shedding tears, read the letter again and again.

CHAPTER 27
(6th July 1946 – Saturday)

Christine and Paul landed in Brussels from New York, and Jennifer, Dorotea, and Carlos flew to Brussels from Madrid. They all arrived almost at the same time. Jane and her cousins picked them up. The reunion was warm and emotional; most of them were openly weeping. The meeting between Jane and Jennifer was especially very emotional. They embraced each other, openly sobbing. It took them nearly one hour to calm down a bit. Both Jennifer and Carlos were as tall as Jane and Jennifer was very strongly built. He was rather shy but communicative. From Brussels, they proceeded on to Waimes. Sarah, Victor and several adult residents and orphans heartily welcomed them.

On the next day at around two p.m., all the orphans and adult residents from both centers and some hundred people from the surrounding communities gathered in the spacious courtyard of ON to celebrate the end of the war and their happy reunion. Altogether there must have been around four hundred people. Fortunately, the weather was fine and warm.

Karin announced the beginning of the ceremony and read the program of events.

"Good afternoon, everybody! I'll read out the program once more even though we've distributed it among ourselves. Paul will first deliver his speech. And then Christine's speech will follow. The next speech will be Carmen's, which will be followed by Christopher's. Carmen will speak on behalf of the orphans and Christopher on behalf of the adult residents. They requested that Jane make a speech, too, but she politely declined; instead, she will read out the short report that we've prepared. After that, the orphans will sing as a choir, and then the adult residents will also sing, followed by a combined choir. A the end of the ceremony, Bishop Martin, the Reverend Adam, and Rabbi Abraham will lead three prayer services. After that, it'll be dinner time. Now, Paul, would you please come up and deliver your speech?"

Paul stood up and went to the microphone.

"Good afternoon, everybody. I greet you from the bottom of my heart. I won't make a long speech since everybody knows what we all are feeling and thinking today. First of all, on behalf of my beloved wife Christine and myself, I'd like to thank Jane, her close friends, cousins, all the staff of the two centers, the medical personnel, the part-time and full-time volunteers, and the volunteer teachers. They all have selflessly and tirelessly performed great works for the relief of those who were – and still are – in our care during the past six years. We accomplished these things not just through our efforts, but due in great part also to the work of innumerable people who supported and trusted us and thus enabled us to run our family business successfully for three generations. We're so happy that we're able to repay our debt to them in this way. In closing, I'd like to tell those we've been caring for not to thank us personally. As a gesture of your gratitude for what we've been doing for you, please do similar good things for other needy people. If you do that, we'll be enormously happy, and we'll have eternal peace of mind. May God bless us all. Thank you."

There was roaring applause for several minutes and a standing ovation as well. Then it was Christine's turn.

"Good day, everybody. Since my husband has already said much of what is on my mind, I would like to wish you all good health, happiness, and long-lasting peace for yourselves and all humankind. As a Christian, I'd like to thank Almighty God for giving us a long and healthy life so that we could give a helping hand to those less fortunate than us during the past few challenging years. Thank you so much. May God bless you all!"

There was another resounding round of applause. Now it was Carmen's turn.

"Good day to everybody. My fellow orphans and I have discussed what I should say today on behalf of us all, and we agreed on a few sentences. First of all, we cannot express how lucky we have been and how grateful we are for what Christine, Paul, Jane, and all the others have done tirelessly and selflessly and with great patience for us during the past six years and what they're going to do for us in the future, too. By 'all the others' I mean the medical and office staff, the part-time and full-time volunteers, and the fourteen volunteer teachers. We owe you our lives, and we cannot express our gratitude in words. You all were like our own parents, sisters and brothers, full of love and patience. On behalf of all of us, I'd like to humbly beg you to forgive us for all our wrongdoing. We'll always remember what Paul has just said, and we'll try to do good things to other people in need. And we do not doubt that the Almighty God will reward you with eternal life in His kingdom. Thank you so much. May God bless you all!"

More rapturous applause. Carmen's words moved everyone to tears. It was Christopher's turn now. He was about seventy years old and so severely handicapped that he used a wheelchair.

"Good afternoon, everybody. Just like Carmen and the orphans, we have discussed what to say and agreed to say only a few words because everybody already knows what is in our hearts. First of all, our deepest gratitude to those who have been giving us protection and taking care of us selflessly and tirelessly and with great patience. We humbly beg you to forgive us if any of us has said anything unpleasant or behaved in an inappropriate or ungrateful way during the past five or six years. We owe you a great deal for our survival. Although we're no longer in a situation to repay our gratitude on this earth, may God bless you for generations to come. Thank you so much."

After further applause, it was time for Jane to deliver her report.

"Good afternoon, everybody. We have prepared a detailed record of what we've been doing from the time we set up the two centers to this day. You can find copies of this record at both centers if you're interested to see them. In this record, you'll see our financial expenditures in detail as well. For the time being, I'll read out only a few important facts. We've given protection to about 300 orphans during the war. Out of them, more than 120 have been cared for from the beginning of the war to this day. We've given protection to more than 350 needy adults; of them, we're still taking care of 130. We've sheltered 52 Jews since they were rounded up and deported to concentration camps; of them, four died from natural causes, and the rest are still alive and well. Our permanent medical staff consisted of six doctors and twenty nurses who were working as volunteers. The medical personnel performed several medical services for people in the surrounding communities as well. And we've got about ten paid permanent office staff. About thirty men and women helped us as part-time and another thirty men and women as full-time volunteers. And fourteen teachers volunteered to work full-time. I must also mention that many people from these communities were also tremendously helpful to us in many different ways during the war. We're so grateful for that. We plan to make a special program soon to show how grateful we are to them. Altogether we've spent a total sum equivalent to a couple of million Swiss francs until now, and we reserved some extra funds for the next few years until we can make some arrangements with the state. Concerning the arrangements that we have for the adult residents and orphans, you can read my father's brief message from the first two celebrations we held last year on 7th April. And now I'd like to assure you all once again that we'll keep taking care of you until we find appropriate alternatives. Finally, on behalf of all those responsible for your protection and care, I'd like to beg you for your forgiveness for any mistakes that they may have made inadvertently. And on behalf of my parents and my children, I'd like to express my gratitude to my close relatives, friends, and other personnel of the centers and the volunteers. Let's hope this was the last major war in our lifetimes. I wish everybody present here good health and long-lasting peace. Thank you so much."

The onlookers gave Jane a standing ovation. Jane's words deeply moved several people to tears. They had their dinner at six o'clock, and the ceremony happily ended at ten.

It was now on 7th July, at Jane's home within the compound of ON. The time was seven p.m. After dinner, Christine, Paul, Jane, Jennifer,

Carlos, and Dorotea were sitting in the living room. Jane initiated the conversation.

"Jennifer, Carlos, Dorotea, excuse me for not having much time to speak with you in the last two days. As you know, we were so busy with the preparations for the ceremony that we could barely sleep. But now we can talk a bit longer. First, Jennifer, you wrote to me saying that you three would be able to stay here for about three weeks. Your oma told me that you've spent some hours with her and your opa and that you'll stay some days with them at their home. I'll also spend some hours with them in the coming few days – and of course with you, too. So what are your plans during your stay?"

"Mama, we don't have any special plans right now. The most important thing is that we are all alive and can see each other again. I want to visit the graves of Sister Hanna and Auntie Elizabeth and Uncle David, and the site where Papa was killed, if it's marked. And I'd like to lay wreaths. I want to read Sister Hanna's last letter, too, and I'd like to hear how you went there, and so on. When I received Papa's letter, I cried a lot. But I'm very proud of him. I'm eager for the day when I'll meet him and my opa again in God's kingdom. I'd like to see Sister Hanna's parents, sister, and brother, too. And I'm dying to read your novel, Mama."

"You can read my novel this evening. You'll surely cry a lot. I haven't visited Sister Hanna's grave yet. We could go there together and lay a wreath. But I'm not quite sure if I'm strong enough to go to the site where your papa was killed. During the Ardennes Offensive, Sister Hanna's parents, sister, and brother were severely wounded at their home in an aerial bombing. They're being taken care of here and are still receiving medical treatment, but they're getting much better now; the doctor in charge hopes that they can go home in a few weeks. So you can see them as often as you want. They'll also be delighted to see you again."

"I'm so sorry to hear that. I'll try to see them as soon as possible. But Mama, why do you think you might not be strong enough to go to the site where Papa got killed?"

317

"Because every one of his belongings and every place we visited together still remind me of him and make me sad."

"But Mama, you have written to me that you're very much influenced by Buddhist philosophy. And if you're deeply influenced by it, it shouldn't be a big problem."

"Jennifer, I don't know if I could ever be completely influenced by it. There is a war within me – a battle between rationality and emotion. Let's think about it over the next few days. By the way, tell me, darling, how do you feel about the emotion I've shown in dealing with you now? In one of my letters, I wrote that I might no longer be able to show you the warmth that you were used to while we were together …"

"Mama, I realize that you're much more reserved than before, but I can still feel your warmth. It's okay, Mama, I can live with it."

"Now, tell me something about Carlos and your plans for the future."

"He doesn't want to tell me much about himself. He only says that the great majority of the people are impoverished and that there is injustice everywhere, and that he came from a small village. He's an only child and was orphaned when he was very young. He's living with the family of a paternal uncle who has been living in Spain since thirty years ago. I don't know much about him aside from that. I used to ask him to tell me more about himself, but every time I asked, his voice began to break, and his eyes filled with tears. So I dared not press him. But I learned from his uncle that he witnessed his family being brutally murdered by gunmen who were believed to belong to the government. He said that the Mayan population's poverty was extreme and that the injustices they are suffering were beyond description. An active leftist movement was in the offing there, against which the CIA allegedly heavily active. So several poverty-stricken landless Maya peasants took up arms sporadically and demanded justice and land reform from the government, but they were ruthlessly suppressed. As the conflicts are slowly escalating, many people believe there could be a full-scale civil war sooner or later."

"Oh, I'm so sorry to hear about that. But both of you want to study medicine and help the poor in his country, don't you?"

"Yes, that's what we're planning. But before we move there, we'd like to work in Spain for some years to get experience in a hospital. I think we'll finish our studies about five years from now. That will be some time in either 1952 or 1953 if nothing interrupts our studies in the meantime."

"Jennifer, before you leave for his country, don't you want to see some European cities and famous museums and palaces and castles, and so on?"

"No, I don't want to see such places, Mama, except for art museums. We don't know how many innocent people had to pay for the construction of palaces and castles with their tears and blood. I have only one wish, and that is to visit Switzerland. You took me there with you once for a week when I was five or six years old. I'll never forget those breathtaking landscapes."

"Yes, let's go there again soon – next summer, perhaps. Carlos and Dorotea can come with us. A cousin of your oma is married to a Swiss farmer, and their daughter, Magdalene, is working as a tourist guide. She's much younger than me. They have a hotel with some forty rooms so that we can stay with them. It's called the Alpenrose, or Rose of the Alps. We'll ask her to show us the most beautiful parts of the country, okay? The best time to visit is between June and the end of August. So come back next year toward the end of May or early June, and we can discuss it again."

"Oh Mama, that will be one of the happiest moments of my life."

Christine and Paul listened to Jane and Jennifer's conversation without comment or interruption. Jane told Dorotea that she would take the next opportunity to speak with her more in detail and excused herself for not being able to spare more time for her at the moment. Jane could also communicate with Carlos in rudimentary Spanish. Now, it was nine o'clock, and they would all go to bed. Jane gave Jennifer a copy of her novel. Jennifer went to her room and began to read it right away. The next morning they all were seated together for breakfast in the dining room at nine o'clock. Christine and Paul also joined them. Jennifer told her mother that she had cried a lot and liked it very much. She said she especially liked some of the conversations between her and her mother in Chapter 1.

"Mama, whenever I read the first conversation between you and me in Chapter I, I cannot control my tears. May I read it aloud to you after we've finished our breakfast? It's one of the most beautiful and heartbreaking parts of the whole manuscript."

As soon as they finished their breakfast, they moved into the living room and seated comfortably. After some moments, Jennifer started reading it out; her voice began to tremble, and tears began to stream down her face.

"Why are you crying, Mama?"

The small girl's faint voice was filled with sorrow. She meekly stood at the door of a living room, quite spacious, luxuriously decorated, and dimly lit. The woman quickly dried the tears on her cheeks and turned toward the little girl.

"Oh, my dear, I didn't know you were there. Come hug me."

The girl was about six years old and biracial, African-Caucasian; she seemed to have slightly more prominent African features than Caucasian. She went to her mother, who was sitting on a large sofa. Her mother, who held a book in her hand, put it on a nearby table, stretched out her arms, and took the child tenderly to her side. Outside it was not yet fully dark. The clock on the wall read nine o'clock. The woman was in her mid-twenties and Caucasian. In a soft voice, she asked her child, "How often do you see me crying, darling?"

"Quite often. Whenever I see you crying, I feel so sad, Mama."

"My child, women are very odd beings. They cry for many reasons. They cry when they are happy; they cry when they are sad; they cry when they reminisce about old memories, good or bad; and they cry when they see beautiful things. Sometimes they cry without even knowing why."

"Really?"

"Yes, you will know when you grow up and become a woman."

"But why are you crying right now, Mama?"

"I'm crying right now because I'm so happy to have a lovely and intelligent daughter like you."

"I don't believe I'm intelligent and lovely. All the boys and girls I meet on the streets call out, 'Hey, you ugly, stupid nigger.'"

"Don't take them seriously. They're just children like you."

"Even adults call me the same thing."

"Oh really? I'm so sad to hear that. But try to be strong, okay?"

"That's what I've been trying to do for years. I have secretly cried alone many times because I don't want to make you sad with my own sorrow."

Upon hearing these words, the woman's eyes filled with tears that she could barely contain. With a trembling voice, she said, "I've always thought so, my child, but I never dared to ask you."

Both of them sobbed for a long while. Then the child spoke with a broken voice. "Mama, you said you were crying out of happiness because you've got a lovely, intelligent daughter like me. Would you still cry with happiness if I were an ugly, stupid child?"

"Even then, I'd still cry out of happiness, my child."

The woman was interrupted by her daughter. "I don't believe that. You just said you're crying out of happiness because I'm a lovely and intelligent child, but that means you'd not cry out of happiness if I were ugly and stupid."

"Even then, I'd still love you because you're mine. Beauty and ugliness are superficial things. For example, you might see a stranger, and you might think they are beautiful or handsome at first glance. But if they said or did something awful to you, you wouldn't find them beautiful or handsome anymore. In the same way, you might find a stranger ugly at first glance, but if he is kind to you and does nice things for you, you'd find him ugly no more, and you'd like or even love him. To you, he could become the most handsome guy. The most handsome guy in the world is the one who likes you, who loves you, who cares for you and who helps when you're in need."

321

"Do you really mean it, Mama?"

"Yes, I really mean it. But you'll find out that it's true when you grow up and have more experience in the world. Sadly, countless people leave the world without having ever having learned this priceless lesson. Just one example: If I saw your papa on the street somewhere, I wouldn't find him handsome or attractive, although he's not ugly. He was not the type I'd fall in love with easily. If he had not saved my life, I'd have been hit by a car and most likely killed on the spot, or I could have been handicapped my whole life. When I discovered his kindness and warmth, he became one of the most handsome guys in the world to me. And I wonder if my love for him is also partly the result of my feelings of pity for his hard life. Some people say that if you love someone out of sympathy, it's much stronger than a love that is the result of physical beauty or attraction..."

As Jennifer read, everyone could barely hold back their tears. Then, after a long pause, she continued, "Mama, you're right. Now I have enough life experience to realize that the most beautiful person in the world is the one who is kind and good to you. Mama, your conversation with Lt. Robert also moved me to tears. Have you ever contacted his wife?"

"Yes, at the ending part of last year, I sent her condolence and asked her about their situation. Her name is Emma. I sent her a copy of my novel, too. In my letter, I offered her financial help if she ever needs it. She wrote me a thank-you letter and said she cried several times as she read the novel. At the moment, she said they could survive with the special arrangements of the US government, but she would let me know if their situation becomes precarious sometime in the future. That's all I know about them until now."

After a few days, Jane, Jennifer, Carlos, Dorotea, twenty orphans, and twenty adult residents of the orphanages went to see the graves of Sister Hanna and Elizabeth and David and laid wreaths at the sites. As they laid wreaths at the spots where John, Lieutenant Robert, and their other comrades were killed, which were marked with flowers, tears were streaming down their faces.

During their stay, Jane observed Jennifer and Carlos closely and sensing that they loved each other so dearly, she was full of happiness. But Jennifer was quite sad and disappointed with Sarah because Sarah did not show any affection toward her, although she was quite amiable with other children of her age. Jennifer even asked her mother a couple of times if Sarah mightn't be a bit racist. Jane advised her to be patient with the girl, as her behavior might still change when she got a bit older. In contrast to this, Victor liked Jennifer very much, and they were nearly always together. They played together and walked together around the neighborhood. It made her happy.

Before Jennifer, Carlos and Dorotea left for Spain, Jennifer visited Sister Hanna's parents, sister, and brother several times. Jane offered Dorotea a place in her house for the rest of her life, when and if she might need it. Jane and Jennifer learned through official channels that John and all of his comrades from his unit had been awarded the prestigious Bronze Star Medal, the fourth-highest award for heroism. And Jane was officially informed by the American Battle Monuments Commission in Washington, DC. that John's remains would be moved to the Ardennes American Cemetery and Memorial in the village of Neuville-en-Condroz, near the southeast edge of Neupré, some twenty kilometers southwest of Liege. The cemetery site was liberated from German control by the U.S. 1st Infantry Division on 8th September 1944, and a temporary cemetery was established on the site on 8th February 1945. After the war, the Ardennes site was designated a permanent cemetery, becoming one of fourteen permanent cemeteries for the American World War II dead on foreign soil.

CHAPTER 28
(30th August 1946 – Friday)

Jane was at home alone, busily sorting out old files in her study. It was two o'clock in the afternoon. Suddenly the doorbell rang. She got up and went to the door to see who it was. There stood a woman in her late forties or early fifties, escorted by a young girl from the orphanage. The stranger had a small suitcase and a handbag.

"Good afternoon, Mama. This young lady wants to see you."

Jane put out her hand, and as they shook, the guest introduced herself.

"Good afternoon, I'm happy to see you, Ms. Jeanmart. I'm Catherine Vogt from Germany, the mother of Captain Vogt. When you met him, he was still a lieutenant. Just before his disappearance in Russia, he was promoted to captain."

On hearing the name Vogt, Jane was shocked.

"Hello Frau Vogt, good afternoon. I'm delighted to meet you. Please come in!"

Frau Vogt took a seat opposite Jane in the living room, and they discreetly sized each other up for a few moments. Frau Vogt immediately made a very good impression on Jane. Although she was in a casual outfit, her gestures were elegant and dignified. And she was friendly. She was a bit smaller than Jane. Jane noticed that she looked much like Daniel, or the other way around. Frau Vogt initiated the conversation.

"Could we call each other by our first names, Frau Jeanmart? Please just call me Catherine."

"Of course, Catherine. You may call me Jane."

"Okay, thank you, Jane. I knew that it'd be a great surprise for you to meet me. Please let me make my long story short. I got a letter from my son through the military post about two years ago. It was written back in the middle of 1940, from somewhere in France. But I had to wait to see you until now because I was not sure whether you'd want to see me. I was afraid you might hate us Germans. Finally, I decided to write to you, but my letters were returned to me marked 'addressee unknown.' At last, I gathered all my courage and decided to come here personally. In his letter, my son mentioned your brief encounter with him here in Belgium and asked that if he did not survive the war, I should come to see you to find out if you conceived a child with him ..."

Jane began to get the message and impatiently interrupted Catherine.

"I see. Where is he now – have you any news of him? When the 10th Panzer Division came through here after the Russian campaign on its way back to France in 1942, I made inquiries about him, but I was told that he was either killed in action or went missing during the Moscow Campaign."

"I've also made inquiries with the 10th Panzer Division Headquarters, and the German Defense Ministry and the German Red Cross. I got the same answer from them. They said that it could take a few more years to discover the true circumstances. So we'll have to wait and see and hope for better news. It could even be that he was captured by the Russians and became a POW, or was shot dead."

"Actually, just before we parted, he wrote down his Service Number, your address, and a few other bits of information for tracing you, but I lost the piece of paper soon afterward. If I hadn't lost it, I would have contacted you. I'm so sorry; I panicked when I lost it, but my cousins persuaded me that it wouldn't be difficult to trace you since he was not an ordinary soldier. So I was much relieved then. If I recall, he said he came from a small village called Obersdorf or Olbersdorf on the German-Czechoslovakian border."

"Yes, we were originally from a small village called Olbersdorf, near Zittau, very close to the German-Czechoslovakian-Polish border. Fortunately, I was able to sell our farms and forest before the war broke out, but far below the market price at the time. Soon after the war was over, I moved to West Berlin, and I'm living there now. I bought some apartments in Berlin with the money that I got from the sale of farms and forest."

"Thank you very much for your explanation, Catherine. Now everything is clear for me. Please let me explain why you had difficulty contacting me. I instructed my secretary after the war to return all mail from Germany. I don't blindly hate all the German people for what was done in my country and elsewhere – we have also done many awful things to countless innocent people in our colonies. I can very clearly differentiate between individuals' and institutions' acts, and I'm not emotional when I need to analyze situations or people. And Catherine, I'm just a frail woman. Even if I hated you all, what could I do? Besides, I'm deeply influenced by Buddhism. So I'm very philosophical about this life of ours. But yes, all personal mail from Germany was returned to the senders."

"I see. Before we go on talking, I'd like to tell you how I so suddenly appeared here today. I tried in vain to get your private telephone number a couple of times. I got your company's number, but your secretary told me that you weren't interested in receiving personal phone calls from anybody whenever I called it. So I took the risk to come here and see if I could meet you personally."

"Yes, what my secretary told you is correct: I don't want to get to know any new people. At the end of the war, I let two of my cousins take over the company's business activities; there is a lot to do in terms of the restoration of war-damaged buildings and contracts for new construction, but I'm retreating into my world. I give guidelines and make final decisions on crucial matters. But I need my peace of mind as much as possible."

"I see, Jane."

"Good, Catherine … There is a possibility that Daniel still might reappear someday, like a ghost. Who knows? I've got happy news for you. I bore him a child, a son, and I named him Victor after my elder brother, who died from his wounds in the Great War. Victor was born on the 1st of February, 1941. That's five years ago."

Catherine was suddenly overcome with great joy and said with a loud voice, "Oh really? What good news!" Tears of joy streamed down her face.

Jane continued, "He's very healthy and strong and intelligent. He's on a trip with some other children in the countryside near here at the moment. You'll see him when he gets back. But what did Daniel tell you about us in his letter?"

"Jane, I'm so sorry to hear about your brother. Well, Daniel told me nothing much. He only wrote that you had promised him that you would contact me to decide what to do with the child if Daniel didn't survive the war and that you and the child would be entitled to inherit half of what we received from the sale of the farms and forest. Do you understand German, Jane?"

"Yes, a little, but not enough for serious discussions."

Catherine took an old envelope out of her pocket and handed it to her. "Jane, it's his letter. You can read it yourself."

"Catherine, thank you very much for your trust in me."

Jane unfolded it, read it, and understood what Daniel had written. It was only one page. "Catherine, I'm glad that he wanted to share half his inheritance with me, but I don't need it. I'm also an only child, and I've got more than I need. Victor can have the whole inheritance. I've never been materialistic, you know."

"Oh? I deeply admire you for that – I mean your lack of interest in material things. I'm like you, too, in that case. It's such a pity that in this world, so many people accumulate wealth that they cannot consume, often at the cost of the tears and blood of innocent people."

"Yes, that's true, Catherine. And I'm so glad to know that you're like me."

"How shall we arrange it then, Jane – I mean with Victor?"

"Just tell me what you have in mind."

"As Daniel may have told you, he was my only surviving son. When he was conscripted into the army, I nearly died of heartbreak. Now I live alone and think of him all the time. I feel so lonely. So if Victor could live with me, it'd be a great comfort to me. But to take him away from you would be very unfair of me, Jane."

"How old were you when Daniel was born?"

"I was about twenty. I was born on the 1st of January 1895."

"Catherine, I fully understand your feelings of loneliness. My deepest sympathy is with you. I myself have gone through similar experiences. I've been writing a novel for several years, quite autobiographical. Just relax for the next couple of hours, and after dinner, I'll let you read it if you would like to. Then you'll understand what I'm talking about. By the way, how long can you stay?"

"I can stay as long as necessary. But you're writing a novel? I'm already dying to read it. And thank you so much for your sympathy, Jane."

"So far, I've finished twenty-seven chapters. Our time here together will become the twenty-eighth. And you can stay here as long as you want. Life in this house is very relaxed. I'll let you know when dinner is ready."

"Thank you so much, Jane. You're so kind."

"You are welcome. Catherine, I must tell you one thing in advance: I'll introduce you to Victor as his paternal grandmother. My cousins and close friends started a rumor that his father was a former boyfriend of mine named Philippe from somewhere in France and that he'd come to live with us when the war was over. We felt that to have a baby with a German in the middle of the war could damage my image. So nobody except my closest cousins knew the truth. Since the war ended, Victor has asked me a couple of times when his father will come to us; I told him that there was a reason why he couldn't come yet and that I'd explain when he was a bit older."

"I see. That's fine, Jane."

"I wouldn't mind if you took him with you and brought him up …"

On hearing these words, Catherine was overcome with joy again and thankfulness, and her eyes filled with tears. She could barely believe her ears. "Oh Jane, I cannot express how glad I am to hear these beautiful, kind words."

"When Daniel and I met, it was love at first sight for both of us. I've never fallen in love with anyone else in my life like that. You'll learn more about it when you read my novel. So I'd like to do him this favor. But there are a few issues that we'll have to think about …"

Jane stopped and thought about something for a while. Catherine was curious. "For example, Jane?"

"No … let's do it like this: you stay here with us and build up a close relationship with him. When he trusts and loves you enough, then we'll persuade him to go with you and stay with you for a while. Then you can both come here as necessary. And I may come to you every now and then. Although, if I'm honest, I don't feel like coming to your country."

Jane continued, "Are there some friendly children of his age whom he could play within your neighborhood?"

"Yes, there are, and they'll surely like each other. I'll help him find some good playmates."

"Are there good schools near you?"

"There's a private school very close to my house, and I've got a good relationship with the teachers. Victor would surely feel at home in this school immediately."

"Very good. The next problem is, he'll want to know more about his father as time goes on. How shall we deal with that?"

"I think when we're back in Germany, I could tell him the truth … Jane, I did not dare to dream that you'd be so generous as to allow him to live with me. I cannot express how thankful I am. He's still such a small boy, and I cannot imagine how much you'll miss him."

"Sure, I'll miss him … By the way, did you see many children and elderly people in the courtyard when you entered the compound?"

"Yes, I did."

"Well, we set up two orphanages – one in the south and one here – just before the war began, and we've been taking care of a few hundred orphans and almost the same number of sick and elderly people. So I've become a surrogate mother to the children and a daughter or sister to the adult residents. They all love me, and I love them. And many of those in the communities around here are either our close relatives or friends. So I'm leading a fulfilled and happy life. I

329

wouldn't suffer that much without Victor. And one of the main reasons I understand your feelings is that my first husband was a black American. We had a daughter, and I saw how much discrimination they had to bear. My daughter disappeared without a trace, and my husband joined the U.S. forces and was killed in action not far from here during the Ardennes Offensive in December 1944. When my daughter disappeared, I tried to find solace in Buddhism. Since then, I have become very philosophical about human existence. You'll find out more about me in the novel."

"What a so fascinating life! I'm so sorry to hear about the fates of your daughter and husband. You have my deepest sympathy. On the other hand, as you've just said, you live a fulfilled life. What wonderful people you are – you and your parents. It's no wonder you're so kind-hearted, Jane."

Catherine continued, "Just a thought: If Victor would prefer to stay with you, what shall we do?"

"I could tell him that I'm not his biological mother; that his biological mother died when he was still a baby or something like that. It sounds heartless, but he might be able to accept that since all the children here are also orphans who have lost one or both parents."

"Would you dare say that, Jane?"

"I think I could. We can still tell him the truth when he's older. One of the reasons I could do it is because his presence makes me both happy and sad at the same time. It makes me sad because it reminds me of Daniel and happy because I feel like Daniel is with me all the time. Victor looks very much like his father."

"I understand, Jane. By the way, it's not my business, but may I ask you another question?"

"Sure."

"What are you going to do with the orphans and adults in your care?"

"Broadly speaking, we'll give up the children for adoption to childless couples or those who lost their children during the war if they meet our very strict criteria. As for the adult residents, we'll discuss how best to restore their broken lives with welfare institutions. But we won't force anyone out of our care against his or her will. We'll go on taking care of them. That's our plan at the moment."

"Jane, you and your parents and relatives are exceptional people. I know God will bless you lavishly for your kindness and noble deeds."

Victor came back from his excursion just before dinner, and Jane introduced him and Catherine. They liked each other immediately. He asked her many questions about her and his father. She tried to answer candidly, although she had to make up some answers to suit the situation. At about eight o'clock, they went to bed. Jane gave Catherine a copy of her novel to read.

It was nine o'clock in the morning. They had just finished their breakfast. Victor and a couple of Jane's cousins, who had breakfasted together with Jane and Catherine, had just left the room. Catherine began the conversation.

"Jane, it's an unputdownable novel. I read it through to the end, and it had me in tears. I've read so many novels, but I've never come across one that's similar to yours. It's so unique. I'm sure that it would become a bestseller. Now I understand your life and present situation. I have begun to see various things, especially certain religious and philosophical concepts, from a completely different perspective. The ideas in the book will occupy my mind for my whole life. Thank you so much. I've also read your parents' messages for the two provisional celebrations from 7th April, and their speeches and your report from 6th July. I cannot express how much I admire you all, Jane. I wish Daniel were alive to read it. Do you think you could live with him as wife and husband if he reappeared someday?"

"I've never really thought about that. Soon after my discussion with the Buddhist monk, I stopped torturing myself with wishful thinking. My strongest wish is to leave this world as peacefully as possible, without suffering physically and mentally."

"You don't want to reincarnate or have eternal life in heaven?"

"No, I don't want to wish for anything at all."

"Have you become a Buddhist already, or do you intend to deepen your knowledge of the teachings of different Buddhist schools first?"

"No, I haven't become a Buddhist, and I don't intend to pursue it further. It has given me a very high degree of consciousness in many fields and great peace of mind. That's enough for me for the time being. But what I'll do with it in the future, I don't know yet. War is still raging within me between emotion and rationality."

"Have you had any contact with the monk after the war?"

"I tried to contact him a couple of times, but I was told that he died in a car accident not long ago. I was shocked because I would have liked to visit him at his monastery someday. Well, that's our karmas."

"How could he leave Belgium and reach his country?"

"As soon as I added the 26th chapter in my novel, I sent a copy of it to him early this year. He wrote a brief letter back telling me how much he was moved by it. It was a great relief for me that he could read it before his death. Professor Fleming once told me during the war that the monk was able to leave Belgium soon after our discussion with the help of some influential diplomats. He went to England, where he stayed until the end of the war, and then went back to his country in June last year."

"And the professor and his wife?"

"I called him two or three times, and we want to see each other soon. But we have not decided yet when that should happen. I want to wait and see how my thoughts, especially on religious matters, develop."

"You could perhaps call and simply ask them on the phone?"

"No, that would be too superficial, I think. I'd need to sit down with them and discuss things in detail. On the other hand, I'm not sure if I'll ever do it. I'll have to think about it. If and when we meet each other again, I'd like to ask them if they've found the right school."

"Jane, excuse me, may I ask you a very personal question?"

"Yes, sure."

"Do you have any idea what happened to Thomas in the end?"

"I have no idea. And I don't have any intention of finding out. But I'm not bitter about what happened between him and me. It was probably our karmas."

"Thank you for telling me all this, Jane. May I have a copy of your novel, by the way? I'll surely read it again and again."

"Sure, but first, I have to write Chapter 28. You may add or delete parts of that chapter. There might be something I've forgotten to include. You'll get it in one or two weeks."

After staying with Jane for three full months, Catherine and Victor left for Catherine's home. Christine, Paul, Jane, her cousins, and nearly all the remaining children from the ON saw them off at the railway station. Victor was thrilled to go with his grandmother. Jane tried not to shed tears, although she felt sadness deep down in her heart. But at the same time, it was a great relief for her because she had made Catherine and Victor happy.

CHAPTER 29
(10th July1947 – Thursday)

It was four p.m. at the St. Vith railway station. Jane, a few cousins of hers, Jennifer, Carlos, Dorotea, and twenty orphans – half of them girls and half boys – were preparing to leave by night train for Interlaken-Ost in the Bernese Highlands of Switzerland, via Luxembourg, Frankfurt, Basel, and Bern. The train would leave at 5:55 p.m. and arrive in Interlaken-Ost at 10:30 a.m. the next day. They all were so excited. Jennifer, Carlos, and Dorotea had come from Spain a week earlier for the tour.

In early March, Jane had informed the orphans, who still numbered more than eighty, about her plan for a hiking tour with Jennifer, Carlos, and Dorotea in the summer, and told them to let her know if they were interested in joining them. She had three conditions:

● Since it would be a hiking tour in a mountainous region, the minimum age must be twelve.

● Only ten girls and ten boys would be taken.

● If there were more than twenty interested persons, lots would be drawn.

When the list was finally closed in early June, more than fifty had given their names. So lots were drawn. The losers were very disappointed, although they were later much relieved when Jane assured them that they would get their chance next summer.

A few days before their departure, Jane had gathered them at her house and read out a letter from her cousin Magdalene, from Interlaken, Switzerland.

Hello, Jane and everybody who will be coming to Switzerland. I'm thrilled that you all want to come here for a hiking tour to enjoy our unforgettable landscapes. I promise to show you one of the most beautiful corners of the land. It's called the Bernese Highlands in English or Berner Oberland in German. The region is small, but the landscapes are full of contrasts. They are stunningly beautiful. You'll see a lot of snow-capped mountains that rise to more than four thou-

*sand meters above sea level. And there are waterfalls of different siz-
es everywhere. Five of Switzerland's best-known waterfalls are located in this region: Staubbach Falls, Engstligen Falls, Reichenbach
Falls, Truemmelbach Falls, and Rosenlaui Falls. And wildflower-
covered meadows and alpine pastures are everywhere. You'll see a
lot of cows and goats and sheep, and several kinds of wild animals
such as mountain goats, ibex, marmots, etc. The moment you leave
Bern for Interlaken, you will see the snow-capped Bernese Alps in the
distance. Since you will stay for only about eight days, I've made a
rough plan for our excursions, as follows (I'm sending you thirty copies so that everybody can study it to get a rough idea of the journey):*

Day 1: *When you arrive in Interlaken-Ost, you all will be rather
tired, although you'll have slept throughout the night. My parents and
I will pick you up at the station and bring you to our hotel, the Alpenrose, which is located within walking distance. You'll rest for a couple of hours, and then at about five o'clock in the afternoon, we'll do
a sightseeing tour of the town.*

Day 2: *We'll travel by train to a village called Lauterbrunnen early in the morning. It's only about a twenty-minute ride. Lauterbrunnen is a village located in a majestic valley among some of Switzerland's most spectacular scenery and the entrance to a fantastic world
of valleys and mountains filled with waterfalls and glaciers. When we
enter it, you'll see a big waterfall called Staubbach Falls above the
village. At the height of nearly 300 meters, it is one of the highest waterfalls in Switzerland, dropping into the Lütschine River. It is a stun-
ning sight located above the picturesque village of Lauterbrunnen.
And it is one of seventy-two waterfalls in the Lauterbrunnen valley.
From the station, we'll walk toward the other end of the valley. After
we've walked about three kilometers from the station, we'll come to
the spectacular Trümmelbach Falls on the left-hand side. We'll go
inside the mountain to see them. Staircases, walkways, and platforms
were built for viewing the falls. The ten glacier-waterfalls inside the
mountain are made accessible by tunnel-lift. The Trümmelbach alone
drains the mighty glaciers of the Eiger (3,790 m), Monk (4,099 m),*

and Jungfrau (4,158 m) and carries 22,200 tons of boulders and other detritus per year. The amount of water flowing per second is 20,000 liters.

After seeing these waterfalls from inside the mountain, we'll keep walking almost to the end of the valley – it's about five km. At the end of the valley, we'll go by cable car up to a small mountain village called Gimmelwald. From here, we'll walk on to the next village, Mürren. We'll spend a few hours there having lunch and enjoying the breathtaking views around it, including the Jungfrau, Mönch, and Eiger in the distance. From this village, we'll walk to a funicular railway station called Grütschalp. It's about five km from Mürren. Along the way, we can enjoy the landscape on the other side of the Lauterbrunnen valley. Then we'll walk down to Lauterbrunnen. After a few hours there, we'll go home by train. This will be enough for the first full day since many of you may not have previous hiking experience.

Day 3: On the third day, we'll go by train to Lauterbrunnen again, and from there, we'll continue our journey up to the Jungfrau, the top of Europe, by narrow-gauge train. We'll pass lots of jaw-dropping scenery. It's one of the most beautiful sights in the entire Bernese Oberland. On the way up, we'll pass through the beautiful village of Wengen. From there, we'll continue up to Kleine Scheidegg, passing through vast landscapes full of wildflowers. From halfway up, you can already see the snow-covered Jungfrau. From Lauterbrunnen, it will take us about fifty minutes to reach Kleine Scheidegg. We'll have our lunch there.

Kleine Scheidegg is a mountain pass at an elevation of 2,061 m, situated between the Eiger and Lauberhorn peaks. In winter, Kleine Scheidegg is the center of the skiing area around Grindelwald and Wengen. In summer, it is a popular hiking destination. At Kleine Scheidegg, we change the trains for Jungfraujoch, which is about 3,450 m above sea level. It is the highest train station in Europe. The train goes through tunnels, and it'll take us about forty minutes. The views around it are breathtaking. And when we come back from there, we'll change trains at Kleine Scheidegg and then head down to Grindelwald, a small resort village. It'll take us about forty minutes. Or, if you prefer, we can hike down to Grindelwald. The distance is about ten kilometers, so we'd need about three hours. Looking down at the Grindelwald valley from Kleine Scheidegg is unforgettable. You can decide which option you'd prefer when we're at Kleine Scheidegg.

Day 4: On the fourth day, we'll leave early in the morning for Grindelwald by train. We'll need about forty-five minutes to reach it. We'll then go up by chairlift to First, which is located at an altitude of about 2,166 meters above sea level. It'll take us about thirty minutes. It's a trendy hiking area. You're fortunate that there's a chairlift so that we can reach our destination without much physical endeavor. This chairlift system was officially opened on 15th June this year.

From up there, you get beautiful views of Alpine pastures all around, including a medium-size waterfall very close by. At First, we'll have our lunch in wildflower meadows. After enjoying the beautiful scenery around it for a couple of hours, we'll hike to a place called Grosse Scheidegg, located at an elevation of 1,962 meters, some seven km away. We'll probably need a little bit more than two hours. Along the way, we'll see marmots, ibex, and chamois. When we arrive at Grosse Scheidegg, we'll rest for a couple of hours, enjoying the views in the directions of both Grindelwald and Meiringen. From Grosse Scheidegg, we'll slowly hike down to Grindelwald, which is about ten km. At Grindelwald, we can do some window-shopping for a while and then head back to Interlaken.

Day 5: On day five, we'll go up to a place called Schynigge Platte via Wilderswil village by narrow-gauge railway. It'll take us about ninety minutes to reach our destination, at an altitude of 1,987 meters. The views on the journey are breathtaking. From there, we'll see both Lake Thun and Lake Brienz and the Lauterbrunnen valley and the Monk and Eiger and Jungfrau summits and the Grindelwald valley and other surrounding snow-capped mountains. There is also a botanical garden called the Schynige Platte Alpine Garden, which was built in 1928, with more than 600 species of plants native to Switzerland. It is very close to the rail station.

A shop run by the garden society at the entrance sells guides to the garden and other related merchandise. An adjacent exhibition contains information on the geology, botany, and zoology of the Schynige Platte. The journey will take us about fifty minutes.

Day 6: On this day, we'll go to Grindelwald again by train, and from there, we'll continue our journey up to Grosse Scheidegg by a Postauto or PostBus. Grindelwald and the Grosse Scheidegg are ten kilometers and will take about ten to fifteen minutes. Grosse Scheidegg is a mountain pass connecting Grindelwald and Meiringen. The road is closed to most traffic but is used by the PostBus Switzerland service from Grindelwald to the pass's summit, with some buses continuing to Meiringen. Hiking over the pass is popular.

From Grosse Scheidegg, we'll hike down to the quiet mountain hamlet of Schwarzwaldalp – about seven km, for which we'll need about two hours. We'll see a lot of cows grazing in flower meadows and alpine pastures. Here we can see the Rosenlaui glacier gorge. As we enter the Gletscherschlucht, we'll first notice the powerful Rosenlaui waterfall that carries the Rosenlaui glacier's waters through this ravine. There is a footpath ascending through the narrow ravine, surrounded by up to eighty-meter cliffs. At the end of the gorge, a forest trail will lead us back down to the entry point.

After resting for a couple of hours, we'll continue our journey down to Meiringen by Postauto. The distance between Schwarzwaldalp and Meiringen is about twelve km or twenty-five minutes. Meiringen is famous for the nearby Reichenbach Falls, the place where Sherlock Holmes fell to his "death," but the falls were well-known in Europe long before this. The Reichenbach Falls are a series of waterfalls on the Reichenbach stream and have a total drop of 250 meters. One can walk along the trail through the falls or take the funicular to a viewing point, where you will be rewarded with beautiful waterfall views. We'll decide whether we want to see them close up or not when we're there, depending on our timing and mood.

We'll then continue our journey to a town called Brienz, in the direction of Interlaken. It'll take us about fifteen minutes. We'll take a break for a couple of hours in Brienz, which is located on the banks of Lake Brienz. It is well known for its wood carving business. There are two possibilities to return to Interlaken from there: by train or steamship on the lake. The train ride takes about twenty-five minutes and the steamship a few hours. The railway lines run along the lake's right bank, and the views along the route are breathtaking. Soon after we leave Brienz, we'll see an awe-inspiring waterfall called the Giessbachfall, or Giessbach Falls, on the left side of the lake. The Giessbach is a mountain stream that flows down to Lake Brienz. Its source is the high valleys and basins of the Sägistal-Faulhorn area. The stream plunges over the imposing Giessbach Falls in a series of fourteen cascades for 500 meters.

Day 7: On this day, we'll leave early by train for a village called Frütigen. It'll take us about ninety minutes. On our way from Interlaken to Spiez, the railway line runs along Lake Thun's left bank, with incredibly scenic views. From Frütigen, we'll head by PostBus for a village called Adelboden– it's about a thirty-minute ride. Our main aim in visiting this place is to see the Engstlingenalp and Engstlingen Falls. The Engstlingenalp is a seven square kilometer plateau. It lies south of Adelboden at 2,000 meters above sea level and is covered with Alpine pastures and crossed by numerous mountain streams springing from the slopes. They collect at the exit of the valley to form the Engstlingen Falls, which cascade 600 meters down to the Engstligen valley. It is one of the most impressive waterfalls in Switzerland. Since the 1920s, there has been a cable car. The waterfall is a confluence of two waterfalls. The Engstlingen Falls has one of the highest water volumes of Alpine waterfall and is one of Adelboden's main attractions.

Remark: I think I should not write in detail now about the places and things you're going to see. I'll tell you more about them when we're there. But I should mention here very briefly three of the most important sights on your journey: Lake Brienz, Lake Thun, and Interlaken. Lake Brienz is thirty sq. km, and Lake Thun forty-eight. Inter-

laken is a town located between these two lakes and is a hikers' paradise. Its current population is about 3,000 and it is located strategically for tourism.

Day 8: Return Home
19th July

The group gathered at the Interlaken-Ost railway station at four p.m. The train would leave at 4:55 p.m. Nearly everybody, except Jennifer, was in an exuberant mood. They all enjoyed the tour tremendously. But Jennifer was silently shedding tears in a corner, looking at the snow-capped mountains in the distance. Jane noticed and asked her, "Why are you crying, my dear? Aren't you happy?"

"Mama, I don't know how to tell you about my feelings. I'm so happy and sad at the same time ..."

"Why?"

"These have been some of the happiest days of my whole life, seeing such stunningly beautiful places, but at the same time, I'm so sad at the thought that countless people around the world don't have the chance to see such things whose beauty is beyond description, even once in their lives. I even wonder if heaven could be as beautiful as these views."

Jane tenderly took her into her arms. Her own eyes began to well with tears, and in a very tender voice, she said, "Darling, we'll come back here again and again, okay?"

"Mama, I don't want to go back home."

"Darling, even when you're in Guatemala, we'll come back here every three or four years, and we'll stay much longer."

"It's so sad that countless people will leave this world even without knowing about the existence of such beautiful places. We all become human beings only once. God must have created these places to let as many people as possible to enjoy them."

"Yes, you're right. It's so sad, but what can we do, darling? It's probably their karmas."

Finally, Jennifer stopped crying and boarded the train, which departed punctually.

CHAPTER 30
(14th December 1949 – Wednesday)

The day was chillingly cold, and snow was falling heavily. The time was four o'clock in the afternoon. Jane was sitting in her living room alone and talking with someone on the phone when there was a knock on the door. She called out, "Yes, who is it? Come in."

The door opened, and a young girl's head popped in. She was one of the orphans at the orphanage.

"Good afternoon, Mama. A man by the name of Mr. Thomas Mueller from Germany is standing in the courtyard and wants to know if he could see you."

It was a great surprise and shock for Jane to hear Thomas's name. She suddenly became very nervous and thought for a few long moments, then told the girl to bring him in. Jane stood up and went to the door to greet him. When they saw each other, he stood still for a few moments, not knowing what to say. It was the same for Jane. He seemed to be much older than his actual age. Then, with an effort, he uttered a few words. The young girl left them alone.

"Good afternoon, Jane. Excuse me for coming to see you without your prior permission."

It took a short moment for Jane to respond without any trace of emotion, although she was very nervous, "Good afternoon, Thomas. Please come in and take a seat."

Jane put her hand out, and perfunctorily shook his. He was not sure how to react, but he took a seat near her. Meek and nervous, he initiated the conversation.

"Jane, I'm happy to see you again after such a long time. You're still as charming as ever."

"Thomas, I don't know how to feel if I'm to tell you the truth."

"Jane, I didn't dare to contact you at first. I wanted to contact you much earlier, but since the war's memory was still fresh for everybody, I thought it'd be too early to do so. So I waited until now. Even now, though, I don't know if it is appropriate. But the desire to see you and talk with you about our family has been so intense that I just couldn't wait any longer. A few months ago, I gathered all my courage to write you a few letters, but I didn't hear back from you. And I couldn't find your phone number. I called your office a couple of times, but your secretary told me that you didn't want to talk to anybody. So finally, I took the risk to come to you in person."

"What is the purpose of your coming here, Thomas?"

"I just wanted to see you again and tell you that I'm so sorry for what I did to our family and the others."

"Thomas, you may not believe it, but for me, the past is the past, and I don't think about what has happened anymore. The reason you didn't hear from me is that I cut off many of my former contacts. So unread letters from various people are piling up in the office and here in the house or returned to the senders. I'm now in contact with only a handful of people. And my phone number is not listed. I've also delegated the daily running of our company to a couple of my cousins. I haven't run it since the end of the war."

"I see. Would you please tell me how you feel, seeing and talking with me now, Jane?"

"Thomas, I'm simply feeling blank. I never made an effort to find out what happened to you or where you were at the end of the war."

"That must mean you hate me?"

"I don't hate you or anybody else, but I don't love you either. It's as simple as that."

"Would you at least let me tell you briefly about what's been going on with me since I left you?"

"Thomas, I'm trying to live in the present. I'm no longer interested in the past, and I'm not interested in the future either."

"You must hate us Germans for what we've done."

"Even if I hated you, what could I do? I'm just a frail, middle-aged woman. And I'm not political-minded at all. You know that."

"May I ask you a very personal question, Jane?"

"Ask me."

"Could there be another chance of starting a new life together?"

"Thomas, I don't want to hurt you, but I want to say that I don't have any deep feelings for you."

"Could you forgive me for what I've done?"

"For what? What you've done to our family or for your political activities?"

"Our family. As for my political activities, I know I'll have to face the consequences for the rest of my life."

"If it's a question of our family alone, you don't need to apologize at all. I accept that everything happened according to my karma – or ours. When Jennifer suddenly disappeared without a trace just before the beginning of the war, I got the chance to have a day-long discussion with a monk from Ceylon. From this conversation, I learned a lot about Buddhist philosophy, not only in terms of my own life but everything in the universe. So you don't need to have a guilty conscience about what happened to our family."

"Once again, could I interpret the fact that you don't hate me as a positive sign for a new beginning for both of us?"

"I've got no place for this feeling in my heart or mind anymore."

"Does that mean that you at least still like me?"

"There's no place in my heart for this either. My mind and heart are blank and empty."

Thomas felt dejected, and his eyes were full of tears. Then, with a broken voice, he ventured, "How's Sarah getting on? Where is she now? She must be quite the big girl now."

"Yes, she's growing fast. She's fine."

"Does she ever ask about me? And may I perhaps see her, too, sometime in the next few days?"

"Yes, she once asked me about you. But if I tell you what she asked me, you'll be shocked. So I'd better not. I've always tried to hide the truth from her, but someone must have told her the truth about you."

"Please tell me her question anyway, Jane. I won't mind it at all."

"She asked, 'Mama, is my father a mass murderer?'"

Thomas was so shocked that he could not speak for several

minutes. Tears were rolling down his cheeks. Then, at last, he managed to ask, "How did you answer?"

"I told her that it was a very complex matter and that she should wait until she was older to find the truth out herself. I couldn't tell her more than that, and I don't think it's a good idea for you to see her this time. I'll give you some recent photos of her to keep. She always gets excellent grades at school, and she wants to study either physics or chemistry when she grows up. She's told me a couple of times that she wants to win a Nobel Prize for any of these subjects. I'm going to send her to America and let her study there."

"Oh, I'm so glad to hear that she's such a bright student. By the way, Mr. Becker told me that he had a short conversation with you at his temporary headquarters not far from here. When I learned that he would be transferred to this region, I asked him to protect you and your relatives and your orphanages as far as he could."

"Yes, we met. He was nice. He told me a little bit about these things. Thank you very much for that, Thomas. Where is he now?"

"He and his assistant Mr. Schneider were killed in one of the Allied bombings not far from the Gestapo headquarters in Brussels."

"Oh, I'm sorry to hear that. He told me that he owed you and your family a great deal. What was that about?"

"He was orphaned in childhood, and my parents adopted him. We were like brothers."

"How much do you know about Mr. Schneider? Mr. Becker seemed to trust him absolutely."

"I didn't know him personally. He had been one of Mr. Becker's best friends for a long, long time. That's all I know."

"Thomas, where are you staying?"

"I haven't booked into a hotel yet, since I didn't know whether you'd want to see me or not. I'll go and look for a room. Hopefully, I can still get one."

It was already half-past five. "If you want, you can stay here tonight," Jane said. "We can have dinner together. And if you would like to, you may read the novel I've been writing since John saved my life. You'll find yourself in it, too. It's partly autobio-graphical."

"Thank you so much for your hospitality, Jane. Yes, I'd love to spend tonight here. Are you writing a novel? I'd love to read it. By the way, would you please tell me about Jennifer?"

"You'll find out quite a lot about her in the novel."

"Okay ... Jane, can we still at least be good friends?"

"To tell you the truth, I don't want to make any new friendships. It's so painful to be attached to others. Therefore, I cannot promise you, Thomas. I'm so sorry to have to say that. By the way, Mr. Beck-er told me that you had a nervous breakdown when your former Jew-ish girlfriend was sent to a concentration camp and that you drank heavily after that."

"Yes, that's true. I tried very hard to save her, but I couldn't. We were really in love, but when the Race Law was introduced in 1935, my family and friends discouraged me from continuing our relation-ship. I don't know what happened to her. From the moment she was deported, my view of the Party and the whole system changed, and I looked at it from a very critical perspective. That's why I was classi-fied as an 'untrustworthy person' and was expelled from the Party."

"Don't you want to trace her and find out what happened to her? It's possible that she survived the concentration camp."

"I'm very ambivalent about that. On the one hand, I want to find out what happened to her, but on the other hand, I still am so trauma-tized that I don't dare to investigate it. If I found out that she suffered a terrible fate, I'd suffer even more. The thought tortures me during all my waking hours. Then again, I know that I must try to find out what happened to her sooner or later. Without knowing, I won't be able to lead a normal life again."

"Have you found someone with whom you could fall in love and start a new life?"

"No, I haven't been looking – at least until now."

"You were very popular with beautiful women when we were studying. So why don't you look one of them up?"

"No, I can't imagine any more living with another woman – it must be either with you or Helena. She was very special to me – just like you. She was not perfect, but I've never met a woman like her— except, of course, you. I think I have fallen in love with no fewer than ten women in my life. You and she have many similarities. I don't think any of my former girlfriends could replace her. So no, I suspect I might not find true happiness again because I'd compare my partner with her – and also with you."

"That's exactly what happened to me when John and I were separated. At least unconsciously, I used to compare him with you. And I was sometimes disappointed with you if I'm honest. But since our time together was very short, it didn't disturb me too much."

"Jane, thank you very much for being so frank. Could you please tell me the things that disturbed you most?"

"Sometimes you used to brag about how popular you were with beautiful women, and occasionally you didn't take my emotional needs seriously enough. So I'd like you to think about such things in case you decide someday to live with a woman again."

"I'm so sorry, Jane, that I hurt you in such stupid ways. And thank you so much for telling me all these things frankly and honestly. But I promise you that I've become a new person. Since three or four years ago, I drink alcohol quite seldom."

"May I ask you another question, Thomas?"

"Just go ahead."

"Did you truly love me, or was I just a replacement for your Jewish girlfriend when you called me on your way to your aunt's in Antwerp?"

"You know how much I loved you."

Jane suddenly changed the subject. "By the way, how's your family's printing business?"

"Fortunately, the building that housed it was only slightly damaged during the bombings. So I'm refurbishing and expanding it. Heide, my half-sister, and I will take over the management soon. I think I'm fit enough again to take full responsibility for it."

"How are your parents and Heide?"

"They all survived the war. Thank you."

"Thomas, may I propose to you something?"

"Just say it."

"There are still many orphans at our two orphanages. So when and if you find a new partner and your family business becomes a success, would you adopt one or two of them?"

Thomas was surprised by the totally unexpected the question, and he thought for a very long while.

"Yes, sure, I'd love to. But Jane, they might object to being adopted by a German."

"Yes, that's a possibility. We have stringent criteria for those who wish to adopt. But I could help you overcome this barrier if you decided to adopt any of them."

"Jane, if I'm, to be honest, I'm still being treated by a well-known psychiatrist, although I'm getting much better. It'll be a while before I could adopt."

"May I ask you what kind of disorder you have? If it's too sensitive, you don't need to answer."

"It's okay. It's the feeling of guilt for what I've done to you and Jennifer and Sarah. It was also for becoming an instrument in a system that caused so many innocent people's suffering and death. This feeling makes me feel very unstable during my waking hours. I cannot express my admiration for your noble deeds at the two centers during the war. And even if I'm deemed unfit to adopt, I could at least help out financially in some ways. I promise you this, Jane."

When she heard these words, Jane began to sympathize more strongly with him.

"Thomas, from now on, you don't need to feel guilty for what you've done to our family. It happened as it did according to our karmas. There are surely countless similar cases. The concept of predestination rather influences me, and it could be a great relief for you to know that Jennifer fully understands and forgives you, too, at least for what happened within our family."

On learning that Jennifer understood and forgave him, Thomas's eyes filled with tears again. "Is it true, Jane?"

"Yes, it's true. We talked about it a couple of times, and she said she could forgive you because you were not the mastermind behind the system but were just an instrument."

"I'm so glad to hear that, Jane. Where is she now, and how is she getting on?"

"She's living in Spain, and she's fine. You'll learn more about her in the book."

"Would you please tell her how thankful I am for her forgiveness? I want to try to contact her by letter or see her. And please convey my heartfelt greetings to your parents as well."

"Yes, I'll do that. I'm sure she will appreciate your kind words very much."

"Jane, by the way, I've heard of the concept of predestination, but what is it?"

"You'll get some idea about it when you read the novel."

"I'm feeling much relieved after hearing your kind words, Jane. They mean a great deal to me."

"I'm very glad to know that, Thomas. By the way, did you have any problems with the Allied forces over your activities in the Ministry? Or were you not forced to go through the denazification process?"

"I was interrogated several times by many different agencies, but as my position during the last two or three years of the war was just that of an ordinary clerk, I was exonerated."

Jane prepared dinner at about six o'clock, and after they had finished it at eight, she showed him the guest bedroom and gave him her novel. He suddenly embraced her and tried to kiss her lips, but she let him kiss her only on the cheeks. She felt much more relaxed now than at the beginning of the afternoon. He went into the bedroom and immediately started reading the novel in bed. They both got up at around eight o'clock the next morning, and after they had finished their routine bathroom chores, they breakfasted together. Thomas began to speak.

"Jane, I've never come across such a novel. I couldn't control my tears. Why didn't you tell me when we were together that you were writing a novel? I think your description of both of us is very fair. And I'm sure it'll become a bestseller."

"Thank you for the compliments. If you want, you can take it with you. I've got a few extra copies. You might want to reread it sometime. But I'd prefer to send you a copy later when I've added the next chapter a few weeks from now. What happened here yesterday and today between you and me will become Chapter 30. You may edit it if you want."

"It doesn't have a title yet. Haven't you decided on one?"

"No, I haven't. And it'll remain a secret until the last moment before publication. Which one do you like most out of the three possible titles?"

"Perhaps *Jane*, but *Why Are You Crying, Mama?* could also be fine.'"

"Thank you. Many people liked it most. By the way, I've called the train station and made a reservation for you. A train leaves at eleven o'clock. I'll take you to the station, okay? And thank you very much for your kind invitation to visit you in Berlin, but I don't feel like coming to your country. Maybe I might come someday, though – who knows?"

Jane took him to the railway station at 10:30. They sat in the waiting room until the train arrived. It was snowing heavily. Thomas took both her hands and stroked them tenderly and said, "Jane, do you remember when you sent me off more than ten years ago? It was snowing like this then. The timing and the snow make me so sad. It reminds me of our short but happy time together."

Tears were streaming down his face, and his voice was breaking. Without looking at Thomas and without a trace of emotion, Jane said, "Thomas, the past is the past. After I met the monk, I could manage to delete the sorrowful parts of my life from my memory. Nostalgia about old times that you cannot repeat only saddens you."

It was now 10:50, and the train was in sight. Thomas suddenly took Jane in his arms and looked deeply into her eyes and said, "Jane, may I kiss you on your lips one last time?"

As she did not object, he kissed her affectionately for a few moments, but he did not feel any trace of passion in her kisses. Just before he boarded the train, Thomas gathered his courage and asked her once again, "Jane, do I still have a chance to be with you in this life?"

"Thomas, I cannot rule it out because the human mind is a fickle thing, and we don't know how our fates are predestined or what our karmas are. If we're predestined to live together again, it'd just happen without our making an effort. But I don't want to waste your time by giving you false hope. We could remain friends. Here's my phone number. If you feel like calling me, do so any time. And if you get any information about Helena, I'd be interested to know about it. Please convey my heartfelt greetings to your parents and Heide. Goodbye, Thomas."

"Thank you so much, Jane. I'll do that. Jane, I've surely irritated you by asking you again and again if I mightn't still have a chance with you. Please forgive me. Sometimes I feel that I'm completely helpless and don't know how to behave. Goodbye, Jane."

Jane noticed that tears were streaming down Thomas's face. She tried so hard not to show any trace of emotion, although deep in her heart, she, too, was so sad for the departure reminded her of the last time he had left her and Jennifer. That was before the war, and Sarah was still in her womb. They waved to each other until the trained disappeared around the bend a few hundred meters away.

CHAPTER 31
(10th April 1950 – Monday)

It was ten o'clock in the morning on Monday. Jane was busy sorting out some papers when the doorbell rang. It was the postman bringing letters. She chose to read Thomas's first, feeling a combination of curiosity and anxiety.

My dearest Jane,

Thank you so much for the copy of your novel that I received a couple of months ago. I didn't call you to thank you sooner as I was going to write you this letter anyway. Your description of our last meeting in Chapter 30 moved me deeply, my dear. Thank you so much. I don't think I need to edit any part of it. You have done it so well.

Since I didn't have much to tell you about myself until now, I didn't write or call you. I hope everything on your side is okay. I'm glad to tell you that my condition has significantly improved with the therapy I've been having. After a few more sessions, I won't need it anymore. Jane, I'm writing mainly to tell you about some good news that made me extremely happy a few weeks ago. A friend of mine recently got word that Helena was living with a girlfriend of hers in a remote village on the German-Polish border under a new name: Linda. As soon as I got the news, I went straight to the village and searched for her. After a few days' searching, I located her. How she was discovered was pure coincidence and a long story.

The reunion was heartbreaking for both of us. She survived the concentration camp and is now receiving treatment from an experienced psychotherapist. She was among the very few survivors of the camp, which she refused to name. At first, she was very closed and suspicious of me, but when she knew what had happened to me after her deportation – thanks much to your novel – she slowly began to open up, and we found we could rebuild up a mutual trust. At first, she did not want to believe what I told her, but then I let her read

351

your novel. She said it was tremendously helpful to her, and she was deeply thankful to you for your sympathy. She especially liked the chapter in which you described my visit. She cried a lot while she was reading it. And she wanted to see you and talk with you as soon as possible. She did not want to tell me her whole story because the reality was so brutal that she did not want me to suffer unnecessarily. I'm not sure if I ever dare to learn the entire truth. She confessed that she never intended to try to find me. I can understand why she felt like that, but it was so painful for me.

Her psychotherapist told me that it'd take a few more years before she would be able to have a close relationship again, so I must wait patiently. Her therapist said she was still so terribly traumatized that she used to have nightmares and could hardly sleep until very recently. But I don't think I should burden you too much with such sorrowful information. I stayed with her for four whole weeks, and I'll go to her again in a week or two and try to stay longer. When I was to leave after my last visit, I asked her if she thought she could have the kind of relationship we had before. She said she could not promise, but she would try to wait a few more years if I would be patient enough. It made me so happy. Since then, I've begun to think seriously about how we'd build a future together. As she's already past the age of having babies, I sometimes feel sad at the thought of not having a child of our own. But I'm sure even without a child, our married life would be a happy one.

Jane, I'll write only this much for the time being. At first, I thought I'd call you and tell you about it all on the phone, but then I had second thoughts. Since you're writing a novel, I thought you might want to include this story, too, so I decided to tell you all about it in a letter. Thank you so much once again for your understanding. If there's any further development on our side, I'll let you know. Please convey my heartfelt greetings to your parents, Jennifer, and all our other mutual friends.

Thomas

P.S. By the way, I'm suffering, not being able to see Sarah – just once. I won't mind whatever she thinks of me. She has every right to say whatever she wants about me. I don't know if I'll ever see her again in this life.

Jane was glad for Thomas and Linda on the one hand, but on the other hand, she was sad about their situation. She cried silently as she read the letter. She decided to write back right away.

My dear Thomas,

Thank you for your kind letter. It made me very glad and very sad at the same time. I was so happy because your girlfriend survived the concentration camp and you could meet again and start a new life together. And I'm so pleased to know also that my book played a crucial role in your rebuilding a mutual trust. This fact alone gives me some peace of mind.

But on the other hand, I was so sad about the indescribable hardship she had to go through. I hope both of you will keep getting better and might be able to start a new life soon. My thoughts will always be with you. Why don't you visit me together sometime soon when you're feeling better? Please let me know how things develop.

Concerning Sarah, I think you should try to forget her as much as possible since you'll only waste your energy. Under the present circumstances, there is no chance of her changing her opinion of you. When she gets older and has more life experience – and if she reads my novel someday – perhaps her opinion could change. Until now, she doesn't want to read novels, saying that they're written by dreamers and liars.

I wish you both the best, Thomas. Please convey my greetings to Linda when you see her again. And let me add a few words here concerning a child. You should not think too much about it, Thomas. As I've told you, there are still about forty children with us who are longing to be adopted. They all are kind and loving. Not every biological child is automatically better than an adopted one. I have seen many happily married couples with adopted children. I'm sure you'd find someone here whom you could love as your own child – and who would love you as his or her biological parents. Just come along together when you feel well enough, okay?

Thomas, you'd be among the last to have the chance to adopt children from the two centers. It's sometimes so heartbreaking to see the whole process that we've decided to adopt the rest ourselves soon. One reason we made it a condition from the very beginning is that a potential adopter is not allowed to adopt only one child if they have a brother or sister. All the children love us, and we love them all back. They enjoy living here with us. I've become a mother to them all. After the war, we held a reunion party here for the orphans and their adoptive parents. Nearly all of them came back to celebrate.

And we're going to have the same reunion party every three or four years. Any adopted boy or girl can always come back here until they find other adoptive parents if they don't feel right with their new family. A few of them have decided to stay here and not look for new parents. Some of them have even managed to start their existence with our financial assistance.

Please convey my warmest greetings to Linda, your parents, and Heide as well.

Take care,

Jane

Jane posted the letter and wondered for a couple of days how Thomas would take it. She got a phone call four days later; he had many nice words for what she had done for them.

CHAPTER 32
(7th May 1953 – Friday)

When the postman brought the mail at around eleven a.m., Jane spoke with someone on the telephone in the living room. She hurriedly checked the mail, and one letter attracted her attention. She knew right away that it was from Thomas. She immediately opened and read it.

My dearest Jane,

I hope everything on your side is okay. I want to tell you about some good news from my side. Our psychotherapists believe that we are both well enough to start a new life together as man and wife. So we're planning a civil marriage. We haven't fixed the date yet, but it could either be in August or September this year.

We intend to invite my immediate family and a few close friends, and our therapists. Since Linda doesn't have any relatives, she'll invite her best friend, with whom she lived after she left the concentration camp. So I don't know whether I should also invite you or not. I cannot decide. I've asked my close relatives and Linda's opinion, and they think it's a good idea. But I'm not sure how you would feel about it. If you would come, we'd be most happy. You could bring along anyone you like. But if you don't want to come, we'll also understand. It's entirely up to you.

Soon after the wedding, Linda and I would like to visit you to become acquainted with the orphans we might adopt. As our printing business is quite well, I think we could adopt four children if we find the right ones and they would like to be adopted by us. Two girls and two boys would be ideal. Could you perhaps recommend some candidates?

When we've chosen the date for the wedding, we'll send you an invitation. We'd be so happy if you would come. Take care and goodbye for the time being.

With all my love,
Thomas

Thomas's letter gave Jane a lot to think about. On the one hand, she wanted to attend the wedding, but on the other hand, she was not sure whether it'd be appropriate or not. She decided to answer his letter on 25th May.

My dear Thomas,

Thank you for your letter. I've been deliberating on what I should do. If I'm honest, I don't know how to decide. On the one hand, I'd like to make both of you happy by attending your wedding, but on the other hand, as you have written, I wonder if it'd be appropriate. Since we're now just good friends, and your family and friends know our story very well, it should not be inappropriate for me to come, I suppose. But let me think it over.

Concerning your visiting me, I'm quite excited to meet Linda. A few words about making acquaintance with the orphans: It's strictly against our rules to recommend any one of them to potential adoptive parents. You yourselves must decide who you want to adopt. You can stay with us for a couple of weeks and talk with them. A good tip is that sometimes potential adopters have a problem choosing who they want to adopt, so a lottery system is used in such cases.

Please convey my most heartfelt greetings to Linda as well.
Jane

Sarah had come back from New York City, where she attended a private high school, on 30th June. She had come back to stay for a month with her mother and grandparents. Christine, Paul, ten of Sarah's cousins and friends, and some former and remaining orphans with whom Sarah had an excellent relationship were there to welcome her back at Jane's home. It was two o'clock in the afternoon on 7th June, a Sunday.

After they had finished their lunch, they sat down together in the living room and talked about various topics. At one point, Sarah asked her mother, "Mama, my friends have been talking about your novel. As you know, I'm not interested in novels myself; to my mind, they are written by dreamers. But since it sounds like a good read, may I read it while I'm here?"

"Sure, if you want to. There's a copy on my desk. I'm up to Chapter 31."

"How many chapters will it have in the end, and when are you going to publish it?"

"I have no idea. But it'll probably contain about forty. When will it be published? I don't know yet either. It'll depend on whether I find a literary agent who wants to represent me or a publisher who wants to publish it. When I finish it, I'll look for an agent."

"How much of it is based on reality, Mama?"

"Maybe about ninety percent."

"Okay, I'll probably read it when I go to bed tonight or tomorrow."

They all went to bed at ten o'clock. Sarah took the novel from her mother's desk and read it through the night. The next day Christine and Paul came to the house to join Jane and Sarah for lunch. Just after lunch, Sarah said to her mother, "Mama, I read the novel, and I liked it so much. I cried a lot. I think I'll begin reading novels from now on. I've learned a lot about my father, and I've begun to understand and sympathize with him. I've learned a lot about my sister, Jennifer, too."

Christine, Paul, and Jane looked at each other meaningfully, obviously delighted. Jane was surprised by Sarah's words and said, "Do you really mean it, Sarah?"

"Yes, Mama. They're going to invite you to the wedding, aren't they?"

"Yes, that's what he said in his letter."

"Mama, I'm thinking about giving them an extraordinary wedding present."

"Oh, I'm so glad to hear that, Sarah. What kind of present would that be?"

"If you go, I'll come with you if the wedding takes place before I leave, and I'll tell him that I forgive him for leaving us alone and for what he did at the Propaganda Ministry since he was just a cog in the system."

Jane, Christine, and Paul were so overcome with emotion that they could barely hold back their tears. And Jane could only utter a few words in a cracked voice. "If you do that, he'll be so happy. There could be no greater present for him."

"Mama, if the wedding takes place after I leave, I'll write him a beautiful letter."

"Darling, I'll give him a hint that if they choose a date that's about, say, a week before you leave, I'll attend, and there will be an extraordinary wedding present for them. Or something like that."

Christine found the idea very good. "I think that's an excellent idea, Jane."

Christine then had an idea and turned to Paul. "Paul, I think we should go too. Look, the paths of our two families have been closely intertwined for so long, yet we've never had the chance to get to know our former son-in-law intimately, nor his parents and relatives. And we're all getting old. So this could be the last chance for all of us. What do you think?"

"Without being invited?"

Jane interjected, "He wrote in his letter that if I was coming, I could bring anyone along with me. Papa, I think Mama's idea is perfect. We can all go."

Paul gave it some thought and said, "Yes, that's not a bad idea. But I'd worry that the reunion would be too emotional for all of us, especially Sarah and Thomas."

Christine agreed. "We'd have to control ourselves and not to get too emotional. I'm quite sure Thomas could burst into tears on seeing Sarah."

"Mama, I must talk to Jennifer as soon as possible and apologize to her for my aloofness toward her in the past."

"If you do that, she'll be so happy her whole life. She asked me a couple of times if you're even a bit racist. She was always so sad the way you dealt with her. So every time she asked the question I mentioned, I told her to wait patiently until you're a bit older and that you might have a change of heart."

"Yes? Since I read your novel, I'm so sad that I've misbehaved toward her from my childhood without any particular reasons."

Sarah's words deeply moved Christine, Paul, and Jane to tears.

In the afternoon, Jane thought deeply about what she and her parents and Sarah had talked about, and she realized that she needed to inform Jennifer about the wedding. Coincidentally, Jennifer called her at about seven o'clock that evening. Jane told her about the conversation and asked her if she wanted to give them a wedding present. Jennifer said that she thought Sarah's idea was a good one. Jane asked Jennifer if she might want to go with them and personally tell Thomas that she forgave him. At first, Jennifer liked the idea, but then she changed her mind because although Thomas used to say that he and his parents were not racists, her presence might spoil the party's mood. So she would just send them a present instead. Jane understood. She told Jennifer what Sarah said about Jennifer and that Sarah would call her the next day. Jennifer could not find words to describe how happy she was at hearing the news.

The next day Jane called Thomas and told him about her decision to attend the wedding, and that if it was held in July, she would come with her parents and bring four "extraordinary presents" for him. Thomas told her that he would arrange that the ceremony was held in July and was thrilled that Jane and her parents would attend. He asked her if she could give him a clue about what these "extraordinary presents" might be. But Jane just said they would be something he couldn't possibly imagine – and she asked him if he had any heart problems. Thomas was quite surprised by this strange question and replied that he had recently seen a cardiologist and that the results were normal. He insisted on knowing why she had asked, but she played it down and said there was no particular reason.

Jane got the invitation to the wedding to be held on 23rd July – a Friday. The ceremony would take place at a registry office in Berlin at eleven a.m. At about noon, the reception would take place at Thomas' villa. Jane informed Thomas that she and her parents would go to his villa from the airport at around 12:30 and return to Belgium on the same day, with a flight at seven p.m.

At noon, Thomas and Linda and all their guests were back at the villa, which was quite big and located in the middle of a large compound with several species of flowers and trees. There were about thirty guests. Thomas nervously glanced at the main gate every few seconds. Then, at about 12:20, a taxi entered the main gate, and Jane, her parents, and Sarah got out. Everyone came to greet them. They warmly hugged each other, one after another. Thomas was so shocked at seeing Sarah that he was speechless. Jane said, "Sarah, this is your father; Thomas, this is Sarah."

Thomas and Sarah embraced each other tightly, and both of them burst into torrential tears. All the women were also sobbing, and the men's eyes too were full of tears. While they were still embracing, Sarah said to Thomas in a choked voice, "Papa, I've forgiven you for what you did to us."

Thomas could not utter a word. He just kept on weeping. It took him several minutes to finally say, in a choked voice, "Sarah, thank you so much. Today is one of the happiest days of my life: my wedding to Linda, your forgiveness, and the presence of Jane and Christine and Paul. When your mama said on the phone that she'd bring four extraordinary presents, I had no idea what they could be."

When he had calmed down, Jane handed him a package and a card and said, "Thomas, these are the second and third 'extraordinary presents' from Jennifer."

Thomas was very excited and immediately opened the card and read it aloud.

Hello my dear Linda and Thomas,

I wish you both a joyous and long-lasting married life. At first, I wanted to come with my grandparents, my mother, and Sarah. But then I changed my mind because I thought my presence might spoil the mood. I've forgiven you entirely for what happened in our family. I hope to see you both someday soon. All the best to you once again.

Your beloved Jennifer

By the way, since you've got everything that one might wish for in this world, I'm sending only two humble presents to you both: two sweaters. I knitted them for you myself. I know that red is your favorite color, and I remember your size, so I hope it fits. As for Linda, I asked Mama to find out her size and her favorite color – which is pink. I hope it fits her, and she likes it.

Thomas and Linda's eyes were full of tears. They both then tried on the sweaters immediately and found that they were the right size. They asked Jane to convey their heartfelt thanks to Jennifer and they said they would also call her the next day. In the next moments, Jane said, "Now the fourth present. Can you imagine what it could be, Thomas?"

Thomas was perplexed because there was nothing in Jane's hand. He admitted that he had no idea what it could be. Then Jane jokingly said, "It's me."

Thomas was even more baffled now. Jane then added, "Thomas, I mean my presence here."

Now everybody realized that it was a joke, and they all broke out into laughter. Sarah and Linda hugged each other and wept for several minutes. The scene was so emotional that it took them nearly two hours to calm down and start talking. They had their meal at three o'clock. Sarah took a seat between Thomas and Linda, and they conversed together without pause. But when Jane, Sarah, Christine, and Paul were about to leave at six o'clock, it became quite emotional again.

Thomas and Linda agreed that they would visit Jane to interview the few remaining orphans for adoption. There were only about twenty-four still living at the centers. Thomas and Linda visited Jane at her home in early September and made the acquaintance of the orphans. They all liked each other very much, but as Linda and Thomas had had difficulty choosing the four orphans – two girls and two boys – they wanted to adopt, lots had to be drawn. Their adopted children's ages ranged between ten and fourteen. A week after their stay with Jane, Thomas and Linda happily went home with their newly adopted children. Jane decided to adopt the remaining twenty, for she felt the procedures were too heartbreaking.

CHAPTER 33
(15th April 1954 - Thursday)

Hello, my dearest Mama,

I want to tell you what I'm up to now. As I briefly mentioned on the phone, we both passed our examinations with excellent grades. What Carlos and I want to tell you is that we wish to combine our graduation ceremony with our weddings (civil and church) at the same time to save time and money. Tentatively, we would like to do it between the 15th and 25th of this coming June, here in Madrid. I'm so sorry to inform you of the timing on such short notice. There were some unexpected and unavoidable circumstances.

Initially, we wanted to do it either late this year or early next year. Two reasons for the change of plan that I can tell you about now are that it seems I've conceived, and half of our best friends with whom we'd like to celebrate will be moving to other countries soon. I know that it might be too short notice to organize things on your part, but we can't postpone it any longer.

I wonder if you and my brother, sister, oma, and opa can come? We intend to invite Linda, Thomas, and their four children, too. And also only our closest friends. I'm sure you'll have some good ideas for the occasion, so we'd appreciate it very much if you could share them with us. Another important thing is that we'd like to celebrate as simply and cheaply as possible, with the money we've been saving during the last few years.

Mama, I hope to hear from you again soon.

Your beloved daughter

P.S. Mama, the church ceremony will take place in a small Methodist church nearby to which we belong.

Jane read Jennifer's letter as soon as she got it. She thought for two days before replying.

Hello my darling,

We are all happy beyond description to hear the good news. Sarah and Victor are so pleased to be coming to the ceremony. But unfortunately, your oma, opa, and I will not be able to come because we've got some important plans for our family business which we cannot postpone.

When you're married, do come here with Dorotea, and we'll celebrate together again. If you want, you may bring your best friends, too. Marriage is a once-in-a-lifetime event for most of us, so I'll try to do my best for you. Although I understand your wish to combine the two occasions as simply and cheaply as possible, I'll send you a few thousand dollars to smooth the way. I think your idea of inviting Linda and Thomas and their children is very thoughtful, and I'm sure they'll appreciate it very much.

The rest we can discuss on the telephone. Take care!

Your loving Mama

P.S. Why don't you spend your honeymoon in the Bernese Highlands, darling? Let's discuss it when you come here, okay?

The civil marriage took place on 17th June, a Friday, and they made the church wedding on 19th June, a Sunday, at noon. The celebration started at three p.m. and ended at nine. Sarah, Victor, and four former orphans from ON, with whom Sarah had a good relationship, arrived two days earlier to participate in the festivities. What made Jennifer so happy was Sarah flew extra from New York to Belgium and then to Madrid to attend Jennifer's wedding party. Linda and Thomas and their four adopted children had wanted to attend the ceremony in Madrid, but Thomas could not get the time off because his printing business had received several orders at the last moment, and Heide and her family were on holiday. Then, on 24th June, a Friday, Jennifer, Carlos, Dorotea, the four orphan friends, Victor and Sarah, flew back to Brussels and then proceeded to Waimes. On the next day, Jane, Christine, Paul, Linda, Thomas, many former orphans, and several old friends of Jennifer's from the neighboring communities celebrated it once more.

On 30th June, a Thursday, Jennifer, and Carlos flew from Brussels to Basel to honeymoon for four weeks in an Alpine hut in the Bernese Highlands. They spent most of their time hiking. Dorotea flew back to Madrid from Brussels, alone.

As they wanted to work first for a couple of years in a hospital to gain some experience before starting their work in Guatemala, they sent out applications to several hospitals in Madrid and its neighboring regions. Then, after a waiting time of more than one year and many rejections, their applications were finally accepted by the Hospital Universitario de la Princesa in Madrid, which opened on 3rd November 1955. They made a five-year contract with the hospital with the possibility of extending it another five years. Sofia, their first daughter, was born on 24th December 1956, and their second daughter on 15th October 1958. They named her Isabella. Calle de Diego de Leon 62, the hospital's location, was quite close to Dorotea's house in which they all lived, so Dorotea could happily babysit the babies nearly every day. They all visited Jane every six months for a couple of weeks, and they spent their summer holidays every year with Jane and Dorotea in the Bernese Highlands. Christine, Paul and Jane had also visited them twice in Madrid.

Because of the two children, Jennifer and Carlos had to postpone their initial plan to go to Guatemala to thoroughly study the local situation. They had to collect the necessary information they needed through various channels. For instance, they learned that from 1954 there were no more social improvements in health care. The focus on health care was thus generally abandoned. The total GDP expenditure on health care was only about one to two percent. Therefore, some NGOs and community organizations appeared on the scenes to provide rudimentary health care for the general population.

Jennifer, Carlos, their daughters, and Dorotea visited Jane, Christine, and Paul between 10th and 17th October 1960. During this visit, they thoroughly discussed their plan for humanitarian work in Guatemala. As the ruthless civil war was now rapidly spreading to several parts of the country, they agreed to wait some more years to see how the political situation further developed. And they decided to concentrate more on post-civil war humanitarian and development projects instead of making a strong presence during the war. But meanwhile, they would open an office in Guatemala City, permanently staffed by about five people, collect information, and prepare for their future projects. Jennifer and Carlos would visit this office once every year, or more often if necessary. Christine and Paul would establish a non-profit foundation in the family's name soon with a starting capital of a couple of million dollars. And it would make some contributions through the International Red Cross and Guatemalan Red Cross until Jennifer and Carlos could implement their own projects.

CHAPTER 34
(13th December 1960 – Tuesday)

The time was about eight o'clock in the morning. Jane and Victor were preparing at her home for a journey to Catherine's place in West Berlin. As Jane was afraid of flying, she always traveled only by train or car, but this time they would fly, at her relatives' insistence, and partly to shorten the traveling time. Another reason was that she did not enjoy long-distance journeys by train or car anymore. Christine, Paul, and some of Jane's cousins and friends came to her house to say goodbye. At ten o'clock, two of her cousins took them to Brussels airport.

It was only the third time she had traveled to Germany. The first time was when Victor celebrated his passing of the university entrance examination. The second time was when she and her parents and Sarah flew to West Berlin to attend Linda and Thomas' wedding party. This time, she had agreed to attend Catherine's sixty-sixth birthday party on 1st January 1961. Since she turned fifty, Catherine had begun to have a special birthday party every five years, inviting her closest friends. She had wanted to celebrate her sixty-fifth birthday the previous year, but due to certain unexpected events, she could not do it. So she wanted to celebrate it with her family alone this time. She promised her friends that she would celebrate with them again on her seventieth birthday. Actually, Jane did not want to go, but Catherine insisted that she would be so sad forever if Jane were not there. So Jane very reluctantly agreed to fulfill Catherine's wish. Victor came to pick his mother up. Since going to Berlin to live with his paternal grandmother when he was five or six years old, he'd commuted very often between St. Vith and West Berlin. The flight from Brussels to West Berlin was not as bad as Jane had expected, and the plane landed punctually in West Berlin. They arrived safely at Catherine's home at around half past three; Catherine and a young girl were already waiting for them. They all greeted and embraced each other warmly.

"Thank you so much for coming, and I'm so glad to see you again, Jane."

"I'm also so pleased to see you in good health after several months, Catherine."

Catherine then introduced Anna, the young girl, to Jane. "Anna, this is Jane, Victor's mother. Jane, this is Anna, a Russian girl who is visiting us. She doesn't speak German, but she speaks English."

Jane and Anna shook hands and exchanged a few phrases in English. Then Catherine ushered Jane into the house.

"Jane, we've decorated the house for Christmas and New Year and my birthday. We'll relax for a little while, and then I'll show you the surprise present we have for you – an exceptional present. At about six o'clock, we'll have dinner."

"Oh really? I'm dying to know what the surprise is! Is it a Christmas or New Year present?"

"No, there'll be separate Christmas and New Year presents for you later."

"I'm so curious. What's it for, then?"

"You'll know why I wanted to give it to you when you see it."

"Okay. Let it be."

Catherine showed her around the house, and they chatted for nearly ninety minutes. Then, at about five o'clock, they all took seats in the living room. Catherine said to Jane, "Now I'd like to show you your present. Don't be shocked, okay?" Then she called out quite loudly, "You can come in now!"

Suddenly, there was the sound of footsteps somewhere behind a wall. Then, after a few seconds, Daniel appeared at the door and greeted Jane, smiling.

"Hello Jane, I'm Daniel."

Jane could not believe her eyes. She thought her heart would stop beating. She could not utter a single word. Daniel walked slowly toward her, she stood up to greet him, and he took her in his arms, and kissed her affectionately on the cheeks. Tears filled their eyes. Catherine, Victor, and Anna were also overcome with emotion and wept.

Jane and Daniel took seats on a sofa that had been reserved for them. They held hands tightly, still speechless, and longingly looked into each other's eyes. It took Jane several minutes to speak in a choked voice, her eyes still full of tears. "Daniel, you *did* survive the war! How did you manage it?"

"Yes, I did … but it's a long and heartbreaking story, Jane."

"How long have you been here?"

"Just over a few months. Jane, you haven't changed much."

"Thank you, Daniel, but that's not true. Let's be honest: We have all changed quite a lot in the last twenty years. Your hair has turned white, and we both have got some wrinkles on our faces. But you still have your charm, Daniel. Would you please tell me what happened to you in the war?"

"Thank you very much for your comment about my charm, Jane. Yes, you're right; we have changed quite a lot in the past twenty years. But your charm and beauty and elegance also remain. Well, first of all, let me thank you deeply for taking care of Victor and letting him stay with his oma. And my mother let me read your novel up to Chapter 33, which she got some years ago. I now know what a wonderful person you are. I was moved so deeply while I was reading the manuscript. I could not control my tears at times. I'm sure it'll be a bestseller. It made me think very seriously and critically about several vital themes, including religion and philosophy. Yours has been a very colorful and fascinating life, Jane.

"But yes, I'll tell you about myself very briefly. We had surrounded Moscow in the winter of 1941/42 and captured several Russian soldiers; countless people were dying from their wounds or hunger and cold. Fortunately, as I was a medical officer, provisions were at my disposal for the wounded and sick on our side. There was a prisoner named Alexander, who looked as old as my father and could speak a little German. I could also understand and speak a few Russian words. I asked him about his life. He told me that he had a young daughter and that his wife was mentally ill, so she had to be confined in the house. He said, 'I'm a sick old man. And we are all in a helpless situation. Whether we both survive this war or die, the outcome of the war won't change. So why don't you let me go or kill me right now? I can't bear the cold and hunger anymore.' That was what I barely understood. It convinced me that we both meant nothing in the grand scheme of things, and at the same time, what he said shocked me deeply. I couldn't kill somebody in cold blood. And I sympathized with him when I heard his family story. I asked him whether he'd be able to find his way to safety if I gave him some food, and he said yes. So I gave him some food and a dry blanket. He disappeared into the darkness of the night. As everybody was out for his own survival, none of my comrades noticed his absence.

"Not long after that, several of us were captured by the Russians. Then, just before I was to be executed by a firing squad, the man I had helped escape appeared and recognized me and spared my life. I later found out that he was a rather influential political commissar attached to a military unit. He and his comrades were quite impressed by my knowledge of communism. I had to thank my father for that knowledge. My father was a socialist. I heard very often all sorts of terminology and the basic doctrines of communism from him. Later I got to know Alexander's family, including their daughter, Alisa, who later became my wife. But she passed away a few years ago from blood cancer. Anna is our daughter and fourteen now. My wife and I waited until the end of the war and then got married in late 1945. As I had the chance to work in many military hospitals, we belonged to Russia's privileged class. And by the way, my father-in-law will visit us here soon."

As Jane listened to Daniel's story, tears were rolling down her cheeks.

"Did you get back to Germany without any difficulty?"

"Before I answer your question, I'd like to tell you how I was able to survive the war. My desire to see you and the baby and my mother was so strong that it gave me the strength to endure all the hardships that came my way. If I hadn't had that burning desire, I'd probably have committed suicide at the beginning of the Moscow Campaign.

The heartlessness of the soldiers during that campaign cannot be described. Thousands went totally insane, and many committed suicide. So yes, to come back to your last question, there were a lot of bureaucratic obstacles, but I overcame them with the help of the German and the Soviet Red Cross."

"Daniel, could you tell me something about your late wife?"

"I was like a son to her parents. And they were like my parents. I lived with them in an apartment, became part of the family. I was working in a military hospital, and my wife worked as a nurse there, too. She was not an intellectual, but she was so intelligent and kind. We rarely quarreled. To cut the story short, her disease was detected very late. Fortunately, she did not suffer any pain at all before her death. And she died in my arms. That was about four years ago."

While Daniel was telling his story, tears were silently streaming down on everybody's cheeks. It was several minutes before she could ask Daniel another question. "I'm so sorry to hear that, Daniel. I do understand how much you must have suffered from her loss. Now, could you perhaps tell me what your most bitter experiences in life were?"

"I lost faith in the humanity of the great majority of humankind, but within this multitude, there are still a few with a noble heart: you and your parents and your close relatives, my father-in-law, my mother, and my late wife, for example. Such rare examples give me some hope."

"Do you have any information about General Ferdinand Schaal, by the way?"

"Yes. It was one of the things I wanted to find out most urgently, and soon after I arrived here, I made inquiries with the German Red Cross. You've probably heard of what is known as the '20th July Plot'. He was involved in this resistance movement and then imprisoned until the end of the war. Here's a little bit of its background history, if you haven't heard about it. On 20th July 1944, Adolf Hitler and his top military associates entered the briefing hut at the Wolf's Lair military headquarters, a series of concrete bunkers and shelters located deep in East Prussia forests. Suddenly there was an enormous explosion, which killed three officers and a stenographer and injured everyone else. This assassination attempt was the work of Colonel Claus von Stauffenberg. The plan was to assassinate Hitler, seize power in Berlin and establish a new, pro-Western government and save Germany from total defeat. An estimated 7,000 people were arrested, of whom approximately 4,980 were executed. Among those executed were three field marshals, nineteen generals, twenty-six colonels, two ambassadors, seven diplomats, one minister, three secretaries of state, and the Berlin police head. I heard that General Schaal is now living in Baden-Baden in southern Germany. I think he was born in 1889 or 1890 – that means he must be about seventy now – just four or five years older than my mother."

"I wish I could see him again to thank him for giving us our chance. If he had not been there, we would never have met each other. Or it could also be that we were destined to meet each other thanks to our karmas."

"Yes, he's such a kind-hearted person. Without his blessing, I don't think we would ever have become lovers. Or, as you've just said, our karmas might have predestined us to meet each other in this way. Who knows? I'll try to contact him to talk with him and thank him. I'm sure he'd be interested in meeting us again. I'll let you know if I can contact him."

Catherine interrupted their conversation.

"Excuse me, Jane and Daniel, for interrupting you, but we'll have dinner in a few minutes. After dinner, you can continue to talk for as long as you want. These are my plans until we celebrate my birthday on 1st January: At about eight o'clock this evening, Anna, Victor, and I will leave for Switzerland by night train for a short skiing holiday. We'll come back on 24th December, and we'll celebrate Christmas together here. We'll then combine my birthday and the New Year celebrations once again. We won't invite anybody else. Victor told me that you'd be able to stay for at least three weeks. Can you?"

"Don't worry about that, Catherine. I can stay for as long as I like."

"Thank you; I'm pleased to hear that, Jane. There's a grand piano if you'd like to play some Chopin again. Victor, Anna, and I want tonight to be an extraordinary reunion for you. In case you'd prefer to listen to records instead of playing the piano yourselves, the record player and records, including the Ballades and Nocturnes and Pachelbel's Canon, are on the table over there."

Daniel was pleasantly surprised and thanked his mother lavishly for her thoughtfulness. Jane also had some nice words for her. They uncorked two champagne bottles and toasted to mark their joyous reunion when seated in the dining room. As soon as they had finished dinner, Catherine, Anna, and Victor left for the train station in a taxi.

Jane and Daniel sat tightly together, and he shyly began to caress and kiss her, first with tenderness and then with passion. After a short pause, he asked her to play the piano. "Jane, would you play the Ballade you played twenty years ago or the Canon that I played?"

"That was the last time I played that piece, Daniel. Every time I heard them both, they made me so sad because you came into my mind. So I never played them again."

"I longed to hear those pieces again during the war, but there was no possibility. Soon after the war ended, I bought a secondhand record player and some old records of Chopin."

She leaned into his arms and shed silent tears as he was telling his story.

"Daniel, let's listen to those pieces instead of playing them. Maybe we'll play them in the next few days, but not now. Okay?"

"Yes, that's okay, Jane. Let me put something on."

Daniel stood up, put a record on. It was the Ballade that Jane had played twenty years ago when they met each other. They quietly listened to the pieces of music, silently shedding tears. They could not talk, for they were feeling sad. At the end of the first record, they began first to cuddle each other tenderly and then passionately. Then after a long while, he began to undress her. But he was shocked and irritated by her unexpected question. "Daniel, please don't do that yet. Before we do it, I'd like to ask you a few more questions."

He replied nervously, "Ask me anything you want."

"Why did you fall in love with me the moment you saw me? Was I so beautiful to you?"

"The reason was easy. It was your charm and your husky voice, which I thought very erotic, and the way you moved. You emitted an aura of elegance and tenderness. And why did you love me at first sight, Jane?"

"Thank you very much for your kind comments. Nobody – I mean none of the men I've ever fallen in love with – has ever complimented me on my husky voice. Well, the first time we looked at each other, your gaze was so intense that it bored deep into my heart. I don't quite know how to describe it. And when you told me about your life – your father and sister dying from their wounds – it reminded me of my own family, and I immediately felt a deep sympathy with you."

"Thank you very much, Jane. We still have more than two weeks together, so let's go to bed, okay?"

"Daniel, would you be offended if I slept alone in your mother's bed? She told me I could take it if I preferred."

Daniel was visibly surprised and disappointed again by Jane's words. "Why do you want to sleep alone, Jane?"

"Because I'm not sure if I can build up a strong emotional attachment with you again, although I still love you so much. I'm longing for the warmth of your body, but at the same time, I'm very afraid of becoming too emotionally dependent on you again."

"Jane, don't worry about that. Since you're very much influenced by Buddhist philosophy, why don't we try to enjoy every moment that we have together?"

At last, they agreed to sleep together in Daniel's bed. But just before they went to bed, Daniel asked Jane some more questions.

"Jane, if I'm honest, I've only slept with two or three women in my life. And my wife was very conservative in bed. So I'm afraid I might disappoint you since you are surely much more experienced than me."

"Daniel, please don't worry about that. If I have the warmth of your body, your love, your tenderness, I won't have any inhibitions. The physical part we can always discuss; we'll openly discuss in which ways we can maximize our mutual desires. Okay?"

"Jane, you can have them for as long as I live."

The next morning, they got up at ten o'clock and breakfasted at eleven o'clock.

"Daniel, you're still full of energy and quite expert. When you told me last night that you've only slept o with two or three women, I didn't expect such expertise from you."

"Honey, you are even more energetic than me. Thank you very much for your kind comment. I was only experimenting with what I've ever read in the books. I wish we could have such blissful moments eternally, don't you?"

"Let's exchange our expertise and experiment without any inhibitions and then try to catch up as much as possible what we've missed for so long, okay?"

They enjoyed the ensuing days and nights until Anna, Victor and Catherine came back from their holiday. They were so delighted to find Jane and Daniel so happy. And they were even more glad to learn that the pair had decided to get married. They also agreed that they should not make it public until everything had been arranged on both sides and that they should not live together openly until the marriage had taken place. Until then, they would visit each other discreetly. Daniel told Jane that he had to keep a low profile so that the local news media would not get a whiff of his presence. She also learned that Anna wanted to study medicine and specialize in psychiatry, mainly due to the mental disorder that her grandmother suffered. She wanted to devote her life to such people, which Jane appreciated very much. And Jane told Daniel that she was a bit disappointed with Victor because he was more interested in studying literature than economics or business administration; he had been inspired by her and wanted to become a writer. But Jane wanted to groom him to take over the family business one day. Daniel assured her that he would try to persuade him to change his mind.

They celebrated Christmas, Catherine's birthday, and the New Year without a single outsider. On 4th January 1961, Victor accompanied his mother back to her home in Waimes.

CHAPTER 35
(14th July 1961 – Friday)

Jane and Daniel chose 14th July for their civil marriage in Waimes for two reasons: First, it was Jane's fifty-sixth birthday; and second, they would be able to combine her birthday and their marriage anniversary in the future. Since her fiftieth birthday in 1955, Jane had decided to have special birthday celebrations every five years with her relatives and close friends. But she postponed her fifty-fifth birthday celebration, which was due in 1960, for one year so that they could combine it with their wedding party in the future. And since she and Daniel did not belong to any religious groups, they decided upon a civil marriage.

For celebrating her birthday and their marriage parties, they invited several people who had been important to the Jeanmart family for decades as special guests. Among them were five local politicians; a few representatives of charitable organizations, including the Belgian Red Cross; a few Catholic priests and nuns, Protestant pastors, and a rabbi; Professor Fleming and his wife; Thomas's parents and Heide and her family; Linda, Thomas, their four adopted children with their families; Jane's former classmate Barbara from Brussels and her husband; John's two American and Belgian friends with their families; Sister Hanna's parents, brother, and sister; three journalists; and a camera team with four movie cameras. Many TV stations requested Jane to let them transmit the event live, but she declined. Instead, she hired a movie camera team to record it for the coming generations.

The preparations for the occasion had begun a few months earlier. Also invited were the orphans who had been adopted and the elderly residents who had moved out of the two centers at the end of the war, and a few hundred from neighboring communities as well. Although the remaining OS residents had been moved to ON soon after the war's end, some facilities still remained intact at OS so that many former orphans who came back with either their adoptive parents or with their own families, and some former adult residents of the centers could stay there. Most of the other guests were lodged in hotels at Jane's expense. Jane had also invited Anne, Betty and her family, and Edith, but they could not come because Anne felt she was no longer fit enough to make a long journey, and Betty had to look after her. So they sent presents and wedding cards instead. Jane learned from Anne and Betty that Edith had not conceived with John, but she had been treated as a family member and looked after by them through Jane's generous financial arrangements.

The marriage took place at the registry office, as planned, at eleven o'clock. The day was sunny, and the temperature very pleasant. The formal procedure lasted some forty-five minutes. Besides the special guests, Sarah, Jennifer, Carlos, Dorotea, Victor, Catherine, Christine, Paul, nearly all the office and medical personnel of the two centers with their families, the part-time and full-time volunteers and their families, and the volunteer teachers were also present. Birthday and wedding anniversary cards and presents piled up on some long tables in one corner. As usual, a stage was erected temporarily for the occasion in the hall; some special guests and the elderly celebrants were seated on it.

The ceremony began at two p.m. in the spacious courtyard with the reading of a message from the reigning monarch. It was followed by champagne bottles' uncorking and a toast to Jane's good health and long life to the couple's marriage.

Jane then greeted the guests with the following words:

"Good afternoon to everybody! First of all, I'd like to thank you all from the bottom of my heart for coming to this combined party. At the same time, Daniel and I offer our heartfelt thanks for your good wishes for a happy and long-lasting married life. And we're so thankful for all the beautiful cards and precious presents as well. Since all of you know what we are thinking about in our minds, I won't make a long speech, so let's start the ceremony right away."

Karin moderated the ceremony as usual. Brief speeches by the special guests followed Jane's short speech. Nearly all the speeches were about how various people or organizations had come into contact with and got to know the Jeanmart family. Then Catherine spoke for about five minutes, briefly mentioning her family life, including how Daniel had suddenly reappeared out of the blue. Dorotea expressed her gratitude to Jane for her promise to take care of her if she ever needed it; she also recalled how she had raised Jennifer. It was then Jennifer's turn. She spoke about her childhood and mentioned how good her relationships with her maternal grandparents, her parents, and her half-sister Sarah and half-brother Victor were and how lucky she was to be born into such a loving and generous family. Then she went on to say how lucky she was to meet such a loving and caring person as Sister Hanna, and finally, how loving and caring her adoptive mother, Dorotea, was. She also mentioned how lucky she was to find her future husband, Carlos. She briefly mentioned their work in the Hospital Universitario de la Princesa in Madrid and their plans to contribute to humanitarian and development projects in post-civil war Guatemala and also in some of its war-torn neighboring countries through the non-profit foundation which her maternal grandparents and her mother would set up soon.

Sister Hanna's parents, brother, and sister also briefly recalled Hanna's life and Jane's relationship with her. They thanked Jane profusely for taking care of them at one of the centers until they had recovered from the wounds they had received in one of the bombings by Allied warplanes just before the end of the Ardennes Offensive. The speeches brought words of lavish praise for the family's humanitarian works during the war and best wishes for a happy, harmonious, and long-lasting marriage for Jane and Daniel.

Once again, Jane briefly told the assembled audience about Jennifer, Carlos, and Dorotea's planned journey to Guatemala via the United States on the coming Monday. Meanwhile, she and Daniel would fly to central Switzerland on Tuesday to honeymoon in an Alpine hut for six weeks. She concluded her speech with these words:

"When I asked Sarah if she also wanted to speak to our guests, she said she wanted to say something that would surprise her mother – that's me – as a special wedding present after all the cards had been read and the presents opened. So we'll start with the reading of the cards and unwrapping of the presents. And then let's see what she has to say. Hopefully, it'll be a pleasant surprise!"

Presents and wedding cards from those who could not come had started arriving a few days earlier. It took nearly two hours to finish reading the cards and opening the presents. Now Jane turned to Sarah and asked her to deliver her message.

"Good afternoon. I want to thank you all for coming here to celebrate the wedding of my parents. Mama and Daniel, I'd like to introduce Mr. William Beckert from New York. He will tell you who he is and why he has come."

Mr. Beckert took his turn. He was a tall and jolly man – probably about 180 centimeters – and in his late thirties or early forties.

"Good afternoon, everybody. First of all, may I wish you, Jane and Daniel, a long-lasting and happy married life! I'm so glad to have the opportunity to attend this very special wedding. I'm tremendously enjoying the day. Please let me get to the point right away. Sarah and I got to know each other through a common friend about a year ago. She told me one day about the existence of a novel written by her mother. I became curious and asked her to let me read it. The moment I read it, I fell in love with it and showed it to my colleagues. They also liked it very much. And we decided to offer you – may I call you Jane? – a seven-figure advance on sales. I'm the chief commissioning editor at Random House in New York. I came here especially to make you this offer. Jane, you may address me by my first name, William. Sarah and I have been on first-name terms for a long time now."

The joy upon hearing Mr. Becker's words was overwhelming for one and all. Jane was speechless, and her eyes were full of tears. It took her some minutes to calm down and reply to Mr. Beckert.

"Thank you so much, William. I don't even know what to say about your offer and how to describe my happiness. It's one of the happiest days of my whole life. But what I'm going to say now may sound arrogant to you. The amount of money itself doesn't impress me, for I'm not materialistic, and I've got more than I need in any case, but I cannot express how happy I am at the thought of becoming a recognized author! But you may be disappointed if I tell you something."

Mr. Beckert was a little bit taken aback but tried to hide his concern. "Jane, please tell me whatever it is!"

"The truth is, I wanted to wait and see what happens with Sarah, Jennifer, Carlos, Dorotea, Victor, my parents, myself and Daniel, and all my best friends and close relatives between now and my seventieth birthday; only after that do I intend to publish. That means waiting until 1975, fourteen years from now. That's a very long time, and perhaps too long for you to wait."

Mr. Beckert was visibly disappointed, but he tried to hide it. "Jane, does seventy hold a special meaning for you, and if yes, could you tell me why?"

Jane replied casually, "It may sound silly to many people, but I think I'm quite influenced by certain mystical numbers, like my father."

Mr. Beckert was now rather amused by her answer. He continued, "How many chapters more do you intend to add to the existing thirty-four?"

"I don't know yet for sure. It'll depend on what my karma and my family's karmas in store for us over the next fourteen years. But there won't be less than four or five, I imagine. What is happening now, for instance, will become Chapter 35."

Mr. Beckert thought for a few minutes, then his face lit up, and he made a suggestion.

"Couldn't you perhaps fictionalize the last few chapters?"

"No, I won't do that; it's an autographical novel."

Mr. Beckert pondered again, and then his face brightened once more. "Jane, that's okay. We've been in this business for decades, and we intend to be in it forever, so we can afford to wait. We won't put you under any time pressure."

"Thank you very much, William. But are you sure that you can wait that long? Don't you need to consult your colleagues?"

"I'm sure they'll agree since your material is so unique. Don't worry about that. We can discuss it in detail later."

Jane had an idea and made this proposal to Mr. Beckert: "William, what I can do for you is I could fictionalize the last few chapters so that if anything happened to me before the fourteen years were up, you'd have a complete manuscript in your hands. What do you think about that?"

Mr. Beckert was highly pleased. "Jane, I think that's an excellent idea."

"I'm glad, William. May I ask you a question?"

"Please go ahead!"

"May I know your conditions before I accept your offer? If I'm honest, I've got no idea how book contracts are structured. I thought I'd study them when I finish my manuscript, and it's ready for publication."

"Jane, you don't need to worry about our conditions. As one of the leading publishers worldwide, our terms are always absolutely fair. You can see the contract later and consult an experienced lawyer in the field, and if you aren't fully satisfied, you can withdraw at any time. One of the great advantages for you is that you don't need to go through an agent. We'll be able to help you with your negotiations for other rights as well if you want. And you may have the advance at any time."

"You've convinced me, and I'd be glad to accept your generous offer. This recognition as an author is a great wedding present for Daniel and me and my parents, our children, relatives, and friends. But since we're financially secure, I won't need payment until the book is published."

"Jane, I promise you that we will adjust this sum to the market rate at the time of its publication. But I can assure you it will not be less than what we're offering you now. Our discussion today will surely be spoken about a lot in the coming fourteen years, and it could even gain us good publicity without advertising the book at great expense. But may I suggest that you don't make any more copies or distribute it to your friends until its publication? If you don't have any objections, we can help you edit it with the assistance of our best in-house editors."

"Thank you very much for your understanding and valuable suggestions. Yes, we can discuss such matters in more detail later. Most of what I've written up to now is in the first-draft form. So it'll surely need to be polished with the help of some experienced editors."

"Believe me, Jane, your existing draft is already good for a first-time writer: the pacing, your narrative voice, the plots and sub-plots, the points of view, and so on. We probably only need to polish the prose. By the way, are you going to write more novels in the future?"

"Sure. I've got some ideas for a few more. Right now, I'm working hard on a fairy tale and another romance, although it's not a historical novel."

"Jane, we can discuss these works as well in due course. We'd be very interested in them, too."

Jane turned to Sarah and took her in her arms and thanked her profusely. "Sarah, this is a wonderful wedding present for us. How thoughtful you are, my dear. Thank you so much."

Daniel warmly hugged and thanked her, too, and all the guests congratulated Jane and embraced her one after another. Their eyes were filled with tears – tears of happiness. It was now Jennifer and Carlos's turn to congratulate Jane on her success. Jane spoke to them in a low voice because she did not want the entire audience to hear what she said. "Jennifer, I'll contribute a large part of my earnings from the sales of this book and its related rights, including the film rights, through the Jeanmart Foundation. We'll talk about it in detail in the coming days, okay?"

Jennifer and Carlos were thrilled to hear Jane's words. It was now 4:30 p.m. Karin announced that dinner would be served early at five o'clock and that the program would continue at six. All the guests had to move into the Assembly Hall, which was filled to the last seat. It was here that the Christmas and New Year feasts and concerts had been held during the war. It could accommodate up about 300 people.

The program had been designed so that everybody could ask any questions they wanted of those who were seated on the temporary stage. On the stage were Christine, Paul, Professor Fleming and his wife, Daniel, Catherine, Mr. Beckert, Jennifer, Carlos, Dorotea, Victor, Anna, the parents and siblings of Sister Hanna, John's two American and Belgian friends, Jane, Jane's cousins and friends who had been responsible for the supervision of the two orphanages, the medical staff, and the volunteer teachers. A few of the part-time and full-time volunteers were also there. Linda and Thomas were asked to sit on the stage, but they politely declined the offer and took their seats in the back rows among some former orphans with their spouses or their adoptive parents and many former elderly and disabled residents.

Karin acted as the moderator. As the proceedings opened, a young female journalist stood up and asked Paul this question:

"I've read Jane's discussion with the Buddhist monk from Ceylon, and I've also spoken with many prominent people with a Judaic-Christian background. So I'm very curious to know if you've found any satisfactory answers to the great mysteries you've been investigating for almost your entire adult life. We'd be very thankful for any answers you may have."

Paul was delighted by the journalist's question.

"Thank you very much for asking me this question, although I'm afraid I might have to disappoint you. The problem is that the more I think I know about these mysteries, the more mysterious they become. So I don't know how to proceed with my search from here on in."

"Does that mean you've given up your search?"

"I'd say yes."

"In that case, do you regret it?"

"Far from it. Through my research, I found out so many invaluable secrets about so many things in our world."

"For instance?"

"To give you just one example: I'm fully convinced now that there are other dimensions that we humans are incapable of knowing. But

I'm sure they influence our daily lives and the major events of this world in either a positive or negative way without our knowing."

"Can you prove that?"

"The fact that we can know our future to some extent through various methods of divination – for instance, astrology, numerology, palmistry, mediumship, dreams, prophecies, et cetera – shows that invisible forces more or less influence us. If we were merely the products of pure evolution, such things would not be possible. And look at the concepts of good luck and bad luck, or what we call 'fate' or 'destiny.' Whether what we call good luck or bad luck or fate or destiny is the work of invisible beings or is just some kind of coincidence, we don't have the mechanisms to find out. Oh, the list is endless."

"What do you think about the concept of predestination or determinism in Christian theology?"

"I like what the monk said on the subject. We have quite similar ideas on this topic. I discussed the theme with John, Jennifer's father, back in 1927, when he first visited us; I think the conversation is described in detail in Chapter 4 of Jane's novel. I don't think I can make any further interpretations. Of course, I could say something about it, but it would just be speculation and would benefit nobody."

"May I say that you seem to believe more in creationism than in evolution?"

"Because of the many great mysteries that science cannot yet adequately explain, I think creationism is more plausible, as the monk also said. In other words, it seems easier to believe in creationism than in evolution. But I don't know how much creationism has to do with the Judaic-Christian version of creation. I find the Buddhist monk's ideas on creationism fascinating."

"Do you think you might be able to persuade scientists who believe evolution to be the absolute truth to accept creationism to some extent?"

"I don't think I have to do that. I think it should be the other way around: They should convince us of how living beings could come into existence if male and female organisms didn't exist at the same time."

"Would you say there is wisdom in the other dimensions you talked about?"

"There must be wisdom in those dimensions - with perhaps different forms of living beings and with capabilities that we cannot imagine. In fact, what we call wisdom on this earth may be nothing compared to the wisdom in those dimensions. If those in other dimensions are not much superior to us in many ways, we might not exist at all in the first place."

"Speaking of prophecies, which do you think are the most fascinating? You must have studied Nostradamus's prophecies, for example."

"Sure. But although I find his prophecies fascinating, I won't discuss them with you here. Right now, our time is too limited. Above all else, prophecies – both divine and non-divine – have been so badly manipulated by so many people throughout human history for their own benefit that I prefer to keep my thoughts about them to myself. I use the existence of prophecies only to argue that invisible forces are influencing us – whether we like it or not."

"There are some people who believe that the Great War and the Holocaust had been foretold in both the Bible and by Nostradamus. What would you say about that?"

"I won't make any comment. It's too dangerous and too sensitive to make such wild speculations."

"You sound quite religious, Paul."

"Well, I was never an atheist. I have been fascinated by various religious concepts since childhood. My only problem has been that I didn't want to accept blindly what I was told."

"Do you believe that we humans have souls?"

"I'm now convinced that we've got souls. I have no doubts about that anymore."

"Have you perhaps secretly become a Christian again, Paul?"

"I'll only say that I know what is best for me. But I won't tell anybody else what they should or should not believe."

"Thank you very much. Another question, if I may: How much did Jane's discussion with the Buddhist monk influence your religious thought?"

"Well, it helped me to look at several religious concepts from different perspectives and very critically. I've read some books on Buddhism by prominent Buddhist scholars and monks, but I don't think I've ever come across similar ideas. I admire him for his honesty and sincerity."

"Do you think the Buddhist monk may have attained some sort of enlightenment?"

"Well, as he said, there are many kinds of enlightenment; I cannot answer your question. But what I can say is that he had profound insights into various religious concepts. And I found his explanation of enlightenment fascinating."

"What do you think of his various interpretations of Christianity – the biblical verses?"

"I find them fascinating, too. I've got the feeling those interpretations would give Christians – or those who are interested in Christianity – food for a lot of new thoughts."

"Do you have any message for mankind as a whole?"

"It'd be too much to say that I've got a message for the whole of humanity. I can only say what I truly believe – that is, if we do good things in this world, we will be rewarded in our next existence. I won't say in what form. It could be eternal life or higher status or a more comfortable existence in our next lives on this earth or in some spiritual domains. I'm absolutely convinced that there are other forms of existence beyond our earthly experience – it may have to do with the soul as we generally understand it, or consciousness."

"But we don't know the forms in which we'd continue to exist beyond this life?"

"No. We can only speculate. I don't think we'll ever find out in our lifetime."

"But aren't the descriptions of heavenly beings in the Book of Revelation, for instance, concrete proof of the existence of some form beyond this world? If we can accept them to be true, I don't think we need to make the kinds of inquiries you have made."

"Well, I wanted to find out if the existence of the heavenly beings as described in the Bible could be proved or disproved by occult means. But we may not need to burden ourselves with deep inquiries if we can easily accept the biblical descriptions, as you said. That means we may most likely retain our human form since the heavenly beings in the Book of Revelation, for example, seemed to look, feel, and behave exactly like us human beings."

The young journalist was visibly satisfied and thanked him. In the next moment another journalist stood up and asked him, "Would you advocate for any particular religion?"

"No, I won't do that."

"Do you have any regrets?"

"Yes, sure. I'm very sad that I didn't go to India to look into Palm Leaf astrology. I've asked several trustworthy people about it and what they told me was very convincing. It's a pity. The main obstacle was that I'm not too fond of long-distance flights anymore as I'm physically handicapped to some extent. But if it's true, it could be proof of the existence of predestination or determinism. The fact that I could not fulfill this wish itself might have been predestined."

"Do you intend to write a book about your research into the great mysteries?"

"Yes, I'm thinking seriously about it. But I'm not sure yet if I'll do it."

Nearly everybody begged Paul to write a book as soon as possible. Then a middle-aged woman stood up and turned to him and said, "I think what we're talking about is extremely interesting and very important, not only for us but also perhaps for millions of others. So I'd be very grateful if you could recommend a few books on occultism. There are so many on the market, and I don't know how to find the best ones."

Paul was very pleased with the question.

"I'm glad you brought this up. For beginners and those who don't have a great deal of time, I'd like to recommend some books written by a man called Cheiro."

He then took a sheet of paper from his files and read aloud, "His name is William John Warner (also known as Count Louis Hamon according to some sources), popularly known as Cheiro. He lived between 1st November 1866 and 8th October 1936. Cheiro is derived from the word Cheiromancy, meaning palmistry. He was a self-professed clairvoyant who learned palmistry, astrology, and Chaldean numerology in India during his stay there. He was celebrated for using these divination forms to make personal predictions for famous clients and foreseeing world events. The following are some of his books: *Cheiro's Book of Numbers; Cheiro's Language of the Hand; You and Your Hand; Cheiro's Palmistry for All; The Cheiro Book of Fate and Fortune; When Were You Born?; Cheiro's You and Your Star: The Book of the Zodiac,* et cetera. If you want to know more about him, here are a few passages from the Introduction of one of these books: *Count Louis Hamon, 1866 – 1936, better known to millions as Cheiro, was considered the greatest and most successful seer of modern times. He retired from public life after forty years of continuous occult research work. He is still regarded as the foremost proponent of the science of palmistry – that is, Cheirognomy and Cheiromancy. He did not confine himself to any one branch of occult study – numerology and astrology were equally taken into account in his remarkable predictions.*

By turns lecturer, public speaker, war correspondent, and editor of newspapers in London and Paris, Cheiro traveled worldwide. Early in his career, he chose to live in the East to study what he described as the Hindus' forgotten wisdom and the mystics of other races. When he set up his salon in London, the world's famous were among his numerous clients.

He was commanded to read the hands of many of Europe's crowned heads, presidents of republics, and leaders of commerce. Many subsequently testified that Cheiro's power of prediction from a study of their hands' lines was akin to the miraculous. Cheiro pre-

dicted the date of Queen Victoria's death, the year and month when King Edward VII would pass away; the grim destiny that awaited the late Czar of Russia; the assassination of King Humbert of Italy; the attempt on the Shah's life in Paris. And also for many others, he foretold with equal accuracy the outstanding events of their careers.

Several people thanked him profusely and many people asked nearly all the personalities on the stage various questions on different topics, and most of the answers were fascinating, exciting, and informative. Some doctors and nurses, teachers, and the full-time volunteers also reminisced briefly about some interesting experiences of their own. When Professor Fleming was asked whether he had become a Buddhist, a Christian, or an atheist, he said that he and his wife were still in the process of analyzing various religious concepts and that they were at a crossroads. However, they would have to make a decision about this while they still lived and breathed. A woman asked him whether he had found the right Buddhist school for them; he replied that he and his wife were still in a great dilemma about the one that would be best for them both—alternatively, they might well become independent Christians without a denomination. A journalist asked him what had happened with those who participated in the discussion between Jane and the monk. He replied that so far as he knew, about half of them became Christian while the rest remained Buddhist. But he declined to answer precisely the Churches that they joined.

Several people wanted to know more about Daniel, but he replied that he did not want to recall the military campaigns in Russia, for they were ruthless beyond description. He admitted that he became a Communist Party member out of political conviction. Still, when Nikita Khrushchev, the First Secretary of the Communist Party of the Soviet Union, criticized Stalin in 1956 in what was known as the "Secret Speech" he began to carefully and critically look at the ideology and those who implemented it. As a result, he became disillusioned entirely with those in power, but not with the ideology itself. Even today, he said, he still found the ideology very sound, but he had lost hope in the competency and moral uprightness of those who implemented it. He compared it with the Bible. He said the messages of Jesus, for instance, were about love, forgiveness, compassion, and peace, but countless Christians had even waged several wars against each other in his name. And he added that there were two other crucial factors that radically let him look at those who implemented the ideology: A book called *The New Class: An Analysis of the Communist System* by Milovan Djilas of Yugoslavia, which was published in the West in 1957, and the Hungarian Revolution of 1956, which started on 23rd October and ended on 10th November 1956.

A young man in his mid-twenties stood up and asked him, "Could you please tell us a bit more about this book?"

"The author of this book was a high-level official in Marshal Tito's communist government; he was eventually disillusioned with the system and became a Social Democrat. The theme of the book is a critique of Communism. It was not available in the Soviet Union, so I got it from a diplomat friend."

When he was asked if he was religious or not, he said he had just begun to do serious research into possible existence beyond this human life, thanks partly to Jane's discussion with the monk and his numerous conversations with Paul. A young man asked him to explain to the audience what the "Secret Speech" was. He took a piece of paper out of his pocket and read it, and at the same time, advised those who were interested in it to try to seek out the full text elsewhere.

"Here's just a bit of background information on it," he began. "The twentieth Party Congress of the Soviet Union was opened on 14th February 1956. In the opening words of his initial address, Khrushchev denigrated Stalin by asking delegates to rise in honor of the communist leaders who had died since the last congress, whom he named, equating Stalin with Klement Gottwald and the little-known Kyuichi Tokuda. In the early hours of 25th February, Khrushchev delivered what became known as the 'Secret Speech' to a closed session of the congress, limited to Soviet delegates. In four hours, he demolished Stalin's reputation. By the way, Klement Gottwald was the leader of the Communist Party of Czechoslovakia from 1929 to his death in 1953, and Kyuichi Tokuda was the Chairman of the Japanese Communist Party from 1945 to 1953."

A young woman requested Catherine to say something about her life. Catherine said she had nothing much to add beyond what she had already said, which was also mentioned briefly in a chapter of Jane's novel. Thomas and Linda were requested to say something about their lives. Linda told them how she and Thomas were so happy with their four adopted children. She thanked Jane profusely for her sympathy and help in many different ways during their hard times. (Linda and Thomas had politely declined to be seated on the stage from the beginning; they took their seats in the back row.)

A journalist in perhaps her late thirties asked Jane what made her generously spend a large chunk of the family's fortune on welfare during and after the war. Jane replied that her grandparents and parents had never been materialistic, so they could afford to be generous. She added that they owed several people for their fortunes since her grandparents had established the family business and that helping those in need was a way of repaying their contributions. A young woman asked her what Jane would do with the remains of her late husband, John. She replied that the construction of the Ardennes American Cemetery and Memorial, where John was buried, would be completed in 1962. She would hold a special program to commemorate the 18th anniversary of John's death next year with her family, relatives, and friends.

The question-and-answer session was very lively from the beginning until it ended at ten p.m. Several guests stayed on until Sunday, and there were more gatherings on both Saturday and Sunday. The last guests left Waimes on Sunday evening.

CHAPTER 36
(10th January 1966 – Monday)

Jane was lying cozily on a couch by the fireplace in the living room, reading the letter from Sarah that she had received that morning. It was snowing heavily outside. The time was two p.m.

Hello Mama and Papa,

I could have told you on the phone what I'm going to tell you now, but since you will surely want to keep it in your archives, I'm writing a letter instead. Let me get straight to the point. I've been dating a senior American army officer – he's a lieutenant-colonel, a graduate of West Point Military Academy (Class of 1955) – for about a year. His name is Samuel Thompson. We got to know each other through a mutual friend. He's about ten years older than me, and he comes from a family that has produced many outstanding and high-ranking military officers for some generations.

Very recently, he asked for my hand in marriage. I asked him to let me have some time to think about it. I like him very much for many reasons – for instance, he's a good conversationalist and very caring; it's never dull to be with him. He's not that handsome, but still attractive somehow, and he had a commanding yet pleasant voice. He took me a few weeks ago to meet his parents. They were very nice to me. Despite his social background, he's not arrogant at all. And he's not inquisitive about my family background. (By the way, as I've been maintaining a low profile since I started studying here, even my closest friends have difficulty detecting my real family background.)

Mama and Papa, I told him that if he knew the truth about my family, he'd be disappointed. He then said he wouldn't care whatever my family background was. When I finally told him that my father once was a high-ranking functionary in Dr. Goebbels's Ministry, he shrugged it off and said the past is the past and that he was hoping to marry me, not my father. And he said that he cared only about the present and the future and the qualities of a person's character – es-

pecially when it came to his future wife. His attitude means a great deal to me. But I didn't tell him much about our family because he might think that I was trying to impress him with our social standing and humanitarian work during the war.

The only problem for me is his arch-conservative political and religious views. He's a staunch anti-communist, for instance, and his religiosity sounds rather like fanaticism. I may be wrong. But I can live with these views since he has never imposed on me to think like him. He has often told me that I have complete freedom regarding my views on religion and politics.

As you know, I'm not that liberal in my views either, but he is a bit too radical for me. So I'm sometimes doubtful if I'd be able to compromise with him on such things in the long run. I wonder if I might find his views suffocating someday. Meanwhile, he's patiently waiting for my answer to his proposal.

My question to you now is: May I come home with him this summer? He'll have a couple of weeks' vacation. He loves beautiful landscapes, so we intend to travel around Switzerland together. I told him about our hiking tours, and he was fascinated. I'm glad to tell you that I've just delivered my doctoral dissertation, and I'm quite confident that I will graduate magna cum laude or even summa cum laude. I'm still dreaming of a career as a chemist, either at one of the top universities here in America or at a well-known research center somewhere in Europe.

I hope to hear from you soon. I miss you both always. Take care.
Your loving daughter,
Sarah

Jane showed Daniel Sarah's letter and drafted a reply after dinner. She posted it the next day.

Hello, our dearest darling,
Thank you very much for your letter; we're so glad to hear the good news, both about your boyfriend and your dissertation. We wish

you all the best. We'll do everything we can to help you have a happy married life. You know that my parents also always supported my decisions, including marital matters.

If we're honest, we're a bit disappointed to hear about his arch-conservative political and religious views. But that is not our business. It's not hugely surprising that someone with his background has such thoughts. If you believe that you can find happiness with him, we'll be happy. And people's views can change during their lives, so his political and religious outlooks may change someday. But it would be best if you did not let yourself be disturbed or influenced by our opinions.

We'd be pleased to meet him and get to know him. Just let us know in advance when you're coming. We wish you all the best with your dissertation. We're fully confident that you'll manage to achieve your goals soon.

Take care, darling. We miss you a lot, too.

Your loving Mama and Papa

Sarah and her boyfriend landed in Brussels in the last week of June. They were met at the airport by Jane, Daniel, Victor, and Anna. Jane subtly tried a couple of times to discover the real political views of her future son-in-law. Still, he said that he always tried to be a good soldier and did not want to say anything either way about the governments' politics in power. One thing Jane and Daniel strongly sensed was that, precisely as Sarah had hinted in her letter, Samuel was indeed a staunch anti-communist. But they understood each other. Every time Samuel wanted to know about Daniel's experiences on the Eastern Front, Daniel politely dodged the subject, saying that he did not want to dredge up his traumatic memories. As he was just a medical officer, he was not interested in political and military affairs. Deep down in his heart, he was thoroughly fed up with these topics.

Samuel told Jane that he had heard she was writing an exciting novel and asked her if it was true. Jane told that it was true, but she would need several more years until she could publish it, for she was still collecting new ideas. He did not ask her any more questions about it after that. Jane's family and friends had kept what she was doing confidential since she'd signed the contract with Random House. They told Samuel only what was necessary for him to know about themselves. They did not tell him, for example, many parts of Jane's personal life.

Samuel had many discussions with Christine and Paul on Paul's search for answers to the great mysteries of life. When he learned of the two orphanages and the good works that had been done by these centers during the war, he was deeply impressed and showed his admiration and respect for the family's humanitarian spirit. At the end of their two-week stay with her parents, Sarah was happy to know that her parents and grandparents believed she and Samuel had every chance of leading a stable and harmonious life together. During their stay in Belgium, they visited all the war museums, American war cemeteries, and well-known battlefields during the war. Jane, Daniel, Anna, and Victor sent them off at Brussels International Airport. The couple flew to Zürich from Brussels for a two-week sightseeing tour in Switzerland.

Sarah accepted Samuel's marriage proposal on 24th December the same year. And they began the preparations for the wedding immediately. He wanted to get married in Washington, DC, where his parents and most of his closest relatives and friends were living, and she readily agreed. As both of them were regular church-goers, they planned to have both religious and civil weddings. And they made a list of the people they would invite. Samuel wanted to have a big ceremony and intended to invite at least 170 people. Sarah wanted to have about 60. Finally, they agreed on 150 in total.

The marriage ceremony took place in a Presbyterian church in Washington, DC, on 16th June 1967, a Friday, at noon, after the civil ceremony at a district registry office. They then held the wedding party at the residence of Samuel's parents. Among the guests were Victor, Anna, Jennifer, Carlos, Betty and her husband, Edith, John's former girlfriend, Daniel, Catherine, and four former orphans from the orphanages, who always had a very close relationship with Sarah for years. Since Jane was afraid of long-distance flights, she could not attend. Christine and Paul felt they were no longer fit enough for the long-distance journey, so they sent a wedding card and a check with an undisclosed amount.

Dorotea was also invited, but she could not attend due to illness. Sarah wanted her father and stepmother to come to the wedding, too, but they could not leave their work, for Heide was away on a business trip, but they sent them a beautiful card they had created themselves and a present. More than twenty of Sarah's friends were also among the guests. The rest were Samuel's close relatives, a number of his comrades and former classmates, and his closest friends. The party ended happily at eight p.m.

A week after the wedding, Sarah, Samuel, Samuel's parents, brother and his girlfriend, sister and her boyfriend, Daniel, Catherine, Victor, Anna, Jennifer, and Carlos flew back to Belgium to celebrate with Jane, Christine, Paul, their relatives, and friends. The party took place at Jane's home on 24th June, a Saturday, starting at two o'clock and ending at eight. This time, Thomas, Linda, Dorotea, and nearly a hundred people from the neighboring communities could attend.

Jane, Christine, and Paul repeatedly expressed their gratitude to Samuel's parents, brother, and sister for their thoughtfulness in coming to celebrate the wedding once again in Belgium with them. During this time, they had numerous discussions on all sorts of topics. On the seventh day after their arrival, Sarah and Samuel flew from Brussels to an undisclosed island in the Pacific to honeymoon in seclusion for three weeks. Samuel's parents, brother and his girlfriend, sister and her boyfriend flew to Zürich for a sightseeing tour in Switzerland for a month. A week later, Jennifer, Carlos, and Dorotea flew back to Madrid.

CHAPTER 37
(12th July 1975 – Saturday)

It was a lovely day. The sky was blue, and the temperature pleasant; it seemed a good omen for Jane and Daniel's future. At three o'clock in the afternoon, they gathered with several people in the Assembly Hall in Waimes to celebrate Jane's seventieth birthday combined with the fourteenth anniversary of their marriage. The couple had decided to make special celebrations every five years by combining her birthday and their wedding anniversary since she turned sixty in 1965; the second time was in 1970, and now was the third time. (Normally, they celebrated their other birthdays quietly with close friends and relatives.) As most people in their friend and relation circles were getting old, Jane and Daniel wanted to make it an extraordinary reunion.

Altogether they invited more than three hundred old friends and their contemporaries from the neighboring communities and former orphans and elderly residents of the two orphanages and their families. The Assembly Hall was full to the last seat. Jane had spread the news that she would deliver some special news for her own family and several other people. So everybody was extremely curious about what it could be. Among those present were Victor with his wife Juliane and their two teenage daughters; Anna and her boyfriend Henry; Catherine; Thomas, Linda with and their four adopted children with their own families; Samuel's brother and his girlfriend; Samuel's sister and her husband (Samuel's parents could not participate due to their poor health); nearly all the former medical and office personnel; several of the part-time and full-time volunteers and their families; all the full-time volunteer teachers; Paul, Christine, Mr. William Beckert, and his wife; Barbara and her family; Sarah, Samuel, and their two young daughters; Jennifer and Carlos with their two teenage daughters; Dorotea; Betty and her husband (John's mother had passed away in 1970); Professor Fleming and his wife, and a few Catholic priests, nuns, rabbis, and pastors. One of the most conspicuous former orphans was Carmen and her husband and their two adult children – a son and a daughter. One of John's American friends and his wife and John's Belgian friend with his wife also attended.

Many of Jane's friends and relatives would not be around in a few years due to advanced age. Several people who had attended her sixty-fifth birthday party could not come anymore. For instance, Christine and Paul were already ninety years old and confined to wheelchairs, although still very alert. One could see the changes in the physical features of many. But although the signs of advanced age were visible in most of them, they were all in an extremely exuberant mood. Birthday and wedding anniversary cards and presents piled up on some long tables in one corner. A stage was erected temporarily for the occasion in the hall, and on it, the elderly celebrants were seated.

The ceremony started at two o'clock in the afternoon with champagne bottles' uncorking and a toast to Jane's good health and long life to the couple's marriage. She then greeted the guests with the following words: "Good afternoon to everybody! First of all, I'd like to thank you all heartily for coming to this seventieth birthday party of mine. And at the same time, Daniel and I would like to offer our heartfelt thanks to you for your good wishes on the fourteenth anniversary of our marriage. We're so thankful for all the beautiful cards and precious presents as well. Second: I'm so glad that my beloved parents are still in good health. I wish them also good health and happiness in the years to come. Third: As every one of you knows, ours is a happy and exciting married life; it's so perfect that it's even boring sometimes – no, I'm just joking…"

A burst of loud and hearty laughter suddenly broke out. Daniel widely smiled and was quite amused. Jane continued, "We thoroughly enjoy life every second, every minute, and every hour. Fourth: Daniel and I'd like to thank all our children and grandchildren and their spouses for their love and care. We wish them success and happiness in the decades to come. Fifth: My heartfelt thanks to my aunts, uncles, cousins, and close friends for their love and support throughout my life. Sixth: On behalf of my parents, our children, and relatives, I'd like to thank all the people who have given us their loyal support for generations, which has, in turn, enabled us to give back to the needy during the last two wars. Seventh: On behalf of my family, relatives, and friends, I'd like to express our profound thanks to those who have shown their gratitude for our help during the wars by giving a helping hand to other needy people in various ways. Eighth: There are untold numbers of people whom I cannot name but who contributed to our humanitarian works before, during, and after the two great wars; so on behalf of my parents and myself, I'd like to thank all of them, too. Ninth: I'd like to express my deep gratitude once again to Sister Hanna, my late best friend, for what she did for Jennifer and me. I'm quite sure that she and her boyfriend are with us right now, joining in from their new home up there. Tenth: My heartfelt thanks to my beloved husband, Daniel, for his love and understanding in making our marriage a very happy one. Eleventh: I'd like to thank, on behalf of my beloved parents, Almighty God, for His blessings on our family and relatives for generations.

Twelve: Jennifer has frequently asked me if I have begun to believe in Jesus because she wants to be with me eternally in God's place on high, but up to now, I've only ever answered her ambiguously. So I'd like to assure her that I now accept God to a great extent. However, like my father, I still have difficulty understanding the many great mysteries of this world – for example, why he created different skin colors and the concept of predestination, to name but two. I promise you, Jennifer, that I'll study Jesus' teachings more thoroughly from now on so that your wish may be fulfilled. Thank you so much, everybody."

There were deafening applause and a long standing ovation. Her words moved everybody to tears, including Jennifer; she ran to her mother and embraced and thanked her profusely.

Jane continued after a short pause. "I'd like to inform you about four more things which I'm sure you would like to know about: One, Jennifer and Carlos's humanitarian and medical works for the poverty-stricken in Guatemala – she will briefly explain in a few minutes about their work. Two, I'm pleased to announce that Samuel and Sarah and their children will be stationed at the NATO headquarters in Brussels soon. And as you already know, Samuel was promoted to brigadier-general very recently. Three, Sarah has got offers from some prestigious universities and research centers in Europe. Four, Mr. William Beckert from New York will tell us some very exciting news a little later.

"And last but not least, I must add that I hope all of you will still be in good health when we gather again to celebrate my birthday five years from now. Whether it's the result of my own karma, or the blessing of some higher being, or just pure luck, I'm so glad that I've reached the age I am today and am still healthy. Daniel and I would like to live as long as my parents have. And we wish the same for all of you. Thank you so much once again for everything. May God bless us all!"

There was once again tumultuous applause. At the end of it, Jennifer made a short announcement.

"Good afternoon, everybody. I'm so glad that you all are here today. Well, I'll make a brief speech with regard to our humanitarian works in Guatemala. We've also prepared a detailed report, so if you're interested to know more about our projects, you may get it from us. As many of you know, my maternal grandparents established a non-profit foundation called the Jeanmart Foundation five years ago. Since its inception, we've made some contributions for the Guatemalan people through the International Red Cross, the Guatemalan Red Cross, and a few other charity organizations. Initially, we intended to concentrate our humanitarian and development projects in the post-civil war era. But the war is still ruthlessly raging everywhere, and we don't know when it'll be over. The existing Guatemalan health care system, in general, is composed of a tiered hierarchy of treatment. This system operates at four main levels: specialized hospitals at the national level, department hospitals at the regional level, health centers/posts at the municipal level, and health promoters at the hamlet level. Unfortunately, a range of key problems limits the system's success. Rural, indigenous populations are least likely to receive adequate health care due to a lack of available transportation, language barriers, mistrust in the providers, and continued reliance on local curanderos and traditional healers. Local and municipal health care is administered in large part by promotores de salud or health promoters.

"We'd therefore start with some minor projects in a few more secure areas. For example, we'd open a small 50-bed clinic on the outskirts of the capital as a pilot project, with the sole aim of giving treatments only to emergency patients who cannot really afford to go to a private hospital or clinic. The government-run hospitals and clinics are hopelessly overcrowded. Our pilot clinic would be staffed with three or four doctors and a few nurses. Our immediate aim is to recruit a few doctors and nurses locally. We want to stay there as long as we could, and we might expand our operations to a few neighboring countries in the region soon, for the poverty in those countries is almost as serious. So we may need to be as frugal as possible. We'd give treatments only to the downtrodden. We know that we'd be confronted with a lot of heartbreaking experiences. But we wouldn't be able to afford to be so generous and kindhearted all the time to every needy person. We'll stay there for about six months at a time and then spend six months here. So our long-term plan is to train the local people in basic health education in cooperation with other organizations. This foundation would completely finance our projects. As sorrowful news from there is flooding out into the world every day, I don't think I need to go into detail. Thank you very much, everybody. May God bless us all!"

There was long and rapturous applause, followed by some more words from Jane. "Now, anybody may say anything he or she wants. When those who would like to say something have finished, I'll announce the good news that I know you are all eagerly waiting for!"

About ten older people and the same number of former orphans described their new lives and lavishly expressed their gratitude to the

Jeanmart family. It took them nearly two hours to finish their speeches of thanks. In the end, Daniel stood up, turned to Samuel, and politely said, "Samuel, as we all know, the Americans lost the Vietnam War a few months ago. It's still the hottest news around the world. So it would be very interesting if you could tell us what you think about it if it's not too sensitive a subject for you as a career soldier."

Everybody turned to Samuel in great expectation. He stood up and replied, "Daniel, thank you very much for asking me this interesting question. It is indeed a very sensitive issue within the highest military echelons, and it's hotly debated among us. But I think I can say something about it as a private person – and also as a Christian."

As he spoke these words, Jane and Daniel exchanged a quick, worried glance. Samuel went on, "First of all, may I *officially* wish you, Jane, a happy birthday and a long life ..."

All the guests broke into laughter at his use of the word "officially." Samuel smiled widely and continued, "See? A career soldier can also be humorous."

There was more laughter. Then he continued, again, "And I wish you both a happy married life for decades to come. Well, I hate people who praise themselves, but my Sarah used to tell me quite often that she loves me for just *one* thing – my sense of humor."

Another hearty burst of laughter. "Now, let me be a bit more serious. I want to say a few words that I can't keep in my heart. It's a very personal matter, but I think I should share it with you all, for many of you have been Jane's friends for several decades. When I fell in love with Sarah and decided to get married, Jane was not very happy at the thought of her daughter being married to a military man. She made it very clear to me that it had nothing to do with me personally, but that she was against anything military in general. I could fully understand her feelings, which were very much influenced by personal experience and the various religious and philosophical concepts that she had come across in her life. I always hated communism, and so I fought in Vietnam and was highly decorated. I have been a staunch anti-communist my whole life. If I'd had the power to do whatever I liked, I'd have dropped some nuclear bombs on the communist countries. But then I lost my youngest brother, whom I was very close to, in Vietnam five years ago, and now we've lost Vietnam to the communists, after having sacrificed tens of thousands of precious lives and hundreds of billions of dollars. It's so painful to think about it. The bitter lesson I learned from all this is that you cannot see things clearly until sorrowful things happen to your own family or loved ones. In other words, without such tragic events within one's own immediate circles, it's hard to see things from a critical perspective. The degree of my sorrow is beyond description.

"Now, it's said that the Vietnam War was a poor man's war because the children of the wealthy and influential could dodge the draft by using various tricks, both legal and illegal. My family line has produced many high-ranking military officers for some generations. My brother with such a background could have avoided the draft , but he preferred to serve his country with dignity. My family is very proud of him, although his loss indescribably saddens us.

"I was brought up to be a good soldier, never questioning the leadership of those in power, and until now, we have served our country loyally, without ever questioning the politics of our governments. I now think about many things related to my country's political and military affairs from a very critical perspective. Yet, as a military man, I've got no right to express publicly what I'm thinking. It is the first time I've admitted my thoughts so openly. I'm so sorry to hear about what has been happening in Guatemala; however, I won't comment on it because I'm not sufficiently informed about it. I can, though, say something about communist ideology from a Christian point of view – from the point of view of Christianity as I understand it. For many people, my views on these matters may be simplistic, perhaps even naïve, but it seems to me that if those who regard themselves as good Christians shared their wealth more generously with the poor or underprivileged, there would be much less injustice and suffering in this world and communism might never have come into existence in the first place. And as a result, the world would be a much more peaceful and pleasant place to live. I even wonder if it might not be more effective to spend a large part of our annual defense budget to fight poverty around the world as our strategy against communism, rather than putting our faith in more and more sophisticated military hardware and technology. Sadly, though, I'm sure that many powerful people and institutions don't share this view. But I'm saying these things not as a politician or even a military man, but rather as a believer in the messages of Jesus Christ. His messages, after all, are love, peace, justice, compassion, and humility. I wish every one of you a healthy and peaceful life from the very bottom of my heart. Thank you."

There was tumultuous applause once again and a very long-standing ovation. Everybody was surprised by Samuel's words, and several people's eyes were filled with tears. Daniel, Jane, Thomas and Linda went to him and heartily congratulated him. Christine and Paul joined them. And Jane embraced Samuel tightly and spoke to him in a choked voice, tears rolling down her cheeks. "My dear Samuel, you don't know how happy your speech has made me. I've never dared to dream that you might think such things deep down in your heart. Today is one of the happiest days of my life."

Jane needed several minutes to compose herself before making the next announcement. She turned to Mr. Beckert and said, "Now, William, would you please tell us your very exciting news."

Mr. Beckert stood up and greeted everybody in the hall. "Good evening, everybody. First of all, just like General Thompson, may I also *officially* wish you, Jane, a happy birthday and a very long life like your parents …"

His words were interrupted by the audience's uproarious laughter. Mr. Beckert continued, "And my heartfelt wishes for a long and harmonious married life for both of you.

"Everybody, please kindly allow me to introduce myself briefly. I have come from New York to deliver some special news to you all. I'm the chief commissioning editor at Random House. I came here fourteen years ago when Jane and Daniel got married. Some of you may remember. On that mission, I offered Jane a seven-figure sum for her novel, *Why Are You Crying, Mama?* - a romance based largely on her own life. But she could not accept the deal on that occasion because she wanted to wait and see what would happen to Sarah, Victor, Jennifer, Carlos, her parents, and herself before publishing her novel. We have, therefore, waited fourteen years. You'll read about it in detail in Chapter 35. The novel contains 37 chapters now and runs more than 500 pages. We have successfully negotiated the various rights – film rights, foreign language translations, paperback rights, et cetera. For instance, 20th Century Fox has bought the film rights for an undisclosed sum and wants to bring the film out within five to seven years. We'd work feverishly on this project so that we'd be able to publish the novel within this year. And I've got two more bits of good news for you: Jane and we have made a deal for her two other books – a fairy tale and a normal romance novel – which we plan to publish next year. We'll help her to negotiate for the film rights and foreign language translations for these two books as well soon. You'll learn more about all these in the media soon. We're quite confident that Jane's novels will become bestsellers worldwide and that the film will also be a big hit. Ms. Jeanmart will be an internationally recognized author. Congratulations, Jane!"

The applause lasted several minutes. Then Mr. Beckert surprised everyone with these words: "Jane, I've read your latest draft while I've been here, and it seems that you've forgotten to include some crucial facts – or perhaps you intended to integrate them later, in your final draft? I'm quite sure that without these facts, your novel might not truly be complete."

Jane was visibly surprised by this and thought for a moment. "Oh really? You mean, perhaps, about Victor, Anna, and the awards we got for our humanitarian work during the war? But what the other missing facts could be, I cannot figure out."

"Yes, three of them are, as you've just said, about Victor, Anna, and the awards that the reigning monarch bestowed upon your parents, you, your six assistants, the twenty-six medical staff, the thirty full-time volunteers, and the fourteen volunteer teachers."

"Thank you so much for pointing out these omissions, William. Well, I intended to add Victor and Anna in my next draft. Here's what I'd write about Victor: Daniel did persuade him to change his mind in time, and he's working in the family business after he got his MBA more than six or seven years ago. When his uncle and aunt, who are my first cousins, retire from the business's management, he'll take the helm. He's a very balanced and considerate person in his dealings with all the people he comes into contact with, regardless of any differences in their social, cultural, religious, political, ethnic, or philosophical outlook. And our generations-old humanitarian spirit very much influences him. Not only that, but he possesses a strong business acumen as well. So we're confident that he'd be able to lead the family business successfully for many years to come. There'll at least be another page dedicated to him and his family: he got married to his childhood girlfriend three years ago, and now they've got two young daughters. And I'd write about Anna that she has been happily working as a psychiatrist at the Ochsenzoll Psychiatric Hospital in Hamburg in Germany since 1972 and that she's going to get married next year to a fellow psychiatrist from the same hospital by the name of Henry. There'll at least be a full page about her."

"Thank you very much, Jane. I think these lines will be fine. And how about the awards?"

"We all have been thinking a lot about them, too. But we were afraid that we might appear vainglorious if I mentioned them. So I decided to drop the whole episode."

"Jane, I fully understand your decision and respect your humility, but since you did not embark on your humanitarian works in the expectation of any such awards or rewards, I'm sure nobody would be suspicious of your motives. I think your readers deserve to know the truth in full."

"Thank you, William. I think you've convinced me. Now, are still there some missing facts?"

"You don't mention whether you went to India to have your Nadi leaf read or not. It could be very interesting for your readers as well."

"Oh yes. I forgot that, too. Well, I'm so sad that I didn't manage to go there for many reasons, but later I tried to console myself that I could not fulfill this wish because of my karma. But I haven't given it up yet."

"And your readers will surely want to know what happened to General Ferdinand Schaal."

"Oh, thank you so much, William. That is truly important. Well, General Schaal passed away on 9th October 1962 in Baden-Baden. If he were still alive, we would have invited him here today. Daniel contacted him and told him by letter about us after our wedding, and he was so pleased. He hoped to see us as soon as possible, and we promised to visit him in Baden-Baden. But then so many urgent things intervened that we could not fulfill our promise in time. When finally we were ready to visit him, we learned that he was no longer in a position to meet us. We were so saddened by it. It's a great pity. When he passed away, he was still quite young – just seventy-two years of age. We didn't expect that he'd leave us so soon, so we didn't make any earlier inquiries about his health. If we had known about his deteriorating health in time, we'd have tried to see him as soon as possible at any cost."

"I must confess, I could have quietly reminded you about these missing elements when we were alone together, but I felt that everybody here would like to hear about them, so I raised the questions now."

"Thank you very much for that, William. After this conversation, I can enhance the story more than if I had just mentioned these episodes somewhere in brief, in one or two chapters. I'll tell you briefly about the awards that the reigning monarch bestowed on us. The *Order of the Crown* is awarded in five classes, plus two *palms* and three medals: First, there's the *Grand Cross*, which has the badge on a sash on the right shoulder, plus the star on the left breast; then there's the *Grand Officer*, who wears a star on the left breast and may also wear the neck badge; next, there's *Commander*, who wears the badge on a neck ribbon; then *Officer*, who wears the badge on a ribbon with a rosette on the left breast; and finally *Knight*, who wears the badge on a ribbon on the left breast. My parents and I were honored with the second-highest award, that of *Grand Officer*, and my six assistants and the twenty-six medical personnel who had worked as volunteers throughout the war and the thirty full-time volunteers and the fourteen full-time volunteer teachers received the status of *Commander*."

"Thank you very much, Jane, for enlightening us."

Several people rushed to the stage to congratulate Jane. Among them were Jennifer, Carmen, Dorotea, Sarah, Victor, Daniel, Catherine, Anna, Linda, Silvia, Veronika, Linda, and Thomas. As Jennifer was about to embrace her mother, Jane suddenly broke down into a flood of tears – to everyone's bafflement and shock. They did not know how to react. Then, in the next moment, Jennifer tenderly took her sobbing mother into her arms and asked her in a broken, distorted voice, "Why are you crying, Mama? Why are you crying, Mama?"

As Jane kept on sobbing without an answer, all the women's eyes also began to be filled with tears. Then, after a short while, Jane replied in a choked voice, "This is one of the happiest and, at the same time saddest, days of my life."

Jennifer tried to console her mother. "Mama, I know that it's one of your happiest days, but why should it also be one of your saddest?"

After a few moments, still weeping, Jane said, "I know how a lucky person I am – I've got loving parents, a loving husband, children, cousins, friends, and relatives who I can love and who also love me equally. But countless innocent people around the world are dying from hunger and war and disease every hour, every minute, every second. I feel so sad that I can't do anything for them."

"Mama, you've done quite enough for several people, and you're going to do a lot more in

the future. I promise you that Carlos and I will continue to do similar good deeds for the needy people as long as we live. And I know that Sarah, Anna, and Victor will also do the same, as far as they can. So please don't feel so sad, Mama. Okay?"

It took everybody several minutes to overcome their shock and sorrow. The birthday-cum-wedding anniversary party finally came to a happy end at nine p.m. Before it was over, Jane announced that she would make generous donations from her income from the book's sales to the Congress of Freethinkers, the two orphanages, and the Maha Bodhi Society of Ceylon. The book was published in December 1975 and instantly became a bestseller in many English-speaking countries. Ten foreign-language translations were simultaneously published, and they all became bestsellers, too. Thus, Jane finally became the internationally recognized author she had dreamed of being for so many decades.

Lightning Source UK Ltd.
Milton Keynes UK
UKHW041835050421
381487UK00001B/45